Among the Veils

Book I of the Paper Thrones Series

Bret Alexander Sweet

Among the Veils
Book I of the Paper Thrones Series

ISBN: 0984493859
ISBN-13: 9780984493852

Library of Congress Control Number: 2013940702
Lexingford Publishing
Belvedere, California

Lexingford Publishing
www.lexingfordpublishing.yolasite.com
New York   San Francisco   Hong Kong

Acknowledgements and Dedications

Many good souls worked tirelessly to ensure this project came to light. I will not remember you all in time for this book so forgive me if I do this in stages.

Inspiration

Mr. Sweet - Every morning is a struggle to process the wonderful gifts you gave to me. I am going to spend the rest of my days with an unease about the cost. I would have traded places with you in a heart beat. You are the most brilliant, prescient, charismatic and noble man I ever met. I hope you feel your student has added on to the lesson. As much as I treasure your leadership, I think it splendid luck that I am also one of your children. This is our victory, together.

Dr. Sweet - Any time we left the house I had an empty pad and a writing tool near me. Thinking back, I only recently figured out why you would say "Well, instead of complaining you could always just write your own". You have balanced being my first fan and asking really hard questions for decades. Even if you weren't the smartest person I know, I would still think it quite fortunate that I got to be one of your children.

Yamma - I thought I was the most loyal human a person could know until I met you. You were correct: it was unfair to keep this all in my head. You are one of the people who told me this book had to be written. Thank you for the sacrifices you made to ensure that it did.

Iteration

Brother - We don't say thank you and that has been the rule. You saved my life. This one is for you.

Sifu - The older I get the more I realize how easy teaching comes to you. I remember when you helped me write my first short story. Now look at us.

Sis - You were a fan from day one. Thank you for inspiring everyone's favorite character

Implementation:

The Sorceress - You did acupuncture on the copy and opened up everything so it could flow. Somethings have changed but your loyalty did not.

Taylor and Khoury - This story could not be told without your help.

Art - Thank you for the challenge and the platform. I needed your push to write like this.

Roger - You are still the greatest American writer to me. I tip my hand to your mastery. One day they will see how much more science fiction can do that other mediums.

Nishant Vats: kudos on a cover design that brilliantly captures the spirit of the book.

CHAPTER ONE

"Careful what you wish for."

-Clay

I don't remember ever having a night of good sleep. When I do sleep, I dream. If they're good, I don't remember them. When I do remember them, they are horrific. Therefore, I don't sleep. I smoke a lot of cigarettes, drink a lot of coffee and end up unmoving but conscious on couches. I don't sleep, though. My foster parents tried everything short of medication to give me a good night's rest. Hypnosis got me to stop biting my nails but it did not help me sleep. Exercise was good for a nice swimmer's cut along the midsection in my teens but ineffectual for rest. No strategy has proven itself.

That's why I enjoy the work I do. Most people sleep to avoid what they do during the day. I work to avoid what I see at night. My foster parents, if I spoke to them, would be fairly proud of me. I have a grandmother who resides in an assisted living facility. She adorns her walls with awards and articles knowing full well that I'd put such things in recycling if not for her.

My pack sits in the right breast pocket of my coat. They are a friendly reminder of my mortality. I smoke because the scent in my nose helps me concentrate and the intake helps with my longings.

I miss my family.

I don't mean parents or siblings I've never known because I've simply never had that. I miss something I know well yet can't remember for the life of me.

I am a psychiatrist. I treat children who suffer from severe cases of psychological trauma. I've done enough reflection and self-experimentation to know that my insomnia, my smoking and my yearning for something, or someone, is related. I don't know why or how. My head is a place of answers for other people, but confusion for myself.

I don't have any friends I can speak of. I have keepers--people who I rely on to show me the line between reality and living in my head. I can't say there is a cadre of chaps I meet for beers every Friday night and discuss sports scores with. I pretty much keep to myself. Sometimes I think I'm living someone else's life, a guest in another man's body. My voicemail and answering machine fill up. I listen, pick and chose whom to respond to and whom to delete. If its not related to my work, I find most human contact to be a sad a substitute for something I can't have.

There it goes again.

That whispering ache in my head reminding me exactly of what cannot be explained. Time for another cigarette.

It was raining that night. The smoke from my lit cigarette drifted off the cherry and reached like a hand across the front wind shield of my car. I met my eyes in the mirror and reminded myself to at least attempt to like what I saw. The weather made my complexion almost gray where as with some sun it was normally a light coffee color. The dark had shaped my eyes towards a dark brown. In the direct light I can find some contrasting specks of green in near the pupils. My hand held no rings with long nimble fingers and cuticles like the frayed edges of packing tape. The frost from the cold wet Alaskan winds that paralyzed San Francisco every winter chilled my blood and inspired my frame to pack on thirty more pounds than I'd like to carry around. I feel more comfortable at one sixty but I was carrying about one eight five on my six foot frame. Nina Simone's "Misunderstood" drifted softly through the front speakers, my radio tuned to the "Quiet Storm." Old music for my old soul. I cracked the window on the passenger side to let the smoke out without getting any water on my face and turned up the defroster to compensate for the warm air escaping.

I saw him across the street looking both ways on an empty, wind-torn Tenderloin Avenue. The rain had not only washed away the bodily fluids left from the unspeakable waste that exists on those streets, but it had also dispersed the human trash that creeps about looking for victims. The rain drove them into holes and away from the light like roaches in a tenement kitchen.

He always treated every day the same--wary. I guess that's why we talk. I wouldn't call him a friend, nor would he count me on his Christmas card list, but there was a mutual respect we had for one another. Unspoken.

He knew the door would be unlocked for him. Cops always have that certainty. It doesn't come from analyzing details, it comes from the thrill of authority the badge brings. He poked his head in, spilling rain from the hood of his navy blue poncho on the dark grey upholstery of the passenger seat and foot well. His face recoiled from the smoke as he pulled back his hood, nodding as if asking permission to sit. I opened my door tossing the freshly lit cigarette on the damp pavement. The overhead light flashed revealing features of the Detective's face. There was a young man hidden somewhere behind intense thought lines and laugh folds. He was young in the sense that his chief was well over fifty, while the officers running the beat were in their late twenties. He had moved to San Francisco from Pomona in the early 80's to go to school, met a local, fell in love, got married and joined the force to make a difference. The thick, sporadic patches of gray in his beard reminded me that he had seen enough to be a qualified vet. The lack of gloss to his eyes reminded me that he held to a bitter humanity. He existed because he refused to go, as opposed to most who are . . . searching.

"Those things are going to kill you," he said in a low growl that came from his throat and crackled on the last syllables of each word when it hit the air.

"Twenty two years?" I asked, checking to make sure the fan was drawing air from outside and shooting it in just before I closed the door. The car was dark again.

"Twenty three," he corrected me.

"You don't miss it?"

"Yes, but it doesn't call me. My family calms me."

I sat back and thought. John Avalos was balanced and funny about it to boot. His voice often switched from a blend of rolled 'r' sounds and over-pronounced consonants as if his vocabulary was a conversation between his Mexican and Anglo grandparents. Is that why he's a cop? His biracial heritage gave him a leg up when it came to walking between worlds. Family gives him a tangible sense of love that exists outside of the tool belt and holster he wears. I remembered that I trust police just about as much as I trust criminals. I chose to work with John because a friend told me he was good to know. And he always has been.

"Speaking of which I have a message for you," he said.

That was when I started feeling like I wasn't myself. As if everything I told you before didn't make you think that something was odd, there came a point when I realized that I woke up that morning not sure of what was happening. The victim of an inside joke. Avalos was too up-front to be coy. Even when he was telling me something he wasn't supposed to, he at least coded it better than that. He was trying to get me to recall some conversation that I'd usually remember. But this time, I didn't.

"Okay. How does one respond to that?"

"Take out that expensive toy in your chest pocket and set an appointment."

Avalos resented cell phones. He came from a time when you got the job done without gadgets. The smart phone in my breast pocket was a waste of time to him. I reached into my coat, retrieving the device and opened my calendar.

"Okay," I said, holding up the stylus in a sign I was ready.

"Tomorrow. The Atlas Café. 4:45 P.M."

I recorded the appointment, griping in my mind about the lack of parking in the Mission.

"Want to help me with a categ--"

"Get the fuck outta here," Avalos sputtered, enlisting a smile from me.

"Just checking. Anything else?"

"We got a call of screaming about 45 minutes ago. I arrived on the scene about 30 minutes ago to find forced entry and multiple homicides."

"That's not my deal."

"There's a survivor."

"A kid?"

"Yes. Very young. There's some things upstairs he shouldn't see and forensics just arrived. I have a very special window for you to be allowed on the premises to help me think this one out."

"What am I going to see?"

"Pieces of human."

"Jesus!"

"No, he's not upstairs, but that kid is. How do I get him out of the bathroom he's in?"

"Let me walk him out."

"Okay," Avalos said, reaching into his stomach pouch and producing an ID card. He was practical. He kept a badge for me but never let me hold on to it. Paranoid, yet pragmatic. He handed me the white laminated paper, the lanyard trailing from his pocket. It had my picture, a reflective patch of material/barcode, and an SFPD logo/badge on it. It was an older photo with my hair cut closer to my scalp and signs of dandruff forming at the widow's peak. The angle of the camera made my nose look much thinner than its regular curve and point. Very official. "When you get to the door someone from the criminalistics will give you the run down. Do what they say and nothing they don't."

"Its your kingdom. I'm just a travelling bard," I answered back.

"Great. What are you going to do?" Avalos asked.

"My magic." That made Avalos laugh.

"Sometimes you get the job done so well, makes me think you really are a magician," he said.

Magic is what people call things they don't understand. I get children very well. I know what its like to be afraid of being abandoned and how to admit when its happening. In the morning, I sit through kids explaining why they set the science lab on fire, their mother's convinced the kid is crazy rather than upset about her absence or not being on her job in general. At night I work with the city, whenever they have a child in need of protective services that needs evaluation. I treat children like they have a valid opinion despite their age. I'm not sure why they feel compelled to, but children like me and want to talk to me.

"Careful what you wish for," I said opening the door. My umbrella and coat sat in the backseat. I grabbed them quickly, first throwing on the jacket, then fighting to open the umbrella against the cold, unforgiving rain. We crossed the street away from the beach, walking parallel to Golden Gate as we headed to the crowded apartment building surrounded by the pneumonia prone residents who insisted on staring at scene along the street in short sleeves and tank tops. They crowded the streets, held into clumps behind the yellow tape. The wind kept those who stared from their cars trapped behind the safety of their windows. I followed Avalos past the long, haunted faces of police officers and paramedics, past the glare of flickering blueberry strawberry lights and into the halogen bulbed hallway of the tenement.

I noticed that the building, though old and weathered, looked far too well maintained for the amount of spider webs in the corners.

I hate spiders.

They are the creepiest creatures on the planet and work in the same way corruption does—tricking its prey, poisoning it, then consuming it over time. Just evil. I shuddered at the thought.

Avalos started up the stairs and I followed. He stomped along going heel toe as if the sound pushed him forward. I wanted a smoke at the third floor but I could see from the sheer number of bodies and the snapping sounds of cameras that this was the scene.

I once arrived to an apartment in the Geneva Towers where a mother of three had been cutting and packaging coke for a local dealer. It appeared the woman had dipped into the product with her nose and even rocked it for consumption when she was supposed to step on it with an additive and bag it up for sale. She was in the middle of a binge when the dealer came over to collect his product. The two began to fight, but her kids had gotten into the stuff too. Her three sons, all under the age of 7, decided to defend their mother.

We found the supplier in front of the building; his body was a mangled wreck punched into the roof of the car he had landed on.

The boys had lifted and thrown him off the balcony. I was asked to calm them down so nobody would have to shoot someone their kids could play with. That was the first time I saw something my eyes couldn't explain to my mind. As we approached the apartment, I had an overwhelming feeling that it wasn't the last.

It was much colder as we got to the door and the first thing I noticed were burn marks on the floor tile. There were no open windows anywhere in sight. The air smelled old but had more bite than the wind outside. Investigative team members walked to and fro collecting samples. There was the distinct smell of burnt metal like after a horrendous car crash where the fire trucks have contained the flames but the chemical compounds have turned into airborne elements. I got the sense of something being left open that should have been closed.

There were two youngsters waiting for us at the top of the stairs. They were kids per se, fresh out of the academy. Their postures still danced with the dreams of the break through that might earn them their own reality show. They always put me with the young ones who don't know any better. Its a sign of esteem and confidence in my discretion. The seasoned members of the team won't be taken away from where they're needed most in lieu of baby-sitting someone like me who's proven my effectiveness time and again. I have a job to do. The one on the left reminded me of the awkward cousin from "The Fresh Prince of Bel-Air," with a jherri curl I thought deemed illegal in 1992. The one on the right looked like the lead singer of the Cranberries with long blonde hair she tucked under a cloth SFPD cap.

"Mr. Durward," the blonde said, extending her hand forward for an awkward handshake that was too low and stiff to be appropriate for anyone besides a midget. "I've heard . . . SO much about you." I received her hand and shook it, bringing it up to an arm positioning that didn't sprain the elbow. I made sure it was quick and painless so she didn't get any ideas in her head. It's not that I expect to be treated like a physical specimen, but I am aware that I have enough safe features to make women wonder for a while when they stare. My cheeks are high on my jaw with a clean complexion. My belly doesn't poke past my belt and my teeth lack any abnormal spacing. My features are non-offensive. Her disposition told me that dwelling too long in the greeting might fool her into thinking something meaningful had happened. I turned my hand to her companion. He just nodded, an overt indicator that a handshake wasn't necessary considering my civilian rank. He was going to be the stalwart dickhead that Avalos had taught him to be to make sure no evidence was contaminated. I looked back and forth between their badges practicing their names in my head a few times.

"Nice to meet you . . . T-AH-IM," I said over pronouncing his name and doing a sarcastic nod. I could see him scrunch his nose in preparation of replying. I turned my attention back to his partner. "Don't believe too much of what Lieutenant Avalos tells you about me Detective Porter. I only make him look good when he has an off day . . . which is never." She laughed while her accompanying penis attempted to disapprove until he realized his boss was standing next to me and putting a hand on my back as he chuckled.

"We've taken care of everything from the bathroom to the main entrance," Detective said to Avalos. I could tell you his last name but I enjoy calling him Detective Tim much better.

"Great," Avalos said. "Can we walk him through yet?"

"We're all clear," Detective Porter said and then turned her attention to me. "Please follow the red and black tape and don't touch anything in the main rooms."

"Yes ma'am," I replied. "Will Detective Tim be accompanying us?"

Before he could reply, Avalos cut in, "Porter will help us with the interview." I smiled at his concealed anger, and raised my eyebrows to Porter. She smiled and turned on heel, walking into the scene like a tour guide at a museum.

As I approached the room, a familiar salty iron smell greeted me. I knew it well from walking the streets near meat markets.

Blood.

There was lots of blood.

It was an average two-bedroom apartment. Not the size I would expect from a flat in a building of this kind; tenements were usually shallow one bedrooms without a bathroom door. The floors went from the mother of pearl colored, precisely set diamond-shaped tile of the hallway over the wooden door jam into dirty hard wood floors. There was a strip of black of electrician's tape accompanied by a strip of red leading from my present position along the room to a closed door where light peeked out from under it. About 2 feet to either side of the tape was yellow caution tape stapled to the walls to create a rope bridge between myself and my destination. The walls at one time had been white. Now they were covered with strange writing, primitive pictures, some things I thought might be runes and what appeared to be complex mathematical equations. Judging by the orange brown color on the walls and soaking into the hardwood, I would say the writings on the wall were drawn with blood. Human and old.

Scanning the room, I watched the other forensics agents tag and place pieces of what appeared to be human body parts into large zip lock bags. Every piece of furniture in the room was shredded with the couch showing large gouge like cuts. There seemed to be footprints on the wall and ceiling. The window to my right looking down to Laguna would have shown a great a view of the Transamerica pyramid had the window sill still existed. The entire area had been removed as if blow out by an explosion or a wrecking ball. There was not a hint of plaster or broken glass any where near the opening. Still there was the smell of burning chemicals.

"What the fuck did I walk into," I asked, covering my nose and mouth.

"You need one?" Avalos asked.

"Yes," I replied closing my eyes and shaking my head. Although mortified by what appeared to be the worst slaughter my mortal eyes have ever seen, something whispered that I had seen much more. There was a vindictive satisfaction I could not explain. A feeling as if someone had gotten what they had coming and my horror was unfounded.

"Alicia," Avalos asked turning to Porter, "can he smoke in here?"

"You smoke?" Porter asked looking at me disappointed. "It should be all right."

I nodded and fished out my green pack. My hands shook as I did. Tim smirked while Avalos cocked his head, watching me. He was a stone against the storm of the scene. It was the first time he saw me overwhelmed.

"You going to be okay?" Avalos asked.

"Yeah," I said taking a deep drag and letting the smoke find its way out of my nostrils. "Any sign of assault?"

"No," Agent Tim replied, "but we have a rape kit just in case."

"You should probably let Porter take care of that," I corrected him.

"Its not a girl, Durward," Avalos corrected me.

I nodded and motioned with my head toward the door. Porter walked ahead of me, watching between the caution tape and my hand that was holding the cigarette. I stopped at the door and handed it to Tim.

"Hold this," I said without asking. "I'm going to need it after."

I nodded to Porter. Her gloved hand pushed the door open to reveal a mildew streaked white wall with a single nozzle showerhead above a bathtub with a dingy curtain. There was a white porcelain mounted washbasin that had matched the color of the floor in the 40's. There was an old toilet with the low flush volume, probably installed during the California water droughts. The room was window-less and fan-less. It smelled faintly of bleach and mildew yet it suspiciously lacked any signs of water damage. I used the heel of my shoe to close the door behind me and searched the room for the signs of a little person. It seemed empty.

I closed my eyes and listened to my breathing. It drowns out the sounds of radios, conversations, cameras and electronics designed to track evidence in the background. It overpowers the sirens, buses, car alarms, horns, traffic and rain splashing down below in San Francisco. Breathing like it was the most important thing I could be doing. That's when I could hear the shallow breaths of a scared heart. There was a low murmuring along with it. A whispering to one's self. In my mind I could picture the room and feel the breaths. It drew me forward to the cabinet below the washbasin.

I opened my eyes and walked softly towards the washbasin, listening to hear any change in breath. My knees popped as I crouched down, putting my hand on the bronze knob and opening the cabinet doors. Tucked into a little ball, with his knees inches from his faces, was small boy. His eyes were closed and he was murmuring to himself, much too low to pull words from. Probably saying a prayer. He had a gentle face framed by unkempt hair that was an assortment of long spiral curls and short tight spring-like curls in a rich brown that reminded me of cinnamon and chocolate. He had long nimble fingers despite his short arms, a sign of agility and his ability to use tools. As I studied him his big eyes opened wide and watched me. There was fear until he focused on my face.

"Hello," I said with a smile. "I'm not going to hurt you."

"I know," he said quickly, not moving anything more than he had to.

"My name is Clay."

"I know."

"What is yours?"

He smiled at me for a time. A bright and cheerful smile with a hint of mischief,

"You're silly."

"Why do you say that?"

"You know my name."

"I forgot. Tell me again, please?"

"Its Desta."

I smiled at him again. "Okay, Desta, my friends and I want to talk to you outside but I need you to do me a favor. Is that okay?"

"What is it?"

"I'm going carry you out of here and need you to look at my handkerchief until I say stop," I said, pointing to the folded lavender decoration in the breast pocket of my suit. "Can you do that for me please?"

"Yes."

"Atta boy." I took off my overcoat and held it in my left hand. I reached my right arm out to Desta and he grabbed onto it, wrapping himself close to my chest. I pulled the coat over him, covering his entire body and making sure I drew it over his head. I took my right hand to the back of his head pushed his face against my chest. He wrapped his arms around my neck and I stood up. I gauged him to be no more than 7 or 8 but he was definitely on his way to being a big boy. He nestled in my body and held still. I backed my way to the door slowly and tapped on it with my heel. I felt it open behind me and turned around to see the two newbies with Avalos. I walked towards Detective Tim, held my mouth open, nodded my head as instruction, waited for him to place my cigarette on my lip butt first, clenched my jaw and took a drag. I kept walking, leaving the cigarette in Agent Tim's hand which he tossed out the torn opening in the wall. I had the proof I needed that the SFPD littered as much as the rest of us. I made my way out of the apartment, carefully and steadily, my hand keeping Desta's head against my chest the whole way. I lifted the coat a bit to check on him when I got outside. He was sound asleep against me, his little chest pushing against mine in unison with my breath. I looked back to the scene to see Avalos approaching with approval in his eyes.

"Looks like you made a new friend, huh?" he asked with a slight smile, his eyes falling on the boy.

"Looks like it. Thanks for calling me by the way."

"No problem. The benefit of bringing in the best is that my job goes easier."

"Well, if picking up a kid is the hardest thing I do for you tonight, then looks like it will be a quiet month for you." Avalos looked over at me, his eyes bothered and restless.

"Not likely."

"What makes you say that?"

I knew the sight of the cigarette stuck to the web did not sit right with me. "I fucking *hate* spiders," I found myself saying. I avoided thinking about spiders and tried to read the sign on the roof of the building across the street to prove I wasn't scared. I counted in my head long enough to keep appearances. Just as I began to turn to leave, I swore I saw something moving on top of the building. I assumed it was a pigeon made angry from the Blondie's pizza crust it regularly dined on. I couldn't take being in the crime scene any longer and decided my mind was seeing things to get me to leave. I motioned with my head to warn the officers assembled that I was heading for the stairs. I knew if I talked, my voice would shake and I also needed to show some confidence to the child in my arms. I was careful but I also didn't play with the stairs down to the street. I got about nine stairs down before Avalos began to follow me, giving instructions to his team to continue upstairs and then leaving the scene to escort us out. I stood outside of the building, happy to get the smell of blood drying out of my nose. It bothered me that I knew the smell. It bothered so much I sneezed which stirred Desta slightly so I adjusted my grip to hold him a bit tighter. I found my eyes going back to the neon sign on the roof across the street, still unable to shake the notion that I was being watched.

"Looking for something?" Avalos said from the doorway approaching me.

"I don't know," I replied. My first instinct caused me to pull Desta closer but my second was to try to recall how I arrived downstairs. I protected the kid from the drops but the trip back to the car was a blank. Third instinct was a squint of my eyes to scan the street after the rooftops. Nothing. The neon sign wasn't even blinking. "I feel like someone's breathing down my neck."

"Me?" Avalos asked with his trademark sign of genuine skepticism. It was then that I noticed he had been in fact looking at me for a bit, intent upon my eyes like an impromptu DUI stop. Maybe I was blinking too much. Too much coffee not enough water.

"Of course not," I shot back, "I just feel like--watched." I looked down the avenue toward the end of the block by the mail box. *Nothing.* Back up the block again. Nothing. "Ya know what . . . maybe its nothing."

"All right. Tell you what. Let the detective do the looking and the shrink do the healing right? I'll send a car around for a sweep and let you know if anything turns up. You can ride with me. It will ease the kid on the ride over."

"Not necessary. I'll follow you."

"Well c'mon then. Street is empty and it's raining sheets," Avalos countered. "That's not good for the boy."

"I know," I answered. "Maybe I'm just shaky. Its been a long night. I will take him by the center and can do his intake myself." I look back up to the neon sign.

"Suit yourself."

With the door open, I handed Desta off to Avalos. He was a father himself and was not a stranger to making sure children got inside cars without banged heads. I started toward my car wondering why I thought that Avalos' offer to send a car around was pointless. I noticed an alley I had not paid attention to before. I felt a primal sense of fear, like a small child being asked to take out the trash and not able fathom what might be in the dark. I hadn't felt like since the night my parents left. I kept walking none the less, lighting a cigarette and keeping a strut to prove to whatever I was afraid of in the dark that I was not scared. My jaw was taut, biting down my back teeth and putting my tongue to the top of my mouth, chin down. I took a drag off my cigarette and stopped in the middle of the alley's mouth. The way that the light, the shadow and the deep dark contrasted each other against the inside walls of the opposing buildings formed a shape; a tuning fork with no shaft. I heard what I thought sounded like my Dad's voice.

Clay.

Something brushed my neck, just behind my ear.

Don't be afraid.

I twisted, swatted the air with my left hand and brought my right hand up in a fist that snapped my cigarette in two. I heard myself scream and then realized my mouth hadn't opened. First, there is the silhouette of a person, then only garbage cans and bad smells. I prepared my mouth to call for Avalos and jump when something touches the back of my leg. Spinning on my heel, I saw a black and orange alley cat walking away talking to itself after having rubbed up against my Achilles heel. I unlocked my car and paused before sitting inside. I looked back at the alley before I got in the car and felt worse than I did scanning the roof tops. The things I saw did not sustain when I blinked and tried to recall them to memory. In fact, couldn't recall how go from the building back to my car. I decided I had better get inside some familiar place before I had a black out while behind the wheel. Rather than risking it, I locked the car twice for paranoia's sake and walked back over to ride with Avalos.

Spinning through the great void of space, third in orbit around an ancient star was a planet the inhabitants called Earth. On its western hemisphere was a large continent known as North America. Along the western strip was a 1,500 mile long state called California. In its northern region, at the tip of a peninsula surrounding a deep bay was a city known as San Francisco. This is where the Hunter chose to place himself on the rooftop of a building.

Place is the only accurate word to use as it neither climbed nor flew to the rooftop. It also did not fall. He chose where to appear and it was the rooftop under the neon sign. It stared across the street at the hole in the side of the building that had been covered by a web. It knew that the web went against the natural order of the land. Its vision shifts to the silhouette on rooftop parallel to himself. The Hunter turns its attention back to the hall in the wall across the street where two men can be seen walking past the opening. One of them is a police lieutenant, the other is its first target: Clay Durward. Clay stares out through the hole into the night searching with his eyes and finding nothing but rooftops and neon signs. The Hunter stares back at Clay, maintaining its camouflage in the night even when the neon on the building is not flashing to reveal its outline.

The Hunter notes when Clay and the policeman descend the steps of the building. To the Hunter, there might as well not be a hole. It could see through walls as easily as a shopper looks at a store display through glass. Seeing that its intended target was unescorted after handing the child off to the policeman, the Hunter mutters to himself that "It is clear." It speaks to himself out loud to separate his intent from the voices in its head that seek to betray its subconscious. The Hunter cleared the tail of the duster from his side as it crouched, tucking his elbows against his knees to rest his chin on the back of his hands. "My tasks are complete," the Hunter states under his breath, taking note of how the statement tightens the muscles at the back of his neck.

The Hunter continues to watch the building entrance and shifts his crouch to sway in place as a warmup. It reaches his hand out to focus its attention, drawing a line down to its target from its own outstretched finger. The Hunter's eyes relax and become steady while its head pivots. The way the Hunter's head twists and jerks on its neck is reminiscent of a bird hunting its prey from the air. Clay makes his way out of the building, clutching a large object wrapped in jacket to his chest. The Hunter finds it unfortunate that it is alone and the target is accompanied by a bodyguard. It causes the Hunter to long for his own companion.

The dark and unmarked sedan was the signature of plain clothes police detectives from coast to coast. Constabulary should be a welcome sight to the Hunter but that night the police presence was a sign of constriction and inevitable danger. Clay eyes scan the rooftops above him, pulling a cigarette from his coat pocket and attempting to shield it from the rain. As he lit his cigarette, Clay found himself staring at the neon sign above. The Hunter tested its camouflage with a wave down to Clay, finding his antics wouldn't be detected.

"His eyes fail him," the Hunter comments to himself with a tinge of relief in his voice. He looked back to the empty rooftop, believing his periphery caught movement along the eastern rooftop--a ripple in the Veil. The Hunter begins to fumble through the pockets of its own coat in search of it cigarettes, coaxing itself to find no alarm in how much its hands shook. The shakes were as much a companion to its rampant mutterings as the Silhouette was to the Hunter. The voices and the shakes were the cost of the Passenger who constantly throbbed in the Hunter's head and threatened to rule its subconscious. The Hunter finds its fingers into the pockets in search of something to smoke. It detested every moment of the search as it was a reminder that this was the only way it knew to silence the Passenger for a period of time. Its cousin had proposed the temporary measure but circumstances had made it permanent. As much as the Hunter resented the method for its harm to his Carrier, it respected the results. It allowed the Hunter to be in one place at one time with one mind.

Horace was the name the Hunter would find on his birth certificate if he needed to look. He answered to it less and less as the days went by. His fingers found the packet of Newport 100's and brought one to his lip. Circular splatters formed along the stem as the rain announced its subtle next movement. This draws in his attention, Horace's eyes relax further so that world can lose color and become mercurial until all that remains is a two toned palette of dim red and liquid silver. The air around the cigarette begins to waver like the sun bouncing off the asphalt in a southern summer. The moisture evaporates from the Newport as the rogue drops of rain hit the small orb around the cigarette and instantly become steam.

A spark followed by a flame and it has a fiery cherry at its tip. His eyes fall upon on the destitute building across the street and the unspoken thoughts of its suffering tenants.

"Purge it now . . . be done with their infantile lot," Horace mutters out loud with a dangerous and guttural sound in the back of his throat. As soon as the words leave his mouth, his eyes reveal a state of panic and craze. He burns himself with the tip just below his left wrist. The smell of charred flesh matches his flinch which adds a watery rain to his gaze. As the pain increases the madness subsides in his eye. Horace drags the cigarette, staring at the wound on his forearm. As fast as his reflexes are, Horace senses a presence in his proximity he hadn't seen coming. His own periphery senses a ripple in the Veil and his panic sets in. He spins with a slight movement in his shoulder as he rises, folding his injured arm into a lateral elbow that will decapitate anything standing behind his right ear. His assault arm meets nothing but the killing air and finds no target. Hearing the weakening of his Passenger, Horace slowly returns his gaze to the street below by rotating on the balls of his feet and returns to a crouch. He raises his right hand and places them on the burn on his left arm. Horace catches his reflection in a small puddle of water near his right foot and watches the sign of terror, then pain disappears from his own face. His Passenger retreats to the back of his mind and lurks in a corner. Horace nods in understanding, squinting away the small tears with the smile of a child.

"You know this is how wars start . . . right?" Horace asks the night, hoping anyone who cares hears him. Flitting his eyes from the street to the roof top again, Horace catches sight of the cigarette that hung in the air after he dropped it to attack. His eyes go wide and Horace fixates on the cigarette suspended in the air, failing to hide his surprise. A distant gong sounded from somewhere causing Horace to switch his expression to the self-disgust of a kid dropping his tray in the cafeteria. Horace grunts like waking from a nap and quickly snatches the cigarette from the air.

"Sorry," Horace murmurs his apology out loud, "the Carrier forgot." Dragging the cigarette hard, Horace breathes out and continues to address his himself. "These works were more exertion than I anticipated." Horace removes his hand and walks to the edge of the building, shaking his left arm to loosen the muscles. He watches his arm where there had once been a burn as the rain resumed on to the skin of his forearm. He looks down at the target intuiting his target's unease. Clay Durward looks up from the street below, his eyes drawn to the source of the digital gong coming from the rooftop opposite him where the neon sign cast through the rain drops. Horace stares back, testing his own sense of camouflage against the target's eyes. Noting his target's upward gaze, he understands the concern. "He is not completely aware," Horace reassures himself when the target looks away. "We still have the time needed."

Horace nods and then points again. He follows the pointer finger's suggested direction to a shape make its path along the gutter pipe running from rooftop to the same sidewalk that Clay Durward and Lieutenant Avalos stand on. Although more than thirty feet away and the size of a thumbnail, Horace's eyes do not miss the detail of the creature. Horace watches the silver spider climb the waterspout as the target separates from Avalos. Clay Durward walks toward his car while his police friend warms up his own vehicle. Shortly after, another shadowy figure grows in size as it is projected on the wall near the mailbox down the avenue. Pale, bald headed, long khaki raincoat, the familiar black suit, blood red bow tie and small wire rimmed sunglasses at night. Horace walks past the gutters to step off the rooftop into the alley. His fall is more of a circular parachute orbit rather than a direct plunge, landing him on the balls of his feet on the wet asphalt. He walks the alley away from the target to its end, finishes his cigarette and replaces it with a long blade shaped like a sharp hockey stick.

"Long night," Horace mutters as he leaves the alley via a ground level door in the building he had just drifted down from. It takes him through a hallway, into a courtyard, through another hallway, into a courtyard, through another hallway, past a laundry room and on to the street again two blocks away from where he started. Horace's underground maneuvers have delivered him behind the figure with the bow tie and khaki rain coat that is walking toward the crime scene from the mailbox. Feeling eyes watching him again,

Horace scans the alley way and finds nothing. Horace shifts his focus, his body language intent on the khaki raincoat stranger who stopped in its tracks and was reversed its course toward the alley. He paces slowly, knowing he is just one piece of a plan involving two operatives. Content that the other operative is free to complete its task, Horace continues on. He backs himself into the alley, covering the space until he left only a sword stroke between his back and the mouth of the alley.

Horace pauses, scans the alley, scans the distance to his secondary target and then the sky. Horace assumes his partner can hear him but refuses to acknowledge him. Testing his theory he finishes the thought, "you would tell me that it's the days that'll kill you, though." Nothing but the sound of cars driving through water replies to Horace. He decides he is being watched by his mischievous companion who refuses to reveal itself. Horace smiles and adds on. "It's now."

"Good hunting," Horace says and walks off in pursuit of the stranger in the khaki coat.

CHAPTER TWO

"What I look like?"

-DeAnthony

The sun shines its light across 93 million miles to be captured in every aspect of the planet Earth. This light is opposed by the darkness of empty space that balances against the light as the hemispheres of the planet turn away from the Sun. The result creates a station the inhabitants of the planet named shadows. Of all the cities in the world, San Francisco attracted the most shadows, ranging from its fog covered peaks to its mysterious urban corridors. From a bird's eye view, the shadows connected into two unique puzzles that are distinct in formation depending on whether day or night ruled the city. In each of the city's shadows, hidden from an untrained eye, lurked the Silhouette of man. It heaved its chest with a breath but drew no air. It stepped along the streets and leapt from the rooftops, yet it made no tracks that could be followed. It reached out and massaged the items it interacted with and left no finger prints. It stalked and hunted its prey without ever losing a trail. Though elusive to most, that night its target was easy to track despite the Silhouette avoiding specifics. That night, the Silhouette had to two targets and its first was Horace.

Horace was hardly passive target. He could be at any location he chose, neither coming nor going. When Horace arrived on the rooftop, his clever eyes found no sign of the Silhouette, although he sensed he was being watched by some thing. The Silhouette crouched in mirror image of Horace, on the building top just east of where Horace crouched, hidden between each drop of rain. The Silhouette followed Horace's gaze down to the street below, staring into the heart of its secondary target. Watching Horace step off the building's edge to the alley below, the Silhouette followed Horace to the street below, disguising itself as a shadow cast by the neon sign above against the drainage pipe running down from the gutters.

It continued its hunt, tracing a path along the cracks between the buildings, finding the fault lines in every structure and running the course like an ant in a tunnel. Horace stepped quickly through the mazes that connected each street level complex for their complex, keeping pace with his agenda. His instincts told him to duck under the vent that released steam from the laundry room into the air. The Silhouette amused itself as it passed out of the pipe and hung in the vapor behind Horace's head. At the end of the his trek, Horace stood in the alley and drew his ancient blade as he eyed the Stranger across the street. Muttering to himself for comfort, Horace began his hunt and set off after the Stranger.

The Silhouette waited in the alley several breaths before it moved again. It was tagged into its primary target, the seasoned man child hiding in the body of a thirty-year-old killer. The Silhouette followed Horace with its sigh, keeping deadly still so it remained camouflaged against the stain and rainfall of the alley wall. It afforded itself a smile at the irony of stalking Horace while he stalked the Stranger. The Silhouette paused until both were out of sight and playing chase with one another before it pulled away from the wall. The Silhouette counted each of its steps along the puddles, motor oil and dried beverages that mixed together with the rain's assistance.

If it had a face, the Silhouette could relish the moment with a childish grin seen when small humans reach for cookies they are not supposed to have. Free and unrestricted, the Silhouette giggled to itself as it stepped in between each drop of rain falling from the sky. It enjoyed the challenge and reward of avoiding the wetness.

Walking on its tip toes for no reason, the Silhouette came to the mouth of the alley and focused on its target. The Silhouette studied Clay Durward as he walked down the street, starting with the man's gait and the rhythms of his steps. The Silhouette mimicked these nuances with a split precision: part composer and part mime. Then the Silhouette matched Clay's posture, mirroring the man's tendency to hang his head as he walked while swiveling his head on his neck from side to side in search of the threats he couldn't find. The Silhouette matched his target's breathing, timing itself to match the flow of electricity through Clay's body down to the beat of every pump from his heart. In complete parallelism, the Silhouette was an absolute doppelganger of Clay's experience which served to make Clay a perfectly defenseless target.

Clay suspects something watches him as he passes the alley. Finding nothing with his senses, he tells himself the crime scene has made him excessively jumpy and he requires a cigarette. This is when the Silhouette strikes and reaches out its shadowy arm. The Silhouette touches Clay on the back of his neck. Clay turns in place, facing the Silhouette and shrieking. The Silhouette matches Clay's screams and cradles his head. They make synchronous blood curdling sounds of fear and pain in their throats. They build in crescendo and take on a beat. The screams grow in loudness until they are broken by an underwater gong.

The handheld Avalos teases me went off. It was morning. 6:10 AM. The alarm sounded like it was screaming. I turned it off and I realized I managed to get some sleep. Sleep. Eventually I have to succumb to it. I remember this one. Let's write it down and add it to the ones before. I'm writing them down now so I remember. This was definitely a voyage into thinking I might not be awake. I might not be asleep either. I remember lying down but I don't remember falling asleep. It's amazing how I can move my shoulder despite all my weight being on my chest and face against the cushions of the couch but still can't motivate my legs and waist. Oh well, I think to myself and roll onto the floor. My head hits the crinkly nylon of the carpeted floor that is strewn with photos, printouts I had requested from Avalos.

When did I become an investigator?

Oh yeah. I was an Egyptologist once. In undergrad, before salaries mattered, I studied dead languages and cultures. Moving my head to orient myself, I stare at pictures of crudely drawn symbols and glyphs in dry blood.

Creepy.

Time to shower.

The water was hot and the steam clung to my face. The water comes directly from the Sierras, melted snow picking up minerals as it runs a series of streams and rivers before being piped into the Bay Area. My hair was getting too long. The water washed the widow's peak of confused curls into my face. I became aggravated with the idea of going to salons and being trimmed while thump bass music played in the background and men who date men advised women on their marriages. I was also feeling too old to wait forty-five minutes to get my head clipped by razor as the barber talked on his blue tooth and watched sports. I was impatient with my hair. I remember being smarter recently and just shaving my head but somehow I had allowed this growth to form. I turned off the water and stepped on to the bath mat, pulling the towel around my body. The mirror was free of steam. I use an open window and a fan to drain it from the room. Saves time.

My eyes were intense with exhaustion. There were rings around the lids, as if my face had grown tired of bags and moved on. I would remove the scruff and briar that had taken residence on my face as soon as the water from the sink was hot enough for shaving. The brown was drained from my eyes, allowing room for the amber flecks within muted green. My skin looked pasty and clammy like tapioca. I needed sun and more sleep; less artificial lighting. I should be a couple shades darker like the color of oatmeal or the clever hands of the young boy I pulled out of a hellhole last night.

My eyes drift over to the picture of my parents' wedding that Granny kept on the couch side table. I have my father's build and shape of eyes. I was cheated out of his gorgeous complexion of oiled and treated black leather by the cross pollination of my mother's pistachio complexion. Her partial Puerto Rican heritage also gave me her cheekbones and lips. They found consensus on my hair, giving me long curls that I can comb back straight when my hair is wet or covered with gel. The Muslims selling bean pies on the T-train often comment I resemble Fard Muhammed, an idea I find hilarious.

I lathered up, covering my face, then pulling out a disposable razor from the package. I had to teach today, then I had sessions, which I'd end early to make sure I could check in on Avalos and see if there were any leads on finding Desta's guardians. I suspected that any blood relation to the child was spread between several examination trays at the bottom of 850 Bryant's crime lab. The process of waiting for social services to get him placed would be long and painful. Avalos was checking on the chances of him staying with me until proper channels opened.

I took the hair off my cheeks in broad strokes, ignoring any shadow of a shave or line up from before. Today would be a bare day. It felt like a new year. A day after heavy drinking when you promise yourself something new. But it was just another day.

Sometimes I feel too tall for my own good. My body feels a bit larger and awkward than I'm used to. Almost a sense of puberty that's never left me. I envision myself as shorter, in the high five foots. Looking at myself in the mirror, I appreciated my over six foot my stance. I felt light and cagey like a monkey. I am proportional and wiry, some where between 170 and 180 pounds when I remember to eat. I watch my arms flex as I move and feel compelled to throw a few punches.

What am I, a little kid?

No. I know how to do some things I tell myself. I make sure not to fight so that when I have to I can use my all. I still wrestle with the fact that I smoke. When I can't sleep and there is nothing outside my door to keep me occupied, I exercise, believe it or not. No gyms or awkward changing rooms for me. Push ups, sit ups, crunches, whatever I can do within the confines of my home.

Ouch.

I knicked the area of my neck where the Adam's apple creates a valley against the bottom of the jaw. Focus.

I allow the deodorant to dry and the cologne to settle before dressing. It's sunny today or will be soon judging by the sun peaking in the through the east window. I won't be fooled, though. The wind will be high by 11 am and the water will be back in full swing by dark. I'd need to be in layers today. Tonight the water will keep the crowds inside their homes. I had no such luxury, so I tucked a umbrella into the back outer pocket of my satchel. I threw the strap of the satchel over my shoulder, doubled checked the stove to ensure it was off and made my way out the front door. After about a minute of securing all billion locks on the door as well the security door, I walked down my front steps to the street. It was about three blocks to Third Street where the train ran and as luck would have it, my route brought me to a stop without having to do much more walking along Third.

The platform was sparse this time of day and the train pulled up shortly after my arrival.

I checked my phone briefly for the quote of the day that usually arrives by email subscription. "Psychological freedom, a firm sense of self-esteem, is the most powerful weapon against the long night of physical slavery," I heard myself say in my head. I read the quote again and smiled at how my own mind recreated the quote in the original author's voice. Martin Luther King Jr. wasn't a bad voice to have rumbling around in one's head. Feeling inspired, I turned my thoughts toward prepping for class.

I spoke to myself in my head, using the rhythm of the wheels against the tracks to rehearse my lecture. Feedback loops. Today, class, we are going to discuss why you argue with your parents who pay for your education, housing, meals, clothes and drugs. We are also going to explore why you fight with your boyfriend to prove that he cares. Examples. Examples, dear friends. The message is sent from the broadcaster. It is received by the participant who processes, filters and responds. This response is feedback. When your special someone tells you to grow up, you speak to him but your feedback is for the male authority figure who has made life so hard for you.

Feedback comes in both positive and negative forms. One of the purest examples is economics. Positive feedback loops in one's income and consumption occur. This positive feedback continues in that your consumption translates to profits for a firm and these firms translate those profits into wages for their employees which becomes income. If only negative feedback mechanisms are governing a system, we call this loop "imploding." For a rather exaggerated example, think of a person who loses appetite when preoccupied. Once she starts to worry, she loses weight, therefore being even more preoccupied as she sees her state and loses even more weight, and so on. If nothing else stops this vicious circle (e.g., societal help), an imploding negative feedback loop leads to the self-destruction of the system. As I understand it, the larger the income per capita in say San Francisco, the more I see people consuming. The more they consumed, the more they gain the ability to consume and that same income per capita grows. Ceteris paribus, this machine will continue without pause or maintenance. The feedback loop in its most positive form.

I hate spiders.

No idea where that came from. I looked up from my hands to look around the car of the T-line as it chugged up Third Street, stopping at King to let off the UCSF medical clientele and pull in the Cal Trans commuters who blend nicely with the high priced downtown condo crowd. Who buys a condo next to a ball park? Who does such things?

My scans of the room show me nothing. I can't tell if the voice was in my head or if I said it out loud. Usually San Francisco is great about eye contact but this morning nobody has the energy. Moving away from face to face encounters, people are consumed with the iCulture and making sure they stay in their bubbles. We are avoid each other on this train. The city aide, the paralegal, the sculptor, the city college student, the MUNI observer, the homeless mother, the finance officer, the thug staring at me, the future independent movie director, the before 10am stoner skater, the line cook at Farmer Brown's, the barber—wait.

My eyes scanned back to the deep chocolate, mid-thirties, tattoo-clad young man sitting with arms folded at the back of the car. His eyes did not leave me and his face showed no indication of approval or disdain. It was a normal San Francisco morning in November; somewhere less than 55 degrees before the fog pulled away and either gave a hint of sunshine or gave us a sheet of rain. Cold. I had on three layers plus a thick ankle-length trench coat made from wool in Macedonia, sold at Macy's in Times Square. Gloves and a scarf, too. It was by no means a warm morning or any day to plan a car wash.

The gentleman still staring at me wore a black tank top and jeans, the type of gear appropriate for a picnic. His body showed no sign of response to the cold despite his dark hue that I knew to be better acclimated to the heat. I wondered if the knit cap he wore over the doo had anything to do with his resistance to the arctic winds coming off the China Basin. I also realized I was staring again. Okay, Clay, let's focus. We have work to do in the head.

Negative feedback loops exist as well. It is hard to imagine because it's extreme to say that only a negative feedback mechanism is governing a system. However, when it does, we see the loop imploding. Let's take an over-the-top one. Let's say that one of you in this classroom loses your ability to want food whenever you become distracted or occupied by something. Could be a lit cigarette, could be a text or could be your own vanity.

As you start to worry, your body begins to lose weight. As you lose weight, you become distracted or occupied by the weight loss itself. Therefore, the more you fret, the more you lose. If only it worked that way, right? What's wrong with that, huh? Well, what stops this cycle? Is there not a point where you are occupied by the loss that you lose weight to the point of your body beginning to break down. Please do a Wikipedia search on bulimia or anorexia. Point being, the imploding of the loop leads to the ultimate breakdown of the system it carries itself.

Where do these loops start? That question is coming. I know this lecture well enough to know that question will either come up or have to be prompted to connect the dots. We start our loops from symbols. So let's ask ourselves, "why are there symbols?" Homework. Bring in a pre-Christian story of how a group of people use symbols to explain the creation of the universe. We will discuss. Extra credit to those who can provide links or pictures of these symbols. Submit your answers electronically and I will combine all your submissions to show some patterns and disparities.

You should have followed him.

Okay that's the fucking voice again.

I looked up toward the back of the car where the temperature impervious black man had disappeared without a trace. Was I so involved in my head that I missed him walking off the train? The gloom of the Embarcadero tunnel pulled a cloak over the windows and kicked on the internal car lighting. I admitted I was a little sleepy from the late night, but it was impossible to conceive that anyone in the car had walked past me while I was rehearsing. Maybe I am that out of it. How would I know if he had passed by and I was that lost in thought that I missed it? Why do I care? Long day. Day hasn't even started. I needed a cigarette before the next bus ride.

Montgomery station isn't nearly as ritzy as Embarcadero but its closer to a bank I use and its got more bus stops. The 5 goes directly from Market up Fulton to where I need to be. Somewhere along the way I would dip through the Fillmore where my African American counterparts join the bus route for eight stops to exhibit their favorite stereotypes to see what kind of response they get. I remember once asking a colleague who was also black if he felt they would act differently if we didn't wear suits to work. He asked me why I would want to rob them of their routine and we both had a good laugh.

I slid my FastPass through the turnstile and made my way upstairs. The wind had picked up, brisk and clean. Not the subsewer cleanout usually reserved for early mornings in the city nor the oiled fishy smell of the Bay. Just a cleansing wind full of salt. I lit a cigarette and pulled out my phone. Scrolling through the previous text messages, I found the familiar name.

You: (7:48 am) Need a session.

A couple drags and exhales. Another cup of coffee would be great right now. Just fucking lovely. Of course I should have thought of that before I lit the cigarette. Amazing that my eyes can scan Market Street, find three Starbucks, but none of them will bring coffee out to the people who still practice taboos.

"Ay, I got dem CDs for—" the kid starts, moving his shoulders back and forth as he ramps up his sales pitch. I hold my hand up to stop him and start digging in my pocket.

"What's your name, man?" I asked quietly with a smile.

"Why?" the kid replied with a snap to his lips.

"I like to know who I am speaking with," I replied.

"DeAnthony," the junior salesman informed me.

"Listen, DeAnthony," I say and dug into my pocket. "Here's a twenty," I said quickly, producing the Jackson. "I don't want a CD. I want a cup of coffee from inside, tall, half calf, three sugars, enough milk to match my skin. The change is a donation."

"What I look like?" DeAnthony replied, face twisting into a baby snarl.

"Change will be $18.50 and the line looks 5 minutes long," I continued. "That's $222 an hour. Better than what a lawyer or accountant starts at." I made eye contact. "You look like a business man."

"Three sugars?" He said, taking the bill.

"Three."

"Got another square?"

"Businessman is starting to sound like hustler." He smiled and waddled over to the doorway into Starbucks, pulling his pants up as he opened it. I started to offer another twenty for a belt when the phone went off.

Xochi Cervantes (7:52 am): You OK?

I typed in my response.

You: (7:52 am): Long night. Voices on the train.

"That was real quick," said the young entrepreneur holding two cups. He handed one to me. "I got myself some chocolate. Thanks."

"Glad to help."

Xochi Cervantes (7:54 am): I'll come by your afternoon class. We can take a walk afterwards.

I guess even shrinks have shrinks. How small is that?

CHAPTER THREE

"Sooner we start, sooner we finish."

-Xochi

"So what you are saying is the Egyptians didn't have gods?" she said, her forehead wrinkling with the question.

"Not in the sense of omnipotent or all encompassing creators," I answered. I pursed my lips, a sign of I was trying to rearrange in my brain to make sure the example I gave made sense. "Think of them as ancestors . . . historical figures who lived and exemplify lessons we want to take note of. Any come to mind."

"George Washington, the cherry tree and honesty"

"Good, any more?" I pursued.

"Gandhi and nonviolence"

"Excellent. More?" I continued to push.

"Jenna Jameson. Being sexy"

"Okay, that's reaching but I'll take it," I said with a chuckle that encouraged the nervous energy in the room to disperse as the class laughed along. "Now let's add in that these concepts also identify scientific principles. Can we come with other examples?"

"Thor and war?"

"Okay, that's more social science. Do stories of Thor have any other scientific law or theory?"

"Electromagnetism?"

"Why?" I asked with feigned ignorance.

"He throws lightning?"

"Exactly. So these ancestors are about not only explaining why things are the way they are but also how we can use these aspects." Politics. This is where the lines between ones job as an educator and personal truth-seeker become blurred. I give this lecture once a year every time I teach this class. It was easy to get the main point across that showed a linkage between how cultures decided the universe was created and how those civilizations evolve to see their place in the world. The same linkage could be made between how one's background or upbringing and how that person approached the world. The danger was suggesting that beliefs were made up, especially at a school founded by priests. Even worse would be to feed into the rebellious undergraduate notion that they can abandon their tax paying parents good faith and works by dropping out of school to become a born again Viking. That's what gets you a private meeting with Dr. Cervantes with your employment contract on the table as well as your student and peer reviews in her hand.

"But they have statues and monuments and idols all over the place," another student chimed in. "How can you say they nobody worshipped them?"

"Who are they?" I asked, drawing the class into the repetitive drill I'd become accustomed to. Maybe I was buying time. I suspected I knew the right answer. Not my opinion, not what I wanted to hear and not the opened ended thinking the school's mission provided. This time I had a sense there was one answer. Something nobody ever sees. Okay, that's eerie. Focus, Clay.

"The ancient Egyptians," the Ed Hardy-clad douche bag sans gold chain in the back row says without looking up from his Mac book screen. Must be a fierce game of online poker.

"Ancient, huh? Which Egyptians in which period are we talking about?" I said, maintaining my coy tone as I crossed the room to the other side so I could place a hand on the diagram of dynasties and timelines on the far right side of the smart board. "The Nubians," I queried starting at the inception and resurgent dynasties. "The Hixtsos," I continued circling my hand down to another range of dates, "The Greeks? Romans? Caananites?"

"I don't know," douche bag responds with a shrug, still intent on Facebook pictures from the weekend.

"Well, I don't either," I said flatly, enlisting another chuckle from the mostly female class. *Yes you do.* Focus. "But we can make one exceptional leap of logic. We can first trust our professor to say it was the Nubians who founded Egypt or KMT."

"What?" she asks and her shirt is open. Inappropriate for class but she knows no better. Her papers have more typos than is realistic and she sits too close during office hours. Playing stupid is not attractive, young lady, but I'm here to teach you psych, not gender redefinition.

"Ka-met," I reply making sure my eyes see nothing but hers. "We write it KMT but vowels were added for pronunciation by years of linguists."

"Oh, okay."

"So this leap we will take. Of the contemporary societies surrounding KMT . . . Greece, Rome, Phoenician and Sumerian . . . there is no explicit text to suggest these deities were nothing more than metaphors. In fact, it is the priesthood in times of economic crisis that begin projecting the notion of deification." Your job, Clay. Do you like it? You want to keep it? The room is in long pause as the wheels turn in the head of students. Light bulbs have not ignited yet. *Go for it.* "Yet in the Book of the Dead excerpts we read, also known as the 42 Declarations . . . clearly . . . CLEARLY . . . it states that no deism properties should be applied to the Ntr."

"The what?" came from the back, attractive Thai girl but too much mascara and I never found jade-colored eyelids to be realistic.

"Was in the reading," I fired back, with a little condescending twist to boot. "Help me out here." Silence and page turning.

"Give a hint?" jade eyelids asks like ordering a drink.

"Guess that's a queue for audio visual." I cross back over to my laptop and with a few clicks, the LCD was filled with statuesque photos. "The infant Heru suckling from his mother Auset. Auset's not only the feminine principle of man's growth and storage of knowledge but also the symbol of the throne. No man can rule the kingdom without equal division of power with a woman but birthright is more determinant of your mother than your father." Giggles. The women seem to agree.

"Oh yeah," mascara chimed in, "the Black Madonna, right?"

"Right," I continued, "Djeuti working tirelessly through night and day to create a text from the divine speech that mankind could use to track its developments. Bonus points. This language is called?"

"Med Nahtur," douche bag says finally looking up from the screen. I feel obligated to apologize to him for calling that. "Scott . . . my savior . . . very good, but the pronunciation is Med doo Net tur."

"What was the pronunciation for the divine speech?" the bright red hair with glasses and freckles asks. I remember her name as Sherri because she raises her hand, is polite and seems a bit excluded from the rest of the student cliques. I like the outsiders.

"Med doo Nef fur," I throw out there, "great speech." I keep clicking through slides. "Khpr transforming Ra's thought into intent and design as Ptah. Drawing the blueprint of the universe and setting the stage to begin forming the world.

Therefore Ntr are to be understood as ancestors. No different than your great grandfather who came to this country as an immigrant and built the company your parents work at. You look to that ancestors example as how to be hard working. The Nubians looked to the beetle Khpr as how to bring about transformative change."

"So if they aren't gods, Professor Durward, "what are they?"

Metaphors," I replied. "Guiding metaphors." The buzz in the left coat pocket of my jacket indicated the mark of class's end through the silent alarm set on my phone. Of course, the alarm was for my own benefit and not the students', who were nearly militant about packing up on the dot.

"Warm up for next time," I said, picking up a green device that served as a place holder for a dry erase marker. I began writing in free hand, assigning the speaking points for the next class.

"What does your world soul look like?" I said as I wrote. I made sure to underline "look" twice.

"Is that the Ka thing from Monday?" I heard from behind me, over the right shoulder and to the back of the room. Searching my mind, I couldn't place voice to faces in the classroom.

"Yes," I replied and turned on heel to find no student's hand raised. Instead, they were either writing, closing laptops or packing bags. At the end of the sloping agora like classroom, arms folded in front of her chest with a sarcastic grin and holding perfect posture was Xochi.

"Ladies and gentleman," I said, somehow drawing attention from the herd of savages intent upon getting out of the room. I was surprised to find so few words could deaden the movement and silence the crowds. Thank god I decided on that second cup of coffee. "You all know Dr. Cervantes. Please say hello to the Dean."

Waves, smiles, nods, sniffles, limp handshakes and shuffling. She was a fan favorite and the people's champ. Child prodigy extraordinaire who had a doctorate by the time I finished my master's besides being four years my junior. She taught, lectured, was a research partner, and renowned for award winning theories in treating sexual abuse in young women. She was also my boss.

The students made their regards to Xochi as they filed out through either door of the education building. They placed me in her department out of a categorization: "Unorthodox, but gets results." You knew you were a faculty favorite when the prefix of the class that you taught matches the building that you teach the class in. You know you are on the shit end of the stick when your office hours are between classes and the classes are on the opposite end of campus. It could be worse. I could be one of the business professors I loaned my room to when they needed a review session for one of their graduate accounting courses; those guys had to ride a bus.

"I always liked this lecture," Xochi said. "Did you manage to suggest that the Catholic church was made up?"

"Considering the stock market in November of the Lord's year 2007," I replied, "no, I think I'll keep my retirement safe." She laughed.

"Don't want to ride unemployment until '08?" she countered sarcastically.

"Will there be anything left?" I said, powering down the screen and waiting for my laptop to shut down. I watched as the computer flitted its light in signal of putting things away from the desk top and saying goodbye for the night.

"Ah, the rain's stopped," Xochi said with a smile as she peered out the window, pushing her glasses back up her nose. "Can we try the mountain?"

I don't like exercise. I have reasons for it. They are never good reasons. Good as in valid. I seldom sleep and sweating type activities make me lightheaded. I am lazy. I admit to my laziness. Xochi, among wonderful services such as listening, suggesting and prescribing medication, also believes in the age-old tradition of blood flow. In fact, she does studies about the change in brain chemicals from waking up in the morning and saying "Good Morning" with a smile as opposed to "Oh Fuck" with a grimace. It's proven the first does more for improving one's demeanor than the second. My brain is working overtime trying to find an excuse not to walk up that fucking hill. I might even lie here. Say I hurt an toe or I wore the wrong shoes. There are multiple ways are out of this situation. I focus on unplugging and wrapping up cords, putting the laptop into the bag and removing any papers from the aisles. "Searching for excuses?" she continues.

"Desperately," I said, throwing the strap of the messenger bag over my shoulder after putting on my coat.

"Sooner we start, sooner we finish," she replied.

I nodded and started out the room, Xochi shortly behind me. Down the stairs, through the doors, and into the parking lot for the education building. Next to us, up the path, the recruits did push up drills in loud repetition for their ROTC sergeants, every single movement translating into loan dollars for their education. We made our way along the pathway, silent as we passed the soldiers, and continued up the sharp incline of drive way toward the administrative building. The grass was like wet emeralds in cut shapes that seemed convenient among the succulents, tall trees and other plant life that was more decorative than practical. I shoved my hands in my pocket and accepted the increase of my heart rate. As I walked, my hands nervously pulled at my coat, reaching for a cigarette and lighter.

"Can you wait a bit longer?" I heard from up above me, Xochi farther up the route, her eyes locked on to the birds who had the courage to return once the rain paused. I nodded. She doesn't like me smoking but she's not the lecture drone that Granny is. I keep trudging along, reminded of the stories of the original priests who had to climb this mountain without soled shoes and asphalt to build their mission on the rock. The very thought of self-doubt and pride pumped out of their every step as the progressed up the mountain. The rigor of self testing leading to self-discovery and therefore developing a new approach in the absence of the blocking brain chemicals that encourage old patterns. The rhythm of the legs seemed to bring up a song only I could hear. The voices of the natives who helped carry stones up this trail like crackling of flame or the sound of hiss of an old vinyl under a needle. The pulsing bass of the voices of former slaves free from the rail roads for the day, encouraging each other with the hope of becoming a gold prospector. The hopes of Chinese writing home, telling their sons about the future of the hills and how the money they sent home would bring them here soon. *You should be proud.*

"You hear that?" I said finally hitting the crest of the hill.

"Hear what?" she said, quickly and sharp. Regardless of whether there was something going on in my head, at least Xochi did the compassionate thing and cocked her head to try to hear what ever was going on for me.

"The voice," I said panting, stopping to place my hands on my knees. I was so out of shape it was ridiculous.

"Are you still just not sleeping or were you up to something?" Xochi asked, examining my face for what I would gather were the signs of my battle. I had a theory that a chart existed some where in Xochi's office that correlated the numbers of hours I rested through a night to a shade of purple under my eyes. Then I thought back to the mascara girl in my class and wondered if she simply knew something I didn't.

"I sleep some . . . couple hours," I said, taking a Bay Guardian from a bin and placing it on the wood bench for me to sit on without soaking the ass cheeks. Xochi seemed to find a spot without a spot of moisture.

"How do you do that?"

"I'll show you sometime," she laughed. "Still . . . you slept some. That's good right?"

"After meeting with Avalos, yes, I did." Xochi turned to stare at the horizon as the western sun began to fall behind the spire atop the campus church and dip into the lavender streaks along the inlay of the Pacific Ocean known as the Bay. Xochi was hiding her expression but the tension in her shoulders, grip of her jaw muscles and palms on her knees told the tale. I'd known Xochi long enough to understand what it all meant. A hope that I would make different choices with the hesitant acceptance when I did not.

"You put too much faith in the system," she said, still watching the water and circling her foot as if she sat in it.

"Avalos is a good cop"

"Um hm," she dismissed.

"How many child prostitution cases does his squad catch and put to bed? A month? A year?"

"There we go confusing the man with the office"

"So you suggesting he's dirty?"

"No. I'm suggesting authority and those who wear it often go home to separate masters."

"So what are we debating again?" I asked.

"Don't change the subject, Clay. The issue is your reliance on systems to make the world as you see fit"

"How many kids come into that center based on referrals? How many young women are returned to a healthy home? How many families are . . ."

"How many more will be on street?" Xochi fired back. "How many are out there . . . right now . . . paying debts to cops much less the pimps? How many mothers will let their daughters lose to the wrath due to brothels that never get touched by those officers, unlike Avalos, on the take?"

"Thank you, senator, for that. No, really. Did you really want numbers on that or can I silence my inner Jed Bartlett?"

"You give that man too much and ask too little," she stated.

"I get what I'm good at."

"Is it acumen? You want a built skill base and acclaim? Working under the radar to achieve glory only you and the . . . wall is aware of?"

"Gee, So-ch, when do we become friends cuz this hater stuff sure is wearing on me."

"Light your fucking cigarette, you baby," she says with a chuckle, rocking back and forth slightly as she brings a few fingers up to clear wisps of hair from her face. I laughed along, following our ritual of watching the three thirty sun shine over the water. I made sure I waited at least forty five seconds silently before lighting a cigarette, which also enlisted a laugh from Xochi at my patterned stubbornness.

"So I'm naive?"

"No. You confuse the office with the man when it comes to Avalos." Short pause for a fire truck.

"So I'm ignorant and naive?"

"Bout who exactly, Clay?"

"Myself."

"Always a good answer when talking to a shrink, right?" Pause. Long. Sustained. I hear muted piano in finger rolls on loop. I remember the sound of Nas opening the most controversial album he released reminding me that I knew the height of the sky, the square mileage of planet earth and the number of Pi. Queens get the money, right? It is easy to fool yourself into one-liners and quick polite responses as you navigate people all day for only a few minutes each. You don't ever stop to interact wholeheartedly so you can get away with the best plug-in repetition and familiarity can buy. This is the purpose of friends. To remind Clay that just turning it in on time to oneself is not enough. In these private moments we accrued with people we value, I collect every precious moment left. It takes energy to fight with Clay Durward and stick in there. Xochi didn't come here because of obligation or pity. I wasn't a lost cause, either. There's a loyalty gained from continuously building up someone and being strengthened by each other. We were siblings in that sense, bonding by a commodity that was impossible to replenish.

"All right. What am I not seeing?" I asked finally.

She turned, switching her entire lower half to rotate herself to face me. Her eyes had changed had changed color then, a reaction to the sun in her face and a signature of the village in Mexico her father's mother came from. Ojos Tapatios, just like the hot sauce. A hail back to Jalisco. The sun cut across her shoulders like a solar sash, the canopy from the giant oak above us cutting a shadow along the length of her face. A slight breeze blowing the second hand smoke away from her, I smelled eucalyptus and not menthol.

"Has it occurred to you that part of you is attracted to the slime under the rocks that good men like Avalos kick over?"

"Come again?"

"He pulls you in on the stuff with kids that makes him worry about the safety of his own children."

"Yeah, so?"

"You are good at it," she said, "very good. Is it good for you?"

"Is it bad?" I asked.

"Voices are back" she countered and I stood up abruptly.

"That's not fair," I said forcefully. "Doing this shit is what got them quiet in the first place. And it was your idea."

"Moderation. Maybe we swung the pendulum too far in the other direction," Xochi replied. Her voice a whisper to match my yells. The breeze picked up and I felt moisture on my face. The air was cooling again and preparing for another storm. A flock of kids walked by us for the stairs down to Golden Gate, every single one with white ipod ear buds blocking them from noticing or hearing a world around them.

"There was a kid last night . . . "

"Clay, I'm serious" Pause again. This time it was me looking off the mountain on to the streets of San Francisco toward China Basin. I watched the cars tear down Fulton, the buses pull along Geary and the tourist appeal of the peaks hide the beauty of the Mission from bird's eye.

"No meds," I said finally, done with that chapter in my life. "No sleeping aids either."

"No meds," I heard Xochi say in agreement. "Clay . . . have you considered that if you keep this up there are doors you might open that you cannot just . . . just . . . what am I trying to say? Walk back through to the same place?"

"Bad analogy, So-ch. Doors goes both ways except in airports, amusement parks and jails."

"You might walk through one and it's you who changes, not the landscape." I haven't visited Granny in a week. I usually never miss my appointments. I've got a failed marriage. My ex's divorce attorney did me a favor during the settlement after realizing the other guy's client did no wrong. My teaching and work at the center pays the mortgage on my grandmother's house in an inflated seller's marker with a ridiculous price tag among a rock cocaine-shooting galleries and rising property taxes. I show up to very ugly places involving kids and keep them from becoming the monsters that damaged them. If I were to change by doing what just felt right, so fucking be it. I needed my grief. It helped me consume the pain of others and gather the bandages of their own self- healing.

"I need this," I said flatly, my voice cracking and dropping the butt of the cigarette to the mock gravel where my Kenneth Coles ground it by the heel. I could hear Xochi exhale; disappointed. *We don't need her . . . she is weak.* There we go again. Almost a whisper like someone gossiping about you at a party in the same room as you except its in your own head. A quick white flash in front of my eyes and the sound of a boom to accompany it like being punched in the nose with knock out force. I straightened my spine in response and felt the muscles of my back pull time. Searching. Waiting. Come on. Talk again, you fucking psycho. Say something. No voice. Just a hand on my shoulder.

"The same little boy you checked in this morning?" Xochi asked. I nodded and started down the path back toward our offices.

"Avalos texts me last night and from its sound, I think it's some kid I need to soak before he points out where the bad man keeps the other kids."

"No?"

"Nah, this was some whole other shit."

Family.

CHAPTER FOUR

"I only need a few moments."

-*The Stranger*

Xochi left me to ponder as she often did, not because I requested it but more because she didn't want to watch me light the second cigarette. I waited until she was out of eye sight before I lit the second cigarette, playing a vicious game with my sense of guilt. The guilt eventually subsided and it converted into considerations about how lazy I had become. The other part about being lazy is that you have to visualize in order to get up from a bench. By visualize, I mean picture hands in front of you that rock your spine back and forth before the momentum builds enough to rise. Once things get in motion, you can swing up and get off the park bench to your feet. That is what life's about, right?

The walk down hill should have been easier than up hill for me, but it was not. The temptation to run down with my eyes closed to just get the whole process over with was far too great. I took the paper with me to keep pace, thumbing through it as I walked. The editorials in the front were a mess of whining sessions written by judgmental hypocrites who had complaints for the very city policies they voted into effect. This led me to whatever passed for news in the next sections.

It was all feel good stuff anyways. A few months ago, Paribas, one of the biggest banks in France, explained that it could no longer find customers at any price for their subprime mortgage bonds. This translated to no customers for these bonds at all. The effect was a huge crunch on credit which was spidering across economies due their global nature. The effect was multiple banks refused to loan money to large corporations, banks being large corporations, because they felt they must reserve loans for their closest allies. I was reminded of the kids in middle school whose parents would drop off food to them in after school programs but tell them only to share with their cousins.

Despite the current president and his economic advisors telling the people we were experiencing five years of a booming economy, data was showing that the real wages people earned were not increasing in comparison to the cost of living. In reality, these wages were actually decreasing. The cost of living was generally hidden under the umbrella term of inflation which left out the prices of food, gasoline and health care, the things people really spend their money on. These items were climbing radically with no evidence of stabilizing any time soon. Some reporter interviewed a woman living in the Bay Area border of the river Delta known as Pittsburg, who was making ends meet by tapping into her savings through securing home equity loans to pay off her credit card debt. The reporter went on to point out that savings rate of the United States was at a negative for the first time since 1933. It wasn't that Americans didn't save, but more that they spent more than they made; the compensation came in the form of home equity loans. Something about my attention fixated on the word equity . . . ownership. The majority of these home owners had purchased homes with adjustable rate mortgages, the same mortgages those "struggling" banks could no longer sell.

I continued to scan through articles, my focus tending to find the really hopeful material. I caught a quote from Epicurus in an advertisement for a website promoting peer learning: "It is not so much our friends' help that helps us as the confident knowledge that they will help us." I wondered if that woman interviewed in Pittsburg had anyone who gave her the confidence that they could help.

Rumors indicate that Northern Rock, the United Kingdom's building society, will need financial support from the Bank of England. Between here and the chaps across the water, money was pulling down the drain faster than the flush mechanisms in the Giants' ballpark bathrooms. All momentum warned of dark times to come. I shook my head at the notion of it all, feeling a migraine threatening to ruin my whole day. Sometimes it was too much to digest. The housing market was falling apart. Prices of homes continued to rise, growth in new buildings had frozen and the money to purchase was being smoked away. All across the Bay Area, signs of foreclosure were taking root as mortgage payments jumped up well beyond what a hard-working family could reasonably pay. To add frustration, student loan debt was climbing as well. The majority of college graduates were saddled with private loans that would accumulate to over three times what they could actually earn in their life time. That assumed they could earn as unemployment rose the chances of a lifetime career got slimmer. The economy was sick and needed medication. The talk provided no solutions and all telegraphed a terrible storm. I rolled the paper into a tight cylinder and held it in my hand, surveying the cross walk in front of me at the bottom of the hill.

I watched each armada of cars, buses and trucks speed along the street in expectancy of the signal to cross. Patterns formed in my vision as I compared the velocities of vehicles to the speed at which the college kids walked across the streets. I edged myself a little farther in front of the pole to avoid being bumped into by the channels of college students on my side of the street. The paper in my hand became a comfort as I twisted and untwisted the cylinder into my palm.

The light changed and I walked with the crowd, alone. The conversations and sounds of my strolling neighbors seemed to invade my space and I longed for another smoke. The cylinder tightened in my hand and I clenched it until I could feel the blood leave my knuckles. Once across the street, I cut to my left and took a long detour to buy myself some solitude. I smiled at my recognition of the avoidance I was putting into returning to the office. A lot of my daily interactions were avoidance, doing something so I could practice not doing another.

I needed to head to the Mission, then back to the Tenderloin to check on the kid. I was debating whether or not to take the laptop with me. If I left it, I could always catch a ride back from Xochi to retrieve anything from school before a ride home. Still deliberating in my head, I decided my moleskin journal and pen was a necessity that could not be left behind. I reached across the desk placing my journal into my bag, along with a foldable parka I could wear in case of the rain. I had a rolled up *New York Times* I carried for flagging cabs and grabbed that in my left. I grabbed my phone charger just in case I found a rogue outlet and decided to leave the laptop here to avoid rain damage when my periphery vision caught the movement in the mouth of the doorway. I left my door open generally since it had an inverse relationship with actual face time spent with students or explaining why a paper topic wouldn't work. Close the door and there would be no end to the flustered undergraduates dominating my office hours. Leave the door open and my afternoons were silent.

I watched the shadow on the ground in the hallway move as if a reflection in a pool of water tested by ripples. Dark, amorphous and tendriled like eight violatory legs of some dangerous smoky bug. I shot my eyes up from the floor, almost expecting to be greeted by some monster in preparation to pounce on to my desk. Instead, I followed the impeccable shine of black, thick-soled shoes that were neither designer or government issue to the crease in the pant leg that hung by the ankles, the sign of a tailored look that came with custom suits. The cut of the jacket hung over the belt but I could barely make out the clasp of suspenders attached at the belt. The shirt almost seemed suited for a tuxedo over casual or business attire, affixed at the neck by a bright crimson bowtie. I was reminded of Muslims of Third Street as they hawked final calls and bean pies. Then the alabaster and dusty pale nature of his skin by the neck that carried to the face as well as head off set any Shabazz like notions I had. There was an accurate goatee of black hair accompanied by side bars that connected to the mustache. His small but pug nose and shiny bald head revealed him as male, at least on the outside. The eyes moved rapidly as he read an article posted on my door but hid behind thin wire rim sunglasses that matched his gloves and shoes in color. It was then I realized, although his front faced my open door, his attention was very much focused on studying me.

"Clay Durward," I heard him whisper with a deep exhalation through the nose and thick accent I could not recognize for the life of me. Russian mixed with Ethiopian? "Your reputation proceeds you. These are quite impressive findings."

Trauma stimulates a fight or flee response in all of us. In children, the lack of sophistication and development with emotional intelligence leads them inside their own head. We all have the shared experience of leaving pants on a chair in our room and awakening in the darkest of the night to see that same chair a terrible dragon. The most piercing dream drives us awake in bed and we pull the covers over our head in some unwritten rule that lack of visibility of the threat creates a loop where the threat cannot see you. Your eyes become stuck open, locked into a wide stare that dries your eyeballs. Your breath becomes trapped in your chest as you hold your breath, causing tension in your neck and a tightening of your stomach. The back of your neck where the brain meets the back becomes warm and tense while your big toes pull up in preparation of running. These were our signs of trauma. Who teaches their children "just hide under the covers?" Where did the evolution of the brain go from its earliest response of "oh shit, a saber- tooth tiger . . . run!" to this later stage where we run inside of ourselves. Children go silent into a place where even sound makes them vulnerable so they dare not make it; they stop speaking altogether.

In the early part of this new century, I found myself working with a lot of volunteers from Silicon Valley's tech hangover. Jobs were scarce, the economy took a hit, and it seemed like we couldn't do enough for youngsters at the center. Programmers, engineers, product manager and designers who had all lost their jobs in the dot com fuckery clamored to the Center for Youth Resiliency after a talk that Xochi gave at that private college with all the trees that someone turned into a podcast. It was about her work with young women as survivors of sexual assault and some of the breakthroughs she had made. Given that most of these stray do-gooders were more prepared to install servers than work with kids, I let them build me a program. We found that with the use of symbols, icons, diagrams, wav sounds, animation and the basic 3-D modeling that we could create an interactive environment that allowed young people to tell their own stories. Sure, they were not the narratives you would expect out some adult telling the triumph over tragedy but instead little people writing their own mythologies of why things are and finding new ways to conquer the monsters in the pages. Some reporter at the *Guardian* got word of it, came by and wrote an article.

In the months that followed, the article was some sort of accidental fishhook that began reeling in mothers from the Marina, the Heights and as far as Marin with young people who had stopped speaking. I was much less comfortable with wealth and the entitlement it came with back in those days. In fact, I resented it deeply. Kids are kids, though. I treated them with the same respect regardless of gender, class or ethnicity. Xochi found me what the average child shrink in the Marina charged and we knocked it down by forty percent as our asking price. For those who could pay, they did and the money went directly to the center. For those who could not, Xochi gave them "scholarships" that the center paid for our time. Then she roped in some of the bright ones from the nonprofit management program at our school and I was told I had stumbled on to a revenue stream. Soon our waiting list spanned a year for appointments with Doctor Durward; I wasn't actually a doctor but the kids decided that was my moniker.

Somewhere after that, I showed up to a bunch of dinners with Doctor Cervantes. The kind where you rent a tuxedo and have conversations with strangers about what you just left at work. Xochi started pulling in the private donors and a consultant whose daughter finally started talking again and admitted she smoked pot as well as avoided school due to surviving her uncle's inappropriate babysitting methods. The father was so touched and impressed, he got his firm to donate time to studying the program and success rates were published in journals but it was the *Wire* magazine article I posted on the door. The piece was on the software, the center and myself but I kept it for the quote I gave that I highlighted for my students: "No one can write our children's destiny but they and they alone." It was a reminder to my students that their excuses were invalid when they crossed the threshold into my office.

"Thank you," I replied, snapping the brackets of my messenger bag closed. I needed to get out of there and this guy gave me the creeps. If I knew my stuff, I'd seen this type before. Probably some pedophile trying to pick my brain for tidbits of children in pain he'd keep in his twisted mind and run home to twist his nipples about. Yuck. "You'll have to excuse me," I continued brusquely, "I was just heading out."

"I wonder if you might be of assistance before you leave," he inserted without acknowledging I had spoken. In standing up, I realized how much taller and wider he was than me in a way I did not see from sitting. I wouldn't be able to eye muscle this one out of my way.

"My time is short." Curt. Direct.

"I only need a few moments," he replied, a smile growing on his face. There was something too perfect and disgusting about his teeth. Repulsive to the point where I wanted to jump out the window behind me. Time stood still and I was aware of not necessarily being in my own body. Flashes of psychedelic Technicolor like the animation panes from the Spiderman cartoon of my childhood, the black skull and crossbones on a yellow palette of poison, the temptation of paralysis, slowing down . . . *Never.*

I got the sense he was looking inside of me like an accountant going through files with an entitlement to my memories. Something in me unnamed and ancient blocked him without me being in control. *No, for you I am here. Show no fear.* The voice had changed in my head. No longer a whispery, tired alternative of my own . . . it was deeper, focused and still. Older and wearied. Determined. Then it occurred to me: there was more than one voice in my head but one was dominant. *Reveal nothing, not even me. Surprise it with your lack of susceptibility. It fears what it cannot trap.*

"Now," he said cocking his head in jerky motions, "I wish to find the child."

"We are not an adoption agency," I said without losing a beat. I saw his smile fade into an open sneer of surprise and frustration. "I'm also going to have to ask you to step out of the doorway. I'm late." *Good.* There was eye contact then. In looking at those dark lens, I stared back with the acknowledgement that those rims hid something sinister. My eyes looked behind him to the posters on my walls, the awards, the cards from students, the pictures from kids, photos of field trips. My life. He nodded slowly and took a step back looking to my left and above.

Emotionless. "Ah, such remarkable creatures." I let my eyes shift to track his vision making sure not take them off of him for a second. Suspending from the ceiling paneling by a single strand of long invisible silk hung a small silver spider at least six inches above his left shoulder. "One has to admire their attention to detail, industriousness and meticulous nature."

My eyes locked on the lens of his face, looking past them into the deep pits of oblivion. I was once again with the voice, the safe one, except I was in my own head and watching as an observer from outside. I both felt my hand moving as well as watched my left arm pull up along straight line vector of his zipper line, arced at his left ear, cut across over his head and smashed the spider against the wall with the rolled up newspaper. The paper smacked again the wall with a resounding smack, splattering its guts against the white paint. I felt myself smile and heard "that was for me."

"Remarkable," I watched myself say and smile.

"Was that completely necessary?" he hissed in a horrified twist of his mouth.

"Completely," I replied rebelliously. "Again, I'm late."

He studied me for a moment. "But of course" and stepped backwards to the hall. I was glad I left the door locked so I could grab my bag and pull it closed without turning my back to him.

"Mr. Durward," he whispered, "I represent many influential and powerful friends that you might find invaluable to your work."

"Invaluable, huh?"

"Yes, in your funding needs. One of my clients in particular is looking for a particular child who may be sheltered at your center." He reached into his coat pocket and produced a photograph. It was of a small boy, wispy curls of hair, high cheeks, thin lips, bridged nose, skin like thai ice tea, bright and very sad eyes. Desta.

"I didn't get your name," I said with a coy blink. That's all I need to start Avalos on his ass.

"I did not give it to you." Yeah, fucking pedophile probably was in that apartment last night.

"Well then, Stranger," I emphasized the syllable *strange* loud enough to attract a look from the admin walking down the hall. "I have to tell you," handing the photo back detached, "we have a number of young people we work with. I can't remember every single one. That's what my program people are for."

"I see." He nodded and backed up a couple feet, body tensing as if to jump again, cocking his head up as if listening to something. Then I saw his shoulders relax; he nodded and turned to walk to the exit. "I hope to see you again," he said loudly as he proceeded down the stairs. I pulled the door closed and watched him head to the door to Fulton.

"I hope not," I answered.

Chapter Five

"Remember to get your passenger looked at, Mr. Durward."

-The Proxy

*I*t's quiet here. Above everything. Time is short again but for now I am safe here. I am waking up but my mind is as cloudy as the scenery. The stonework is impeccable but distant from home. I am walking feeling comforted by the blade at my side. It's a tunnel and it's ending. A dais overlooking several waterfalls, spilling into a wide estuary that trails off to feed the sea. I am excited. I am going to see Victory. She has many names. She allows me to call her by my native tongue rather than that of her own devoted. To them she is the decision they call for when they are without. To me she is gentle and kind. She is also formidable and cruel. She calls me even now. In my time here, I could have known many a woman but none would draw me like her. My steps stop making sound the closer I come to the mouth of the tunnel; I feel as though I don't actually have to walk to travel. Here thoughts float as swift as the air coming from the water. I hear her laugh and know she welcomes me with a sweet supplication in her presence. As devastating as I know she can be, there is a girlish quality to her enjoyment at my arrival. Something I had never known before her.

I can make out her shape now. Her back faces me as she strokes the head of an owl who sits on the banister looking at me. She is looking at me but she has chosen to leave her other hand holding a long spear tilted so that the tip hovered above the floor by a very small margin. Her bark brown hair hangs down casually above where the clasp of her draping white linen covers her body and flows to reveal her physique. Her arm does not show the slightest sign of strain or labor as she holds her weapon. She moves her finger and the owl flies off. I watch the cloth she is covered in catch to the wind, her wind, and pull free. The sounds of reinforced copper hitting the floor told me my garments have begun to unclasp and fall. I forget again. This is her sanctuary. She is all powerful here and all vulner-

47

able. She will strike to the final kill. I panic and crouch, draw my blade and spin to put her at a diagonal in one motion. She nods and whispers, "Don't be amazed."

It's cloudy again. Someone is touching me. Kissing. I am kissing a woman. Her lips are the softness on a ripe plum. Her breath pushes against my bottom lip and I open my eyes to arch my head. She is faceless and bright. Too bright for me right now. It hurts my eyes and I close to remember. Her skin glows in the moon light along with the sweet taste left she leaves in my mouth that seems to pulse. She is pure energy now as am I. I have brought something impure to us and she claws at it to remove it. Her fingers are in my skin as she works her way into my being, ripping out the intruder.

Opening my eyes to my cheek pressed against the glass of the back seat window, I figured out I had fallen asleep. Good timing. too. The cab driver pulled up to the Bryant side, across the street from the Café and away from the mural where a lot of the local eses like to smoke joints. The driver made a sudden jerky stop that caused me to look around for the car he was avoiding. There was none. Just the lonely street of the Mission touched by the rain. I would have thought more people to be inside but the windows revealed a warm night with a few moments indicating a sparse house. I looked forward through the glass divider toward the plastic display and attempted to ready the cab driver's name. There was the Yellow Cab certification but a miniature Palestinian flag in place of where his identification would be. The meter read $16.43 and the clock read 4:39.

"Thank you, chief," I croaked and slid a twenty through the glass tray enough for him to reach. He took the twenty and I opened the door, swinging my left leg out to the street.

"My friend," he said with a thick accent in a short burst as he dug for small bills from the pocket of his Levis and turned his body to the right to stop me.

"That's all for you," I replied, waving my hand once as I stood up and latched on to the strap of my bag.

"Oh thank you, friend," he fired back, smiling wide and nodding his head. I smiled back and closed the door walking into the street to the sidewalk in front of the Atlas. I stopped to pull out my phone and quickly text. I also lie to myself about how much I smoke by saying I'm texting and quickly lighting a cigarette I only puff ten times. I punched in a quick text to Xochi.

You: (4:40pm): Keep a close eye on Desta.

Drag. Exhale.
Drag. Long exhale.

Xochi Cervantes: (4:41pm): Should I be worried?

You: (4:41pm): Mr. Adams.

Xochi Cervantes: (4:41pm): Going upstairs now.

You: (4:41pm): Thanks.

Mr. Adams was a code we use. In a facility that might house over two hundred girls and boys, it was important fear be kept at its lowest. Therefore we used codes that referenced emergency. Mrs. Jameson was the intoxicated parent who thinks their child is upstairs and wants entry. Mr. Frost is how we prepare for a social worker or anyone from the system coming by to interview a ward. Mr. Adams was our general statement for the lengths pedophiles went through to gain access to our kids. Newsflash, ladies and gentlemen: most of these creepy fucks aren't rustic old loons in Vietnam vet military greens and spooky vans. They are generally very wealthy, very put together, have delicate features and carry the false air of high civilization on their breath.

I put away my phone and dropped the cigarette into the gutter. A square of bubble gum and some hand sanitizer did the refreshing. A honk of a car horn brought my attention back up to 20th Street where the cab had pulled a U-turn and was before me with the passenger window rolled down.

"My friend," he called out toward me, holding out what appeared to be a slip of paper. I approached his window to see his hairy thick fingers carried a business card extended toward me: basic white with information as printed at a stationary. Omid Retb. "You need ride home, you call. I be here as soon as you need." His cadence was a machine gun cutting into the misty sunset. I smiled at his enthusiasm and took the card.

"I'll do that, Omid," I said and placed it in my breast pocket, tapping my chest to show it was secure. He smiled back, nodded his head twice quickly and pulled off with screech against the wet asphalt. One of those random acts of culture San Franciscans practice. The outside wall was covered with large murals that looked more like art student work than a community-based mural project. They ranged in topic but all seemed add up the same theme of visually describing members of the Greek pantheon, the center piece being the Titan who held the world on his shoulders. Below his feet, in a clumsy red hand style, someone had spray-painted a quote: "Chaos often breeds life, when order breeds habit." The author had the decency to attribute it to the historian Henry B. Adams.

I thanked my grandmother for teaching me how to use twenty percent to tip as Omid pulled out of sight and headed inside.

The smell of baking bread immediately made me hungry. The café was laid out like a traditional pizzeria with a long counter, salad prep and a kitchen behind the doors. The scene was generally one of those Mac user magnets where they sold world news papers and everyone held the book they were pretending to read up to be viewed. The line for food was non-existent and I saw no sign of anyone I recognized seated in the place, so I ordered the half soup half salad. Clam chowder with a tuna seaweed apple salad that came with bread. I wasn't a health nut or vegetarian, I just tried to swing the pendulum back away from the coffee and cigarettes with my diet. Did I mention I ordered another cup of coffee with my meal. I paid for my meal, folded the receipts into my back pocket and waited for my ticket number. The girl behind the counter, worked around the clock making espresso drinks for a virtually empty shop.

"Excuse me," I said, my voice gravelling over the sound of the milk steamer. "I didn't get an order number."

"Corner table by the doors," she replied matter-of-factly without looking up from her stainless steel pitcher. "We'll bring it to you."

Glancing at the only table next the door to the patio gave me the view of an isolated table where a woman sat with her back to me. I approached from the far side, taking careful steps to avoid her periphery. Familiar, but out of place; wrong context, I decided. Long honey-brown hair over a shoulderless shirt of dark gray material. Solid physique, dancer or an active gym monkey. The skirt cut off just at the knees revealed her legs, short and strong, crossed over one another. Pale skin with the curves bronzed by sun or some tanning salon. Circling the table showed me more depth: high cheek bones, full lips, one of those Scarlett Johansen noses, bright brown eyes that caught my own and sent back a sparkle. In fact, I could see myself in them, and for the first time I didn't like myself. There was a knowing smile from her as I placed my bag down on the floor to lean against the chair leg, sat and pulled my chair up to the table. She was focused on her phone, finishing a text in her smart phone and placed it in the white leather Gucci handbag on the table. I realized my mind was a product placement add for free.

"Well, well, well," she said in a sultry, squeaky voice that reminded me of the drunk socialite from Will and Grace. The name escapes me. "You made it."

"I'm usually good about appointments," I replied cautiously.

"You're late." I checked my watch. It was 4:41pm. The sun had just gone for the night. *Second of all, who did this bitch think she was?* Usually people use a hello, nice to meet you, or even a "my name is." Late? Where was all this aggression coming from?

"I have four minutes."

"Be serious. You are late."

"I was told 4:45, I am here at . . . " I found myself raising my voice. Mystery woman was watching me. She was magnetic. It was nearly impossible not to make eye contact. It was as if my head was being positioned. She raised her chin and moved her eyes to scan me from my head to my waist. I watched her nose crinkle. Then her eyes got sad and distant. The cold fire that she held in her eyes when I arrived had turned to a soft, warm concern.

"If you are testing me it's not funny anymore," she said as her eyes relaxed and she turned her head to look away. I noticed there was a pink shade to her lips that I liked. It was pronounced against her olive-colored skin with a depth that came from its paler shade. Who is this woman and why do I feel like I did something wrong all of a sudden?

"I was told by my friend . . ."

"Don't," she said, bringing her hand up to my mouth. I froze. "Don't say the name." Her eyes locked in on me and swimming pool of rippling autumn leaves. A storm brewed. She was intense and focused. I must have twitched or shrugged because she cracked a smile, just a bit at first. It melted away into a full one as she looked to her hand.

"Oh my god," she said talking to herself, "did I really just touch you? How awkward that must be for you right now." She laughed to herself hearty and cheerful. I found myself smiling at the joke I didn't get.

"My name is Clay," I said, using my hand to take hers from my mouth and shake. She shook it with a diligent look on her face that melted into another laugh.

"What's so funny?" I asked. She continued to laugh and then covered her mouth.

"I'm sorry . . . it's just I've never seen you like this before," she said between giggles. Her eye lit up and I blinked. "I like it." When my eyes focused she sat holding my hand at the table smiling.

"Do I know you?" I asked.

"Yes. You remember the bar you went to about three weeks ago and you picked up a hot young thing to take home? You told her of love, promised her the world, and then didn't call?" Okay. so I go into bars. Yes, I have met women in bars. I don't promise these things. Apparently I had drunken too much that night.

"Sorry . . . um . . . ."

"Well, I'm not her," she laughed again. She looked around the room and used her free hand to rub her face as she yawned. She looked back to me then, looked me up and down again. This time she smiled mischievously.

"I like this one. I bet he smokes too. Let's have a cigarette." She motioned at me with her hand beckoningly towards the pocket that held my smokes as she looked around the room. Glad she mentioned it, but I'm not sure I like her knowing where my smokes are.

"You can't smoke in here."

"And why not?"

"It's illegal . . . despite my own wishes."

"Let's see what happens." Her eyes were beyond sparkles. I saw entire cities behind them. Athens, Sparta, Crete, pyres of bodies and the sound of men yelling at the cry of victory. Something dark and selfish in me stirred. Vengeful and playful. Against my common sense, I fished out the pack and lit one.

Something told me she wanted to share just one. "And he listens. Good."
Another excited smile.

"Who are you talking about," I asked dragging and passing her the cigarette.

"You. You are comfortable now . . . yes?"

"Better," I tried to downplay out.

"You don't remember me?"

"No ma'am." There was another streak of disappointment. The smoke from the cigarette drifted up in column to form a thickening disc above her head. She never took her eyes off me when she bent her head down to drag from the cigarette in my hand, her lips curling around it slow and with a muted smirk. She was flirting with me in a way I wasn't sure I was used to but was strangely aware that I liked. There was the soft sound of metallic drum. Almost a synthesizer imitating a gong from far off in the distance. A dull drum echoing from some remote corner down the way. Her smoke halo grew in depth and I realized nobody in the room was aware something was on fire. She made sure her lip brushed my finger, leaving a faint trail of red lipstick on my finger.

"I missed you," she whispered and licked her lips. The smoke continued to trail into the air, widening the disc above us. The drumming gong raised in volume with metallic and tinny reverb. "You remember how you came to me . . . weak and tired. I had no idea how different that was for you." Something moved in the smoke and I found myself peering into gloom like eyes when a movie screen goes from black to opening credits. A vast ocean spreading for miles, crashing its waves against jagged rocks below a cliff face. Spread into the mouth of a cove lay a white beach, massaged by the foams of the surf. As the waves washed in and out in repetition, I saw a man's body appear face down on the wet portion of the beach. Sputtering. Water and wet sand streaming from both his nose and mouth as he clawed at the sand morbidly. Half alive half dead; the man's burnt bronze muscles glistened and flexed as he crawled from the water trailing blood from cuts all over his body and a pulsing wound of ebon pink flesh that vibrated like a black light where his neck met his back. *Such memories do us no good. Feed and be done with it.* I heard the angry and spiteful voice from inside my head say as it reviewed the memories. The wounded man continued to claw at the sand, weeping, growling, and cursing. Every inch agonized his body until his arms found the sandals which he hugged with all his might before passing into unconsciousness.

She stood before him in a long white robe, hair hanging around her shoulders, a grey owl perched from a rogue branch growing from the rock face, spear in arm poised for the death strike with her face a morph of pity and horror. "I couldn't leave you alone then . . . just like I can't now," she continued and I saw her face in the woman warrior poised in the smoke. *It was a long time ago.* The other voice; my sentinel, it would seem. She posted her spear in the sand and crouched to bring her fingers to the man's neck, checking his pulse for signs of life. She stood again and held her hands a few inches from each other, the palms crackling with azure daggers of energy that surged and bounced between palms. Her hands sent out a pulse that expanded, filling the day with blue light and then retracted into disappearance. "My father warned me you would only invite their wrath but your quest for the life within your immortal blood despite that broken body was irresistible." The gonging is louder now, as if right out side the café on the sidewalk. I could neither turn my attention away from the smoke theater or fully focus on it. Within the scene scape, I watched the woman ascend stairs into a great hall, lined with pillars of half cylinder davits I knew to be a signature of Greek architecture. Assembled in line, stood various men and women in tunics aligned with columns leading to a massive throne. The ceiling was the backdrop of the stars, beautiful and bright shining orbs close enough to reach out and hug. I lay on a cloth palette, feverish, barely able to keep my eyes open, suspended above the marble floor by the graceful and unstrained arms of naked women. Virginal and fierce, I knew them to be my ward's entourage.

Approaching the throne, I watched her present me to its holder, her father and lord of their world. His fingers twisted at his long white beard hairs when she presented her case, motioning to me several times with her long lithe arms. Her father's eyes burned with the fires of his conquered Titan ancestors and the worry of the doom of existence. Resistant, his judgment was impaired at the request of the daughter who sprung from his migraine and threatened to cause another if her wishes were not granted. The lord of Olympus looks behind him and below to the world his people know, staring at the ocean that brought this change agent to Greece. Neither his brother the sea nor his brother the underworld, offer any counsel to provide an alternative. In thought, his amnesty is granted, and his action is seen in the world below.

"When you did heal. You were the challenge I loved failing at," she purred. In a large dais overlooking several waterfalls that fed a lagoon hidden from the ocean by massive cliffs, I saw myself staring into the mist generated when the falls hit the pool. My skin was quite darker and I had lost four inches to my height. My hair was spun into long locks hanging to my back below the shoulder blades. I had adopted the Greek robe in keeping with customs of my guests but clasped the tunic at the chest with a golden emblem of a L and its mirror reflection. A small rectangle box with no lid. I recognized it as the two ninety angles of Ka, the kemetic symbol for the world soul or one's experience on the planet. I watched as swallows danced up and down in air currents in the air by the olive trees that grew by rock face outside of her temple. They scattered at the sound of the grey owl's wings on approach from the southern horizon. It took long circling loops as it descended and eventually perched on the sill, blinking as it watch me with its huge eyes.

She approached from behind, wrapping her arms around my waist and pressing her face into my back. Her fingers traced the blackened bruise on my neck that pulsed with its own breath and did not heal, her very nature baffled by this wound her works could not heal. "Although your mind was with her, your time was with me." The gongs were becoming deafening. I could hear the sound of a painful moaning and a breeze from some where touching my cheek. My eyes flitted around the café expecting its occupants to be staring in awe of the film playing in a platter of cigarette smoke above our heads. Instead it was as if this woman and I did not exist as more customers entered the café oblivious and the ones who were saw nothing.

"But father like so many before and after became infected by the allure of power..." *I stood on a hillside now in a bronzed breast plate that was dented and nicked over a long lavender tunic. My gauntlets and leggings covered in black oily slick blood, the lavender cloak I wore with the olive green Ka symbol of my house, torn and soaked. I clutched tightly to the hilt of a long two edged blade, ending in a symmetrical point, thin and agile. It dripped with the same foul ichor as the as the substance on my legs and arms. Below me in the valley crept a pink rolling fog that growled and flashed with thousands of red eyes that hid themselves when seen. Behind the fog, the great citadel burned, mixing the black smoke of charred bodies with the pink noxious fogs. Towers I had once visited were covered by silk and threads stretching into giant webs of horrific scale. Within those webs sat the shapes of demonic arachnids the size of cottages hissing and shrieking in clogged wicked voices like workmen talking their way through a construction job.* The gong split my ears and hurt my eyes so much I shut them closed as my hands shot to my ears.

"What the fuck is that?" I bellowed out on reaction. I heard a "hmmph" in response. When I opened my eyes, I was aware of a set of bulbous eyes staring at me. They were worn by a small humanoid creature of deep green skin and lightbulb-shaped head. It was without a nose and had a small slit for a mouth. It wore a white t-shirt with a rainbow colored skull reminding me a of gothic Apple Inc. logo with the words "Think Entropic" under it over some cargo shorts and tiny beige Teva sandals. A small messenger bag was strapped over its shoulder and it carried a small vibrating gong in its hand.

"I see I have your attention now," it said, turning its eyes on the woman sitting across from me in a nasally, annoyed voice that seemed to creep out of its mouth. It nodded and placed the gong in its bag, producing a thin obsidian rectangle in its stead. The creature held the small pane up to the woman, looking in it like a customer service agent reading mileage in a return dock at a rent-a-car depot.

"Citizen Athena of Olympus," the little green man stated as if reading a list, "Veil Carrier Contadina Kephalos."

"Correct," she answered with a half smile and winking at me, "but I prefer Dina." He touched his finger to the black stone and nodded. Then suddenly without warning he pivoted on his little legs and turned to me, holding his thin glowing black panel. I saw the slit of his blank eyes and from where his eye brows should be. He tapped the stone several more times with his finger tips, turning its glow to fuscia, then orange, then jade, ending back at black, while looking up and down at me. His left arm moved and he placed his hand in his left pocket as if to announce he found what he was looking for. His eyes relaxed as he made eye contact.

"Veil Carrier Clay Durward," it said peering into my face, "Your passenger does not have a file in my system."

"I thought this was a free zone," Dina said in a hurried tone I had not expected from her.

"Free from Isfet law, but not my lord," the creature replied, holding his arm out to dismiss her. "I have no cause with this citizen."

"Thank you," I heard myself say and assumed one of the two upstairs felt it was necessary.

"You are welcome," he replied after wheeling back to Dina, looking back to his stone which are turned to a bright pink when aimed at her. "Citizen Athena, you are in violation of public demonstrations of works in the presence of mundanes."

"They aren't aware," she said in a passive-aggressive plea. "I have their attention elsewhere, Proxy." I realized I was watching her rationalize double parking in front of the store and catching the tow truck in mid-pull.

"That by definition is paradox, ma'am," the proxy replied in a bored and condescending tone. I realized it didn't like her very much.

"I don't think I would have taken the extra step had I known that, sir," she replied very calmly and somberly, her eyes flashing a hint of azure in the whites around her lens.

"I suppose not," he said tapping fingers again. "Nonetheless, the minor works is illegal here. Please disperse it." The proxy motioned to the smoke ring above her head. I saw her nod and watched it disperse. "Have your fine paid on time. I am not going to escalate this."

"Thank you," she said, smiling, and I smiled to myself at the humor of her somehow influencing him with the same thing he was here to prevent. His stone returned to black and he placed it back in his bag. He looked toward the window to 20th Street while reaching his arm across the table to grab my cigarette out of my hand. It should not have reached without him climbing up on table, but somehow that did not matter. I flinched a bit with surprise as he took a drag, exhaled and then placed the cigarette in his mouth with a deep swallow. Afterward, he opened his tiny mouth as wide as it could go and began to take a deep intake. The smoke in the room coalesced into a single beam the size and dimensions as a workmen's level. The smoke beam drained into his puckered lips until the room was drained of it. He closed his mouth, licked his lips and reached into his bag to pull out a small bottle of what appeared to be freshener. Spraying it around, he waved his hand and took a deep intake. I expected to smell that new car fragrance, but it smelled strangely of baking bread and slightly damp clothes. "Sorry," he said to me as he struggled to get his bag open to replace the bottle, "you can't smoke inside public establishments in the city and county of San Francisco."

"Won't happen again, Proxy," I said following Dina's lead and trying out this new information. He nodded and walked to the patio door. The rice rain stayed frozen in air and I noticed the umbrellas above tables frozen in mid-blow from the breeze. The few people who were getting up from tables to avoid the sprinkling again were fleshy statues that didn't breathe while I just noticed that the random iPod on shuffle was no longer playing *I Don't Trust Myself Loving You* by Jon Mayer; it wasn't playing at all. "Remember to get your passenger looked at. Mr. Durward."

"Will do," I replied, employing my natural-born talent for talking my way out of tickets and into free cups of coffee. He nodded one last time and walked directly into the glass patios doors, dissipating as he did. The bass lick from Jon Mayer returned and I watched the rain hit the ground. Ambient conversations in the café reminded me that the world had been taken off pause. I looked to Dina who was looking off toward the bathroom, arms folded with her mouth scrunched up. Whatever she had thought was going to happen did not go as planned. I knew this much about her. She did this a lot. Most times it worked excellently, but never on me. Although not completely clear on what was happening to my life, I felt as though I had at least an equal playing field with her right now.

"What is that face for?" I asked, looking toward the kitchen to remember that although a hipster green man had stopped the world for a time, he had done nothing to my appetite.

"You really hurt it this time, didn't you," she said nodding her head as she didn't make eye contact but rather was having a dialogue with herself. "I mean . . . I knew you would eventually," she said shrugging it off as I saw the tiny hint of tears and a hurt look on her face. "I just *knew* I was gonna have some fun with you before you broke through again." She laughed loudly slapping her own knee and pausing to rest her hand on her hip. Then she was looking at me with a smile on her face, eyes sparkling in curiosity. "How did you do it?"

I knew I had two names to play with here. My grandmother always taught me that there was a sense of privacy to a name one kept at home and a power to the name one carried in the world. When she greeted salesman at the door, she always called them by the first and last name to indicate she wasn't interested, but when she was really impressed or disappointed I knew she called me by my full name. Citizen and Carrier. These were what the proxy had used to categorize her. I decided to go for a gamble.

"Athe--"

"Hey," she said sitting up straight up in her chair, "what the fuck?" She indicated her head to toward the patio door. Athena is Citizen and that's a no-no in public. Got it.

"Dina," I corrected myself and looked back to the kitchen. "I'm listening. Why are we here?"

"I just wanted to check on you and see how you are doing"

"About to eat," I said, feeling myself angry at her for something I could not explain. My eyes followed the body language of the short Salvadorian waiter bringing a tray my direction. I smiled to make sure I could read if he was in on her little thing, the game I felt I was playing along with. He gave me the eye daps that told me he knew I would bus my own dishes and tip so nothing funny had happened back there with my meal prep. "Bout to leave right after, too." Her nose scrunched and I saw her arms fold again.

"Why can't we just speak to one another," she paused, the last piece a little too long to make me feel it wasn't rehearsed, "like we are . . . "

"Like friends? We're not friends. Friends call me directly"

"You are a real asshole, you know that? A real prick?"

"Want to get a new table?," I said, smiling as the food arrived and grabbing my fork quickly. Maybe I was hungry with low blood sugar but I didn't remember actually moving my arm to get the first bite in my mouth or the next. I was chewing, I could taste the rich flavors between the bit of cinnamon on the apple or the tanginess of the vinaigrette on the tuna but I was lost on how it was getting in my mouth. I blinked as my swallowing seemed to be moving slightly faster than things around me.

"Fine," she said digging into her purse in a huff, pulling out a laptop and a plastic case that held several jump drives. She placed the laptop in front of me with the screen in my direction and flipped her finger across the power button. It was a Macbook, of course. I am Clay Durward, going schizophrenic seeing women who make me hallucinate with American Spirits, getting fix-it tickets from lime midgets and I am a PC! The screen jumped to life from its sleep state and I starred at her desktop. She popped open one of the USB flash drives that I realized was color-coded black as opposed to the usual red, yellow and the brown. She plugged it in and sat back in her chair, producing her phone and looking at it.

The screen had gone white except for a single field. It read Last Name. I looked up to her and received "yours" mouthed from her in return. I inserted the information, pressed Enter and was asked for my first name. That was easy to complete and was greeted with blank field. I looked up again and saw her staring at me. "Your anchor," Dina said, "who you would die to change if you knew you could right now." I haven't seen Granny in three days. When she first got Alzheimer's I promised myself to do everything I could to make money to pay for her care. The more I worked to provide, the less I could get away to see her. Maybe that was my excuse to hide from visiting and being in pain about it. There was a couple times I was drinking and thought I made a deal with God that if he took me then and there, Granny would miraculously get her memories back. After what I had seen, I wondered if I could do such things.

I typed her name into the screen. I watched as the white screen dissolving and I stared at what appeared to be a page to website with threads to folders. I read recently about the cloud computing technologies that had been developed down the 101 at the really good search engine company. Apparently, they had figured a way to make integrated blogs and servers to give each user with one login id their own personal server space thru wireless. This page had no address; instead it read Thrones. I looked at the threads and the massive amount of folders each contained: Start Up, Journals, References, Genealogy, and Dreams. The word start is usually a good guide of where beginnings are. I clicked on it to see a page open a read a description page:

It's going to scare you. I'm not going to lie. Every time we do this we need to make sure we leave a back door so we can ensure a commitment until the end. If you are with us, there is a link below you will need to click. If you cannot finish what you start, then I need you to close this laptop immediately and tell the woman across from you that you like to see her naked.

Granny was seldom critical of me. One thing she did say, though, was I had a bad case of not knowing when to quit. I didn't let things go when I was younger. I not only needed the last word but I was willing to get my ass kicked to get it out there. She called me Pay It Forward Durward as a cute joke because I told teachers they should call her at work because I knew I was going to act up. I didn't win many fights as a kid by being a knock-out king; I just generally did not stay down and did not tire. I looked down at the link and ran my hand over the mouse pad to move the cursor over the link. I just couldn't leave shit alone.

The page changed again and I was greeted by another letter.

This is you. I wrote this to you to tell you how to get back up to speed. How can you believe anything I'm saying. I know. This is crazy. I know. I also know you get teary eyed every evening when the sun sets. I know you really well, Clay. Get yourself around this concept: I am writing to you.

We need not to push things to hard because we want a clean transition. However, there are some things to be done and the longer we wait the less chance of finishing this. I am going to give you nine rules for now. When you get those down, I'll give you nine more and you should move around the next page in Thrones.

1. *You are Sekhem Ka*

2. *Your cousin will never leave your side*

3. *The child is more important than you or the Carrier you are housed in*

4. *Trust the Aztec*

5. *If she uses smoke, you taught her that, just watch people and then feel them*

6. *Your heart answers to Neith*

7. *The Passenger in your mind will do anything to return you to them*

8. *Isfet Propius fears fire*

9. *Log out and ask Greece for the glyph now!*

"Where's the glyph," I said forcefully, trying to make myself proud. I looked to the bottom of the page and saw a log out icon. Clicking the log out icon seemed to further automate the laptop as it flickered the screen to a blank desktop and opened the hard drive. I watched as all the histories and temporary files were erased; the rumors of any key strokes I had made were transferred to the flash drive. The flash drive popped out of the USB and the computer shut down. "Now . . . where's the glyph!"

Dina's eyes narrowed and reached in the purse again pulling a small Fed Ex box. I felt my eyes shift and the world turn mercurial again. The box shrank and leaving a piece of sandstone with a forearm carved in it. *Khepesh. Strength.* She placed the box on the table and I made note to pick it up to place it into my welcoming backpack. I smiled as something in me told me I had something nobody knew about, the trump card that the players didn't know how to use. Dina closed her laptop and placed it back in her back.

"I did my part," Dina said confrontationally. She leaned in, her eyes blazing and focused. "Where's my son?"

"*I can't say,*" I felt something reply. Her nose crinkled and I saw her place her hands on her knees nodding.

"I am being more than amicable," she replied slowly, "but if you want to see *her* again, play with the concept of a mother missing her child more and see what happens?"

"*That a threat?*" I felt fall out of my mouth and realized a part of me knew was no match for me. Match at what?

"No," she said, "but eventually I will grow tired of waiting. I want my Desta."

"*He's safe,*" the other voice said, "*safer than with you or did you forget your choice made him a rogue as well?*"

"Can I see him?"

"*Can you?*"

"Sekhem . . . are you going to push me?"

"*And now we are using proper names are we?*"

She stood up and pushed in her chair.

"This is how you are going to be, isn't it?," Dina asked, putting her purse on her shoulder. I felt myself chuckle and shake my head.

"*Who owes who here?*" I found myself saying, twisting my lip up with a sense of disgust at a woman who any other day I'd walk into traffic to get attention from. This sense of entitlement and arrogant chattel ownership dug at me. It was clear that I needed her for nothing and she should be pinned to wall by every principle for what she did. What was that? What did she do? Did she do something? Was there someone I was angry at she reminded me of.

"How long am I going to have to keep doing this?" she said, looking away, her voice low and painful as if embarrassed and ashamed. I was aware that she knew my thoughts and was ashamed to be reminded of some infraction.

"*Until you choose a fucking side,*" I heard myself say, an ethereal and scratchy authority to my voice. The bass of the tone almost made me believe there was a mouth on my chest.

"I can't say sorry enough, Ka," she said, walking away, "but I fucked up and I know that." I had an ex-wife that said that once but I couldn't remember her name right now. Dina walked past the tables, ignoring every man who turned their head to watch the movement of her legs that stirred the pit of the stomach and made you want to bench press gas stations to be with her. Graceful and sullen, Dina and Athena walked out of the café. I was aware it wouldn't be the last of our encounters. Soup was off the hook, though.

Outside smoking. Again. I don't finish all my cigarettes. I've pulled my parka over me to fight the drizzle. I decided walking up to BART was a better idea than an eight block cab ride. I tricked along, noting the ease which movement came now. It was as if that 15% of the brain humans were supposed to be limited to had just increased. My legs pushed fluidly my head feeling light on my shoulders as if suspended from a thread. In front of me, a youngster in a Niners coat and matching red beanie trudged up the block ahead of me carrying a radio that blared Tupac into the night as he waddled up the street with his pants below his knees. I decided the music would help clear my head and sped up to make sure I could at least sync with its pattern.

His shoulders hunched on his back, unaware that the tension made it that much harder for his neck to continue its rotation in the expectation of trouble. 20th was a neutral zone, unclaimed territory between the northerners who owned 24th up, the brown priders from 18th down, and the portero brothers who crept down from the hill in search of sales that never made their way into the projects. David Hernandez, the son of second generation black migrants from Texas who'd come to build ships for the war effort and the Mexicans who were here when they arrived. He repped his flagrant soldier colors out fear of being *discovered without which was a contradiction to the fear of being caught on 20th with them on. David told himself the rain made it safe and losing himself in the passion of the 7 Day Theory made him safer.*

I was aware . . . I was no longer psychoanalyzing David; I was in his head. I could hear his thoughts from at least two blocks behind as long as I kept an eye on him. Turn my vision to a sign or another pedestrian and David's dialogue ended in my head. Focus on his bop and how he sang along to himself in the night and I wore his skin like a suit. *He powered his way up the street, looking to make it to Mission to see what was awake. His eyes scanned every door way for threats, expecting what he called Scraps or southern-ers, to creep from dark corners.* Given my dinner with spiders hanging from Greek architecture, I didn't blame him. *I was curious why he would choose such a route if it implied danger. Exploring further, I found myself digging into the recesses of his being, David unaware of the answer himself. What he was aware of was the steps behind, his alert for danger acute and nearly feral behind his stoned state. I saw through his eyes as he turned his head to spy the parka clad male a few strides behind him. Examining the sweater, laptop bag, coppery skin, wavy wet afro and glassy eyed look in his eyes as he walked, David decided his temporary companion behind him was no problem. In fact, he looked like some down ass principal or outreach worker, the type all the kids liked but knew not to get attached to because the time line before they were fired was short. I suggested I was safe, David, believing that thought was of his own ideation acted on it by giving the parka man the tough kid nod of "Sup" and turning back to his walk. He wondered if I liked Pac or I was one of those New York back pack niggas his cool teachers all seemed to be.*

Walking at my same pace, was it physically possible I could have caught up to David in such a time? Looking behind me, I decided that three blocks in twenty seconds was possible for a Jamaican track star at the Olympics but not chain smoking Clay Durward. I was reminded of the list of nine I gave myself: *You are Ka,* I nodded, fanatically aware of the symbols in Ke-metic thought but not sure how it applied. *Your cousin will never leave your side,* I have to file that with number one for lack of family. *The child is more important than you or the carrier you are housed in,* this took some reasoning. The child had to be Desta, there really wasn't any other way around it. She had gone as far to name him which confirmed it. In addition, we knew her name was Contadina which applied to a carrier. Carriers must be bodies just as my carrier was Clay. Therefore, the kid was some kind of grand priority and at risk. My mind flew to the pink fog, the talking spiders and the webs in the hotel room. Ugh. I don't like this superhero story so much any more. *Trust the Aztec, I got nothing. If she uses smoke, you taught her that, just watch people and then feel them.* Stories, experiences, memories, in our mutual minds. I thought about David and realized, this is why it was familiar. I was reminded of when I first started working with Xochi Cervantes, she was a wunderkind and I needed a project approved to graduate. It was a quick fix, meet with some kids she worried about down at the Ida B Wells Center and write a paper. It was then my lucked turned against me and I was told about my uncanny knack for getting inside the heads of children. This unfortunate series of events led to further education and degrees. I began to conceive perhaps this talent I had no control over was part of something bigger, an aspect of having "Ka" inside my head. If that was true, then jumping from David's mind to my own could be focused despite it disproving laws of space. Furthermore, if regardless of distance, I could magnetize another's thought and pull myself in, then the space between us for my corporal body could be magnetized as well and pulled along. An experiment was in order.

I tried to see if I remembered my high school chemistry lab. We had a hypothesis, now a test was in order to replicate results and then we would form a law. I scanned as far as my eyes could along 20th, catching the site of an older woman pushing a roller car of bagged laundry down 20th on the opposite side of the street. Letting my eyes relax, I was able to feel the vacuum of inner dialogue pulling at me. Spanish. Mexican....*ojala que llega a mi casa antes de la lluvia . . . me duelan los pies. . . gracias a dios, hay comida de la noche anterior en el refri . . . mi esposo tendria que tomar su medicia, no mas futbol anoche! tendria que dormirse . . .* Clay ball, bounce off wall, corner woman. I found myself drawing a line between David and the woman named Zoila, a long streak only my eyes saw like lining up a shot on an online pool tournament. Meanwhile I imagined a line behind me, tugging at my back in exactly the opposite direction and distance from the woman. Somehow I knew pulling back first made my physics teacher happy and would avoid the proxies. Slingshot loaded. Count to three. Breathe and let go . . . .

Zoila was a little shocked she looked up from her feet to the black man walking past her. She usually knew faces and he seemed like a nice one, she just didn't see him there before. She smiled and he smiled right back. 20th and Mission. Amazing. I looked down Mission and decided there was less foot traffic to 24th then down to 16th. I would head south, sticking to the even number addresses of the street which had less street lights and neon. My eyes searched the street and could make out an older white male pulling himself in a wheelchair using his legs; how come no green men for him? Eyes relax and watch. *Jesse. His spine had been damaged in a steel mill in his twenties; standing ignited all sorts of ache. One of his buddies had turned him on to shooting heroin to kill the pain; both in his back and his wife's resentment when she had to begin working due to his disability checks barely covering the cost of bread. When she took the kids and left him to move up with her mother, he sold the house and followed the love of good horse out west. Hotels, whores and the monkey had long since drained his pockets.*

I made sure as I walked next to him, I reached in my pocket and fished out a dollar. I dropped it in his lap, surprising him as he looked up.

"Hey!" he said, his breath smelling like I don't what the fuck, "I was just gonna-"

"Buy food," I said smiling, "not the stuff. K?" Eye contact, warmth, hope that he could try better tomorrow with a little forgiveness and time.

"I am hungry," he said slowly and tired. "Thank you."

"My pleasure," I croaked and kept walking, 24th Street BART within a block of me. I smiled at the possibility of telling Xochi I would never be late for a meeting again as I crossed the street and made my way down the stairs. Then I was reminded of the growling pink fog I didn't like and loneliness. Better not involve Xochi, nobody should get hurt in this but who was already involved. Who else was involved? I walked to entry kiosks, waving my phone by the pad to have the fare deducted directly from my checking account. On the second set of stairs, I smiled to myself as I remembered not to use my new found fun to jump on a train. The Dublin Pleasanton line came soon enough and I was seated on the car, I pulled out my journal, skipped a few pages and wrote whatever came to mind.

So today I learned to . . . .

What did one call it? The sticky feeling pulling one's self along by connecting people? The ability to soak yourself into a random stranger's thoughts like jumping into a hot tub full of conversation. What does one categorize this under? *Wisping.* Thank you. Today I learned to wisp. I let my mind wander in pause from writing seeing how many head I could bounce through as the train pulled away from the Embarcadero station. I was aware that some thing was attempting to peer into me. My eyes shot around the car to commuters with heads in magazines, iPods, laptops, articles and on the phone. My eyes caught the brown green-flecked irises staring at me from the back of the car near the door. I recognized them as the tank top from the T-Train this morning. I must have looked shocked because he smiled and lowered his chin to peer at me from the top of his head; a boxer's stance. I watched his mouth one word: "Revenge." The lights dropped when we hit the Transbay tunnel and I heard the brakes kick in to slow the train. No. That was not brake. That was a woman screaming a frustrated, humiliated, sick of it all scream. The lights flickered back on. He was gone . . . again.

She was asleep again. I can never catch her awake past dark. Come too early and she's groggy. Come too late and she would be asleep. Sundays were a so-so. You never knew what you would get. She could be ecstatic to see me, patting my arm and mumbling with a bright smile or an agitated impatient stomp that led her around the facility expecting to be followed. Granny was a queen, a community staple who loaned money and helped bring folks in. She hadn't planned for this one and neither had I. I guess I understood why she fought; this is what we did. How does one give over to a condition that seeks to rob you of everything you have been? The few windows of time she had to remember, she thrashed through the illness. The cocktail of anti-depressants, memory platforms, sedatives, seizure inhibitors, blood tests and nurses, the one chance she had to say she was in control.

I kissed her on the forehead and closed the door silently. I starred at the lock for a moment wondering do I dare use my lessons of the day to seep into her head and see. On second though, I wasn't sure I'd make things better. Can I really exist in my own head? Much less, shimmy around in what I gathered were broken photographs of faint experiences, references and lonely islands of meaning separated by oceans of the inability to articulate it all.

What did it mean to do these things I've done? There has got to be some rational explanation for what I saw earlier. If there is not, would I be any happier? Saw and lived now occupied the same definition in my mind. Although I could not access them I knew I lived the life of several men in the course of going from generation to generation. Scattered, shifting in and out, I wasn't sure I was the kid doctor or some fugitive from things I was frightened of in my dreams and still couldn't name. Is this what being outted on a secret nobody knows about feels like?

The walls of Merritt Shores Alzheimer's Center offer no rest. The paintings of lattice, wood work and windows into the white walls do more to remind me of a children's amusement park rather than a community. Each grouping of suites named after an East Bay neighborhood and fashioned by popular landmarks patterned the walls. The kindness of familiarity being the vibrant colors and details, the cruelty of it all in the flatness of the walls and its enclosure. It was here the Clay in me who ensured Granny didn't wander the dark streets of Oakland warred with the grandson who adored his grand mother's dignity and self defined freedom. Even when I won, I lost.

"She adores you . . . you shouldn't hate yourself over it," an older male voice said drawing me out of my reverie. I turned around to see the sitting room that connected the pod communities empty. A nurse walked by from the dining hall into next quarters, flashing a tired smile as she made her rounds. I smiled back and scanned the empty room, making sure I didn't bump into anything in the low light. As my eyes adjusted, I noticed light leaking from under the door farthest on the left toward the central gathering area. I could detect the sounds of movement and made out the faint sounds of music. I made my way to the door, carefully pushing it open into Mr. Wobogo's room.

Harrison Wobogo had been a pure asset to the Bay Area and the black community here for over three decades. Scholar, scientist, linguist, professor, mentor, tutor, speaker, musician and community organizer, Mr. Wobogo had been one the first African Americans with engineering doctorate to work for IBM. He had once been the indoctrinated company man who wore the uniform navy suit, black tie and sung company songs at the start of the day with the rest of his cohort but found his way into a dashiki and volunteering to teach African centered science at a community center in East Palo Alto the same evening. Deep brother. His walls were covered with pictures and sketches, ranging from scenes with students to awards to thank you letters to accommodations to glyphs. I vaguely recognized them as early kemetic writing. I'd always liked Mr. Wobogo. He was a very sweet man, quietly imprisoned by his illness and became comically annoyed at too many doting nurses.

Wobogo sat at his desk with his back to me. His silvery hair had been picked out into a symmetrical puff around his head reminding me a cool Colonel Sanders in a maroon dashiki, sweat pants and slippers. He worked continuously at his "experiment" mixing chemicals and taking notes on small slips of paper with magic markers. What ever he expected to be in each beaker was actually nothing more than either fruit juice, water or a saline solution lest he try to drink his chemistry set. He sat pouring combinations into test tubes held in a wooden rack from beakers and placing each tube over an empty can of cat food he saw as a Bunsen burner. Near my right hand, was a record player on a shelf, near several racks of vintage vinyl. Jazz, soul, classical, gospel, funk, R&B; he had mint condition pieces of entire lifetimes. The record on the turntable was at its end, making the monotonous sound of skipping. I reached down and started it over again, recognizing the artist Billy Paul but not this particular track.

"War of the Gods," I heard from Mr. Wobogo's direction as he stiffened his back. As the song began, I realized this was the most I'd ever heard him say which was probably why I didn't recognize his voice from earlier. I saw him staring at his concoctions, squinting and rubbing at his left eye. My vision caught the glimpse of a pair of glasses on his bed, golden frames with big square lenses. I tip toed over to the bed, retrieved the glasses and walked around his back to face him on his left side.

"Mr. Wobogo?" I whispered, "Do you remember me?" He stopped his test to look up at me. I saw his eyes squint a few times and then reach out his hands to feel the contours of my face. His eyes closed as his rough palms that smelled of grape juice and hand soap palmed cheeks as he closed his eyes. He returned his hands to his lap, opening his eyes to smile and sheepishly nod. I smiled back and slowly placed his glasses on his face.

He squinted and then let his face relax in recognition of sight. I got a little boy smile and then he patted my leg.

Looking down at his notes, there was no words I recognized. In fact, there were numbers and symbols. They were liked nothing I'd ever seen . . . except last night. My mind called back to the strange symbols written on the walls of the apartment drenched in blood. I reached over to grab a piece of paper and marker, scribbling down the fragment I remember as best I could recall and placed the sheet in front of him.

"Mr. Wobogo," I asked quietly, "do you *know* this?" He starred at me with a loose smirk that grew into a smile. "I . . . should . . . *shouldn't I?* But I don't." He patted my leg again and took the marker from me, watching him draw glyphs I recognized. Child, throne, trap, snare, door, immortal, falcon, immortal, fishing net and immortal with backwards beard. I got nothing. I took another marker and began to correct his mistaken beard.

"No," Mr. Wobogo said forcefully, slapping my hand away and scratching out my correction to redraw the symbol: an immortal with a backwards beard.

I'm sorry," I whispered, "I don't understand." His eyes lit up with an impatient fire as his eye brows furrowed to create a little valley of skin above his nose. He wrote words under each symbol: Boy, trap, The Door, Isfet, web, Heru. I watched the words for a while assigning possible orders and conjugations until: "Use the boy to trap the door, and Heru is in the Isfet web?" He clapped his hands and patted my leg again. I nodded smiling and shrugging. Give me some credit old man, this stuff is hard. I circled the last symbol, the misshapen immortal and asked "What is Isfet?"

Wobogo looked away, breathing out and staring into space. His hands drew a circle, attached a curved line, another, another, eight total and dotted inside the circle several times. A spider. A fucking spider. I heard the growl and starred outside to see a strange pink tint to the fog near the water by the Embarcadero. I bolted to the window to get a closer look only to see nothing.

"Meestah Wobogo," I heard a sing songy voice say from the doorway, "Are you disturbing guests?"" I looked to see the kind cherubin face of the Nigerian nurse come to check on him. Wobogo opened his mouth in protest, unable to articulate. Frustrated.

"He's fine," I said smiling at the nurse and resting my hand on his shoulder. "We were just listening to records."

"Well," she said smiling, "that's very nice of you. Mr. Wobogo would like me to come back later to give you your bath?" I saw him sit up in his chair and brush off his chest if getting ready for some event. I chuckled.

"No, I was just leaving," I said walking past her. "Thank you, Mr. Wobogo." He waved at me half-heartedly. Don't worry bout it. I stood in the mouth of the door, catching his eyes as I mouthed "Be back soon." He smiled and turned his attention to his attendant.

On the elevator down, I decided again calling Xochi again. These Isfet things scared me and I didn't need her worried as well. However, it was apparent Desta should be under closer watch. Was I ready to face whatever was coming? No. I would need help. My message to myself had said my hear was linked to a name; Neith. The name was an old kingdom reference to a hunter aspect associated with the place the ocean met the Nile; fluid strategy in the face of difficulty. Could I find this Neith and ask her for help? *Haven't we already found her?* Had I? My mind swam through references. Neith was strategy. The only one like myself so far appeared to be linked to the Greek's concept of warfare planning. It was well documented KMT has influenced Greece from Socrates to Alexander the Great. In fact, the name Egypt came from Herodotus' travel to the black land and confusing the name of a temple with the land it was built in. Was it so far a stretch that Neith and Athena were one in the same? *You give power too freely.* Help me here then. If I asked he, would it be a forthcoming answer? I couldn't keep guessing, there was pressure now. *Use her to return.* Agreed, but where to find her? Avalos. I decided I needed my laptop and I would check on Desta after while putting in a call to Avalos in the morning. As I stepped out on to Grand Avenue, I made out the image of a motorcyclists accelerating toward Broadway. I let my eyes relax and smiled at the notion of a ride without a helmet.

CHAPTER SIX

"Don't want to wake the babies. This is the stuff bad dreams are made of."

-Horace

My phone buzzed to life as soon as I got to the top of the stairwell out of Civic Center. I was expecting to walk up to McAllister and catch a 5 line back up to the school until the text came in.

Xochi Cervantes (1:43 am): Your guest is here.

I remember to relax my eyes when I watch the scenery like before. The timing is good now, a comfortable rush that my body rationalizes as adrenaline. I begin to call it autopilot. It's who I imagine calls the ambulance for you after being stabbed. My vision catches an empty plaza full of UN insignias on shiny stone and silent abstract art fountains. Not even a cockroach or a pigeon being robbed by two seagulls and a rat. Seriously, it happens.

I reached in my pocket for a cigarette. A card fell on to the stone plaza as the pack met the mist. Omid's card. I punched in his number to the hand held while letting the cigarette start and taking a deep drag. I listened to the tinny digital ring tone waiting for a pick up, noticing how strange it was for fog to even hint at being downtown. The fog seemed to compete with a new wave of pink fog. The phone picked up someone speaking away from the microphone and then placing the unit to their face.

"Car service?," I recognized Omid's voice upon answering.

"Hey, this is Clay from the Fulton to 20th and Bryant earlier today," I said quickly with a hope he remembered as I looked around. Something was moving at the back of my brain. It felt like a pulse that started on the base of my spine and ended between the shoulder blades. Muscle spasms. I sit ergonomically incorrect in my office chair when I type at my desk which combined with packing too many things in my bag pulled my shoulders apart creating pain in my upper back. It was easy to draw lines between the dots on the paper and tell yourself that was a line.

"My friend," he fired back, pleasant but impatient.

"Are you working right now?"

"Four children very hungry," he said with a chuckle. I hadn't expected that and laughed along with him. Of course. I think everybody felt like the economy was headed for another dip.

"I need a ride," I spat out, pacing and finally deciding to walk to the part of the fog was still a soupy gray. "Very important."

"Where you?"

"Civic center BART . . . by the Carl's Junior."

"Five minutes." Click.

"Um...great?" Five minutes, yeah, right. *Why did this motherfucker just hang up on me?* Okay. So now we wait. The lights from the tall plaza building shined down cutting into the patches of the shadows between the complex wall and the hypotenuse of the triangle formed by their shape. I noticed between the flag pole and trees on the western side of the plaza a shimmer in the wind. Watching it closer, a foot wide, swinging in the breeze without break was a spider web. My eyes caught the movement of a tiny silver spider and I was convinced it had moved in its web to watch me.

"My friend!" a voice calls to my ears from behind my right shoulder but my eyes stare at the eight-legged beast more than forty feet away. *My mind swims, leading my vision to find the black Crown Victoria with its tinted windows, the passenger side window rolled down, my body still intent on the web and its wicked inhabitant. Omid is in the driver's seat. I feel myself attempt to drift through the open window and am blocked. No. Repelled like a hand ball against a yard wall, back at a slicing angle to the hand. Drifting, I am aware of Clay and back.* I backed towards the car, watching the web and what I swore was the pink fog becoming slightly denser as it drifted off the web like a tiny stage prop. I walked backwards, my hand catching the door handle, pulling it open and dipping down into the backseat.

I looked to Omid when the door closed. "I need to get to Sutter at Larkin. Family emergency." Omid turned around and nodded, tapping his fingers on the steering wheel while rolling up the passenger window.

"That okay with you, Boss?" he asked, looking into his rearview. His eyes weren't aimed at me in the back right corner but directly behind him. Looking over at the mirror, I saw the side of a hand holding a 9mm with the barrel aimed at me. I turned my head slowly to the left to see the gun connected to a tattoo covered hand going along a black thermal covered arm connected to broad shoulders on a wide chest supporting a thick neck that held an oval head which had the same nose, eyes, facial hair and cornrows as the tank top from the trains. He sat comfortably with his back wedged into where the locked door met the frame before the back driver's side wheel well. His left foot rested on the back seat, the knee relaxed half way between touching his chest and pushed against the back of Omid's head rest. On the seat between my left thigh and his right leg was a black duffle bag with what appeared to be semi-automatic machine guns. He raised his eye brows and lifted the barrel in a motion. I raised my hands over my head looking at the gun. The car took off and pulled around the corner. I felt my stomach tighten and Clay Durward decided he was in over his head.

"Omid . . . his window," the gunmen muttered, his accent clearly local with a slight lisp to the depth of his smoke chopped voice box. The window near my right ear rolled down as we drove along Market, the plaza to the right, my eyes catching the web. YAP. The gun went off and barked in his left hand, rolling an empty shell into the wheel well near my feet while his right arm reached across effortlessly pushing my chest against the back of the seat. I jumped in my seat with my ears ringing as the 9mm made the pop sound, throwing a hot melting round out the nozzle, past the windows into the night, across the plaza between the flag pole and the tree, knocking the spider clear of its web. The window rolled up as the Crown Vic picked up speed. The gunmen flicked the safety and rolled it up in his palm with the handle resting on his index and shoved it my way.

"Cousin," he said with a wide smile offering the gun to me. I took it rather then have it pointed at me. I wondered if the youngsters who frequented the liquor store near my house wore pants that were too large to leave room to tuck a gun in the waist line. I loosened a belt loop and put the piece in my waist. Omid crossed 8th at Market and blasted along the cab lane. The gunmen reached his arm around my neck and pulled me into a strong embrace. *Horace.* I felt a sense of safety wash over me. Indescribable, I knew this man. There was the relaxed exhale out like Sundays with Granny when I'd visit and she would cook. That first hug at the door letting you know that the people in your midst accepted and represented you.

Yes, we were cousins; in fact, I knew that we worked together on something. *Thing?* He wore the body of a man a few years behind me in age but yet I felt a reverence from him like an unrealized mentee. Then it trickled into my brain like water dripping off the rain gutters on to the leaves of the ferns I kept potted on my balcony. I had learned to command in this man's service or someone one stored between both of our brains. In his presence, I had known honor that could only be born of continual duty. His embrace ended and he sat back in his original position. "We made it," he smiled to himself looking out the front windshield, massaging his forearms. "Yes, good hunting tonight indeed."

"What did I get myself into?" I stammered after Omid took a sharp right on 9th and zoomed past the City Hall plaza. The gunmen paused from his knuckle cracking to study my face, head cocked as a look of concern crossed his face. His eyes slotted and his right hand reached out, a small olive green glow to his fingers. I felt his hand touch the back of my neck, just about where my back started.

"Light a cigarette," he said, placing his hand back on his lap. "You hurt the Passenger enough to mute it," I found myself digging for my pack. "Your recovery is going to take a little longer than the plan."

"Whose plan?" I shot out, worried, watching the street change as Boalt law school and City Hall gave way to the strip. He laughed looking at me.

"Your plan. Sekhem," he said with a told-you-so melody to his voice. "Light that. I need one." I looked down at the pack in my hand, pulling out two and handing him one. Before I could reach for a light, a cherry appeared in at the tip. The sound of clips punched into position made me jumpy. My companion, intent on his work, pulled at his cigarette. "You always found the good tobacco. These are menthol, too?" Omid shook his head and opened the window by the gun men's head a crack while muttering "fucking Horace." I want to believe that there is a coincidence between the name Horace and Horus. I knew the myth all too well and found this interaction not quite what I had pictured. I could hear me trying to make up my excuse to Xochi's bosses. Something like a bad joke by an amateur comedian on a cruise. So did I tell you about my cab ride with the Egyptian resurrection icon?

"Should the . . . light of the world be smoking a fucking cigarette?" I asked. "Am I going to hell for giving you one?"

"No," he said, exhaling and ashing out the window. "We're not allowed in hell after trying to stop that bomb thing." He said it matter of fact and I didn't think he was going to smile any time. "Besides you gotta be monotheist to see Hell."

"Oh shit . . ." I panicked.

"Tobacco is the only way you've found to block the spider in your neck."

"Fuck you," I said, remembering the images of the seared pink black fish on a former self clawing his way along the beach. I could hear it, the black starfish like arachnid, wrapped around my spin with its nasty little fangs in the base of my brain, beating with a heart that added an echo to my own. Breathing shallow, choking on the nicotine clogging its foul respiration, it lay wounded in my blood stream adding its own fetid liquids to my own. No amount of surgery would reveal this parasite for removal; it traveled as a collar on the other mind occupying my subconscious.

"Pull over, please." I barely got it out. The gunmen tapped the head rest behind Omid who responded with a swooping swerve to the curb. I pushed the door open, I emptied clam chowder and coffee on the street through my nose. Sputtering liquid out of my mouth, I heard the sound of the car door open as tears formed in my eyes. Horace took a seat on the curb, watching me with a bird like twitches to his neck. He held his cigarette clutched in his fingers, eye rolling up as if recalling some facts and then shooting down to check on me. His face read that he was deciding what not to say. "Get out of my fucking sight," I heard myself say between gags.

"Can't do that, homie," he said between drags, pulling a green military handkerchief from his coat to wipe my mouth. "Not a part of the job description."

"Are you enjoying this?" I heaved, feeling my forehead contract.

"No. Why would I?" Horace replied. "What happened, Sekhem? You used to love this."

"Puking?"

"No . . . waking up to *hunt,* Sekhem."

"Don't call me that."

"Oh, I forgot. Clay," he said with a smile. "I wonder, was that Clay Dur-ward or Sekhem Ka of Kemet sling-shotting though the Mission earlier this evening",

"You saw that?" I said, horrified at being outed.

"The eye of Ra sees much," he said tapping his temple and raising his eye brows. His head turned every once and a while to survey the street. Ra had two eyes: Horace and Djeuti. Horace symbolized Knowledge or the capacity to learn, while the right eye was Wisdom or the application of that learning. "But more than that, the Son of Ausar has seen the your works tonight." Ausar, the first born hybrid of both the creator and the creation, which the Greeks would name Osiris for the western world to interpret. Long before this name was popularized, the great teacher of man existed to inspire the cultivation of the earth for crop, the harnessing of measurement to build pyramids and the retention of value to build schools.

"Are you really Horace?" I asked, reaching for another cigarette. "Like... you're the rebirth?" I motioned for him to do his trick again to my cigarette.

"I am," Horace confirmed, "and don't worry. We'll save the fire works for the crawlies . . . when we need it."

"You're missing an eye," I shot back and found my lighter.

"There's that sense of humor I missed," Horace replied, looking at the skyline, "I have his son and he hasn't let me down yet." Horace patted me on the shoulder. Djeuti has a son. Djeuti married Ma'at. *Ma'at weighs the heart. The heart is named Ka. A Sekhem is a scepter meaning power.* Okay.

"Might want to hire an army," I said, staring back at the pistol tucked into my waistband.

"Funny you should say that. I've been thinking the same thing. However, I don't do anything without my bodyguard," he replied, poking my knee with his index, "Been working for 10,000 years. Why mess with the chemistry?"

"How long have I been doing . . . "

"Bout once a generation. Some gaps here and there"

"You are used to it?" I asked.

"Starting over?"

"Yeah?"

"Think about it," Horace replied. I did and considered the Heru myth. Yeah. he was supposed to start over in a way. *It is his hold on reality.*

"Seems very scary."

"I don't indulge the fear. It's self pity in a very nice package."

"I'm not as sharp as you," I argued. Horace laughed long and wise, showing his teeth.

"I should hope not," Horace replied, "or we lost about a thousand years for nothing."

"Huh?"

"Buried in each of us is a parasite which feeds information to the enemy. As we grow in power, it grows in its ability to sense our intent and broadcast or even dominate us with its will. We can never move forward if our thoughts betray us. But you . . ." He stood up excitedly, clapping his hands together. "You, my curmudgeonly cousin of a squire, found a way to silence them. All the benefits of membership without the cost of dues." He peered at me, his brown eyes becoming wide and reflecting the moon in the sky behind me. "You will have to find a new way back to yourself now that your Passenger is damaged without its memories from every carrier you have taken."

"How did I do it?"

"Wish you had told me. I suspect the Monk knows."

"The Monk?" The pink fog had begun to drift north.

"We must go," Horace said looking at the sky and circling back to the car. I nodded and straighten up to the seat, closing the door as he sat next me. When his door closed, Omid pulled us off the curb with a howl from the good years. The streets rushed by as the car flew through the night.

"I don't know much help I'll be," I said, worried and unsure how I felt about rocking the boat.

"You'll be great," Horace said, screwing on silencers to each of his weapons. He removed the 9mm from my belt and fastened a silencer. "Sometimes we just gotta get the hands dirty."

"Silencers? We doing a hit?"

"Don't want to wake the babies. This is the stuff bad dreams are made of." I appreciated his concern and was relaxed to meet another person who got it. Then again I wasn't sure he counted as a person. I also felt my stomach seize again at the notion that something malignant could be so close to the kids. He dropped the silenced piece on my lap as the car pulled up in front of the center. I began to regret even taking Desta here the night before and exposing any of the other kids to whatever was coming.

"Looks quiet," he said.

"That's how you know something's wrong," I said, "only lights on are on the bottom floor."

"Back door?"

"Sure," I said pointing down the alley, "there's a service entrance for Sysco orders and office supplies." Omid nodded and made the sharp left into the alley. Horace pushed open the door before the car had totally stopped moving and tapped the trunk. Omid popped that as well. The trunk slammed with force to vibrate the car, Horace stood in front of the exhaust pipe. I watched him in the back windshield carrying a long curved blade reminding me of a thick Chinese katana. Katana is Japanese. I know that. I'm just saying how it looked.

"Bring the bag," he said to me through the glass. I nodded and used both my hands to lift the duffle which was heavy as shit and made me wish I had the strength of eighty midgets. When I got outside of the car, Horace reached back in to retrieve the pistol he'd awarded me, tuck it into the outside of my messenger bag and lessen my load by taking a semi-automatic from me.

The service door was a screen and solid metal portal, each with mechanical locks controlled from either the front office or a key card. It was only open under scheduled delivery and under the supervision of a program staff. Tonight the door was swung open the wall, an open nostril breathing in thick pink fog. Over the doorway was a thick web of silk, embolden by several silver spiders crawling across it.

"Nids," I heard Omid say and spat from the window, which was usually regarded as a sign of disgust. Horace said something in what sounded like Farsi mixed with Arabic, causing Omid to nod and back the car out of the alley.

"I hate spiders," I said, somehow afraid to enter a building I knew like the back of my hand.

"Hate," Horace said, pulling my cigarette from me in mid-drag, "like fear becomes an excuse."

"How fucking eloquent," I said, "says the giant with the big shiny sword."

"You are Neteru," Horace continued as if I had never spoken yet responding to me directly as he learned into the web, blowing smoking and freezing every eight legged monster who the smoke touched. "The sword is you." He blew at the cherry of the cigarette, sparks licking off of it, catching the web and emulating it in seconds. He handed the cigarette back, "Make sure you really need it, though." I took a drag and dropped the cigarette, following Horace into the hallway.

"How do I do the fire thing," I asked as he cavaliered down the hallway, looking in on the empty dining hall.

"It depends on how the world defines your Aspect," he replied, moving down the hall and opening the door to check the storage room.

"Aspect?" I asked as the storage closet was closed and we moved on to the lobby.

"Your proprietary hold on reality." He stopped before the door to the lobby, which was covered by another web. He waved his hand like clearing dust off a table and the web ignited into flame that burned itself into nothing. "This look right?"

I peered into the lobby which was complete with comfortable chairs, a computer monitor hanging from a mount in the corner of the ceiling, a television screen on the corner mount and a plastic caged window where the attendant on shift lay on the floor. The front door remained locked while the multi windowed room maintained a cover from the outside visage due to the cold moisture in the form of frost on each pane. I walked over to the woman, dropping the duffle outside the receptionist penalty box. Her neck showed the sign of fang punctures and a horrible bruise as she twitched slightly.

"No," I said worried, "this is certainly not right."

"Yeah, man," Horace said, walking behind me. "Watch the door." I turned to watch the hallway, not sure if I could hit spiders with a bullet like him but I was ready to try. The hallways stayed motionless and I felt insecure without the guy who knew to actually use the guns standing between myself and the danger I felt creeping. Glancing over, Horace was crouched with his hand suspended a foot or so above the night clerk's neck. His fingers stroked the air as if working through a fuzzy cat's hair, leaving trails of olive green light. A small black dot appeared near his palm, growing in symmetrical volume as the grainy bits of dark matter drained into an olive green column from the bruise on the attendant's neck. As the bruise lost size and color, returning the attendant's neck to her normal complexion. A pitch-black orb hung below Horace's hand, bobbing in the air as if on a string. He swung his arms near me and I jumped back, gasping and tripping over a chair in the process. Horace laughed loud and then covered his mouth with the back of his wrist, his grip still ice cold around that incontrovertible ass sword in his hand. He looked over at the hallway and then over to me like I was getting him in trouble. He held the blob over a steel garbage can and closed his hand into a fist, dropping the blob into the can. Horace snapped his fingers and the contents of the can ignited in one puff of smoke that smelled like moldy incense and burning bug spray. I picked myself up off the ground and looked to the attendant. The holes in her neck were sealing and she started to breathe normally.

I guessed at what he was. A big kid? Smart kids now-a-days were programming computers at four years of age. Was it so hard to see a young child who is told his father is the people's ability to adapt and that father was slain by the people's ability to use violence? Sure, the kid's ability to absorb all the years of training would be inspired but what about his creativity outside of a predisposed identity? Essentially, when I starred at Horace, I saw the mannerisms and curiosity of a teenager perpetually interlocked with a righteous warrior and savior by automation. He pumped hope into the system but was still just a big ass kid.

"Venom," he said disapprovingly. "There's a big one here."

"That is so *not* what I wanted to hear."

"They must have sent two."

"Two what?"

"Bow ties? Khaki trench, black tuxedo . . . ."

"Red bow ties?"

"You've seen them?"

"One came by my office"

"Minor Isfet. Probably doesn't know who you are. That's good." Horace walked over to the duffle. "Stopping it will be easy; keeping it from communicating what it sees to the rest will be difficult."

"The rest?" Horace picked up the semi-automatic, loaded the chamber and flicked the safety off. He stood with a menacing gun in his left and a sword in his right, his eyes studying the doorway.

"Don't forget the bag," he said and walked toward the hallway. I resorted to a half carry half drag of the duffle, following behind him.

"Don't squires get their own horse or pack mule at least?"

"You chose not to bring your car today"

"Can I have a squire?"

"You'd complain about them too"

"Right"

At the stairwell of one flight, banister to wall was covered with spider webs. I imagined that was how my brain looked before coffee in the morning. Horace crossed his hands in front of him and pulled them back like a tightening of a knot with two ends of rope. A cork screw of light the color of orange and tomato juice shot out of his chest, heading like a dart into the web, spreading like food dye until the entire structure was his signature and converted to flame that dissipated as soon as its fuel was consumed. I heard a hiss, and Horace replied with sprayed silenced shots above his head, a black spider the size of a pit bull falling to the stairs, rolling down and twitching as its body bled. "Come on," he said and started up the stairs. I followed reluctantly telling myself that my gang banging magician would keep me safe. The lights were off, creating a dark and lonely atmosphere so intense that I would not have wanted for a child leaving the bed to use the pisser.

As we climbed the stairs, I felt my eyes adjust between the lighting of street bulbs pouring in through the windows as well as the fluctuating colors of neon from the rooftops. Ascending to the second hallway, my eyes scanned the corridor. The right hallway was covered in art work and posters on either side of the doorway that lead to the dorms where our residents slept. Standing in the doorway to those dorms, in the same jeans and sweater I had seen her in earlier that day was Xochi. Her hair flowed around the shoulders which I was not used to seeing, picked up slowly by a breeze that swam around her as she stood as if lunging. Her hands were in front of her, palms flat, as if pushing a box on to a shelf. At her feet flickering with red edges was an urchin shaped yellow light that resembled a giant illuminated marigold. At its edges, tiny silver spiders scurried back and forth, each brave enough to come close to the edges being licked by the tips and transformed into a mockingbird that flew into the ceiling and vanished. Half way between Xochi and the stairs end, on the left side of the hallway in front of the shared bathroom stood the bow tie from earlier. He stood with his arms in front, each hand clutched as if squeezing a separate and individual orange of its juice. His ankles were hidden in a thick pink fog that blew from the giant web completely covering the door to the bathroom. The fog fell just short of the maize colored light emanating from Xochi. I realized she had wedged herself in the doorway and was blocking his path.

"Quit now, Aztec," I heard the Stranger's voice taunt without his mouth moving, "and we'll consider sparing the rest of them in there."

"I really don't think I will be doing anything you would call quitting," Xochi replied, her tone unfettered and her lips unmoving with a quiet expression on her face.

"Oh, is that so?" the Horace replied, his fog pushing forward and Xochi adjusting by stepping back. She was losing ground but holding what was left. Horace lifted the left hand, firing off the rest of the muffled shots into the Horace's belly.

"Yep," Horace said beckoning to the Stranger with his sword arm, "that is indeed so." The Stranger was unmoved by the shot but turned facing us with his left shoulder to Xochi. The fog redirected and aimed towards us. "Clip", Horace said as the Stranger's eyes found us. "Oh, and the black bag." I scooted back and dug into the duffle, my hands finding the long rectangular magazine which I tossed to Horace who caught it in between his elbow and left rib cage. He planted the blade in the floor, the edge splitting the linoleum to free him to drop the empty magazine and pop in another. My hands found a black plastic bag, the kind liquor stores put cheap wine or old pornos in. It felt heavy and sloshed as I picked it up with both hands. Tossing it forward Horace caught it by the handles of his right hand, planting his back leg and hurling it like sling.

A dark dripping shape slammed into the Stranger and rolled on the floor trailing black liquid. When it stopped moving, I counted over sixty eyes of a decapitated spider head the size of a playground ball. "Don't worry, he won't be alone for much longer." The Horace hissed and stepped back from its broken comrade.

"Son of Ausar," it hissed a whispery throat that sounded like gurgling. "We will enjoy hanging you next to your father"

"I hear you talking," Horace replied pulling his sword out of the floor. "You worried?"

The Stranger hissed again, his legs flying up backwards beneath him as if pulled by some tree snare. His chest rippled and bloated, as a pair of black furry legs pushed out of his ribcage and waist line respectively on either side of his body. His coat pulled tight, covering his body in a hard black carapace, while his bow tie swiveled ninety degrees and spread across his stomach. Hanging upside down on the ceiling, staring at us with several black eyes of despair, was a spider the size of Geo Metro hissing. The creature's head matched the head of the decapitated spider laying on the floor. I just decided screaming and wind milling my arms as I backed up was the best thing I could do in it a moment such as that.

Horace begins pacing, fearlessly defiant as he waits for the creature to move. I knew him to be taking on his Aspect, Horace making room for Heru. It twists its body in response following his patterns as it bounces on its legs across the ceiling. Heru walks again, suddenly doubling back and twisting his hips as his legs change in his stance. An arc of reddish light rips along the floor, knocking the severed head to the left, igniting it as it hits the web on the doorway and starting a fire there. The Stranger retreats a few feet back and makes a sound like ice cubes being cracked out of a thousand freezer trays all at one time. The web turned pink, then a quartz white and returns to a pulsing pink. I feel the area in between my shoulder blades go numb and the web pulls back into a long woven tunnel that seems to go through the shared bathroom into some place in the universe I won't commit to writing. The tunnel coughs and ejects at least six starfish of fleshy black material. Horace is an artist, his left arm spraying in short bursts like a painter that catch their targets in contracted swings while his right arm carrying the sword parries multiple scurries forward by the Isfet across the ceiling or swinging from where it has hung silk. The Isfet scurries back and the tunnel's pulse pauses.

Horace chuckles and resumes his pacing. "That's you? . . . dat's you?" He says, dropping the gun and motioning behind him. I find myself able to throw another gun just before the pulsing begins again. His semi-automatic brush is deadlier and his sword is scalpel that nicks the belly of his opponent. The pulsing stops and he calls for another gun. We repeat this for a few times before I find the last gun has been thrown and the empty bag leaves me but one clip.

"One clip," I scream.

"*Aight*" Horace yells as he dances his blade outward, keeping the horrendous talking spider occupied and on its defense. This is where my mind cracks and I shit my pants in panic.

"*Fucking shoot it, man,*" I scream again, throwing the last clip. He reloads and steps towards the pulsing web ignoring the Isfet who has crawled from the ceiling to the floor at the end of the hallway. His shots are measured as every wave is repulsed. His hand drops the empty gun, leaving the left index and pointer finger to trace an silver triangle in the air that floats as it gains definition forming a small pyramid in the mouth of the Isfet tunnel. The pyramid twirled on its axis as the nearest clip flies from the floor to stick to the pyramid's side. Horace turns his attention to the Isfet which was making a bee line for Xochi. The pyramid gains speed in its rotation, as all the metal on the linoleum is attracted to his magnet in addition to the duffle. Then it let out a loud piercing shriek that reminded me of hunting birds and burst in a bright explosion. I covered my face at the volley, hoping my arms would be enough to protect my face. I heard children screaming and opened my eyes. Xochi was no where in sight, Horace was getting up off the floor from the back of the hallway where he was lodged into a part of the wall.

"*Desta!*" he yelled at me, climbing up. I heard the name, my mind flowed into the dormitory where another long hallway revealed doors flung open and closed. Little people, from age seven in onesies to seventeen-year-olds in t-shirts and boxers, cowered at the end of the hall behind Xochi who was swinging the branch of a potted tree like a whip at the advancing spider while backing up. The Isfet stood in front of an open door which led to a sparsely decorated room where a small boy sat cross legged on the bed. I hooked my hand on his arm and pulled myself through the doorway, over the Isfet who leapt and into the room. I landed just short of the bed as the Isfet transformed back into a human costume mid air, wrapped an arm around Desta and leapt through the window sending shards of glass to the street below.

Horace dashed in, realizing what had happened, and bellowed a sound of frustration like an old man when his team misses the game winning field goal. He paced, gnashing his teeth, almost wanting to curse as if he knew how. Xochi walked into the room, surveying the damage.

"Go after him," she said to Horace. "I'll clean up here." Somewhere in the distance, I heard the familiar digital gong of paradox. It wavered and held in the air, lifting my nose like the way Eddie Hazel could pull your nostril with a lick from Maggot Brain. In that moment as I found its beauty, both Xochi and Horace's somber far away gaze gave me evidence of everything I suspected and tried to rationalize away. The Passenger in my back was one voice in my head no matter where I turned or what life I lived. It was the same thing that Sekhem Ka used to find the next person to Wisp and stick to; me. It would never really produce anything but its own aim, inextricably connected to the horrendous spiders of my nightmares, here to slap me with the very sobering reality that I could not run from this. There was no second opinion. I was not smarter than that moment. In that dose humility I understood that while the Passenger in my psyche would stop at nothing to help its Isfet kindred. It would also risk subverting the very laws of what Clay and people around him called reality in order to bring a paradox that might even the odds in its kind's favor. Its intelligence would sacrifice me to change the game in its favor, and so I would have to see a part of myself as an enemy.

"The strand . . ." Horace started.

"You closed it," Xochi interrupted, looking out the window toward what I imagined she knew the direct of another gong. Horace nodded, stepped back ward a few steps and ran forwards to hurl himself out the window. On the street below, he ran at full clip down Sutter. I turned to Xochi who was surveying the room and looking to the frantic children crying in the hallway. She waved me off with her right hand, "we'll talk later. Don't leave it all up to him . . . you're better than that." I started to say something and shut my mouth in a nod.

My eyes relax and my thoughts find the running mass of my cousin pumping his arms down Sutter, a huge blade folded behind his right hand, tight in his hand with his index and pointer finger pressed against the flat of it. I locked on to him and attempted to pull myself in. Instead the connection became taut and ripped me out of the window. Hung from a string I couldn't see, I floated above San Francisco like a kite at the mercy of Horace's velocity. As he turned sharply at Mason, I swung out like a loose cherry picker on a fire truck yelling profanities and laughing at the same time. My eyes caught the sight of the beast crawling down the side of building, dragging a small cocoon, which ebbed with the same olive light as my cousin. I recognized that somehow despite the Greek's biology, Desta was family; Neteru. Horace, hearing my thoughts, took two giant steps and jumped, appearing to speed up as he ran on thin air. At times he was a giant hawk gaining on the spider, other times a man running on the sides of building as he closed in on the spider that scurried on top of windows and ran to the street as a man. The air vibrated with the third gong. Now it would start again, in faster intervals and closer until the Proxies arrived.

The Isfet paused, aware of the impending penalties for its actions. This pause was all Horace needed to swoop in against the wall; his blade interchangeable with a giant talon slicing with razor accuracy at the knee of the Isfet's left third leg. The member came off in a spray of black juice and the Isfet dropped to the street, limping as the tuxedo monster pervert. Even wounded, it was still quite fast as it scampered down Eddy. Ahead was the over pass into the Powell Street BART, which Horace's trajectory indicated was its destination. He flew up high, swinging me low and directly in line with the speed limping monster man.

I panicked and began to scream, breaking my hold on Horace, flying directly through the air into the Mr. Adams.

Horace dive-bombed down into the opening off the station as my thighs knocked the Isfet over the rails to the platform below. Scrambling I follow behind on a new vector that scrapes me past the nearest pillar taking some skin off my right hand as I try to correct myself. I bounce off the ceiling and land on the tile with skid that hurts.

Horace flies down and lands on his feet, between the shaken Isfet and the paralyzed body of Desta lying on the platform, sword posed as he studied the Stranger. I clinched my hand seeing there was no muscle damage and assured the pillar we would never collide again. I got myself off the ground and crawled over to Desta. He was breathing and silent, his eyes staring into space. I wrapped my arm around him and pulled him close, he responded sleepily and cuddled against me. That was when I noticed the footsteps in the shadows.

Cast down from the platform lights and the depth of the tunnel, shadows stretched across the platform in long banners. Walking along the dark panes, in quiet exact foot falls that made insane steps on its four padded paws was a large jackal. It should be a bear judging on its sheer bulk but it was in fact a jackal. It starred at me with bright brown eyes with hints of blue in it; sniffing at us before snarling without sound. In my periphery, Horace waited for the Isfet's leap, twisting on to his left arm, using his legs to catch its belly on his heels and propel it behind him in an arc, swinging his sword and reversing his legs to sever the spider into two pieces. It landed and twitched until death bled it. There was the stinking of stepping on cockroaches for fun. As Horace landed on his feet and danced like a boxer, the growling jackal turned its head to Horace, whose back *was turned. I heard the pulse of an incoming BART train timed just before a louder ring of the digital gong pattern. Proxies. Scooping Desta close to my chest, bolted toward Horace. Out of the right corner of my eye, the Jackal snapped its jaw.*

I felt the force again my legs, catching me off balance and sending me through the air sprawling. I wrapped my arms around Desta, expecting to bite it hard on my side. Instead a hand caught my ankle, and swung me into the wall. I heard a loud pop as a fiery liquid pain shot up my leg just before my back broke the tile and embedded me in the pillar. The BART train sped into the station behind Horace as he began to turn alarmed, the bald headed peanut butter brittle colored man, side stepping on to a shadow and pouncing like a ripple along floor which knocked Horace into the side of the train. The train car buckled against the force, skidding with sparks and ending in a wreck. The sign of paradox near the near, the jackal smiled at the site of an unconscious Horace, winked at me and jumped on to the track running into the gloom of the tunnel.

"Ah nga," I groaned, surprised I was alive, "when I learn some of that cool shit . . . I'm get your bitch ass!!" I was greeted by fading laughter from the tunnel. I heard a small cough from under my chin and saw Desta wipe the wipe dust from the broken wall off of his face. "You okay?" I asked concerned, dusting his face off.

"Yesh," he said with his tiny lisp, frowning slightly with my hands cleaning his face. Holding him to my chest, I pulled myself out of the wall and stepped down. My ankle shot fire up my leg once again; I was confronted by the reality that my wheel was bum. I sat Desta on his feet and leaned against the wall for support.

"Can you walk?" He nodded and threw up his hand to me to hold. Limping, we made our way around the tiled pillar, to spy at the limp body of Horace in the wreckage of the car, sparking with electricity and smoke. The gong was deafening and almost on top of us. I studied the scene, racking my brain for how I would be able to lift the broken metal off of him with this ankle and make it past the loose and live wires. "You know any magic?" Desta shrugged his tiny shoulders and scrunched up his mouth. No I guess you wouldn't would you.

"We should go," Desta whispered and got my attention. I looked down to his wide eyes and realized the memory. *The child is more important than you or the carrier you are housed in.* With that we headed toward the escalator up to the Westfield Shopping Plaza. The escalator down ran at normal time while the display for train schedules remained stuck in between characters. I noticed a plastic Safeway bag hung suspended in the air as if caught in a gust and frozen in movement. I checked my watch, the seconds hands did not move. As we got closer to the upward escalator, it stopped, and reversed directions. Just then a train pulled into the station, its brakes kicking in to slow its descent. On either side of the escalators, small green men dressed as financial district commuters filled the moving stairways. I heard a nasal and irritate voice announce a seven car Entropy bound train. The doors opened and green men dressed in hard hats and overalls holding tool box flooded the platform.

From the end of the platform, I heard the sound of the elevator announcing its arrival at the platform. The commuters filled up the station, talking amongst themselves, listening to their black stones through white ear buds, reading news papers and holding black stones to their ears in phone conversations. The track side advertisement showed a picture of a Proxy in a trench coat with a dog's face reading, "Only you can prevent paradox!." I heard a clicking and looked down at a Proxy with spiky hair, a black t-shirt of a little bear with a back pack being shot out of a cannon, and white sunglasses that looked like venetian blinds snapping photos of us in a digital camera. "Lego men," Desta said matter-of-factly; the Proxy covered his teeth to laugh.

"Stop that," I said.

The elevator opened to the sight of a churning maelstrom of colors; azure, olive, lavender, black, teal, chocolate, crimson, ivory and silver. I felt a tingle and had an image of lying in a crib as a child; my father's voice with no face. Deep within the storm, a skull consumed by blue flame floated. As I found myself unable to look away, I reached my hand over to cover Desta's eyes. The skull was indeed on a body of glistening and translucent plate mail. The figure rode a skeletal horse with no skin, its internal organs visible and the same blue as the flame, flanked on either side by marching Proxies in legionnaire formation, each dressed in riot gear. The procession filed out of the elevator, a Proxy stepping over to the dark rider with its hands up raised as if carrying a table over its head. The horseman swung its legs over the saddle and stood on the Proxy momentarily before standing on the platform. It was at least seven foot tall, with a chest as wide as two men. Its armor seemed to contract and expand as it stepped, adjusting to its wearer with every movement. On its head was a sinister and dark helm, the face of a gruesome screaming skull.

"Proxy," the thick and terrible voice commanded, "why are there *works* in my free zone?" A green man broke from the crowd, wearing a tie over a white button up shirt that was rolled from the sleeves to its elbows. His arm pits showed the sweat of a work day and his brown corduroys swished as he walked.

"My Lord Entropy," the hurried little man started, "the dark rider, bane of paradox, pain of the hopeful, his exalted arbitration . . ."

"Spare me the pleasantries, Proxy," Entropy spat out and I felt Desta hug my leg. Yes, you're right little guy, this motherfucker is not at all pleasant or tree. For the first time since college, I wished I smoked weed. This would all be so much easier to take in if I was stoned. Why did I ever give up such habits? Oh yeah, I decided I wanted to be responsible and stop living in fantasy world. Good luck that did, huh? Instead, I put my arm on Desta's back not sure who was relying on who for comfort. Entropy turned his dreadful helm and attention to us lifting his finger. "Humans. Why are they not in suspension?"

"The adult has an Isfet passenger and the child is without," the Proxy administrator replied. "We suspect they are devotees." The ghastly helm nodded, considering.

"I smell . . . Neteru," Entropy said, looking at us closer. His head turned to the wrecked train where members of his SWAT team had climbed into the wreckage and dragged Horace out. Groggy as he was, they stood him on his feet, holding him at each of his joints. A Proxy wrapped itself around his ankle, transforming into a large manacle, followed by another ankle, and then each wrists. Standing, Horace stood in shackles, teetering while supported by the rest of the squad.

"The distant one," Entropy said stepping forward, and I caught the reference of the direct translation of the word Heru. "Quite a pickle you've gotten yourself into." Horace flexed his muscles some testing his bonds, unbreakable, he met the gaunt man's unearthly gaze.

"I thought we agreed this is our free zone," Horace replied.

"*Your* free zone?"

"A free zone," Horace danced back antagonistically with his tone.

"My word remains law," Entropy replied dismissively, "and no works in the presence of humans"

"What about Isfet attacks?" Horace motioned to the pieces of spider being dusted, photographed, measured and examined by the proxies in navy blue windbreakers with the letters ESI in bright canary across the back.

"Proxy," Entropy said looking over his should behind him, "what do you know of this?" The administrator pulled out a black stone, gazed it and looked up.

"The son of Ausar is correct," the Proxy admin stated. "In fact, we have over five major works by Isfet this evening as compared to the Neteru's two minor and one major work. To boot, both free Attributes involved were careful to dispose of any sign of paradox." Entropy nodded and looked to Horace he smiled vindicated.

"I wonder, distant one," he whispered in a playful and baleful tone, "where is your Door? I must admit, I am disappointed at finally snaring you without your beloved bodyguard."

"We work hard to displease you, sah," Horace responded with a sarcastic grin in mock slave tones.

"Defiant to the last. I respect that, son of Ausar. It pains me that the Isfet caught your sneaky little squire before I did."

"Don't worry, he'll be back . . . we always are."

"Indeed. Perhaps these devotees you have brought can show me his fate." His gaze returned to us. "I would so enjoy returning them to my realm and allowing my Proxy to jog their little human memories. What do you say Neteru prince? Yes?"

"No!," I heard behind us and turned to see Xochi running down the escalator at full tilt. Dashing in front of Desta and I, Xochi bowed before Entropy as soon as she stopped before the dour giant.

"My Lord Entropy, please spare my pages. They were kidnapped by the Isfet and the Neteru was only aiding me."

"Ah, the mockingbird," Entropy responded with a heinous smile. "Given your fidelity to code in the past, I shall grant your amnesty." I heard a cough and the Proxy with the glasses from the Atlas café approached Entropy. Standing next to him, he reached into his messenger bag, retrieving his little black stone, displaying a series of colors and then looking at me with a smirk. Entropy laughed. "Xochiquetzal....matron of craftsmen, prostitutes and expectant mothers." Really? No wonder our office was in the Tenderloin. Okay. "You would be wise to keep an eye on your pages more closely. I am told the adult was witness to minor works by a citizen earlier this cycle."

"Surely you are mistaken," Xochiquetzal replied, confused.

"No, m'lady," Entropy said coolly. "In fact, he kept company a name I am sure you enjoy hearing . . . Athena of Olympus."

"I was not aware," Xochiquetzal replied, looking at me as if I had flaked on another smoking cessation classes she had signed me up for. "Thank you for informing me, constable. I will see to correcting it immediately." I wasn't sure what I did wrong but the look on Xochi's face suggested I might get a better deal with the Balco skeleton.

"But of course," Entropy replied in his smug whisper. His head turned back to Horace. "As for you, son of Ausar. while I cannot castigate you for your defense of a free market away from Isfet law, this is not your first transgression with my office."

"No it is not," Horace said.

"Therefore, the levy shall fit your aspect most complimentary. I shall not slay your Attribute . . . "

"You are not skilled enough for that," Horace interrupted.

"Be it as it may," Entropy continued right over the top of him, "I leave you to the laws of these humans you cherish so dearly." Proxies in hard hats pulled metal back into its molded shape and reconnected wiring in the wrecked BART car as others took mortar to the damaged pillar and replaced tiles. They worked at furious speeds, erasing any sign of struggle and returning the station to the semblance of normalcy. Entropy beckoned his gauntleted fingers, five of the Proxy commuters stepped forward. Entropy twisted his fingers back leaving his thumb extended and his index pointing out. YAP. I heard the sound of a gun shot and where a Proxy once stood was the bleeding body of a shot BART police. YAP. Another body, flat on its face, bleeding on the platform. YAP YAAAAP YAP. Two commuters bled on the platform, the third with a gun in its hand. He turned his hand to Horace. Horace straighten his posture and looked to Entropy.

"Entropy," Horace said with a smile, "you don't have what it takes to catch the Door. Sekhem Ka will *always* be more ingenious than you." The grim figure shrugged and let off his final shot catching Horace in the chest and slumping him to the ground. The manacles melted off his body, returning to Proxy, who worked their way into the crowd.

"Now how smart was that?" Entropy replied. I felt my eyes relax and well with tears, as I knew my enemy. Xochi's voice was in my head: *No . . . turn around and take Desta up those stairs . . . I'm right behind you.* I looked over at her, following her eyes to the exiting Entropy. I squeezed Desta's hand and limped to the escalator heading to the street. Powell Street, completely back to equilibrium, watching silently as droves of Proxies filled the train from whence they came. Entropy had mounted his steed and let it lead him back to the elevator that should not fit his massive depression of an existence. Xochi stood below us on the escalator, hands on either side of the rails, barring a return to the platform. As the step reached its half way mark between the platform and street level, I heard the sounds a train leaving followed by the sound of a thousand sirens. Looking at my watch, seconds began again while the sight of hundreds of SFPD filled the station in hot pursuit to the platform.

"Get dem next time," Desta said, brushing his cheek again the back of my hand. I nodded and let the tears fall.

Chapter Seven

"No, similar departments, different companies."

-Xochi

ochi pulled the car to the gate, waiting for the security fence to pull back before driving in. I'd always wondered who lived in the gated communities on the San Bruno mountain that divided the south district of San Francisco from Brisbane and the start of San Mateo county. As she pulled down the driveway to pull into the opening garage, I decided I would ding her for keeping such things from me.

"Xochi . . . you been holding out on me?"

"I don't live here," she said, stopping the car and moving the stick into park.

"Who does?"

"You." I looked to the back seat where Desta slept unmoving with his head pressed against the window. I had folded my coat to give him a pillow, which he hadn't moved from since the car began moving. The garage began to close behind us and Xochi turned the ignition off. "I'll grab him, you get off the ankle," she said.

I unbuckled and stepped out, careful to keep off the right leg as I reached down and grabbed my bag. Using my arm to steady myself, I hobbled to the door that led into a lavender carpeted foyer. I decided I didn't have kids or generally didn't interact with mud enough to allow such a bright flooring. The walls remained a smooth arctic white with Dali, Escher and Diaz paintings every five feet or so. I noticed a shoe rack near my lower right and took the time to remove my shoes. More hobbling brought me into view of the sliding doors that gave me the middle of night view of the entire city of San Francisco. Xochi passed me with Desta in her arms, climbing stairs toward the second floor. I hobbled further, turning on lights and settling my sights on the kitchen.

After finding a zip loc bag to place ice in, I discovered I did actually live here. The fridge was packed with food I would eat including my favorite: pre-prepared meals from Planet Organic. I popped out a chicken kebob and threw it in the microwave, ignoring the fact I was heating the side of potato salad. There was an orange juice carton that came with me to the bathroom. We, Clay and Sekhem Ka became quite intimate with the calcium-enriched pulp imported from Florida as I took the power piss of a lifetime. Some reason told me the OJ was the only pleasant thought I had of the state of Florida. As I washed my hands, the timer from the microwave went off and I smelled the end of my hunger. Out of curiosity, I opened the red drawers in plastic cabinet on the floor and found a drawer of bandages. Further exploration gave me an ace wrap and air splint on the bottom drawer. Judging by the sheer volume of first aid supplies, I suspected I got injured quite frequently. The two tabs of ibuprofen was the last piece to that room before exiting.

Making my way back to the kitchen, I waited for the dish to cool down while wrapping the ice pack around my ankle with the ace wrap. I popped the painkillers I had stolen from the medicine cabinet in my mouth and washed them down emphatically with more OJ. I stuffed the food in my mouth, barely chewing and using the juice to soften the food before swallowing. I made short work of the meal in less than a minute, even scraping the container with the fork to make sure I got everything. Limping with my hands steadying me along the stairs, I headed upstairs to explore. There were a number of closed doors. Of the two that were open, one held Xochi tucking Desta into a bed and the other was what appeared to be an officious study. I took the second option, placing everything on my surprisingly clean desk and plopping into the seat with a creak from the chair itself. I elevated my ankle on the desk and leaned back in the chair. The wireless key board near my hand was too irresistible not to turn on which lit up the smart board across the room with a Microsoft Vista loading logo. Great, I wasn't in the Apple cult nor did I start it.

Gulping the second container of juice, I watched the desktop materialize, revealing a quiet mountain range I guessed was either China or the Philippines judging on the color of the sun against the water. The meal lasted a number of minutes before I found myself stuffed, out of juice and belching. My eyes scanned the desk, finding the delight of my days: an ashtray. I riffled through my pockets until I found my cigarettes but realized my lighter was probably sealed inside the reality of a newly renovated BART station. Going through the drawers, I found a lighter and decided I loved the guy who lived here. Lighting a cigarette, I closed my eyes to let out a heart felt fart that reassuringly didn't ruin my underwear. Then again, my BART ride earlier this evening might have given me enough excuse to. I watched Xochi walk in the room and go directly to the balcony door to slide it open. She waved her arms and few times, the smoke changing direction and heading out to the night. Sitting on one of the couches, she eyed the book shelves. I followed her gaze and realized that there were some fairly old titles. Nothing I recognized, but the material themselves did not look like anything printed in the last fifty years. Looking around, she eyed the empty dishes on the floor by the desk.

"How's the leg," Xochi asked breaking the silence.

"Icing it but I can't feel the toes," I replied.

"Can I take a look at it?"

"You mad at me?"

"Yes."

"Then no thank you."

"I'm not mad about what happened back there"

"Okay . . . then fine." She started to get up from the couch and appeared by the desk; unwrapping the ankle. The bottom of my foot was striped with purple bruising. She touched her fingers to the swollen bones and squeezed a bit.

"Hey," I said flinching.

"It's dislocated," she replies, not moving her hand. "Do I have your attention, all of you?"

"Yes, ma'am," I gasped in pain.

"I have been pretty transparent with you, have I not"

"Yes . . .ow!"

"A free therapist for six years or so right?" Her hands glowed a marigold, rubbing her finger tips along the swollen veins.

"Pretty much."

"Wouldn't you think if some woman you showed you something your rational mind couldn't fathom and you began experiencing an altered state, that's the one thing you can tell your therapist?"

"Sure, if you want to be called crazy."

"Name a time when I used that word."

"Fair."

"I don't, so your excuses suck." There was another swift shot of liquid fire up my leg as there was a wet snap like throwing a rotten grape fruit against the side of a concrete wall.

"Ow, mothafuckin mockingbirds!" I screamed as the feeling in my toes returned. "What the hell is your problem Aztec?"

"It was a dislocated ankle," she said coldly, "but it's back in the socket." Her hands had changed to an olive garden the same hue I'd seen Horace wield. She continued to stroke the veins, pulling out the bruising from the top of the foot and dispersing it among the veins. She replaced the ice pack on the ankle and started to wrap.

"Is this a jealousy thing?" Xochi started to laugh, covering her mouth and holding her stomach. I felt I was being serious and transparent, as her face turned beet red and her chest heaved.

"This is funny to you?"

"I'm married, Clay"

"Oh."

"You are, too."

"The Greek?" She pulled my toes and I howled, flailing my arms. It wasn't an answer but whatever it was, it was not a confirmation. "What's your beef with her?"

Xochi strapped the velcro end of the wrap around the ice pack and sat on the edge of the desk. She pushed the ash tray to the other side of the desk away from her and waved her hand, the smoke blew away from her continuously.

"She's ugly on the inside, Sekhem," Xochi said, "and she likes that about herself."

"Don't we all have an ugly side?"

"After what you saw tonight, are you going to tell me that Clay's ugly is my ugly?"

"No."

"I guess you need firsthand sightings before you understand."

"You're talking to me like one of the kids."

"You're acting like one."

"Blame the guy whose body I'm borrowing named Clay," I replied chuckling.

"I'm not laughing."

"You are not."

"I don't mind being here to help you get up and running. I've been doing it for six centuries. I *do* mind your need to play information games with your friends and hand your power away to those who are not."

"I'll work on it."

"No more surprises via the Rider, got it?"

"Deal." She let go of my toes. "So how long have we all been doing this?"

"You and I have been friends since before Colombus."

"Are there others?" Xochi smiled and looked around.

"How much would you believe me as opposed to yourself?"

"Eh?"

"Somewhere here you've left Clay a trail of bread crumbs. You were always insistent upon us taking notes." My mind thought to the flash drives in the satchel bag by the door. "As smart as you are, you required us all to chronicle our steps to Recovery."

"Recovery?"

"The stage you are in. You mind is experiencing new management."

"I'm possessed?"

"Don't be gross. Think of yourself as a company. Before the CEO was Clay and your Passenger handled operations."

"K . . ."

"Sekhem Ka bought the company, moved Clay to operations and moved the Passenger to finance, which it hates."

"Wouldn't you?"

"Clay, if you talk about Excel, I will slap you in the mouth."

"It's a cool program-"

"Clay."

"K. So when the CEO learns the job and draws up the new strategy?"

"Then Recovery is over and my rogue brother from another mother is back."

"We're related?"

"Not directly."

"I found some flash drives. They seem color coded. Any clues?"

"We all have them, again at your insistence"

"Do tell."

"The black are personal information regarding you, your family and your bloodlines."

"Excuse me?"

"Every Carrier we take is at least forty permutations from your original form. We can only bond and recover in Carriers that are direct descendants"

"So I couldn't jump into some Russian because that's not from Kemet?"

"It could be done, but the recovery would take an entire lifetime. You got to ask yourself, how long is the walk from North Africa to north east Asia?"

"As opposed to the West African brought over by slavery. Interesting. The red?"

"The Isfet and the Partisans"

"Partisans"

"Not tonight"

"Yellow?"

"Your Aspect. A catalog of the legends and stories associated with your attribute, Sekhem Ka. Should give you ideas on how it can affect the Veil."

"Veil. I feel a sense of regret at that word. What is it?"

"Don't indulge it. The Veil is the layer upon the world that defines the world we exist in. A system over layered upon a system"

"Defying it brings Paradox."

"Yes."

"Are there places beyond the Veil," I asked, taking a long drag, "where Paradox doesn't come into play?"

"Yes, but it's thick with Isfet."

"Ah. What's the brown?"

"When you are ready."

"Ok."

"Remember to elevate the ankle when you sleep."

"Of course."

"How's the center?"

"Good as new."

"What about the kids?"

"The ones who remember will think it was a bad dream and not mention it."

"Desta OK?"

"Knocked out in one of the guest bedrooms. Sleeps like a rock."

"His mother wants him back."

"I'm sure she does. Better with us than with her opportunistic ass."

"You sure she can't help with . . ."

"She can only help herself. She serves her ego and her sorceress appetite"

"Sounds familiar but I don't . . ."

"She's dog food."

"Lost me."

"You can eat but I encourage you to return to pursuing cleaner options."

"Eat?"

"Sex. Intercourse among Passengers revitalizes the attribute. The more compatible the aspects, the more filling the meal."

"So she is related."

"No, similar departments, different companies."

"I never knew you were married, Xoch."

"Do we discuss Clay's ex?"

"Touche. Divorced too, huh?"

"Not at all. Long distance thing."

"Friend of ours?"

"You'll see."

I let the conversation die down, pushing the cigarette into the tray, extinguishing it. My hands fumbled on the desk for a bit before I opened the center desk drawer to find a channel changer which flicked on the television. Xochi watched me, her face in a smirk as my low attention span drifted away from focus, trying to hide in the nonsense of late night cable to escape from the depth of the conversation for a bit. Flipping channels, I stopped on the local news and its breaking story.

"Drug Deal Goes Bad" read the caption as helicopter footage showed a bird's eye view of the Powell Street BART station where a collection of ambulance, fire trucks, news vans, squad cars and BART police cruisers blocked off Market Street. The right panel showed the visage of the reporter feigning a somber expression while his eyes betrayed his excitement at being the one awake to catch this story. I decided such opportunism rubbed me the wrong way and stored his name in the recesses of my brain for later use. As the graphics revealed, four dead, gunman wounded in critical condition, officers killed. The face of Horace came up on the screen from some earlier incarnation of a mug shot which included the reporter informing his audience that the suspect identified as Horace William Marshall as wanted in connection with a number of drug related murders in the Bayview Hunter's Point district of San Francisco; where I had grown up in Granny's house and still lived. I flicked off the power, sitting in silence for a while.

"He didn't kill those people," I said out loud, folding my hands behind my head.

"I know," Xochi replied.

"But that Carrier, Horace, isn't exactly innocent is he?"

"Wouldn't be the first time."

"Do we have a plan when he gets captured?"

"Never happened before."

"No?"

"Usually its you. Also I want to be clear, your family thing is not my thing. I don't work for you. I just make sure you, personally, transition safely each time. You and I have an arrangement . . . that is . . . as far as it goes. You and I, no one else." Xochi looked at her watch.

"It's a good idea if we both got some rest. You gonna be at sessions tomorrow?"

"Yes, I suppose so."

"Okay," Xochi said, getting up from the desk and heading to the door, "try to get some sleep"

"I will."

"I know you want to think this through like a puzzle and will have more questions. Just entertain the notion, that your best resource is a conversation with yourself."

"Noted, lemme walk you out."

I hobbled down the stairs after her, following her across the foyer into the garage. She gave me a hug and climbed into her car, waving as she backed out of the garage, I waved back at her when she cleared the opening and closed the garage. Hobbling back towards the study, I dragged the satchel bag behind me, feeling the exhaustion setting in. Making my way back to the study with a third carton of orange juice, I retrieved the black jump drive from the bag and plugged it into the USB port on the wireless keyboard. Password entered again, I found myself back in the database. I clicked on the journals and found myself in annals spreading over two million entries. Unsure where to start I clicked through a few pages and found a link the middle of the page. The link brought me to another page divided between text and a picture of an old set of journal pages I assumed were the original scanned in.

We came north when Xochiquetzal told of us the gold in the mountains. The Monk and his refined guardian traveled with us from the old Aztec kingdom which had now come to a new world under the Spanish. I tell myself that the first ships were only looking for new forms of material wealth and I am shamed to dare mention the Isfet followed me from the west over to Atzlan. Xochiquetzal tells me the struggle is inevitable whether at home or in this golden coast. Horace will meet us upon my arrival. He is the martyr's assurance. Unsettled by the loss of the warrior priests in the southern part of this continent, he turned to the struggle of this young nation in its war to end its stain of slavery. Both of us had seen the abominations of slavery in our home and knew it for what it was.

Now with the war over and the promise of a new day for this America, Horace turned to the islands in the ocean between here and the continent we had left. Closer to Oba was a good idea it allowed us to keep the Resonance. We would need to stay quiet for a while, it would be at least two generations before the seeds we planted could grow. This body will have to stay clear of movements until we have settled more roots and have more Carriers to pick from.

To my future selves learning this cycle I ask you to remember the market you are in. Soon we will have established both major settlements in this state as free zones away from Isfet law. Until our voice is heard, we shall remember to struggle. For now, be aware of our endeavor. Should you read this, I ask you to adhere to our way. We do not exhibit works in the world before us without prior approval of Lord Entropy. Nor do we take devotees. We are not to be worshipped. There is one high among you and you are not it. Your service must be affixed. Each of the peaks of the mountains in San Francisco shall be anchored by works placed long ago by you and your allied rogues. Soon we shall return to activate that which will give us domain over the clouds and fogs of the ocean bay. In doing so, we will mask our movements from the enemy and re-energize the market around you.

Our way is to ensure that humanity around you invests in itself.

These farmlands show the promise of a thousand dreams. With help, the sons and daughters of the indigenous who have dwindled away from their once free way of life may find a new path in this temporary system. Imagine if these fields were tended by the same hands who once danced with the bear and deer in the twilights when the untrained eye cannot perceive. The earth was not a thing to own.

In this new world of California I am discovering, I have such hopes for those I know have lived its beauty for ages due to the richness of the soil that was their faces and thoughts. Such smiles come from eating of this land. There is possibility for them in hands of this America more than Spain gave this land. The Monk watches me write with a knowing smile as if finding a way to make me laugh. His disciple's lesson today has left my back sore and I am no Heru to the proper fall. I give him all respect and devotion as my Sifu, but Wukong takes a certain mischievous and silent approach to instruction. Though I have known him many years, in the selflessly way he has mastered, he finds the way to adding to the last lesson over the centuries when it is due.

I can feel her looking for me. Heru tells me it is foolish to deny such feelings. I respect his council but do not have the same strength. I miss her terribly. Fighting it disturbs me. I know she can hear me. She can even intercept this letter from these pages I write. Can I love myself, my duty, my nature and love her when she serves the traitor? How does one fight a war against family when the enemy keeps your heart in its ranks? We cannot kill our collective enemy and we cannot get their leader alone.

I remind Heru we are free to slay any of the other Attributes in his ranks who are not kin and would hunt us under the Partisan banner. My prince does not answer me and once again leaves the matter to its silence. Not even the disapproval I would expect from such thoughts. I can tell by the Monk's face it is time for my meditation. He much prefers that than the strong tobacco I still carry from the Ifa. The days are beautiful if you let them be. Until we are free. I leave to my silencing of the mind.

Remind the Monk that you know he eats meat for time to time.

I nodded and limped into the hallway, opening doors of guest bedrooms until I found the one with the large bed and skylight. Mine. I dropped face first into the pillow and died to the world.

Long hard breaths. I know I usually didn't sleep this long. I would have opened my eyes but I could feel small fingers picking at the crust in the corners. I decided not to move too quickly lest I get my iris poked out. I reached out my hand to find a small foot that giggled when I touched it. Opening one eye, Desta is sitting Indian style, near my head, smiling as my left hand clutches his foot.

"You snore," he said with a lispy whisper I decided to call lispering.

"Your baby breath is powerful," I replied and accepted that it was the next morning. Desta giggled again, his breath smelling like applesauce and stir-fried dog shit. I wondered what happened to small children when they sleep so that their breath turns to a flesh-eating dragon when they start talking the next morning.

"Wakey wakey" he said, using his little palms to slap my cheeks. "I'm hungry." I opened both eyes and examine the world. The clock reads shortly after ten o'clock and the sunlight through the window on my chest felt wonderful. I didn't want to move but I was also starved and could feel the caffeine headache approaching. I started to move and was reminded of the soreness in my right leg around the ankle. Carefully rotating it, I saw and felt the dislocation has turned to a nasty sprain.

"Get me the splint from the study," I croaked.

"Da wha?" Desta inquired.

"The blue and white foot thing from the room with the books." Desta crawled off the bed and ran out of the room leading with his head first. I sat up in bed and wished I hadn't fallen asleep with my clothes on like some drunkard. I was just starting to wake up and looked around the room with the realization I wasn't a fan of furniture in the bedroom. The only fixtures I did enjoy was the bed I was lying in, a couple of closets I hoped had un-derwear in them and some form of altar on either side of the room. I closed my eyes and made a concerted effort to keep the day normal. Despite the pitter-patter of little feet from a small boy I had met two nights ago, saved from a giant spider a few hours ago, today was going to be *mundane*.

When I opened my eyes, Desta stood before me with the air splint in his hands. I smiled, strapping on my fake leg and stood up. I could see his eyes scanning the room recording in his tiny brain through those giant warm eyes of camera lens. I scratched the top of his head with my fingers as I left the room, baby breath following in tow and racing ahead down the stairs to the kitchen. He was ahead of me with the refrigerator door wide open, staring at me expectantly.

"You don't do eggs, do you?" I asked, looking into his blank face as he shook his head, I tried to decide how this balance between authority and unconditional love would work. A stranger I've known my whole life. My eyes caught the sight of a produce drawer full of expensive items with organic stickers. I began putting fruits on the cutting board as Desta sang a song to himself, bopping his head from side to side. I decided I would throw together some scrambled eggs, turkey bacon and English muffins for myself. The youngster and I would share a fruit salad.

Once the eggs were mixed and the bacon sat sizzling on the Foreman grill, I eyed the prep counter for a knife to dice the pineapple I had pulled from the produce drawer. There were blades in a block on the far side of my reach at the right end of the counter. Desta had found a pen and paper, scribbling on it at the small counter as he sat on a stool looking into the kitchen as he sang his little chant.

"Little man," I called out over my shoulder.

"Huh?" I heard the lispering midget respond.

"Hand me a knife, please."

"Mmmkay," he replied cheerfully, excited to help.

I continued to prep, wondering what kind of house I lived in where music wasn't readily available everywhere. All though I was relieved at the absence of iPod technology, I found myself agreeing yet second-guessing my own taste. The kitchen was practical beyond all imagination but lacked any of my need for flair and design.

"Aghhhh," I heard Desta scream, just before the sound of metal clattering against the title. Looking over, Desta stood worried to my right, clutching at his hands crying, a large cutting knife on the floor. Rushing over, my eyes saw no sign of blood and all of his fingers were attached. Asking him what happened only got more tears and violent body shakes as he tried to answer. I pulled him against me with my arm and did my best to squat with my bum of an ankle. He pulled himself close and buried his face into my shoulder. I followed his eyes to the blade on the floor.

"Ba en pet," Desta murmured, clutching at his hands. I looked at his fingers to find first degree burns on his hands along his clumsy grip. Picking the knife off of the floor, the blade was cold to the touch. I put Desta's hands under the cold water for a bit and then sat him back at the counter with the crying subsided. Washing the knife before cutting, I thought of the phrase over in my mind. *Ba en pet.* It sounded very close to a reference between Ramses II correspondence to a Hittite king. Just to be sure, I repeated the phrase under my breath and asked Desta if he could draw it for me remembering my lesson from Mr. Wobogo at Merritt Shores.

Desta was finishing his artwork when I placed the pasta bowl full of bite size fruit pieces in front of him with a fork. I walked back to pour the egg batter in the skillet that looked perfectly sized for omelets and continued to cook. I was ready to eat ten minutes later and the little stomach was craving a second helping. I tried to decide where the food was going and looked for a hole in the back of his neck. Sitting down next to Desta and his sketches, I looked at the images. Wide marker strokes with shaky hands, clumsy, unsure, and unlevel, they resembled glyphs. Desta watched my fingers follow along the lines as I tried to recall. I picked up one of the pens and recopied as best I could remember the symbols.

"Metal from the sky . . . meteorite . . . irons?" I asked the big brown eyes.

"Ba en pet," Desta replied with a deep nod as he continued to scribble trees, rivers, mountains and birds. No trace of iron hewn weapons had ever been found in Egypt in pre-dynastic times. Most historians attribute the multiple conquests of the black land to the end of bronze's dominance and the rise of iron. These same historians overlook the iron found in tools assumed to be used in the construction of all three pyramids at the Giza site while agreeing the smelting technology of ore was mastered south or north of the Delta. It was not a reaction to metal, so much its function that Desta's body rejected. I looked over to the knife on the counter my eyes picking up the branding indicator of stainless steel. The pounded ore stretched into a sharp point and slicing blade somehow seemed opposed to the curious and nimble personality of a child's growth. Sure, little boys played with toy swords and plastic guns but where I was from, that could be a self fulfilling prophecy. I was relieved at the little boy who liked trees instead of weapons.

After breakfast, I hurried Desta through clean up, glad I had the sense to buy dishes and cooking ware that all fit into the dish washer. Then we piled into the car in the driveway, a black Lexus GS whose keys I found with house keys hanging on a hook in the tool room on the bottom floor. Kanye's "Good Morning" sprang to life when I turned on the engine and backed out of the driveway. We pulled along the mountain, taking a short trip to Target to pick up some children's clothes, a pint sized, video-game toothbrush and some toys we could fit into a backpack. Mr. Lispery felt it was his job to talk to every one who passed him which I effectively bribed away by purchasing him a smoothie. I ushered him out of the store and back into the car, heading back into the madness of the Peninsula and daring back to the 101. Ten minutes or so we were back at my second home, using the space to shower and change clothes. I used the time it took Desta to bathe and dress to shut down the computer while locking up the house. There was a safe in the study that opened to my finger print. I wasn't sure how it would know this body but like the other pieces of stone, wood and perhaps even clay already stacked and residing in the safe, I just accepted it. I left my latest stone glyph I received from Dina in the safe and decided the pistol in my satchel bag would be better suited for a storm drain away from remembering eyes. Old habits die hard.

Desta hollered from the bathroom that he was ready to go and I walked up to the bathroom to check on him. A quick knock and he told me to come in where he was dressed in his clothes with his dirty ones on the floor. I even noticed a bit of toothpaste near the drain in the sink, which told me he had adopted his toothbrush. I would have to thank Wario for his help with fighting cavities some time. I picked up his clothes and tossed them on the floor of the bedroom for me to wash at separate time. We hopped in the car once again; I tried the sunroof to make sure I didn't miss the warmth coming from the sun's heat. It loosened the stiffness in the back of my neck. I enjoyed the wind in my face more though. Couldn't tell you why. I was reminded of skin cancer and questioned if that was mother nature's way of being wary of sun worship. Back up the 280, connecting to the 101, down the Hospital Row on to the Central Express Way and a quick dip off the 9th Street exit. At noon, the traffic really seemed invested in attempting collisions or threatening to speed up only to get in front of me and decelerate by ten miles per hour.

I almost saw every movement before it happened, not really surprised when some random utility truck swing into the lane without a signal or fair warning. I could swing wheels too I thought to myself. I could serve this expensive Japanese inception of masterful Toyota auto artwork through lanes along a flow that seemed to be moments before bullshit happened in the rear view on a continuous basis. I slid into the middle lane on 9th, Desta using his eyes to watch the space between cars as if the other drivers should know better. A few sharp turns and into the alley behind the center. Xochi's car was parked in her spot with the remaining two hex marks open for the taking. I pulled in on a dime and killed the engine. He watched the door, which was now closed and secure, with his eyes, his face lost in thought. I was witness to him beginning to watch for the first time yet recognize he was already aware. Something wonderful sprang into my face as I knew how special the rest of his day could be and fear for whatever else was out there for us on this road. I put my hand on Desta's hand to comfort him. He grabbed my fingers and stayed staring at the door. I stepped out of the ride, walking around to open his side, help him out and lock the doors afterward. Our keycard got us in, along the hallways that smelled of Pinesol, Victoria Secret's body spray and the salty air that McDonald's fries makes. I led Desta to Xochi's office who sat with her back to the door at the desk facing her screen. I pointed to the chair against her desk and the boy crawled into it. Xochi continued talking on the phone to what sounded like a foundation interested in the site visit that led to what I realized would be an *inevitable* donation and reached her palm up to Desta as she clenched the phone between her shoulders and her ear. He gave her a quick high five with a dimpled smirk to the right side of his face when she shook her hand as if it hurt. She turned her fingers to a pointer, which made Desta turn, smile, do a pointer, which made me turn and see the clipboard hung on the wall under the sign named Clay.

I walked over to the intake boards and pulled the clip board off to examine. One session, one hour a day, three hours total, two people, one facilitator, one room, three people and one of them not one of the Parchicks. As I tell you this, I still even now have to pause. The Parchicks? . .

. .oh come on, Xochi! Fucking come on, man! Are you serious? Really? Did you not know the night I had last night. Well....now that I've vented and re-vented, I still accept that fair is fair. You really couldn't see the scenario as anything but Xochi telling me she was tired and I had to cover today. She doesn't ask much so when she does you just don't argue. Normally we rotate the mother daughter duo and laugh about it later over beer. Somehow how her rotation got skipped and I was up this morning. Looking up from the clipboard, I saw Xochi wink and look at her watch.

12:58 PM. Two minutes of sanity left before I'd have to go be sane for insane people. No let me not say that. That's biased. Let me be very objective and fair in saying that parents can just be stupid sometimes. Of course kids are going to be stupid, but they are kids. Parents seemed to be full of shit. Not as much as before but still enough of them talk and can't back. So I will have to be the listener. Two minutes to deal. I pulled off my leather quarter length and quickly undid my button up, tossing both on my chair. It would be my intent to walk outside again drag from a cigarette until it was half gone, rush into the session and reek of tobacco. Oh boy! I powered myself up the stairs to the roof, lighting the cigarette when I got a foot outside of the door. I took multiple puffs, exhaling quickly. One minute left. I tossed the cigarette on to the pile of butts I had created on the rooftop over the last few years and slid myself down the stairs with my butt on the rail. Careful not to strain the ankle further, I hobbled back to the office and put on my shirt again. Thirty seconds to go and I was inside the session room. Sure enough, Mrs. Parchick began rubbing her nose when I entered. That's how I told myself I would be objective now.

The session rooms were located on the second floor and tucked away in the hallways opposing the dorms. Small, dimly lit, clean and free of too many decorations, they were built to be a safe haven for our clients to share their thoughts in completely confidentiality. Often it became a place for parents to sneak in attention at the expense of their child's psyche.

"Hello, family," I said walking across the room, using colloquial Xochi and I developed to reinforce out clients were more than customers to us. There is also a joke hidden in there I am sure Dave Chappelle would enjoy.

"Hello, Dr. Durward," Alexandra says immediately with an insecure shrug as she stands. She is a brilliant and gorgeous young woman in her second year of high school that has no idea how powerful she could be with a bit of self-belief. Her eyes give away her relief as the referee has returned to session. She does that awkward knee lock that young women do when they want an embrace and don't know how to ask for it. I reached my arm out and cocked my head, giving her the "don't get weird on me" expression. During the hug, I felt her mind slip out a *thank god* and wondered why she didn't feel the same around her mother. I slipped in a subtle concern about how much cleavage she was unfortunately showing into her head as I let her go and turned to her mother.

"Hello, Clay," Mrs. Parchick said as I extended my hands to that high as weird hand shake she did as Alexandra buttoned her shirt two more top buttons in my periphery. Mother gave the big set up that ended in the limp shake not because she was disrespectful but because she wasn't sure why her daughter wouldn't open up without these sessions. I shook limp fingers and tried not to flinch when she did the two kiss on my cheeks. If she told me ciao at the end I just might throw her to ropes and do flying clothesline that ended in me pumping the sky with my arms and talking to all the warriors. Shut up, you know you watched the superstars on Saturday night too. Despite her repulsion to the nicotine pouring out of the sweat glands behind my ears, Mrs. Parchick's mind reacted to the texture of my hair quote favorably. In fact, she had noticed that it looked a lot more cylindrical and spiraled near the scalp. She connected it with my intelligence and thought of some interesting marketing executive at her job that had my same toffee complexion. I was suddenly aware that her husband didn't argue with her much or even engage, silent complicity followed by some material reward. A buy off. Did you know that tip stands for To Insure Performance which in some countries they call a bribe? She exerted her free will where there were reactions: charity, travel, appearance, her daughter, home, renovation yet for some reason her profession didn't make the list.

The Parchicks sat on the couch with the invisible divider of a cushion between them. I pulled up one of the black plastic chairs I assume Xochi ordered to ensure pain in my Africanized ass muscles which would in fact keep me awake and alert during these sessions. Instead I looked over the typed notes from the previous sessions, my eyes scanning at an amazing rate. The key pieces highlighted themselves as factoids to guide the path. The Parchicks came twice a month for the last year and a half. Alexandra had been caught stoned at school a few times. When moving her from school to school had proven a failed attempt to reduce negative peer influences, (that interestingly enough lived next door) the response was to cut off contact with peers completely. Phone, text, internet, extra curricular activities and leaving the house were monitored. Alexandra simply slipped out of speaking while her consumption increased. In private journals only myself and Xochi were privy to, her usage stemmed from anxiety she associated with the normal pressures of a teenage girl such as her weight, do boys like her, is she good enough and how does she reconcile the hormones running through her body that make her look at crotches of her other school mates. Then there was the constant monotony of her parents bickering and her hatred of who she saw in the mirror. I decided that I couldn't resist.

They begin talking . . . well, no, mother talks. I feel something pull in the left side of my brain above the ear. The seagulls from Ben Harper's Roses From My Friends in my head on some well chopped loop with a new back beat. Mrs. Parchick is speaking in slow silent words that are negotiable depending on how low the right side of my head turns the volume. I already know what she's going to say before she does. *I watch my posture change as both of them move in slow motion. I seem unaffected by the time distortion.* Eyes glassy relaxed, I watch the conversation go as far as it was going to go if I let Mrs. Parchick go down her paths of "I don't understand" while Alexandra continued to say in her head that she could do anything. This was a waiting game with a cycle; a war of attrition. At times, even terrorism makes sense to the victim and her daughter's silence was taking a piece of her life. This was a waiting game with a cycle. A catch in the system and the family was too into the loop to see it for what it truly was. Somehow my brain had opened a program and I could see where ten years later ended for the two seated in front of me. I tried to be an objective participant and allow them their own process.

Then I thought of the preciousness of time lost hiding from my parents as they fought and all the things I should have said if I could have spoken. My pursuit of a world distant from the life on the corner across from Granny's house off below Hunter's Point is what drove me away. Then I was forced to run back to being choked by it. More time with family and less time proving I was better than the manufactured myths of the streets that sold you on being faster than bullets and being the one cat to never get caught. Worlds apart were the Durwards and the Parchicks, one thing linked us; the need for the next generation to find something new that was of value to the table. Was that what I was searching for with Granny? Making up for lost time I didn't know I missed. In this new found power, I found myself a victim to its will.

"Mrs. Parchick," I waited through as I spoke, "can we try something different today?" Her face stopped in mid-word, shocked and in thought. I saw the world changing, the possibilities of tomorrow fuzzy in my mind as just a few well placed words transformed the direction of these two. I rose from my seat and walked over the desk to grab two legal pads. I scribbled a question on one and scribbled another question on the other, bringing the pads back with me along with two pens. Each got a pad and something to write with. "Bullet points only", I said with certainty, handing each customer their respective prompt. "Nothing more than five words long."

Each took their pad, looking at the question waiting for their higher intelligence to respond to something new in the cycle and dug into the alternative. Alexandra went first, uncapping the pen, slow motions, sped loops, then furious strokes when the paper drew her in. Her mother notices, in the way anything that has given birth, sees in its progeny a genuine sign of interest and inspiration. Mrs. Parchick dropped her shoulders, surrendered and began writing. I tried to pity her for her need to control and feeling of being beat down as she accepted this was not a task she was comfortable with but complied. The ball point opened up for her as she left the barriers her mind put up to not remember and flew to a place where pain detached from the ability to watch and accept.

Mrs. Parchick's mascara ran as she wrote, tears forming from glands she had willed closed years ago in pursuit of harder simulacra of herself. I watched her memories form behind her head of the stern and controlling father she was never able to love the way she thought she ought to through his armor of etiquette and predisposed mannerism that let in no affection. The mother who laid time and time again into the child she expected to be everything she was not only to create a genetic replica who's life was everything left over after her husband's identity. No wonder she missed the cues from her now teenage Alexandra who pivoted herself to be every thing Mrs. Parchick wasn't if only to make one choice, no matter how wrong, on her teenage own. Nestled in the back of Alexandra's mind was the memory of some *family member who took advantage of her while vulnerable, though an obstacle she wouldn't let it haunt her. Instead, the ability to choose, to define her own safety became the only focus that stretched every thought of her expanding mind. The idea of her own way became nearly prurient. The two women's voices are like a chorus, loud and turbulent, jumping all over, spinning me through possibility after permutation of where memories meet intention to form decision I until I am choking in the wind like sensation of another's experience.*

"STOP," I heard myself say forcefully, both clients looking up with eyes wide and a ripple to their spines. I put my hand up to press my fingers against the throbbing vein on my right temple.

"Are you all right, doctor?" I heard Alexandra ask, concerned. The room swam for a bit and I felt my stomach turn.

"Yeah, I'm good," I replied closing my eyes and feeling my words in the dark. "I'm fighting a bit of a bug." In the darkness, I can see long and wide. The long column in the gloomy temple is made of fleshy stone, some times lit from a flicker that glints on my eyes. Those eyes never leave the eyes attached to the creeping and sneaky eight legs of the creature wrapped around the column that is my spine. My hand should have something, a weapon at least. Where is my mind in all this? I found myself short of breath and unfocused. I shook my head, returning light to the visualization in my forehead. Opening my eyes, I saw the Parchicks remained in captivity.

I reached forward and took their legal pads from each of them. Crossing the room, I pulled a black licorice scented Marks-A-Lot marker from the pack on the shelf of the easel that held the large ream of a giant Post It chart paper and drew a vertical black line down the middle of the page creating two columns. On the left, I began copying all of Alexandra's bullet points into the left column in green apple while placing Mrs. Parchick's in blueberry on the right. I picked up the grape soda, drawing circles around ideas and then lines to connect. Soon the page was a sea of balloon and there corresponding idea on the other side of the column like a boiling page of hot molecules.

"They are the same," Alexandra mumbled, eyes wide and speech far away as she stared at the pad. Mrs. Parchick looked from Alexandra to the chart, covering her mouth with her hand as she began to cry. I smelled trees near a stream covered with moss and a thick fog, the smell of growth and healing to a burnt land right after the first hard rain. I nodded.

"Alex," I said calmly with my voice hoarse, holding myself up with my arm bolted against the desk. "What was your question?"

"What makes me fight against my mother so much?" she murmured.

"Mine was what would I change about my childhood?" Mrs. Parchick sobbed, her body shaking with the tears. Alexandra looked over at her mother, a look of deep concern which inspired her to slide over across the cough and hug her mother. I began limping toward the door.

"You're, you're leaving?" Mrs. Parchick sniffled.

"Well, we've got forty five minutes left," I said, steadying myself against the door knob. "Now that you two are communicating, it would be a shame for me to get in the way."

When I got to the stairs, I couldn't help but remember the images from the night before. My ankle hurt something fierce, my head swelled like a cold and my back sweat with cold perspiration. Something about this Sekhem Ka entity was killing the Passenger inside of me was directly connected to my nervous system. Each step down reminded me that if the two beings fighting for dominance continued to make my body the battle ground, no matter who won, Clay Durward would be decimated in the process. I stumbled into the office where Xochi sat in her chair, Desta on her lap, reading from a large book that was nearly bigger than him.

"*Accipiter cooperii*," Desta sounded out slowly with a smile. Xochi smiled as well and moved her finger slowly to along the page.

"What about that one?" she asked and I saw the image of a bird in the corner of her eye reflect from a page.

"*Buteo jamaicensis*," he said shaking his little arms up and down excitedly.

"That?" Xochi moved her hand faster now.

"*Spizella passerine*," Desta shot back as his mouth smiled and his eyes grew. He giggled after the answer popped out of his kind face like a bubble.

"You speak Latin, Lisperman?" I asked, feeling like Fred Sanford after a long day as I limp-shuffled to the chair and plopped down hard on my jacket.

"You should have seen him with the book about plants," Xochi said.

"Garden," Desta lispered, happy with himself and tucking his hands in his coat pockets.

"He was telling me how he likes to garden," Xochi chuckled, "in French, no less."

"Must have been the Super Mario tooth brush," I said, folding my hands on my chest and closing my eyes.

"Cheese," I heard Desta say as I returned to the darkness. The column. It. Me. My head. This vein. Focus. *Is he sick?*"

"Garden," Xochi said alerted and awake, *"of course. Thank you, Desta."* I opened my eyes and little man was on the other chair standing up to lean over and peer at me. Xochi stood close as well looking down at me as if she was trying to remove a splinter directly from the top of my head.

"Get down," I said sternly to Desta, who reeled back, pulled down his shoulders and dropped into the chair depleted.

"Hey," Xochi said, grabbing my attention. "Don't talk to him like that."

"It's okay," Desta says putting his hands back in his pockets, looking away. Xochi is still looking over me; my eyes detect a slight yellow to the air like a marigold perfume that you see when you smell.

"We need to see a doctor," she said looking at me directly.

"I thought you said this wasn't covered by my Kaiser," I replied, half joking.

"You're on the same plan as the doctor," she replied. "I need some time to contact him."

"Okay." Her eyes changed and there was deep yellow to the room.

"Ka...I need you quiet until you get to the Monk."

"Yes," I heard myself say and look over at Desta "Sorry," I said, calm on my breath.

"What's a moment ago?" he asks looking off at the floor. "It is what you do after those moments that tells us who you are." I paused looking at him for a few moments wondering how profound it could get.

"We're still friends aren't we?" I asked.

"No." He said with a quick head shake.

"We're family, right?"

"Very much so," Desta lisped back. He leaned over and squeezed my finger. Now I was the scared kid in the front seat.

CHAPTER EIGHT

"We all have our areas for improvement."

-The Monk

I stayed quiet the next few days. Teaching, sessions, reading with the boy and no sign from any friends in my head. I slept well, ate a lot, learned the Latin name of all the trees in northern California from my tutor, iced my ankle and read more of my archived journals. Saturday started with Xochi texting around eleven to let me know she had an appointment for me around 5pm. The address I found to be a found to be a Buddhist supply and eastern nursery retail operation on the plush side of Lake Shore in Oakland. I couldn't get any sense of owners or biography from the website but something in the name caught me for a few minutes: "Too Far West."

I stood on the balcony, smoking as the fog pulled off Twin Peaks and began its slow creep into the city as if the wind pulled it along some invisible tractor. Then I thought to myself, only my reality as Clay that told me of air currents, condensation and the square mileage of the earth moved vapor at certain almost predictable rates. If I wanted to, I could let that slip away and look long enough to find who's job it was to direct that fog. Instead, I said it was both and blew my smoke into the air to join with the clouds.

Too Far West. Someone had joked about that. I relaxed and let the voice loop in my ears. Although I didn't recognize it, it spurred other memories and I found myself in a playful mood. Ever remember a time when you were laughing with friends but couldn't remember the punch lines much less the jokes? The laughter is coming to me stronger and I feel myself smiling. My nose is stuffy and I can hear the sound of rain with the smell of water it touches open flame. A camp fire under a canopy of animal skin that is too assailed by water to be effective. A clearing. Tall trees with thick bark and rolling hills of dry grass behind us. The air is slightly salty so we must be near an ocean. A few silhouettes and flickering faces in the storm. We are laughing at our friend as he shivers, water dripping off his hat into his face. His hands shake as he counts beads and attempts to focus himself away from the cold. He stops to chide, explaining he has seen the floods of China and the snows of Tibet, so our comments are ill advised. Then he sneezes and shivers. We have found his prayer that he may gone too far west in his journey very comedic. He knows he is funny but pretends he is above it.

"The Monk," I heard myself say out loud. I looked around to reassure myself I was alone although still unsettled at this new habit of speaking out loud for no good reason. This would take adjusting to and some monitoring. I guessed that the next time it did occur in front of someone, I'd follow with a burp or fart to keep it awkward. I tried to keep eating, reading on a blog that you could subdue a craving for a cigarette with salty foods. I spent the rest of the day writing. Just forming thoughts in my moleskin to get it out of my brain and on to paper to make space for the inevitable information would be coming my way. I figured I would put all of these journals together one day and maybe someone would want to read it.

Around three o'clock I picked up Xochi and headed over the bridge toward the East Bay. Normally its not that long of a trip but I was wary of cramming in too much so that I didn't leave room to do some necessary recon to soothe my soul. Only so much one can find out about a building from Google maps and street views. The bridge was tame until the 880 and 580 split where the roads left off in their separate directions. I quickly resolved myself to the idiotic stop and go that led up to the slope of the 24, but decided I would dip over to the 980 rather than loose my cool. If I had a quarter for every large person in a SUV or truck on the phone without a headset under the false impression that they drove near safe, I'd be guaranteeing the Treasury. I took the loop and pulled off at the 27th Street exit.

Lispery croaked from the back seat that he was thirsty and with Xochi in the front seat, I couldn't smoke. I pulled over at the market a block away from Merritt Shores to buy Desta a small bottle of orange juice; not the quarter water sugary bullshit either. My eyes caught the sight of a bag of beef jerky dangling from the fastener behind the counter. It was inner dispersed between the bandanas, cognac blunt wraps, phone cards and doo rags. I couldn't help the temptation around the taste of salty and some need to argue with aggression inherit in chewing anything dried. I nodded toward the package with my finger as I laid a twenty on the counter for the subtotal already rung up on the register. The jerky broke the bank bringing the total closer to four than three dollars. I collected my change and carried my items out with me to the car, watching Xochi hold a conversation with Desta in the back seat. I dropped off the juice to the little one and flashed my pack at Xochi. Walking around the corner, I lit a cigarette on the lawn at the grassy shore of the Lake where it met Bellevue.

I looked out at the slow wind at the water, resisting the urge to randomly kick a water bird living off crumbs into the branches of a high tree as a channel for my frustration. Anger. Kubler-Ross states the second stage of grief can be compartmentalized as anger. Yes, I am anger. I am in fact alone with my anger, wondering how to reconcile my spirituality. I am arguing with the doctor who tells me about loss and grief. Around the corner, as I look at the back side of the plush prison my grand mother dies in every day slowly, I realize no Elizabeth Kubler-Ross I don't actually want reconciliation. This is the private conversation I have with the authors of books I read to find new outlooks to loss. Yes after the last couple of nights I have had this week, I am willing to bet God is mad at me and its probably not even due to me being mad at God anymore. In fact, I remember asking God is it possible we leave Granny alone? She gave everything she could. I'll go. I've lied, cheated, stole, cursed, thought of killing someone and I've even smoked a joint rolled in a bible paper. Send back Granny and take me. We can even do an Aaliyah for Brittney Spears swap. Nothing. God didn't even tell me to fuck off. I get subtle signs and friends who step on Bulfinch's head. Yes, I am that guy who is wondering what happened to my faith when I was in need.

I am as well someone who is completely aware of my shortcomings and past transgressions. I have spent the last decade practicing the daily knowledge that if I am a "good" person I will not suffer the ugly hardships of this world. Granny raised me that way but it was I who chose to accept it as my natural state of being. She made it clear that I was a son of my parents, therefore a son of their success not their tragedy. So now we have a full room in my head. Dr. Kubler Ross, my Granny, my mother, my father and me in a session room in my head as I smoke on the north side of the lake which people called Merritt but on maps was named Lakeside. Oakland. Everyone agrees in my head: if we live in accordance with our hearts and the life we could lead after our doubts have dissipated then the terror of the night would pass our door step. Granny lived as if she might not have another chance to make a difference and not a person who remembers her will tell you any different. She went to church; some go to synagogue, mosque, temple or unfortunately burning man. She gave time, did as she was told, stuck up for those who could not stand up for themselves yet and all these assumptions did in fact come crashing down for me when she got sick. Bush will get to pardon John Forte, Cheney will get a retreat in Montana near missiles, Rumsfeld gets a mansion that used to break slaves and Granny gets Alzheimer's Dementia Stage Three. I lost my way when the good, the just, the loving, the healthy, the young, the most needed, or the least seen died on me.

I tossed the cigarette into the lake, hoped Felix Mitchell liked my brand and walked back to the car. I popped open the beef jerky and took a long bite, waiting for the effect to cleanse my tongue of the need for a smoke. Instead, I chewed on salty cardboard that moved against my teeth like saw dust. I spit it out and tucked it in a pocket rather than litter in front of the small child watching me in the rear view of the car even though I had just thrown a cigarette in the lake when I was alone. I make sense to me.

I jumped in the car without looking around, started the engine and quickly threw on a seat belt. Desta told me I smelled as we pulled out of the parking lot so I answered with a loud fart without moving my shoulders an inch. He giggled and clapped, Xochi punched me in the arm without looking at me, which hurt but I didn't admit it. We cruised around Grand heading past the Grand Lake Theater and its prominent display warning of the abuses of absolute power. Up the street past restaurants along the avenue and toward the turn signal that gave us the opening to the parking lot that stood as a connector to Too Far West. When the signal changed, I cranked the wheel to the left and breezed into the parking lot. When I parked the car, Xochi reached back to release Desta's seat belt. Soon as I heard the click, I felt tiny nimble hands probing my hair at the base of my skull.

"Spy rules," I heard the lisper in my ear and smelled orange juice and peanut butter in my nostrils.

"Excuse me?" I said.

"Spy rules" he repeated, tugging at my hair, causing me to wince. I reacted and moved his hands out of the way of my own, running my fingers through the back of my hair and being surprised when the fingers got caught on a tangle. I let my fingertips play at it, realizing it was more than a matte or some briar patch, but a column where the hair was growing around itself three strands at a time. Further exploration found that several patches all over my scalp were experiencing the same phenomenon. I pulled out a long one near my temple, eyeing the beginning stages of what I knew to be dreadlocks. I felt the tiny hand on my shoulder and its weight as a small body learned on my shoulder to point at the hair in my hand.

"Spy rolds," he whispered.

"Spirals?" I asked.

"Yup," he replied and returned to his seat. I felt eyes on me and turned catch Xochi's blank gaze.

"Looking familiar are we?" she asked.

"Am I?" I replied.

"How do you feel?"

"Like I hate doctors, dentists and shrinks."

"This one is different."

"I'll have to trust your judgment." She patted me on the knee and left the car. I stepped out myself to open the door for Desta. He hopped out and sped around the car to catch up with Xochi. I locked the doors and wondered why nobody waited for the hobbling patient. The inside of the shop immediately made me think of a green house, controlled humid climate and smelling of potter's soil. The windows were synthetic Gaussian, a plastic tinting to promote the capture of ultra violent rays. The floors were gravel stones placed over the hair of red wood bark with a wet rich brown earth adhesive which supported the racks and multiple boxes of dark green plant life growing on all sides. High trees that climbed tall enough to threaten to tickle the ceiling, succulent ferns, herbs, decorative flowers; the entire warehouse reminded me of a grotto. Somewhere I heard the sound of trickling water and far away birds.

"Oh cool!" Desta cried out and ran off into the foliage. Xochi smiled and followed slowly leaving me along on the stone block pathway with its fluorescent green moss where it met the running boards. The path led to a smaller show room made of lacquered wood panels with a number of friendly indoor lights that contrasted with the interior lights of the display cases that held the high end statues of Buddha. The lights reflected rainbow patterns across the floor from the green, blue, purple and brown jade casted upon the very clean wood floors. I heard the sound of wind chimes in the distance. I searched the room and the high ceilings for a sense of breeze. There was none and I found myself slowly pivoting in place as I took in every detail of the room in its size and infinite sense of calm. I felt eyes on my back and followed them to their source staring at me from a door way I did not see when I entered.

He was shorter than me, not but much but he definitely made up for it on the x and z coordinate. Judging by his wide nose, rusty colored skin I guess him to be southern Chinese from either the country or Hong Kong; perhaps even the mountain. His black hair was thick with grilled back streaks that ended the length just behind his ears. He seemed to be masterful in his ability to control a smile or laughing despite something being tremendously funny. He wore thin wire rims over his eyes which had an intensity about them that did not match his conservative garb and demeanor. Although I was impressed with the store front as well as the small forest in the next room, I wondered if the sale of trees and statues generated enough cash to afford the elegant cut of blue Armani he wore over his Italian leather shoes. His hands were folded in front of him just below what I assumed was his navel. He motioned with his head in smooth pull to the hallway behind him, turned on heel without changing his level and walked down the hall.

I followed, the heels of my shoes making squeaks on the treated floor boards until I hit the carpet of an anteroom. We passed through an office, warm, bright and slightly reddish in tint as the sunlight passed through a stained glass window depicting an island in the sea. I followed him through the doorway into a larger office, wider clear windows and sparsely decorated. He stopped at the door, closing it as I passed into a large open space in front of an empty desk. Above the seat attached to the wall by something I couldn't see was a large calligraphy piece hung on the wall in flourished Chinese characters.

"So you're my doctor?" I said to the silent guide who watched me with silent eyes. The corner of his mouth pulled down and his eyes fell upon the calligraphy on the wall. *Do not believe in anything simply because you have heard it. Do not believe in anything simply because it is spoken and rumored by many. Do not believe in anything simply because it is found written in your religious books. Do not believe in anything merely on the authority of your teachers and elders. Do not believe in traditions because they have been handed down for many generations. But after observation and analysis, when you find that anything agrees with reason and is conducive to the good and benefit of one and all, then accept it and live up to it.* I heard in my head from a voice that wasn't any of my own. He opened the door again to reveal a long ramp aside columns leading toward what I heard as running water and could make out more foliage. I followed him through the causeway, feeling a half smile from face as the Cantonese Willy Wonka led me down the slope through a moist cave top and into the bottom of a large open grotto. The path gave way to a floor smooth jade forming a wide open clearing. The platform was a large circular island extended into a waterfall fed lake by a single walkway. Along the walls grew plants and foliage nestled around large flame lit lamps that hung from the metallic shiny looking rock. On the banks of the lake grew thick bamboo, oak, and redwood among the black sand of the lake shore and the chocolate cake looking rocks sticking up from the azure blue tint clear water. Seated at a table at the center of the platform, a man focused on brush strokes across a parchment. There was the soft sound of erhu that most people just told themselves was the violin the Chinese favor playing from some where as he occasionally looked up from his writing to stare into the space at a nine o'clock from his chest with a meditative smile as the sun light from the open ceiling staring at the California skyline sent a ray on his face. The guide bowed extending his arm to lead to the seated scholar. I nodded and walked along the walkway to the platform, standing next to the desk.

"Have a seat," he said calmly, eyes still intent upon his work as his head made a slight nod to an empty chair I hadn't seen before. I took a seat and studied the doctor. He was not as dark as the other gentleman but definitely southern Chinese as well with the broader nose, wide lips and round forehead. His head was a smooth bald, free of dots, razor bumps or regrown fuzz. He wore a black tunic of silk, fastened by red ties and long sleeves that hung off of his wrists. His pants were of the same silk yet he wore white Adidas shell toes. *Very comfortable and practical* I heard in my head and placed the voice from the walk down to the voice that greeted me at the table. There was youthfulness to his face, what you would expect of one in his twenties but his focused and relaxed eyes showed the patience of someone much older and developed.

"Have you been writing?" he asked, dipping his brush in the small ink well at his desk and dripping it to the right absorption before writing again.

"Just started back," I answered, "keeping a journal, if that counts."

"It does," he said with a smile, "and your dreams?"

"If I can remember, I write them down"

"Good. Are you eating well? Mindful of the cigarettes. How many do you smoke a day?"

"Nine to ten" I said shifting in my chair, feeling the contents of my pockets scratch against my thigh.

"Almost a pack, as well as can be expected. You are decreasing which is also a good sign," he said. I reached into clean out my pocket, my fingers falling upon the package of jerky from earlier. I fished it out and placed it on the desk.

"I go back and forth with the smoking," I replied.

"We all have our areas for improvement," he said, examining his lines closely as his hand waved over the package the silk at his wrist draping over it. When he moved his arm again, the package was missing from the table. "Well let's take a look at you." He said and placed his brush on the table. He produced a stethoscope from the other sleeve and placed the ear buds into his ears. I tried to relax as the doctor pulled up my shirt and placed the instrument on my chest. He instructed me to inhale and exhale a couple times which surprisingly I could see my breath puff out of my mouth and drift into the mist coming from the waterfall. He removed the stethoscope and made notes on his parchment. Once he was done, he instructed me with "lay on the table."

"Which table?" I asked looking at his writing skeptically even though I did not read any Chinese.

"The examination table of course," he replied and I followed his eyes to a massage table in the center of the platform. Somehow we had moved our orientation from the center of the chamber to its rim just before the walkway back up. I shrugged, got up and made my way over to the massage table. I sat on it and placed my hands down to help me turn over to lie on my stomach. "Remove all your upper garments please," I heard from behind me. I sat back up pulled off the jacket, pulled off the t-shirt over my head and pulled off the tank top. "Remove your shoes and socks as well" he added. I followed orders and folded my clothes neatly, placing them with the rest of the pile. The Monk spoke in Chinese, quick and loud. I searched for somewhere to store my clothes and was greeted by the sight of my guide snatching up my garments from the exam table so he could carry them off toward the cave tunnel. I pulled myself on to the table all the way and placed the back of my head into the cut out to lay bare chest exposed. I stared at the platform below me and realized it was actually a circle of smaller circles. Each was colored and followed pattern of white, blue, green, red and brown in repetition from the center to circumference. My nose caught the smell of sandalwood just before my eyes saw the return of shoes. I also heard the sound of soft Chinese being spoken followed by a prick just above my right shoulder.

"What's that?" I asked, feeling the cushion pushing into my neck and slowing my speech.

"Small needle," I heard the Monk say. I felt another needle on the other side of my body in exact same spot.

"Another shot?"

"Not shots. Acupuncture. Now please relax before I am forced to ask Wukong to beat you." The pricks continued from the bottom of my neck, then my chest, a few in my stomach and a couple in my ankles which made me yelp loudly. I was about to object when the needle went into my forehead between the eyebrows and I lost speech. A final needle went into the top of my head and I slipped away. I heard the two of them talk in soft Chinese I wish I spoke as my back filled up with pricks. I felt light as if the weight of my skeleton was removed from my frame.

Drifting, I feel my mind float, away from the grotto and into the sky above. High into the clouds and soaring, feeling my body left behind. I reach my fingers out and scrape clouds inadvertently missing so I somehow over-extend and wobble. My nose catches the cumulus and courses into my face, causing me to spiral into a barrel roll. Then I curve down, breaking the cloudbank and streak over the plush green hills, past the stretch of desert and back to the grasslands of my home. I knew it was home because I can clearly see the largest of the three pyra-

mids with its white cap staring back at me. The day turns into night, I am pulled back into the sky. The night fades away into the blankness of absolute black.

My relaxed eyes refocused on the center of the cup of dark steaming liquid held in the hands of Wukong. He was propping up my upper body with one arm unstrained as he held the cup in the other.

I felt sweat rolling from my forehead into my eyes. Lethargic and heavy, I lifted my arm to wipe my brow and saw my body was covered in it. I clutched at the cup still too weak to pull it to my mouth, Wukong helped to pour the liquid into my mouth. I shivered before he did and I saw his hand move in rhythm with my mini-spasm to ensure not a single drop was wasted. It tasted like ginger ale and smelled like a mix of the marsh off 101 by the Sun Microsystems campus mixed with Bengay. I found as it went down I could think clearer and a tingle started in my arms as if pulled up by small strings. I wrapped my hand around the cup and drank on my own. Wukong nodded and produced a towel. I wiped my mouth and pulled layers of dirty sweat from my upper body. I smelled wet cigarettes.

"Nicotine," Wukong said looking at the towel, "was blocking many meridians."

"Isn't that what its for?" I heard myself say.

He shrugged and handed me my clothes. Dressing and sipping tea, I watched Wukong who watched the Monk. He stood in the center of the platform, sans any tables, moving in slow continuous motion. It looked similar to the exercises I saw old Chinese do in parks in the mornings as the hotels walking distance from the wharf and Chinatown began there mornings. The Monk held a scabbard that he used though his motions. His eyes never left the tip as he stepped, rolled in his waist and pushed through level. When he was done, he stood for a long time in one place with his eyes closed. Finally he spoke in Chinese again, most of it I could not make out except for what I knew to be the Cantonese word for Egypt. Wukong became attentive and turned to me; motioning with his hands he would take my arms for support if needed. I waved him off and made my way across the platform to the quiet acolyte. Wukong lifted the table from the platform and moved it to the walkway.

"You're the Monk," I croaked, when I was close enough to enough for him to open his eyes. He smiled knowingly and nodded.

"I am," he said confidently, "you are the Door."

"I don't understand that yet," I said defeated.

"How much of the form do you remember?"

"Form?" I said thinking out loud.

"The Shape Mind Boxing." Did I know martial arts?

"I'm not sure if any," I replied.

"Give it a whirl." He stared at me, unimpressed in advance of any response I might manufacture. His assistant stood at his side, the same look of anticipation. Nodding I placed my cup on the ground and walked to the center of the platform again. By now, I had gotten used to the concept that when there was a need for space I would be moved to the walkway and expected to walk to the center. Standing, on the spot, I tried to do what I saw I'd seen The Monk start with. He shook his head at me and indicated I should start over. I closed my eyes and relaxed my hands at my sides. I saw visions of an axe cutting through wood. Then I let go. *My weight shifts and my hands come up, falling into fists at my center. The hands open with the back foot and I step out into a fighting stance; hands over my feet while my palms push away the earth. The front hand returns to my center, I shift again. My weight goes to the front foot and my stance is long as my hands come up into fists along the center line. This draws my back foot in near my front in a chicken step, my weight dropped low. Then my backhand drops over the front and it cuts through the air. I repeat on the other side. I cross the room with repetition, turn around following the same pattern and return to where I started from. Then I close and look to the Monk.* I felt finger tips at my neck and saw the arm of the Monk.

"As I thought," he said solemnly, "you may have cut it off from the Nest but it is not going to let renew yourself while it is out of contact."

"It?"

"Your Passenger."

"Have you seen this before?"

"No. None of us has ever cut off a passenger."

"You have one of those spiders in you too?"

"We all do except for him," Wukong said quickly, indicating the Monk.

"Although free from their law," the Monk interjected, "we are still connected to their chains."

"Would make one ask what's taking so long," Wukong asked, looking at me directly. "Is he done indulging yet or has he grown up-"

"Wukong!" the Monk growled sweeping his arm back toward the assistant. Wukong frowned at me, bowed and stepped backwards silently. "Forgive him. He is impatient with your Reconciliation. You-"

"Reconciliation?"

"It is the process your body is going through as you and your ancestor become unified."

"So I'm related to Ka?"

"You are a descendant of his house just as I can trace my surname to the family of the first monk"

"So we can only reconcile with blood descendants"

"It can be done with others, but its never as potent as your bloodline. The benefit of your progeny is while your Reconciliations are always slower; it has come with some added benefits."

"Such as?"

"Your people are fairly resistant to Isfet venom"

"Oh really?"

"In your last Carrier, your body was better at fighting it than your cousins"

"That's actually reassuring. Thank you...seriously"

"Its my job brother." I was intrigued at the use of the word and sensed at deep tone not only in the sense of family but in the sense of the way an older cat raised in the sixties might refer to his fellow black American on a good day by the water cooler during Kwanzaa. I was relaxed.

"Do you know how this started?"

"Yes it was here. You asked me to use the chamber to extract the chemical from your blood that was secreted when you were bit. We did so and I injected it directly into the Passenger."

"Was it this body?"

"No." I felt a sense of responsibility for something terrible and horribly wrong.

"What happened?"

"We have our theories but you will have to fill in some blanks...it has been some time."

"How long?"

"1988"

"Okay. So how often do the rest of you all change bodies?"

"I sailed over from China in this body. There was still gold in the hills back then...but not tennis shoes." He laughed hard and I laughed with him enjoying his calm and focused intelligence.

"So we obviously made the bug sick, and now its cut off"

"Precisely. Except now it is starving itself in order to starve you."

"Starve?"

"Your body is composed uses an energy known as ATP for energy. Depending on ones genetic make up, we each create, process, refine and draw energy differently."

"And in our respective families we do all that better than most human beings?"

"Exactly. However what you should know is that unlike most humans, your body has Sekhem Ka in it, who has his own source of energy in addition to yours"

"Where does he get it?"

"From behind the Veil," the Monk said looking off into space.

"Or among it," Wukong added.

"I'm still having trouble with this Veil concept," I said, "Xochi introduced me to it recently."

"The Veil is the system behind the system. In Kemet, where Sekhem Ka was born is where your family draws its power."

"And if he isn't connected to that, what happens?"

"He will fade and be broken down by the Proxies for redistribution. Think Chapter 11."

"Huh?"

"It's an economy. A very complex economy of energy, I believe your elder Khpr can explain."

"I'm going to need more than that."

"That's what I have. I'm not an economist. I'm supply chain expert."

"Meaning?"

"My specialization is helping you move the resources you need from behind the veil into it so your attribute is healthy"

"So your basically saying this is a job"

"Yes"

"Here?"

"The entire planet Earth. Perhaps farther. Where does reality stop?" He let out a chuckle.

"Like a demi-god almost."

"Careful with such words, Sekhem Ka is fairly adamant about not being referred to as a god."

"But you mean he is actually the embodiment of a force of nature."

"Absolutely."

"And the passenger is starving him to death...why?"

"We need to ask."

"Tell me what to do." The Monk looked to Wukong who walked off on an errand. When Wukong had disappeared into the tunnel, the Monk brought his hand forward with the hilt of the sword in offering to me.

"I don't know how to use that," I pleaded.

"Might want to learn," he said sucking his teeth.

"Why?"

"Because it's yours," he said cold and flatly, annoyed. "I thought you wanted me to tell you what to do"

"Right."

"From what you have told me of the chamber, you will need it."

Gripping the hilt, I followed its shape with my eyes. My left hand came up to hold the scabbard which was covered in gold filigree in Chinese characters. Something told me that was rare for Chinese blades to have engravings but the faded lavender of the scabbard was even rarer. I recognized the color as associated with my house. Pulling the blade from its scabbard, I followed the grain from its curved top down both of it sharp sides to the hilt where it was inscribed with two glyphs: a scepter and two ninety degree arms. *The power of the world soul, Ka.*

I remembered my dream of the night's past and was brought back to the ruined hillside over looking a defeated Athens, body covered in Isfet blood with this very sword in my hand. Somehow I knew it was native to Heru and I but had been given as a gift for me alone. I thought of the journals and remembered the California coast. In doing so, I realized my bond with the Monk and his companion was much older than this state and older than its road's built by missionaries and gold hunters. In my hand, I held irrefutable proof of contact between ancient Chinese and pre-classical Nubian kemetic civilization. In fact, the technology inherent in smithing a sword of that kind that incorporated aspects of both cultures was a sign of private and sentimental innovation.

"Did we meet in China," I asked, smiling at the weapon in my hand, feeling myself studying my arm against its weight.

"India," I heard from Wukong behind me.

"It was not called that then," the Monk corrected.

I found the scabbard had a fairly sturdy clasp and attached to the belt loop on my jeans over my left leg. Drawing the sword gdave a crisp sliding sound like watching meat being sliced at a deli by machine. I pivoted on heel and walked to the center of the platform without instruction; standing tall. Looking at the Monk, he nodded impressed and walked to the walkway to join Wukong. Once there he turned around to face me and bowed. I did the same.

The walkway detached from the platform as well as the pier at the tunnel mouth and sink into the water. Once the pier was submerged; I felt movement under my feet. Looking at the center, a yin yang symbol lit up as if being projected on the surface of the platform. I bent down to touch it, in doing so the symbol faded followed by the first white jade ring spinning slowly clockwise. Four jade lines later, the next line turned blue and moved counter clockwise at the same speed as the first. It was followed by the next in the sequence, turning green and moving clockwise at a faster speed than the first as the pattern continued. Soon all the jade lines spun creating an audible hum. I felt a tug on my sword from all sides as if a giant magnet grabbed at it. Shiny pieces of the cave wall began to rip off and spin around the platform growing in mass to form a cloud. When the cavern was stripped, the cloud streamed like a bee swarm towards the center of the platform. As it came down, it formed the Chinese character metal and was sucked down as it turned into a vanishing mist before it touched me. When the last was absorbed into the center, a white wall formed around the circumference of the platform.

Next the blue jade ring began. Once all of the rings spun on their clockwise to counter rhythm, the water swelled around the platform and swirled into the air forming another cloud. The cloud spun and formed the Chinese character for water before funneling to the center followed by a blue ring lying on top of the white wall at the platform's circumference. Next was the third green jade ring which pulled the leaves as well as bark from all the plants and trees around the grotto into a cloud. The cloud formed the character for wood and was drawn into the center leaving a green wall on top of the blue. This led to the fourth red jade ring starting its spun which drew the fire from the lamps, circling into a cloud, hanging as the character for fire and pulled into the center. As soon as the red wall formed on top of the green, the final yellow jade ring spun which pulled the rocks from the drained lakebed, disintegrating them into gravelly dust. The dust formed a cloud, creating the character for earth and funneled into the center leaving a yellow wall up. All five walls spun at the same time in unison and opposition. The spinning shot a column of light high into the sky as well is deep into the ground like a needle through the very fabric of the universe. As the light increased in the platform, the world outside became impossible to see through the walls spinning that reached critical mass, exploding in a flash of bright yellow.

When I opened my eyes, night had enveloped the world. The grotto had disappeared leaving only constellations as far as the eye could see. The wall around the platform had a translucent feel, just a thin glass between myself and the oxygen free void. The platform was clear as well, looking down upon the spinning earth below us connected by a pillar of light with origins in what would appear to be the north western area of the United States. I was reminded of my memories of being presented at Olympus and understood I was somewhere on the other side of reality.

Standing across from me on the opposite side of the platform stood the reason for my ignorance. The buried and shaming memory I practice to avoid. We share the same height, build and facial structure. His body is covered by tattoos from his forehead down, glyphs of the same structures I had seen on the walls at the murder scene Avalos brought me to. His eyes show no pupils, two orbs of smoky quartz that blinked as he watches me. When he smiles, I see he missed teeth except for fangs on his top jaw. His hair is long dark brown locks, looking matted with something foul, ending in cruel metallic hooks that seem to move on their own volition and life. Bare chested, he is immensely muscular, wearing bracers of dark black and red metal, a smoky black cod piece and leggings of a slick loose vinyl material tucked into his black spiky boots. Held in his right hand is a large cleaver, the size of a brake flap for a 747 that steamed with a pink mist. Behind him, in complete mirror movement of him, stands what looks like an Isfet arachnid with a tail that was the size of a pack pony. When he begins to pace in place, the Isfet slowly scurried to match every movement keeping him between the two of us.

"Son of Ma'at," I see his mouth move but knew the voice to be the Passenger behind him.

"Bastard of Chaos," I reply, hoping that this was the snappy come back that would really hurt his self esteem, forcing it to delete its MySpace, seek therapy and join a hiking club on Sundays for moral support. It takes a step forward.

"Shall we have another of our games?" it asks, waving its cleaver like an invitation. "I do so enjoy your idea of chess."

"If you don't tell me why you are starving him.......you are going to get split into 8 by 8," I reply, finding myself wheeling the sword with my wrist.

"If we cannot eat," the Isfet Swordsman replied inching closer, "than neither shall thee."

"I suspect your myopia will fool you again," I hear myself say, "but continue to come closer and I'll plate you on your arrogance toward oblivion."

Then I counter step or a version of me does. The self I remember from the hillside above Athens, wearing the same garments as I do now, counters with a saber in its right hands and its left hand flexes into two fingers. I begin the game, my mind a controller on the coolest and most frightening rock em sock em robots ever played. The two met, The Door and the Swordsman, speed and strategy matched by might and fury. As their metal clashes, it is impossible to see how this could ever go past status quo. Evenly matched, the Swordsman is too strong and ferocious for The Door to disarm while The Door is too nimble and forward thinking for the Swordsman to land any blows upon. I expect the melee to continue forever until I notice the break in the pattern; while I stand stationary almost willing The Door with my thoughts, the Isfet on the other side has begun moving. I step to the right as The Door and the Swordsman exchange slices that end in parries and push backs. Sensing treachery, I watch the Isfet crawl up on the clear wall and then vanish. Running straight toward The Door, I know I will need to cover his back. In doing so, I watch the Swordsman cut low at his feet which The Door leaps backward from to avoid. I leap as well, my trajectory aimed to intercept to where The Door will start his arch downward. My periphery can make out the outline of the coat we are both wearing before the rush of air in my ears signaled the appearance of the Isfet out of thin air in a pounce of its own. I saw its wicked eyes.

The stings punches into my left side between my lungs and kidney. I fall shaking as the venom hits, watching The Door slide and slice to remove two of the

legs so that the Isfet scurries away trailing foul blood to hide behind the Swordsman. The Swordsman swings wildly, stepping in front to cover the Isfet's retreat.
The world is becoming smoky white before my eyes as it fades out. The darkness
again. Alone in a chamber. My eyes adjust and I make out ten columns before me,
five leading along the left and five leading along the right toward a goal I cannot
perceive in the dark. I step forward along the dark pathway stopping between the
first of the first pair of columns realizing there are statues in front of each. The
ones at my flanks are a man and woman each with blue green skin. At the foot
of the male is a stone frog, the female a curled snake. Reading the glyphs at the
cartush on the other side of their feet, I say the woman's name first out of respect.

"Naunet," I speak into the gloom and the statue became outline with a quartz
white energy. It lit up the chamber even more and I could see hundreds of spiders
crawling on the walls which seemed oblivious to us.

"Address my husband," a strong, powerful, deep feminine voice commands. I
am stunned, feeling as though I just met Angela Bassett.

"Nun," I say, watching a yellow outline on his statue.

"Son of Ma'at," I hear the voice say, though now masculine, level and sharp.

"Have I died?" I ask.

"Do you wish to discontinue?" he replies.

"No," I say quickly, "I have so much more to do. Free me of this bug."

"It is not clear the Isfet have made the impression upon your family that they
should," the female Naunet spoke.

"I am not my family," I replied.

"No, you are quite different," Nun booms with an aquatic feel that reminded
me of being spoken to from a bathtub. Nun, the primeval waters from which all
life had sprung. His counter part and counter heaven, Naunet, the measure by
which things end and decay.

"The Isfet are part of you," I say to Naunet in realization, "you could stop this
at any time."

"The Isfet are far beyond our realm of control now," she replies, "our hope was
that you would see the error before it evolved this far."

"But the infighting perpetuated it."

"Indeed."

"I can alter it."

"Then son of Ma'at, meet us again in our home."

"At the source," Nun adds, "we shall remove the Isfet from you."

"How do I get there," I asks as the light began to fade into darkness.

"Find your way home," they say in unison and my eyes shoot open on the platform. I look into my own face standing over me concerned, extending his arm to help me up. Clasping his forearm, I am pulled up to stand eye to eye with myself. We hold hands for a moment and then there was only one of us. The walls of the chamber shift to yellow while the center spits out dusty rock particles that fly into a cloud and return to the dry lake bed as rocks. The flame next, then wood, then water and back to the metal lacquering the rock face. The chamber stops spinning and the walk way rises from the waters.

The Monk and Wukong walked briskly over as I sheathed the sword on the ground and began to pull off my upper garments. My left side felt like fire and there was bubbly bruised in a wide puddle across my rib cage. The Monk held out two fingers, the tips lighting up with olive green, as he rubbed his fingers over the sting swapping unmolested flesh in lieu of bruised.

"What's that?" I said, pointing at his finger nails.

"I don't have a good translation for you," the Monk said, "I remember you called it Kooket."

"Ah," I said catching the reference from the Ogdoad which was birthed from Nun and Naunet, "light, photosynthesis, all things living."

"Yes," The Monk said with a smile. I knew that Kwkt as well as Kuk were in that chamber somewhere and somehow I could connect with the entire Ogdoad that rose out of Nun and Nuanet to affect the laws of the universe around me. I was watching the Monk do it and his marvelous machine. I had seen both Xochi and Heru do it as well. It was inside of me waiting to be found.

"Did you find anything about removing the Passengers?" Wukong asked optimistically.

"I was told to go to home to Kemet," I replied with a smile. Wukong looked away disturbed and disappointed.

"In the Veil? Kemet?" The Monk said. "Too dangerous."

"Why?"

"That is free range for Isfet," he said, as he closed the holes on my skin with his hands.

"I'll take my chances," I said.

"Your home land is dominion to a Major Isfet, one of the old ones from the first hatching."

"I'll take my cousin."

"Give me a few days to run some more tests and do lab work," he said reassuringly. "Let's rule out all other options before you take things to extremes."

"All right."

"I will send Wukong to contact you when I know more."

"Thank you."

CHAPTER NINE

"You seem . . . centered but not really here."

--Avalos

The rain was gone and the streets were antsy. I drive through the billows of vapor coming from pot hoes that are reminders that not everything released from San Francisco is over the ground and in plain sight. I am a thinking man. I cannot really avoid that. In fact, I am aware I'm pretty sharp. However, I often feel there is a correlation between the amount of ignorance in the lyrics and the size of one's smile as they drive down a street in a really really nice car with the music turned up really really loud in a really really good system; it only adds more spice if the beat knocks in the subs really hard. Imagine two midgets on a see saw belching every time one of them was up top but the sound shakes windows and makes us other drivers feel you. Its at times like this you notice the detail of the light off street signs that reflect on the hood of an expensive car and you too realize the moment that 50 Cent is appropriate to listen to. I pulled up 6th, poppin' the right on Market, to right on to 5th, to Mission heading south. A Frisco left consist of three rights. Down Mission, I viewed the collage of office buildings, massage parlors, quick Chinese take out, bars and adult video stores that faded away as I passed the court house. On the left the stature of Justitia, in her blind folded contemplation of the sword and scales she carried. Did she know she was really a composite? Maybe she actually had been aware she was a conflation of both the Roman Fortuna for her blindfold and the Greek Tyche for her sword. Of course she knew. She probably robbed both Fortuna and Tyche for their stash like a good stick up kid from Fillmore, now she controls the supply. Next to her in complicit arrogance Athena was with her owl and spear. I smirked and turned up the 50 Cent, daring her to play this on the radio.

I parked in an alley next to the combo dirty jazzercise and ballet studio turned strip club named Barbary Coast, backing in so the front of the car faced Mission in case of an immediate exit. No street behind me so I would need to gun the engine which meant putting the car near the front of the alley but not close enough to make out the car from one hundred eighty degrees looking in. Throwing my hood over my head, I pulled my scarf up covering my face in the cold. Realizing around the corner with the Wisp, I scanned the streets for the signs of life. I reasoned that if Naunet was decay, Kwkt (Kooket) was the organic, then Hh (Huh) would be the spatial. Time and Space. Huhet, the female time, and Huh the male space. In that linkage, I could search for its thread under everything around me. In searching I found an outlining tint to everything as if a blueprint done in spray paint strokes with pale grids. The closer something was the brighter it was in hue, while farther objects were in darker saturation. Lacing in, I relaxed into Amunet and how she related to all things unseen; the mind. As people drove in their blueprint cars, their clothes took on a lavender background to a small screen of all their thoughts and memories. I watched for anything watching for me.

On the street at 8th, parked at a meter, next to the mattress store that had been once been the Guitar Center was a Ford Crown Victoria. Inside the gray American made automobile of Federal issue were the two police officers, Stockton and Porter, from the crime scene. Their eyes watched the glass window of the Happy Donuts that Avalos had texted me to meet him at. Following their eyes, I drew a thin lavender equilateral triangle, the apex starting at the officers' eyes, with the range extending across the block to Avalos seated in a booth at the back of Happy Donuts. This told me the extent of where the officers' line of sight reached and where it did not. Smiling I drifted past Avalos' head to the men's bathroom in the back with its air pump operated self closing door. It was simple to place myself there. I washed my hands and walked out of the lavatory wiping them on a paper towel for posterity. I passed Avalos and sat in front of him at the booth. His eyes watched me and I was disappointed he was not more alarmed at my arrival.

"If you were going to bring friends," I started, "we could have just had me come by your office"

"I came alone," he replied, reading his New York Times.

"Stockton and Porter are watching the back of my head," I said pulling down the scarf to show my face, "and she still has a Cranberries haircut."

"Not my hand."

"No?"

"That would be repaying a favor," he replied, turning the page of his paper and briefly looking at the window as he did.

"Oh but that's not you, huh?" I replied sarcastically.

"Did I miss something?"

"That meet you sent me on. I was surprised to see where you stood."

"I don't know anything about that."

"Oh, but you can hand me times and locations? John, I thought we were deeper than that."

"I'm here about the kid."

"Tell your sponsor the conversation is closed."

"Sponsor?"

"Again, man, we had a certain understanding, you and I, before all this started."

"What's between you and I," he said sipping his coffee through it small rhombus shaped opening on the lid, "still stands. I should have mentioned I was just delivering a message I was pulled aside to give."

"From the bosses?"

"As a favor," he restated.

"Then do us a favor and make sure the powers that be stop asking about the kid . . . keep him out of the databases. He is in danger. Tell them the same child they are looking for came out of their sponsor's womb."

"What are we talking about here?"

"Laws of governance"

"Cute."

"You sure you need to know, John?" He looked at me long and hard for a while studying my eyes. I thought about his wife and kids, telling myself in my head that he would sleep a lot better in this world if he didn't see what was happening behind it all.

"Are you okay? You seem . . ."

"Abrupt? I'm all right. I am here right now, aren't I?"

"You seem . . . centered but not really here."

"Let me make this easy for you. Put your people on local cults." Avalos pulled out a stenographers pad and mechanical pencil, scribbling down notes.

"Any focal points? Psychographics?"

"Affixation with Mediterranean to Fertile Crescent ancient civilizations"

"Got it."

"Oh and spiders. They are going to leave paper trails. Money. Enough to purchase exotic and poisonous spiders. Think snake cults. You also will find them donating to charities. I got a hunch you can cross reference any leads with any one donating large sums to direct service providers to local teens?"

"Pedophiles?"

"Not directly, their kick is terror, by any means necessary but the target market would appear to be teens." Avalos, writing and putting down bullet points. "You will need to outsource the language. Cross reference Mdw Ntr, classical Chinese, Latin, Gaelic and possibly Aztec scripts" He continued to write nodding. "You owe me now"

"Do I?" he said putting the pad away and folding his newspaper to lay it at his left.

"You do," I replied. His body was fluid and minute as he grabbed the manila envelope from the seat next to him and slid in into the middle of the New York Times. He tapped his finger on the paper once and I matched his subtly by resting the palm of my right hand on the edge of the paper. Through the creases in my skin, through the dry waxy feeling of ink on printer paper, through the smoothed roughness of manila and into the envelope I perceived a stack of developed eight by eleven glossy photos that one might get from a high quality digital printer or fresh out of a photography lab. The top portrayed me entering a black crown Victoria at civic center BART. The next photo is of Horace entering the same car earlier that day while Omid talked on the phone. The next of Horace at a pay phone.

"Horace William Marshall. Wanted in suspicion over distribution over most of the Bayview and spillage into Lakeside. We suspect his finger behind twenty murders over the last five years and directly in charge of the muscle that has dropped three times that along Third Street weekly."

"Okay," I said blank as my face.

"A few night ago Marshall was picked up at Powell Street station after killing two BART officers and three passengers....one of them holding a briefcase in over twelve kilos of high purity cocaine. DA will go with drug deal gone wrong. This is the same night you two had you car ride," he said, staring his eyes directly into mine with a finger raised. I blinked, flipping in my mind to the fourth photo which depicting Heru standing over me as I smoked and puked on the curb.

"Got anything more?" I asked.

"Film wouldn't develop past the fourth shot."

"Saw something did we?"

"I don't sleep well. It doesn't add up, Clay"

"What doesn't?"

"A month ago, Horace was caught on tape at a stash house explaining he had a no bodies policy until he said other wise. He didn't want a single shot fired. It was as if he was avoiding violence. His rules would make our ballistics department look lax. A few weeks after, we see him handing wads of cash to kids, to keep them off the corners. Hundreds for not showing up for work, thousands if they could prove they went to school that day."

"Local drug dealer gives money to kids? Gee is that so suspect in the Bay Area?"

"No. The final hint comes into play a few days ago. We followed him to The Jewel on Third Street. In the parking lot, we watched him avoid the blunts, the dust and the liquor, sticking to the occasion cigarette. When a conflict jumped off, he had the numbers and still walked away. Going out of his way to diffuse violence."

"Meaning?"

"Horace was neither sloppy nor did he show any signs of radical profile change over the last month. A shooting gallery on BART doesn't fit his m.o. or his new profile."

"That on record?"

"On record, he is at the Moreland facility of the San Francisco county jail awaiting sentencing before transfer to a maximum security prison. DA is going for death penalty and will get the jury to do it. Meanwhile word is anyone looking to get even with Marshall and his past while on the inside, is looking to beat that death charge's date." I nodded and tapped the top of the newspaper, watching it slide across the table and fall into my lap.

Once there it was easy to move it under my sweat shirt with just a thought. I fiddled with my hood pulling it down more over my face as I rose from the table.

"If you want to go back to sleeping at night, you should start soon on forgetting."

"What photos......we're even."

"Makes sense. Tell her I'll be in touch soon."

"The favor?"

"Sponsor." I pulled the scarf over my mouth, threw a gloved middle finger behind me to the street and made my way back to the bathroom. As soon as the door closed, I was back in the alley standing next to my car. When I got in I relaxed, turning on the engines without head lights, watching in my head as Avalos walked to his car which was parked on Mission by the Happy Donuts, get in and take the sharp left turn to u-turn to pass me on mission headed north. The crown vic at 8th made the hurried illegal left and followed then cars behind Avalos in a sloppy shadow. I smiled, turn on the head lights, and made the right on to Mission south. Hahahah. Police. Hahahah.

Saturday was ending with Sunday beginning soon. The sky was calm but the flicker of lights down in the City suggested turbulence for the evening. Stepping back, if I wanted, I could spread the lavender shade over the sky and listen to as many minds as I could reach through out San Francisco County. Given the distant sounds of fire crackers, gun shots, car alarms, dogs barking, sirens, and blaring music, I wasn't sure I wanted the unfiltered input of over 700,000 people cart wheeling through my head.

Time to play with the puzzle in my head. I arrived at a murder scene at the request of a friend to help get a kid out of a traumatic situation. I am good at such things and have done them before. The scene is covered by pieces of body parts, no apparent murder weapon other than cryptic runes and a spider web. The kid is released to me to take a shelter specializing in trauma cases that I also happen to work at. The same friend who headed a major crimes unit, would involve me anytime there was a kid at risk, referred me to an anonymous contact I assume is a lead to another case dealing with kids. Some where I tell my boss and best friend Xochi, who reveals her mistrust of the cop I am in contact with. Leaving the office, I am interviewed by a creepy pedophile who is looking for the kid. Meanwhile being followed by a 10,000 year old deity in the body of a gangster rap celebrity in training, I meet with a catty white woman who is not only the mother of the child I'm guarding but is also the avatar of the Greek goddess Athena. Undecided on whether she wants to attack me or turn me in, she is given a warning ticket by an agent of Entropy for using her powers to try and seduce me. At the end of this, I see she is a courier for an older version of myself which has occupied bodies in my family before and currently is inside of me. In learning this, I become entrenched in the forces of nature which allow me to read minds and travel without moving by using people. Not to be out done, I visit my grand mother who has raised me since my parents murdered one another in the last of several brutal fights. I learn that her less advances stage of Dementia room mate can speak to me in diagrams, glyphs and pictures. In doing so he can help translate the script for the murder scene, identifying it as used by the Isfet, the ancient Egyptian concept of chaos embodied in a race of sentient and demonic spiders. Returning to San Francisco, I am informed by Xochi that the same pedophile has shown up at the center looking for the kid and hurriedly calls me for help. I request a ride from the cab driver earlier in my day while the transport turns out to be my cousin Heru, the modern day embodiment of the Egyptian principle for rebirth and king of the land by birth right. Informing me of my own duties, I find the entity inside of me is his squire and has been his companion since time was measured. Following his lead, we go by the center to engage in a fight that reveals the pedophile as an Isfet and Xochi as an Aztec deity. Fight becomes chase, ending at BART where Heru defeats the Isfet but not before we are both injured by a shape-shifting jackal. In the wreckage, I am saved from Entropy's judgment by Xochi but Heru is framed for murder for defying the natural laws of nature.

The kid, named Desta, reveals himself to be not only wise beyond his years but seemingly of the same family as Heru and I. In playing with things the next few days, I find I'm more likely to use my works than not, the process of fighting it not only out of my control but draining me. Concerned, Xochi takes me to visit a doctor, who I have known previously as

The Monk. Suspecting he is a principle as well, I find he has been studying the process of removing the parasite in my back for centuries. Our latest endeavor has wounded the Passenger from contact with its kin but has pushed it to block my body from healing. In realization, I directly confront the creature, learning I must visit my ancestors directly to be freed. While a break through, it sounds impossible. A meeting with Avalos revealed while he is no servant of Athena, he is certainly not under anyone's thumb but his own work. He gives me the location of Heru, making it clear that he is in danger and Avalos can smell dead fish.

Lost in thought, I do what anyone in my shoes would do. You've probably guess it by now. I lit a cigarette and smiled at myself for dramatic pause. This balcony is the gateway to my memories. Looking out at the City I know I can sit here and also watch the city from the peaks comparing the two sets of landscapes simultaneously. Clay is on the balcony, looking toward the city of San Francisco. Sekhem sits stop the shed on Twin Peaks. They both live in my head.

Its warm over on the San Bruno mountain with the sun having risen over the water to the east but casting its light through the soccer field in the valley below while on the peaks with their charter bus of tourists and quarter powered pole cemented binoculars it is foggy and cold. The freakish weather I grew up to make comments about soon as I left the gloom of the city for some random errand one to two miles out at Serramonte or Tanforan's blazing hot safari sun was not so freakish anymore. It was becoming logical as I watched the peaks. I could smell the faint traces of Heru . . . then the Monk . . . Xochi lingering as I sat on a rooftop of some utility shed atop Twin Peaks overlooking downtown from San Francisco. There was no light at this height, the kids smoking and having drunken promises to get panties off in cars were clueless I sat in the shadows on the shingles above. I did not recognize the other two signatures up here.

My phone which is on the makeshift table I've created out of a cafeteria tray over twenty four empty Pabst beer cans, the contents of which I've put into my body as I struggle to get drunk sitting on the balcony staring back at myself from the south side of the city. The phone delivers a text from a number I don't recognize.

5108976517 (12:04 am): Waz good?

I try tracing back through the line but only get a fuzzy image in the mind and warped voice like someone explaining an alien sighting in anonymity before Robert Stack tells me the unsolved mystery about the prime matrix. I know this a principle where I need to work. Niaw . . . maybe Imn. I'm guessing by the structure and wording some kid got a digit wrong therefore hitting my Carrier's satellite on accident. Back into meditation, I slide Avalos's piece along the board trying to find a fit. Why wouldn't Athena contact me directly instead of reaching out through him. Her method led me to believe while she didn't mind being seen with me, she ensured it always seemed coincidental and distant, keeping contact reserved to back channels; complicit of something but what?

Why then would I choose her to deliver startup documentation for my own reconciliation? Did I not trust Xochi, Heru, The Monk or even Wukong? What if each of them was in reconciliation, who would guide me? Someone outside the circle would be my thought or you'd have a loop. Ah ha . . . Constadina. Safe enough to courier but shaky enough to be ignored due to her own ambitions. I remember my last words to her and deduced that somewhere between us and the Isfet, she dangled in the middle. That left me to question, if we were not willful sufferers of the Isfet, then what were we? Xochi had mentioned that attributes who retained their influence over how the world was seen under Isfet law were part of some formal body known as the Grand Concord. In a grammatical sense, a concord was a form of cross-reference between different parts of a phrase. Aside from good grape juice, a concord was also an agreement between things, a mutual fitness or harmony. Seriously, look it up. How did we operate separately and at what price?

> 5108976517 (12:04 am): Waz good?
> 5108976517 (12:06 am): U dere?
> 5108976517 (12:12 am): Dis a Door?

Probably a changed number that someone wasn't informed of. Although, I've had this cell number since I bought my first cell plan. I also queried my mind for the rest of the family. Why had I seen Heru and no other signs of Neteru. Wait....there was the jackal in BART; could that be related. Interestingly the Isfet had referred to Heru and I as Neteru, meaning principles, as opposed to Nehesy, the Nubian colonists who walked north to found Kemet. Then there was a definitely some disconnect between how we see ourselves and how history states our existence. For years, I gave the same lecture, hammering in the principle architecture nature of the Neter as compared to the Greek Olympus, Nordic Asgard and the Ifa Orishas. Now, embroiled in the conflict, I struggled to make sense of how it fit together.

> 5108976517 (12:04 am): Waz good?
> 5108976517 (12:06 am): U dere?
> 5108976517 (12:12 am): Dis a Door?

I had heard Lord Entropy refer to me as that before. "The Door." Searching my mind, I was reminded of the images of windowpanes and doorways inside tombs that curiously led to nowhere. Archeologists labeled these as "Ka Doors," symbolic of Ka being a doorway to the afterworld in which the people regarded as the life in the West. In this regard, the Ka was the door but I couldn't wrap my brain around what it would lead to in context now.

> 5108976517 (12:04 am): Waz good?
> 5108976517 (12:06 am): U dere?
> 5108976517 (12:12 am): Dis a Door?
> Me (12:12 am): Yes. Who is this?

Had Wobogo been placed at the home by coincidence or was his presence there forethought? Perhaps, he like Granny, was family and there was some innate connection between their dementia and our struggle. Terror struck my heart and I queried if there was a sign of what happens to carriers that have damaged their passenger to a point of ultimatum. Could Granny and Mr. Wobogo both be discarded husks for experiments I conducted a generation earlier? Was I that ruthless?

> 5108976517 (12:04 AM): Waz good?
> 5108976517 (12:06 AM): U dere?
> 5108976517 (12:12 AM): Dis da Door?
> Me (12:12 AM): Yes. Who is this?

5108976517 (12:16 AM): Quit playin. You doin 2 much
Me (12:16 AM): I asked your name. If you want to be ignored....keep skipping answering my questions.

Heru. Why hadn't he just snapped out of his handcuffs and flown away? Did he respect the laws of humanity that much that he would martyr in the face of adherence? Did Entropy have something on us I didn't know about? I got the sense from both Xochi and the Monk's silence that there was a somber inevitability to the situation. Back to Xochi's words, while we were friends, my family's business was exclusive to my family. In that knowledge, I decided I would need to talk to Heru soon, before a trial had him less accessible and under more scrutiny.

5108976517 (12:04 AM): Waz good?
5108976517 (12:06 AM): U dere?
5108976517 (12:12 AM): Dis da Door?
Me (12:12 AM): Yes. Who is this?
5108976517 (12:16 AM): Quit playin. You doin 2 much
Me (12:16 AM): I asked your name. If you want to be ignored....keep skipping answering my questions.
5108976517 (12:19 AM): Ah . . . my nigga. Dat is you! How come you ain't answer the emails?

I put out the cigarette and dropped the butt in one of the empty Pabst cans, picking up my phone as I pissed over the railing of the balcony into the back yard. Had the kid been awake, he would have wanted to join my barely buzzed mischief but lucky for me he slept like a rock. Stepping back into the office, I sat at the desk and waved my hand over the smart board to turn off the screen saver. I followed by opening a browser and clicking the email icon in the upper right corner. Playing with keys on the board, I found the "T" key had a cookie and selected that to input. Signing in, I saw several emails from phone numbers with wireless carrier addresses as endings leading me to see the link between this email address and numerous phones via text message. Judging by the chat window, there was over a million previously used addresses connected to phones. I opened a Compose Mail window, entered in the last phone number with its carrier address, left the Subject blank and wrote in the body "was away from screen." I clicked Send and waited.

The reply came in a few minutes after that. "I seen the news. Fuck happened to him?"

"Who?" I replied and sent.

"Horace" was the reply thirty seconds later.

"You believe everything you see?" I replied and sent. Five seconds.

"Y'all said not to."

"I'm learning that more every day," I typed and fired off.

"We ready. When can we meet?"

"You tell me," I replied.

"Tomorrow. In front of W Oakland BART when they close the gates"

"Who am I asking for?" I sent back.

"Wally Mac my nigga."

"Tomorrow then."

"Bring muscle."

"Got chu."

I didn't sleep much that night. I stayed up reading journals and trying to pull jewels out of notes. In particular, I tried to find any references to Huh to help develop myself further. There were specs few and far between, making quote to doors which made notes back to Ka. Vaguely circular and circuitous. One piece I read described in venomous ridicule of researchers puzzled at a Ka door the size of a drive in screen at the entrance to a temple in the Mastaba tomb of Ti. Puzzled, the researchers struggled with the scale of the door and its functionality. A door the size of my own balcony doors might even be too big for the average occupant so what would a door the size a sound wall be needed for. Unless the monument was not to move one person alone--large enough to march an entire army through.

Sitting back, I attempted to put my awareness to somewhere I had not seen before. Visualizing, I thought of the Koret Center gym, letting my mind do the walk from the front door past the check-in turn stile, down stairs, across the walk bridge, over the Olympic-sized pool, past the ellipticals and in front of a locked door I'd never seen in the past. Relaxing, I let my eyes fall on the door to my office while my mind stayed at Koret. Drawing a shape, I saw the blueprint outline form in front of me on the office door jam, static, flickering, and jumpy. I picked a paper cup off the desk and tossed it at the door way; it was zapped by blue gray energy and bounced back against the locked door skidded on the floor. Progress.

Standing, I pushed a finger through the doorway, feeling a cool sensation as it passed through slowly and then became warm as it touched the warm humid air of the gym in its late hours; I smelled chlorine. Removing the finger, I sat in my rolling chair, with the back aimed at the Ka door. Putting my feet on the desk, my knees were cramped against my chest like giant springs. One more check to ensure a path was clear and I pushed with my legs full force away from the desk. I hit the Ka door a second later, launching back across the room in a flash of mercurial blue light. I landed on my chest, the chair rolling against the wall and falling over on top of me. I stayed on the ground giggling as I always do when I have a ridiculous fall.

"Whoa," I heard the lispy voice gasp. Lifting my head, Desta and his Dora the Explorer onesies stood in the doorway. Puzzled. I was clear of any signs of Huh works and the little one looked concerned. I pushed myself up on one arm, beckoning with my head.

"I'm okay," I said with a smile as he waddled closer, putting his hand on the side of my face. He cocked his head unsure, making sure I wasn't saying what was expected of adults to quiet him as he examined my body for signs of damage. "I'm fine buddy," I said kissing the palm of his hand as I moved to stand up.

"Wha was dat noise?" he asked, still alarmed and shaken awake,

"I was playing with some toys," I said pulling the chair to its rightful standing, "but I think I broke them."

"Das wha Momma says when I think something wrong"

"Think wrong?"

"Yeah, like one time I was pettin the kitty . . . "

"Wait, you were petting your mom's kitty?"

"Yesh! The kitty cat," he said, annoyed, his eye brows furrowing like an emoticon. I don't think he got the joke but he was right to object. I looked down at the floor and let go of my smile letting him know I was ready to listen again. "I tried to make him listen when I talked but he scratched me."

"Yeah, cats do that."

"But den she told me I was gonna break it if I kept forcing it."

"Ah. That is another way to look at it," I exclaimed.

"Ruh verse ah sum sen."

"Reverse assumption?"

"My kung fu is great," he said clapping with his cherubim smile.

"Mine is greater," I smiled, tousling his hair and circling the desk, to open a few drawers in search. I found some string for binding newspapers and cut three feet worth so I could fasten it to the bottom of the chair. I wrapped the other end around my right forearm, relaxing my eyes to find the doorway again. Slowly, tile by tile, the blueprint appeared in the doorway and I saw the locked doors inside Koret.

"Desta," I said, splitting my attention between the Ka doors and making eye contact with Desta. "Want to help me?"

"Sure!" he said, rubbing his eyes.

"Sit on this chair for me," I murmured. Out of the corner of my eye, I watched Desta place his hands on the back of the seat pad, yanking himself up with a hop that caught with a knee on the front. He pulled himself up on the chair with a bunch of grunts as his tongue poked in the corner of his mouth. He was seated on the chair with his legs swinging over the side. I leaned over and pushed a hand against the chair guiding it through the blue grey pane. Slowly there was resistance and then it gave away to suction. I let the chair roll as the scenery changed to the empty basketball court hidden by the locked doors, the frame of the door retaining its blueprint out line as the string pulled through my hands like a sinking anchor. Finally when it had reached its length, it pulled tight and taut.

"Desta," I said, "can you hear me?"

"Huh?" I heard back from him, watery, elongated and distant.

"Walk back along the string to me," I said. He nodded and stepped off the chair. The alarm sounded at the motion of something in a secured area and he looked at me panicked. I watched the door way crackle. Losing focus. "Desta . . . NOW!"

He looked at me worried as if holding back a loud fart in front of a cute girl, closed his eyes and ran forward leading with his head the way young boys do when they run. Crossing the threshold, I scooped him up in my left arm. I switched feet and pulled with the right arm. Desta scrambled with his arms trying to help but only got slack since I moved too fast. The Ka door began losing its outline; I tugged with both hands at the last moment, bringing through the chair, toppling to the floor.

"Ha! It works," I exclaimed, pleased with the results as the outline faded away into the doorway of my house.

"You need to draw faster," Desta said, unimpressed. His hand drifted over to the fallen chair that was missing a wheel and at least two inches from one of the four stems at the chair's foundation. I could also feel wetness seeping into the sleeve of my left arm as I carried him.

"I'm gonna count it as a success."

"Can I go to bed now?" He whined flatly.

"You need to be changed."

"Bath too?" he said excited.

"Sure," I said, letting him down. "Go start the water." I smiled and watched him pad out of the room towards the bathroom closest to his room. I laughed at the broken chair, dragged it out of the way and took a piss before going to the dryer to find Desta clean onesies. After his bath and some new pjs, Desta knocked out shortly in his room. I took a piss myself and curled up in my bed. To give myself another giggle, I waited until I was lying down before I turned off the light in bedroom . . . and the office.

The next morning I used my email to send a message to the phone, hoping it got to Wally Mac. I was told from a new number they were in the parking lot waiting to go into Moreland County jail visiting hours. I sent a reply email to Wally Mac to tell Horace I would see him before tomorrow started. I also instructed Wallace to get as much detail as possible about his cell, location, and any landmarks he could see from inside. The chair was left on the curb in front of the house, moments before I popped into traffic with Desta to drop by office supply store to replace the chair. I bought him a Jamba juice at the shopping center at 16th and Potrero, leaving him to smile at the staring women as I sat and wrote in the sun. A few hours later, I dropped him off down 16th at Xochi's condo of glass and lights overlooking the Metronome dance studio. From there, I headed over the bridge, parking at Merritt Shores. I took the time to order a bagel and lox from the local coffee shop, watching people as I chewed silently. Then I walked into the park, finding a quiet clearing free of the melodic smoke from the rastas in which to practice the forms the Monk suggested I brush up on. I did what little I could remember of the movements, multiple times until the ache in my ankle was too much to work through.

Granny was too busy doing sing-along with Mrs. Hotchkiss, Mrs. Bermudez and the nurse to notice me. I resisted the temptation to smoke, walking from the dining hall to the elevator that only opened by secured ched attached to my keychain. My eyes caught Mr. Wobogo standing in the doorway of his room beckoning. His eyes darted side to side, ensuring nobody viewed us when he motioned to me. I dropped my head like I didn't see him, letting the elevator open and stepping inside. Once the doors closed securely, I slid myself into Harrison Wobogo's room just after he closed the door to his room.

"Your hair," I heard his voice in my head, *"bit more like yourself."*

"Yes," I said out loud, "how are you?"

"Less agitated. I was wondering when you would return," Wobogo said, looking with bright eyes.

"Sorry, I've been close, just haven't been upstairs. My cousin is in trouble. I've been . . . "

"Heru?"

"You know him?"

"I'm the one with dementia. What game are you playing, grandson?" he said, looking stern and impatient.

"None. I've just recently sort of woken up, you could say."

"Of course," he said in my head, raising his arms in realization before sitting down at his desk. *"I was wondering why you couldn't hear me previous visits."*

"Who are you?" I asked, pulling a chair up next to him at the desk.

"I am Harrison Wobogo" he said silently and proud, *"while I am also what you know as Khpr."*

"Grandpa!"

"That is what you two have often called me but I am more accurately your greatest grand father. I was also one of your managers in the family business."

"And what business would that be?" I spat out loud in shock.

"We sold an intangible commodity packaged as a durable good known as order."

"I'm really not liking this talk about business," I thought to him.

"*Oh, but it is,*" he shot back excitedly, his eyes lit up. He pulled a piece of paper and marker from his stack of supplies on the desk. His hand started on a building another message to me. It started as pictures which I assumed would be more glyphs. Instead it was two buildings. He labeled the one that looked like a factory as a "Firm." *My mind calls to the sight of workers spraying some fluid into bottles along an assembly line. Now it is watching those bottles being placed into cases. Cases are shipped, salespeople touch phones, accountants adding up the bean pulls and stores loading their shelves with cases from the truck. These were firms.* He labeled the building that looked like a cozy bungalow as "Household." *This pulls my mind to a smiling couple standing in the doorway of the bungalow Harrison just sketched. One of their children plays in the yard to my right, the other hugs to their parents' legs. I can hear their dogs bark from the back yard. Their refrigerators carried bottles from the factory.* He moved his head very close to the page, as he poured into drawing a flow chart where Households flowed into Firms and those same Firms flowed back into Households. "*Firms,*" he said pointing to B, "*sell things from cars to time in an Alzheimer's facility to the consumer.*" He points to C. "*But consumers work places, at businesses or firms. Therefore the money businesses pay employees circles back and is therefore-*"

"Circular flow," I interrupted, "yeah, and . . ."

"*Slow down, boy. You will miss the details. I taught you better. Where as I-ah...*" and he drew a similar diagram substituting B for Creator and C for Creation. "*As the Creator births creation, Creation recognizes it's not the progenitor and follows its best facsimile of the Creator.*"

"*Circular flow,*" I thought.

"*Where would the injections occur?*"

"*There would have to be some form of government.*"

"*Ah . . .*"

"*Neteru . . . the local presiding body*"

"*Take a step back,*" he cautioned. "*We know for the consumer income equals expenditures. What happens to those incomes?*"

"Well," I thought back, "*it's split between taxes, consumption or savings.*" He moved his hands on to a new page of paper. In the lower left corner he drew replicas of an icon of a family to represent the consumer, fed by an arrow of income, with arrows reaching out to each stem displaying taxes, consumption and savings with his color-coded stems. He traced the same diagram again on another piece of paper leaving the stems without destinations or labels. I watched the papers pile up and was glad no hybrid owners were there to find how very unsustainable we were being. I also realized how powerful labels were in binding me to reality. How very powerful a selection of agreed-upon words could be toward shaping what I accepted from moment to moment.

"Back to our struggle," he thought to me and I was aware he could hear not just what I consciously said to him but also my inner dialogue. Part of my mind searched for the mute button as the rest interacted. *"The split is the same, except watch where the flow is distributed."* He redrew the model, replacing the consumption with *Exertion*, taxes with *Belief* and savings with *Fear*. *"This is not how it has always been. I can only show where we are now."*

"No older models?" I asked out loud.

"I was only reconciled in 1956," he said solemnly. *"There is still much to learn"*

"Where were you before?"

"Between worlds." He let it hang and I felt disturbed, watching his eyes gloss over as if sad. *Then I saw the painful long sleep. The psychotic, psychedelic dreams. The bites. The sounds in your head like shaking ice cube trays and wet maracas. The raw toxin in your blood as your very life is sapped away. Trapped dead and alive in a cocoon. Long. The cycle. Then a sword cutting through the silk. The faces of your family, young and quite different from the bodies you saw them in last. Being carried quickly while the sounds of death surround you. The intensely bright light and the penetrating darkness that follows. Opening your eyes in the body of a young man that was not your own and looking out into the streets of Chicago just after the world was at war for a second time.*

"Heru and I?" I asked.

"Yes," he said rubbing his beard and couple times, a softness returning to his eyes.

"I'm trying to see the parallels but I think I'm close."

"Let me draw it more accurately." He started with what looked like similar to circular flow between firms, product markets, resource markets and households. He looked over to me and I nodded to signal I got it. He winked and then pulled another piece of paper, drawing a similar diagram. He replaced households at the top with *Individual* or *People*, at the bottom firms became *Aspects* and *Pantheons*. Where a product market should have been between firms and households, he labeled it *Humanity* as well as *Other*

People while replacing the resource market with *Environment* and *Earth*. In the middle, which in the former model had been Government, he simply put *The Veil* and appended it with *The Grand Concord*. "*The average individual pursues community from his or her fellows in exchange for their own exertion toward a task.*"

"Building a library or planting crops," I murmured following his hand from *People* along to the right to *Humanity*.

"*Humanity as a whole binds together under precepts provided by their celestial guides in the form of civilization,*" Khpr continued. "*In return these guides provide a certain order to things.*"

"Our family" I interrupted, "we were . . . corporate officers? The company provided order."

"*Yes,*" he sent, smiling. "*However, by the same token, that average individual is not an island interacts with the planet.*" His hands traced from *People* left to the *Environment*. "*The Environment provides sustenance in food, clothing, shelter and travel. In exchange, the individual uses their faculties to aid the earth in symbiosis.*"

"*Planting trees, fighting fires, building levies,*" I stated.

"*Precisely,*" he agreed, "*but the environment dictates how the individual can interact.*" He traced his hand from *Environment* down to *Aspects*. "*A fellow in balance, well within the limits of the earth's environment, knows equality. The exchange is the range of limitations that define reality.*"

"How so?" I asked. He laughed.

"*You should know, son of Ma'at.*"

"That's not helping."

"*Your mother is reality itself, boy.*"

"Getting colder?"

"*Eh?*"

"An expression, I'm losing it."

"*In 4000 BC,*" he lectured, "*is it conceivable that a man should leave six miles of atmosphere to walk the moon or sail ships that pass under the ocean's surface?*"

"No?"

"*Why not?*"

"There was no NASA, no submarines, that's just the reason . . ."

"*Ah!*"

"Oh!"

"*Over here,*" he began, placing his finger near the right side labeled *Humanity,* "*we see an exchange. Through The Veil, the Grand Concord supplies humanity with a system to structure ideas of themselves.*"

"Ideology," I said, nodding.

"*For morality, it would seem,*" he sent to me, disappointedly, "*humanity's imagination tests our very ethics as symbols of right or wrong.*"

"How so?"

"*Bring fire to one population*" he sent skeptically, "*and they cook meat, make tools and ward off predators. You become a savior. Bring fire elsewhere and when the neighbor's house burns they ask why your aspect has cursed them.*"

"Yeah, but that's interpretation, isn't it?"

"*Very much so.*"

"And this exchange?" I wondered, pointing to arrows from *Individual* to the *Veil* and *The Concord.*

"*The Veil absorbs belief in taxes and in exchange The Grand Concord authorizes works.*"

"Wouldn't that provoke Paradox?"

"*Not if the works were say . . . approved by The Concord, say a painting on a ceiling, a leaning tower.*"

"Okay, so they are like grants or transfers."

"*You can say that they help fill in the blanks until individuals adapt to the new way of thinking introduced by the works, minor or major.*"

"What's the difference?"

"*Minor is our conversation at this moment, without use of sound. Major would be that remarkable wall in China.*"

"Okay. From environment to Concord would be an exchange of evolution for influence over the planet."

"*Yes,*" he said placing his hand on my shoulder, "*and tell me why?*"

"This market is a resource," I said slowly as it came to me, "how both people and Aspects interact with the limitations of the planet. The Concord regulates . . . how people adapt to nature as well a society's degree of alignment with the planet, all predicated on the amount of control."

"*And what else?*"

"As the population adapts to the environment it increases in size because its odds have increased."

"And therefore."

"Increased revenue to the regulatory body."

"And this final exchange?" he asked, pointing to the flow between the *Concord* and the *Aspects* at the bottom.

"That's where I'm stuck."

"As Attributes or in our collective Pantheons we pump in the universe's primal energy into organic growth and the inanimate material you know as Kwkt and Imn."

"What do the Attributes get in return?"

"Theoretically, the Veil returns the vital essence used to shape the universe."

"Nun."

"As well the influence over other Attributes . . . even Pantheons."

"What do we call that?"

"Niawt."

"My head hurts, Uncle."

"That's a lot for today," he said smiling, "I need a cigarette. *That thing in my neck is kicking."*

Chapter Ten

"You talk funny."

-Cornelius

I waited, smoking at the corner, starting at 7th Street in Oakland with its slow moving traffic. The black Ford F250 truck pulls up to the curb, the sound of heavy bass playing from its subs. It's a pickup, new, dealership plates with deeply tinted windows for the windshields as well as in the back cab big enough to seat three. The driver's side door opens with no passenger exiting. I look around to see who is watching. No one. I walk around the front of the rig, hopping up into the driver's seat. The door closes and I smell thick heavy weed smoke. When I reach to crack the window, I also realize the blaring music is making it hard for me to think and rattling my teeth in my jaw. Turning down the volume, I catch all the eyes in the rear view mirror. Not the black or blood red eyes of the maddening Isfet, but the brown and green bright eyes of youth. Teenagers. Teenage boys. Hooded sweatshirts, Rocawear jeans, white t-shirts, M&M jackets, doo rags, beanies, fades, dreadlocks, gold fronts, tooth picks and crooked teeth. Seated in the seat next to me was a young man, no more than fifteen, hair cut to his scalp, toothpick on his lip and a glazed smile on his angelic dark face.

"Stop starin, my nga," I heard a shrill yet raspy, beautiful little voice say from behind me on the driver's side cab door. Hair pulled into a pony tail, thick cheeks, full cracked lips, a pretty smile, Raiders cap on the front, tilted on her head with the brim flat and a pea coat over a white t-shirt was a young woman the same age as the first child nudging her companion in some form of manners.

"Shut up, bitch," says the youth in the passenger seat next to me to the girl in the back seat.

"Bitch ain't what my momma named me, Corey," she says back to him, pushing his head. He starts to retaliate and I hear it from the back.

"Yo . . . cut that shit out, you two," from the back. The voice is steady, powerful, wise but young and undeveloped. I recognize the voice somehow and meet his eyes in the rear view. He was just hitting a weed wrapped in a cigar before passing it to the kid next to him in back. He was the phone with me last night, except when he texted I pictured someone nearly ten years younger, muscles from shoulder to shoulder, and an AK-47 for a tooth pick. Instead, he was an early teen, a black sweatshirt, dark jeans and a pair of Timberlands. His locks hung near his shoulders and contrasted evenly against his rich chocolate tone. I took the second look at his features start-ing at his eyes, then nose, forehead, chin, lips and finally his mannerisms; I thought fondly of my cousin.

"My name is Wallace," he said extending his hand to shake. I returned it and was surprised at the firmness and focus of his clasp. *In touching, I saw a flash of images: Heru in a county orange jumpsuit in the left pane of sight. He is staring up toward a window and the window is part of a booth with a phone. The glass splits my awareness to the right pane in my vision. In the right pane is Wallace who is hiding tears, nodding to a woman who is seated staring into the glass that separates her and Horace. She gets up from the chair, stepping away into a living room she has decorated. She is speaking to a small child that walks slowly along the carpet in diapers. She lies on the couch and becomes dressed in a gown. The couch is now a bed in a vanilla white room to match the wristband on her arm. She holds Wallace as a baby in her arms, sweat drying on her skin from her encounter. The sweat becomes a layer and Wallace is gone. Horace hov-ers over her in the dark while she reflects back with a scrunched face of prurience that turns to relaxation. The room is dark around them and holds any secret they choose to leave there. This young man is connected to Horace.* "My daddy told to me to call you when I got stuck," he continues, almost suggesting he was giving me time to probe.

"I see why," I said with a half smile. "I thought I asked you to bring some muscle."

"I did."

"I see children."

"Aintchu heard, cuzzo?," said the light-skinned kid with burgundy tipped locks and frog Louie Armstrong groan to his throat sitting next to

Wallace. He is squat and low to the ground, his voice coming from some-where close to the earth's core. "Whitney said the children are the future, ma nga."

"Hella dumb," says the girl behind me at the window, shaking her head with a smile. All the kids are laughing now, except Wallace who still holds my gaze with a cocky smirk.

"Quantity or quality," he asks me. *Wallace has the eyes of his mother and the nose of his father. He pulls me in with the same sentimental gravity as Harrison. Wallace senses my fear and replies with the recognition of his own. So many decisions in such a limited space. He has started high school and is not impressed so far. He almost didn't show up. His father showing up regularly has him wavering between at school and not. Even when he is there, his mind is somewhere else. Still his instincts appreciate his father's consistency. It tells Wallace that the absence of a relationship is more of a burden to his father than the relationship itself. His father is a balance between apology and unquestionable authority. They share the mandate that something is meant to change. Horace is ready to be an example, not an older brother. To be Wallace is to feel that the three other children, his father and his mother are is his world.*

Puberty. Wallace is faster and stronger than kids much older than he. He picks up information more quickly and seems to recite it faster to get the expected response from teachers, but only when he chooses to. He works to ignore the voice that tells him he is smarter than any child at his school. This is also why he limits his participation in sports to dabbling. Competing with other children makes him feel guilty and he attempts to find an identity that is him and a much more watered-down version. He rides the hills on his bike long after his friends have turned back either from curfew or being wiped out. He puts the bike on its lowest gear so he can break a sweat and smell like his peers. Wallace still reconciles why he never gets tired. He can sleep for a while if he chooses but he seldom feels exhaustion. He rides the back roads when the rest can't keep up.

People. Girls notice Wallace now and it makes him optimistic. A part of him wants them to look at him the way his mother does at his father. The majority of him continues his policy of not speaking, afraid that what comes out of his mouth will make him look like a complete ass. He learns from me that most people consider such things, including myself. Wallace respects his elders, whether they are aunts or play aunties. Everyone he knows seems to know either his mother, his father or his grandmothers. He has never been out of his neighborhood but he knows the world is bigger than eight square blocks in Oakland. He is processing the consideration that many of his parents' extended family share a pattern of giving him instructions that do not match with their actions. Wallace's closest friends sit in the car with us. In one manner or another, they are all related. He knows they expect much out of him and Wallace works hard to provide the guidance he believes his friends expect while hoping not to disappoint. They made him a leader; this was never his idea. Candace might have started it with her calls and visits to the house, looking for advice. Wallace seldom believes he is right but what he speaks from his heart seems to be the answer Candace needs to hear even if it isn't what she wants to hear. Corey loves to believe he is the reason everyone comes around even if he knows he is not. Corey tended to be the moody one of the bunch but he brings a lot of heart when tested. Wallace remembers starting middle school and being jumped while walking home from school. All the other kids ran except for Corey. Corey's mom whooped him pretty hard for messing up his school clothes but Corey wasn't willing to leave Wallace behind. Later Corey would begin to understand that Wally didn't need any help, but to Wallace the intent was everything. Nigel asked very little and gave everything. In the days when Wally's mom was still more into drinking and parties than into him, food and the money to buy it were few and far between. Nigel was never broke. Nigel would often buy groceries or meals from the liquor store, meals which Wallace would cook, watching food shows through the illegal cable connection.

Parameters. He understands I can get in a lot of trouble for what I am doing or considering. Wallace trusts me unconditionally and asks me to extend that to him and the young people in the car. I worry for their safety. Wallace believes he has spent more time facing monsters than I have. I cannot argue. I smile back, nod and turn in the seat, release the parking break and cramp the wheel. I turn off the radio and pull the truck forward, making wide U-turn at the intersection of 7th and Peralta.

"I'm Candace," says the precocious girl. *Candace hated her body. It was changing faster than she could keep up with and she found most of the changes to get in the way. There was a time when she could outrun the boys from her neighborhood without her chest hurting. She found herself growing wider rather than taller. It frustrated her that she was no longer standing over most the boys and able to push them around when she wanted. She enjoys the activities other girls seemed fascinated by such as dancing, poetry and fashion. The extent to which these girls spent time on these activities confused her, though. She would much* rather play basketball or run a race than spend all day copying dance moves. She wrote in her journal daily but never any poems. Most of the time her thoughts made her angry or sad, so she avoided thinking about them. Clothes were a problem for Candace. She was far more comfortable in loose jeans and billowing sweatshirts than tight jeans and shirts with her chest hanging out. The girls at school called her hair stringy so she often kept it in a pony tail or hidden behind a hat.

"Dis is Cornelius," she says, shoving the shoulder of the kid next to me who was watching me like a cat watching its food dish being filled. Cornelius hates his name. He wonders what his mother was thinking and couldn't have just kept it to what everyone calls him--Corey. Sometimes he thinks his mother really wanted a girl, what with the way she spent all her time on his appearance. However, it wasn't all bad, he told himself. Corey was aware he usually had better fits than his friends. New jackets and boots before school each year. New shorts and shoes for the summer. His haircut was done regularly while other cuts usually waited for Candace to braid their hair or got a discount cut every two months. Corey would rather be talking to some girls, his wingman of choice being Wallace. Wallace seldom talked, but he made Corey look older when he spit his game. If it wasn't girls, Corey spent his time watching videos and trying to learn dance moves. He knew girls judged him on how he moved. He planned his outfits the night before school every day, practicing his looks in the mirror so he could get the same responses out of girls as the older boys with cars who hung out in front of school. Corey also rapped but he kept that to his chest. His older half brother, Nigel, would slap him for the things he discussed. Corey said what sounded cool but he knew his brother lived it. "You already know Wally Mac and next to him is Nigel." Nigel doesn't speak much because he doesn't have to. He stands on his word just like his uncles taught him. He silently enjoys these type of nights because he's good at his work. He has come a long way in a short period, which now presents the conflict. He remembers being a lookout but he calls himself owning a corner. A corner he didn't inherit without a great deal of work, a great deal of pain and now some things he wished he hadn't done. Nigel knew what it felt like to walk his corner from dusk to dawn, slinging anything that could be bought for a dollar and sold for two. It was better than staying at home and watching his mother smoke up what he brought home for her. He tells himself it was better she copped from him than another hustler but the images still haunt him. Nigel rests his head in a cheap motel down on San Pablo. The

163

room is filled with his comforts: comic books, a television, a dvd player and tons of nature shows. He talks to his pet turtle who keeps him company although he is not supposed to have pets. There are a lot of things you are not supposed to do at the motel that people do anyways, so Nigel has a turtle. He is not supposed to have guns either, but he has been collecting them every since he learned to fire a weapon. Wallace is his cousin on his mother's side somehow. Corey was his half brother, although they didn't have a real mother between the two of them; they have never met their shared father. Candace's mom parties with Wally's mom, although most of that stopped when Mr. Marshall came back around.

"Question," I ask, hitting the right onto Frontage Road toward the 80. "Where are colored parents getting names these days?"

"Why, what's yours?" Cornelius asks offended.

"The Door," Wally says before I can respond. This brings a low hush over the car, the way kids get around authority and fear. You can hear a pin drop matched by the hum of the truck's engine. Cornelius shifts in his seat, having second thoughts about being so irreverent any more. Nigel leans closer to Candace and studies me as if measuring. I chuckle and turn on the radio. I mouthed to myself the fact I was pleased we settled that quickly. I searched the dial with my hand until I found a soul set coming off KPOO's muted pirate signal. Roy Ayers' Ubiquity explained the memory through stabbing synthesizers and a hanging drum pattern that locked me into the groove.

"He like old shit," Cornelius whispers under his breath like I'm not sitting there. Driving. Driving him. Driving his friends. He was speaking to his window in the vehicle, but not me.

"He was prolly there," Wally says.

"I'm not that old," I say defensively.

"Woofin'," Nigel says tossing what's left of the blunt out the back window. The kids all laugh. I found myself smiling at Nigel's reticent nature and near perfect timing. His face shows no sign of laughter and I realize his natural-born comedy. I questioned if this was what Bernie Mack had been like as a child and missed him dearly.

"If I was, I don't remember," I said, catching Wally's eyes in the rear view as I took the left on to West Grand.

"It isn't," Wally paused, "always with you?"

"Yes and no. It's in pieces. Constant work to connect them all in my head." West Grand dipped downward, flattened and inclined as we enter the freeway. "If I think about it too much, it escapes me."

"You talk funny," Cornelius said as his annoyed tone increased.

"Look who's talking," I fired back soberly, pulling into the Fast Trak lane and cruising the dark highway to the empty tollbooths on the far right of the freeway. The kids are laughing again.

"Square ass nga," Cornelius says to the window.

"When I square your ass the fuck out, you can say that shit under your breath then too," I murmured and growled under my breath. The radio turned off without being touched. Corey shifted again and is looking at his hands, plotting.

"Told somebody named Corey," Nigel said, flat and sarcastic, looking over at me.

"Fu . . ." Corey starts.

"Shut up," Nigel said, still staring at me, which gets the whole car laughing again. This time much harder. I realize that despite his age, Nigel is straight fool. The DJ on the radio announces the call letters of the station and moves to the next song. The kids recognize Bill Withers' Lovely Day and sing along. I feel a hand on the back of my neck.

"You have one, too?" I heard Wallace's voice in my head and see his eyes in the rear view.

"All of us," I sent back, passing the toll and powering up the incline of the Bay Bridge.

"Daddy said you can fix 'em, tho," Wally sent back.

"Does it look fixed?"

"No," he sent back with his eyes in his lap, *"but yours look different."*

"I'm close." Wally looked up with a bright smile.

"I was told you're the smartest," he said out loud before nodding and removing his hand.

"Your father places too high a degree of faith in me," I replied.

"Faith can never be too high."

"Really?" I pushed back.

"Yeah," he said, locked into his conviction.

"Oh, you can always be too high fuckin' with me," Nigel said, seeing the punch line and the kids giggled loudly.

"Then why am I driving and your Dad is in jail?" I asked continuing my seriousness. Wally clamped his lips and shrugged, playing with his hair. I watched the road leading toward the tunnel of Treasure Island, paralleled by the construction of a new bridge commissioned by the same governor who had killed Tookie Williams. This was a week of familiar and unknown excitement. To play through the night, and pretend through the day. If I was to keep a semblance of my old self, I would pull over at the island, kick the children out and drive back to the unfinished bridge. To the uncertainty of the day-to-day mundane which demanded I tell a lie. The lie that I told myself: I wasn't aware I was built for something much more impossible and extraordinary. The falsehood that I was only bring something "special" to people. It was as tangible to me in how it was constructed as the new bridge to my right in my peripheral vision. I did good work, but I was only addressing young people after they have been hurt and not before. I was stuck in a mendacious puddle of effect and not cause. My way deeper into the lie was to drop these kids off as soon as possible and speed my way on to the parallel bridge. That would be how I could keep the path of the lie.

To avoid the lie would mean to follow through as I had promised to my former self as I had sworn an oath. That road was this tunnel ahead and into the last stretch of the Bay Bridge on the 101. Although the road ahead was clearly mapped and had been traveled, it would be very different from the times I had driven this bridge before. I traveled with minors with drugs in their blood stream as we planned and conspired to break the law for what we felt was the right cause. The path of no return had been crossed the night at BART already, but this drive would be no return for Clay.

As we sped past the Transamerica pyramid to the north out of the passenger side windows, I knew I was leaving my identity behind. I built that position long and hard to be a different breed in mentality than those who needed me most. I trained myself to be so outside of the drama, the pain and the anguish that I could be effective in removing it. Instead I am angry, lost and alone. I live in the duality of my grandmother's house and the laws of Third Street. As soon as I had gotten my passport in the form of moving away for college, I took it. It was my way of leaving a husk of that same duality on those streets. I was the effective role model known as Doctor Durward because I required the youth I worked with to ascend to my focus rather than cosign the very things that had us relate. We all shared the experience of being stepped on more than other kids and we knew it. If Wallace, Candace, Corey and Nigel could see me at sixteen, there would be no compliance at the rumble of my throat. In a strange way, I'd come full circle. I started as the all-A's student. Then I became the student hustler that every kid from a black neighborhood in San Francisco who survived the 80's was. I ended up a shaper of the very healing needed in families. I manufactured the healing that my own family never knew. I was inserted into exactly the life I was trying to change. Beyond a sense of irony, I found no solace nor suffering in the pattern. Passing Hospital Row, the radio popped back on but the signal on the radio was lost to static. Corey reached over and turned on the CD. I shook my head and rubbed my nose like something stank.

"Why you hatin?" Corey asked sharply.

"Why you lovin?" I asked with a rich, sarcastic smile.

"Use a nut," Nigel said chuckling, inspiring another car-wide giggle fest. I took that as a compliment.

"What's wrong with it?" Candace asked as we passed the Cesar Chavez exit.

"For me," I said over the blare, "nothin'. For you? Blurs fantasy and reality too much. You don't know the difference."

"Oh, like magic," Wally said, cynically.

"Woofin'...ain't no magic," Corey said.

"Oh, yeaaaah," Candace whistled in her chest with her words, "show us some hood magic"

"You hella dingy," Corey said, slapping down Candace's enthusiasm as quickly as it bubbled. "We got junkies, cops and street sweepers. Ain't no fucking hood magic."

"Trippin'," Nigel said is his low froggy croak, "Mac's got it, den dis nga do."

"Show us!" Candace said, her eyes lighting up again. I took the 280 South junction passing the first iPod billboard in the country. I remembered when John Lennon's face adorned it, asking me to imagine. I remembered why I only visited San Francisco during the late nineties. Back then I had no plans of returning. The kids started arguing in loud, hurried, sharp voices that both clashed and blended with the music. It was as if the anger and futility pouring from the speakers was one with their conversation. I felt a ripple in my neck and knew the Passenger was enjoying the argument, perhaps even feeding.

"If I show you," I said as we passed Monterey Ave, "radio goes silent."

"Heck, yeah," Nigel grinned.

"No . . . I mean forever. You can't listen to this shit anymore," I barked. Candace's arm was a dart of light as she leaned forward from her seat, flicked the eject button on the dash, grabbed the cd, leaned back, rolled down the window and hurled the CD like a Frisbee into the night.

"Oh, fock nah," Corey said in disbelief, lips twisting in the angry black boy face I had grown to know attending Thurgood Marshall. I saw him lick his lips and run his palm over his hair, the sign of preparation before he did something emotional that he knew better than to commit. I could feel the discord building.

"Corey," I said, using my voice, feeling a lavender tint outline him.

"Huh?"

"Corey," I repeated.

"What?" he replied, turning his attention away from Candace to me.

"Give me one of your cigarettes," I whispered.

"I don't smoke," he said quickly and dismissively. I could feel all the eyes on me in the car, intent like being at your third Christmas morning ever, about to unwrap presents.

"Good one," I said flatly and counted to two in my head. I mouthed them as I did so. One thousand one Coreys. One thousand two possibilities. Corey started to turn his head back to Candace, angry.

"Corey," I said again, this time his head snapping to attention on his neck to face me. "Give me a cigarette." He inhaled through his nose. A big and long breath. *Corey doesn't know I see his breath as well as his shoulders shrugging before he reaches into his jacket and produces a pack of Newports. I let him know I see the .40 Cal Sig Sauer tucked into his waistline. He fishes out a loosie and holds it up. I briefly reach out with my right hands and place my fingertip on the cigarette's tip. I see Horace's eyes from the night with the Stranger in my head. Under the fabric of everything from the steering wheel to the letter signs of the Serramonte mall out the window past Candace's big-ass head breathes with the motion of Niaw. The spark is as latent as knowing that your laptop is connected to a power strip that runs to the AC/DC outlet* in the wall bringing power to your devices. Motion. *Niaw.* Thank Tesla for that analogy.

A spark touched the tip of the cigarette, burning the paper without having enough force to ignite the tobacco inside. The children make chatter somewhere between "Oh Shit" and "This Motherfucker Is The Greatest." Wally Mac smiled on, pretending to feel chagrin while meeting my eyes in the mirror.

"Agin!" Candace's voice chimed, hitting a note that reminded me of the way women in digital voicemail systems on cell phones sounded. While I waited for her to tell me that the command I had given her was not valid, Corey took a chance and pulled the cigarette back to his mouth. He leaned his head to put the cigarette to his lips. *Niaw.* It lit as he inhaled. The car cheered and I put my hand back on the wheel. The kids set into excited conversation about me and to me. The naysayer of the four had given his trust. In a symbolic act maybe he hadn't anticipated, he pledged his life and his death in bringing that smoke in. I lit one of own, nodded at the exit and promised myself to quit smoking when this bug was gone.

"We all need to quit smoking after this," I said.

"What?" Nigel asked.

"We all need to-" I attempted.

"Let me roll you one," Nigel cut in. I walked right into it and let him have his smile as the little people rolled with deep belly laughter.

"Nah," I said shaking my head, "I'm cool, tho."

We pulled off the freeway, climbing to the foothills above San Bruno. The conversation quieted when we hit the fog, the lights of the truck bouncing back against the thick watery air. I overheard the murmured thoughts as Candace, Corey and Nigel explained how not even the fog by the Port of Oakland got this dense. It occurred to me there was no fog in Oakland flats. Wally added in how his Dad told him the fog is a friend; it hid what might drive most folks "crazy." He even put up his fingers in quotes and I chuckled with his mannerisms to myself. I interpreted crazy as paradox and stayed silent, turning into the parking lot of the junior college on the other side of the mountain from the county jail. The area is cut into a hill or the valley basin below it, I couldn't tell. It was a wide circular expanse to remind me of a lake bed of concrete and yellow lines. The school was built into the part of the hills below the basin that were very shallow in slope. On the other side was an reach of steeper hills that climbed upward in sequence and dropped down to another valley. I brought the truck into an empty spot under the shadow of a tree and killed the engine. I smoked with the windows down silently until the headlights automation turned them off.

"Get dressed," Wally said, morose, and looked to his band of merry fellows. There was a shuffling of eyes and no apparent movement. Corey's mouth turned to say something smart, which was intercepted by a slap to the back of the neck by Nigel. Whatever this signal was, it worked appropriately because Corey killed all protest, rubbed his neck and got out of the vehicle with a stinkface aimed at Nigel. The three filed out of the truck, opening the flatbed as Wally climbed into the front seat. I waited until the door was closed before I spoke.

"How is he?" I asked, watching the fog on the hill begin to thin.

"He says don't do anything stupid," Wally replied.

"Well, glad to hear he knows me well. You get the shopping list?" I checked.

"Everything. It's in back"

"Good man. Relax." Wally stuck out his left hand; I reached over touching my index and middle finger to his wrist as if checking a pulse. My instinct told me a direct connection took less effort than a remote connection. "I want you to start your day from the parking lot until the return trip." There is a flash in Wallace's eyes. It takes me back to the old instructional films in driver's education which warned me about the dangers of accidents. *I am sinking in the ground and move to the muddy flat of the parking lot. It is a cold morning. I see through Wallace's eyes his mother as she leaves her signature at the tower by the gate. Her license is checked and Wally gets a nod because he is a minor. They are back in their car and riding through the construction as the county tears down the old building that faces the junior college down the hill. His mother drives around the newly planted grass patches and concrete dividers that make the road flow to the front of the jail. They both go through the metal check into the facility; pockets are searched and we are escorted to a visiting room. Horace is brought in shortly and embraces Wally at the table. Wallace makes contact with his father. We see a flash of Horace's subterranean cell. The cell has one bed, a frame, a blanket with no mattress, a toilet and a pinhole camera hidden in the corner of the wall above the door jamb. The conversation out loud is flat and coded. Both father and son are aware they are watched; they end their conversation just less than fifteen minutes. Afterward, Wally is retraced through the system and returned to the parking lot.*

I removed my hand, nodding and stepped out of the car, leaving the keys in the engine. I circled to the back of the truck where the kids had changed into all-black outfits, hoods and black stockings over the face with eye slits. I began taking off my jacket, keeping my phone, leaving my clothes in the flatbed in lieu of the black-hooded sweat shirt, stocking and black derby jacket. My shoes were traded for boots, which I found in the duffle everyone was grabbing from. Each child checked to see if their respective pistol was loaded. Wally reached into the bag and tossed a folded ratchet knife to each child but he kept a machete for himself. Nigel held tightly to a backpack. As Wally walked to get the keys from the truck, I spied the long iron pipe secured by plumbers' tape to the flat bed—a pipe ten feet by a four-inch diameter.

The key is to hear yourself say it in your own head, Clay. The amazing thing is how you have skipped over all your life until now. You even got glee out of using it on teachers, hall monitors, officers, judges and authority figures that presented obstacles. You have often found work around solutions by playing dumb. You played so dumb, Clay, that you skipped past your whole life. *Huh.* Corey had taught me a small system behind a system. Here was the baby step I needed: the mind of a child. *Huh?* I saw my saber at home on the floor in that sword's remarkable scabbard. I saw myself grabbing on the piece of metal on the truck. I know that my sword is always with me. Reaching, I grab my blade from the truck, absorbing the raw material of the pipe in the process. The metal hummed faintly. It made a sound that satisfied me. I got the impression it had a taste for the creepy; anything that I cut it with would experience heat slicing through it. Then my conscience kicked in. I looked like a fucking dork with a sword strapped to my waist, like a UPN network movie about the Middle Ages. Kevin Costner is going to be my guide somewhere along the way since I freed him from slavery but his accent will still be awful despite him asking the kids to tell him when to go. Go go go go.

Outfits were folded and placed in the truck, which I found strange for teens. My eye caught cell phones going on vibrate and I did the same with mine. We all stood aware of each other in the fog. I stepped from the truck, under the tree to where the grassy hillside began its ascent upward hearing the opening of that Nas song again from some invisible speaker. I carried my sword in my right hand, which felt comfortable. I turned as the piano in my head rolled. I thought it was in my head. The kids were nodding along and somehow understood the soundtrack. Wally Mac stepped forward. His locks were pulled into a tight pony tail that was tucked under the scarf around his neck which was wrapped over the black bandana that covered his mouth and under the hood of his sweatshirt.

"What's the plan?" I thought I heard Horace's voice ask. I studied Wally's eyes as his body showed no change my eyes could detect.

"I'm going in," I said. "I don't think I can do it in one trip from here. What's on the mountain?"

"Don't know," I heard Wally say. "Let us go up first. We'll make less noise. I'll send a signal."

"All right."

"Spread out," Wally murmured with a tone that stuck out and soaked in. "I'll run center. Call your zones."

"Nine o'clock," I heard Candace say as she headed away from the lot and up the hill into the mist aimed at the Bay.

"Midnightcoreysabitch," Nigel said one breath as he sped off dead ahead, keeping low against the shadow of the back peak.

"Ahhh . . . fuggunigga," Corey snapped back, but his sentence finished too late before Nigel was lost in the fog.

"That word," I said, without making eye contact.

"Yes, sir," Corey said. "I'm on the three." He threw his hood over his head and ran in a faux squat I recognized as creepin'. There should be a pop-up for definitions. It would go nicely with the music, but would probably give us away.

We stood alone, the two of us for a moment, Wally Mac and the Door. Then Wally padded into the fog after Nigel. I relaxed and spoke to myself, saying *Imnt*, feeling my mind reach out to find Wally in the fog at the hill's crest. He was close to the chain-link fence topped by razor wire; he was lying on the ground in the black on his belly. His eyes watched the lit structure below in the valley which held thousands of inmates, property of the city and county of San Francisco. *I swung from the parking lot to Wally, arriving on the ground next to him, unmoving.* Inside through the door, past the visiting room, a hallway, stairs down, check point, hallway, doorway to a cell, Horace was lying on his back on folded blanket laid across a bed frame. His eyes are to the ceiling. They reflect the pane of the window in the wall behind him and the watchful eye of the camera in the corner over the locked door. *It's through the gaze that I swing from Wally to under Heru's bed.* I was on my back with my body hidden by the darkness, which unfortunately did not hide the just-not-right smell. My sword was on my chest like a knight's tomb. I felt for that stunt I could tell myself I'm the real shit here! I reached a finger up past the springs and touched Heru's shoulder.

"*I'm here,*" I sent, sure that Horace could respond.

"There's no microphone," he said, his voice gravel from lack of use. I could see better that his head was resting under his locked fingers with his palms cupping the back of his skull. "And the shadow cuts across my mouth. The camera can't see my lips."

"Oh," I said, feeling dumb.

"We gon kill you, Marshall," I heard yelled from somewhere out on the tier.

"Our voices carry in here," Horace explained in a quieter tone. "No background of TV or anything. All you hear is the voices and the plotting in the dark."

"That's a dead nigger speaking," a random voice added, different from the first.

"That one was white," I said, "and the first sounded black. You're real popular in here."

"Good news travels fast, cousin."

"All the more reason to get going," I replied.

"What are you chattering about?" he asked, confused.

"We're leaving. I'm taking you out of here."

"Don't be silly."

"No," I said firmly, "snap the chains and let's go."

"I can't."

"Why not?"

"Entropy took my works. I can't chant."

"So. I can do a door out of here."

"Explain that to the video and Proxies."

"You were a smart inmate . . . so you . . . "

"On the run? And in Paradox? No, this will not work, friend."

"So you stay in here for life?"

"Look," Horace paused and realized someone inside him was speaking. "Even if I did not kill those people, Horace has killed before. Many times. These may not be what we consider just causes or noble endeavors. The emptiness around him was matched by the emptiness he felt. Rage. The need to hurt others lest he not be able to hurt them. These were the rules of the environment he was in. A quest for dominance is what fed the enemy and led him there. He recognizes this but we cannot ask him to tread near it again for our purposes."

"And man's laws deal with that fairly? He should be here, among this, despite such conditions he could not control?"

"It's man's laws. Do you respect them?"

"It is not as simple as man's laws. Man's law is influenced by the Isfet. They do not respect man's laws. They do not even acknowledge the word respect. So what's respect?"

"Be that as it may, Horace can know peace on our path. No matter where this ends, in here or otherwise."

"*Those threats are real, Heru,*" I said and realized one of my own voices had driven that.

"Should it end here, we will look to Horace's family as we would our own."

"This is stupid, Horace," I said, outraged.

"When you want to be in command, let me know."

"I like being number two."

"This place has Entropy's eye on me." He scans the room with his eyeballs in rotation. "Why are you here, Sekhem? Why are you not with Grandpa and the little one while the eyes are off you?"

"The bug is cut off. But it won't let me eat," I replied.

"Is it blocking during sex as well?" he asked.

"Haven't checked"

"And it's risky. All right." Long pause.

"Don't leave that cell, dead man!" came from the dark. It was a new voice. I couldn't make out ethnicity this time but it was clear Horace was not popular.

"Have you checked in with The Monk?" Horace asked.

"Yes," I replied. "There was a fight with the Passenger. I got stung and saw the Nun in the chamber." I could see his head freeze in its nodding when I said the word Nun.

"You have reached where I could not," Horace said finally, after a relaxed sigh outward that smelled of confidence. "What have we learned?."

"They told me to come to them directly. I need your help getting there."

"Why?"

"The Monk said it isn't safe."

"The Monk worries . . . because he is supposed to. He is a Monk." Horace laughed and kicked his leg out shaking his ankle chain.

"Green light on this mothafucka," I heard from the darkness.

"Cousin," I said, appealing to his emotion, "I'd feel better if-"

"Don't move," Horace interrupted. Something about his voice was different. He was turned on his stomach, his eyes facing me through the frame. I saw the reflection in his left eye of the silk strand descend from the ceiling at the ass of a single silver spider suspended above his left shoulder.

Neteru," I was sure we both heard in that dark voice. Horace's arm was swift, slapping his palm against the wall, crushing the spider with a pop that left juice as a stain.

"Two," I said.

"You should go," he said, turning on his back again.

"I'll be back for you," I stated.

"You better not if you follow orders" he said annoyed. "I am still king."

"You got a terrible fucking martyr complex," I growled futilely, "you know that?"

"I am the martyr complex, Clay."

"Holler," I said and felt my way back to the parking lot, but felt the way blocked. My swing ended short. Wally stood looking behind us at the slope down to the truck, pistol in hand and machete in the left. The fog had curdled near the rim of the parking lot, forming a wall as the hue of the grass lost its green and began turning red. I heard a familiar strange barking and looked to see small flashes in the distance.

"Hey," Wally said, puzzled. "Why is the fog turning pink?"

CHAPTER ELEVEN

"Bodies blink sometimes."

-Corey

"Pull them back and close," I barked to Wally, wishing I had a gun. Instead, I held the sword in my hand like an umbrella after a rain subsides. Wally made a bird sound with his throat three times. Staring into the fog, he pulled off the safety to his pistol. Nigel was back first, padding to a location behind Wally and covering the zone behind Wally. Corey came sloping up soon after, his sig in hand in crouched waddle. We waited.

"Where's Candy?" Corey asked gruffly and sharp. Wally repeated his bird call and the pink fog grew thicker hiding the light from Moreland below. Our soundtrack was gone, only the sounds of wet maracas in the distance. I walked off in Candy's direction.

"Stay," I said, drawing the sword from the scabbard and hearing the hum of the metal again. Something switched over in my mind and I could hear Nas competing with the maracas in the fog. As I stepped deeper in the cotton candy colored mist, I noticed the salty smell of bloody smoke. It covered everything with a sticky, sweet, rotted nature. I heard a girl's scream from the depths and bolted forward on the down the crest of the north east slope near where a street should start. There was a giant spider web fixated in the very night itself, open in the center as a throbbing vein to an accursed nest of pain and torture. Crawling out of it on eight legs were malformed fleshy arachnids, looking as if some twisted cross between man and Isfet. They each crawled from the strand, touching the blood red grass of the hill and standing on their legs. They walked forward to reveal nasty cleaver like spurs at the joints of the rest of their appendages, a thick mucous white carapace like chest armor, bald human heads with no eyes and a mouth of filthy spider fangs. One stood over a fallen Candace whose gun had dropped a few feet out her reach behind the creature. It hissed and shook, bouncing on its legs calling attention to its prey.

I feel myself run, step, bounce off the ball of my front foot and twist with the other leg in the air, swiping up from six to nine o'clock slant, then back along the horizon and twist, drawing the blade back to me. The creature falls in three pieces, my blade steaming from the blood. I grab Candace by the collar and half tug, half drag her back. She slides for a moment and then breaks free of my grip. Running back, she snags the gun, letting off a spray of shots. The first five shots cut into the chest piece of the nearest creature, chopping it down as the next shots catch the remaining creature, putting it down. She runs towards me as the hillside begins to fill up with creatures just as the alarm went off at the jail, of course due to shots fired. I let Candace pass me, and spear another creature as it tries to leap, falling backwards as another spider swings its leg over where my head was, cutting its companion in half. My blade free, I let my left leg swing back into a wide stance, bringing the blade up to sever the leg off and twisting the arm around to bring the stroke down, which took out its standing legs. Turning, I run to find the kids. I hear shots in the pink fog and run toward the muzzle flashes.

Wally was dropping bodies, two shots each that tore through foreheads. Nigel had dropped his pistols and sat crouched with a sawed-off cradled between his thigh, knee and waist. Corey laughed his way into a fit as he caught any creature he could knock the head off in such a way that its body would fall back on another behind it. Headlights cut into the melee from the Sherriff's county-issued truck that had the guts under the hood to drive up the grassy incline to investigate the shots. I wondered if the drivers had the guts to investigate. The truck pulled about thirty yards from Candace as she followed me, crashing into several creatures as the GMC skidded to a stop. The bullhorn told us to freeze, followed by terror as the passengers of the vehicle witnessed the open strand ripped into the sky in front of them. I heard the faint gong in the distance, knowing the Isfet had tipped the alarm out of their favor. Two men stepped out of the truck, holding shotguns.

"No!" Candace screamed and waved her arms frantically. "Get out of here!"

The men took no heed and began firing into the growing army pouring out from the strand. One of them went so far as to call himself brave, telling Candace not to worry as he pumped hot rounds into the strand. His aim would have been flawless, had some bullets into a tear in the fabric of reality mattered. The hot slugs did nothing as the creatures crawled out of the hole leading to the universe's spooky basement. Well, it did something. It took the sheriff's eyes off of his own back as he fired. A creature behind him tucked its legs and spun on the point of its carapace like a top. Its legs were ticked at precise angles as it eviscerated the county's cowboy in an exploding cloud of blood. It ended its momentum to land on eight legs, ejecting a metallic bone-tipped, tube-like spear from its spinnerets that punched through the diced pieces of man flesh lying on the lawn. Once the creature's stinger had speared every piece of the man kabob, it sucked the morsels dry and left desiccated pieces of body as it withdrew its stinger into its body.

The second sheriff screamed and ran back to the truck, grabbing for his CB and calling desperately for backup. He let out frantic yelps that gave off white mists revealing his terror. They floated like smoke clouds behind him. Each terrified thought was tackled by a creature that bound it in a cocoon of razor wire and dragged it back into the strand. His last screams were for help as the entire truck was bound and dragged into the portal.

"All bad," Nigel said, dropping the sawed-off and loading a pistol.

"Last clip," Corey yelled out, firing as the gong in the distance grew in volume and vibration.

"We're surrounded," Wally said to me, scanning the field.

"Draw 'em tight," I yelled over the shots, deciding this would not be a battle won by numbers. The kids drew in around Wally, clumping like puppies around a warm body. I was getting my stride back. Just myself and four kids without ammo were not going to be much against an army that grew proportionally to what it killed. Then it hit me--the notion that I had perfected a skill after years of Granny lectures when I face a fight. The brave die valiantly. The smart find a way out where there is none. The back door to any scenario was where I found my bread and butter.

While the kids kept cover fire, I switched my sword through my hand and sheathed it. I used my right hand to form a smaller blade with my index and middle finger. Grounded in my legs, planted in the feet, twisting in my waist, I pulled my fingers up from the ground. My fingers went high overhead, sharply along the lateral to the right and then down to the ground. When I was done, I carved into the raw blueprint of nature using Huh which cut into the fabric of space as real and unexpected as the Isfet strand. There in front of us stood a door in a blue frame and black, blank pane.

"In!" I yelled, switching hands with the sword, and drawing it from the scabbard again to step in front of Wally, who had taken vanguard position.

"Where's it go?" Candace yelled back.

"Mothafucka!" I screamed back, frustrated at the perfect timing of the wrong moment that came with teenagers. Nigel came up from his crouch, grabbing the sawed off, shoving Candace through the door in a tackle that sucked him in as well. Corey tapped Wally on the shoulder before backing into the door. Wally swung his machete, making no contact but enough to ward off the creatures.

"Behind us?" he asked, backing his way toward the door.

"Your pops is the martyr, not me," I shot back. He smiled and jumped through, yelling "Oakland" before he went through. I bounced on my legs, keeping distance with my scabbard in the left as I backed a bit toward the door. Although new, I was learning these creatures' reactions. They liked to cluster and attack high. I waited for the opportunity, watching the closest one pop up on its spinner. Leaping above the cluster, I popped the scabbard into the ground, bringing my right arm up in a wide arc which cut across, lopping off the creature's right appendages and spinning it in the air. I kicked out with both legs, knocking the creature into the rest with a loud clatter and launching myself backwards into the door, carrying my scabbard out of the grass with me.

There is a darkness that occurs as I swim in nothing. My skin weighs light on the bones, my whole body feeling suspended and less dense. A quiet place. The mind is empty and the flesh is irrelevant. The mind tricks the body. The body thinks the mind is crazy. Right? I feel as if one hand holds me in its palm and another pulls a cord from the top of my head that connects to my spine. There is a stillness. The force from every flicked cigarette, missed punch or false start in the mind finally comes to disperse itself here. One really can't say much about it because there isn't much to say. Words do not exist in this place. Even my thoughts of it are mere copies and somehow less real. I have the knowledge that this place is without thoughts. I am aware of a sense of suction.

I know how to pull myself. I am even more of aware of it now. Floating loses its appeal and I feel a pull from below me as if the hand has dumped me off like a crumb remaining from flaky cornbread. I am falling toward a single sand dune in the darkness that seems almost animated but frighteningly real. I can see the bottom reaching up to swallow me and I sprawl my arms trying to straighten my body to take the impact. It has the reverse effect, sending me somersaulting until I finally hit the sand dune on my right shoulder coming through another roll. Hard, too. I feel it swell over my chest after the impact my back makes in the dune punches a hole in its imperfect dome of grains.

I lie unmoving, the force of the fall knocking all volition from me and I am aware of nothing but silent curses in my head as my body reveals I am not as young as I tell myself I am. I cannot tell you how long I remained there. Only that the sand, if it could talk, would tell you of all the reasons I listed not to continue. Though silent, the arguments to press on were stronger and more numerous, the talking points swaying a jury of its peers. Lost in my own emptiness I saw into the fragile pieces of my body and into an unexplained source. I feel the intake of much-needed energy from a primal place. I see the soft tissues of my swollen ankle. The blood stream carries away the water from shock. Bruised clotted blue replaced with the proteins needed to mend the tears in the tendons and equally weakened muscles. The bone is fused and the excess was sweated out. I feel terribly hungry as if I hadn't eaten for days. Then darkness again.

"Return," I hear her say.

"Neith?" I ask, choosing not to remember.

"He blinked," I heard another feminine voice say. I knew by its youth and rasp to be Candace.

"Bodies blink sometimes," I heard Corey's voice, affirmative and Socratic as he asked a question of his own question. Pause. Some one sucked their teeth. "When dey got Bo he was shakin n shit."

"You would too. Shit a hole dummy round to da chest, my nga?" I heard Nigel's matter-of-fact Southern throaty wisdom correct him.

"Nga, you always knowin something," I heard Corey whine back.

"That word," I groaned, opening my eyes to look up at the moon.

"Told you he wasn't dead," I heard Candace's loud glee, and saw her looking down at me.

"Not yet," I said, feeling my voice in my nose. "Help me up before I look in your nose." She laughed slightly as she dug her hands into the sand under me, finding my left forearm and tugging. With a little help, I was standing up slightly dizzy, looking down at Candace. Behind me stood the crater of the sand dune my body had violated, leading to miles and miles of open desert in the night. The boys stood a few feet away on a patch of dry grass that led into wide plains. I returned the sword locked in my grip to the scabbard in my other grip, knowing it was fairly impossible to separate me from this weapon unless I deemed it so. I hung it on my left side and I deemed it so.

"Where are we?" Corey asks.

"Candy's good with maps," Nigel delegates.

"I dunno," Candy answers. "The Door knows."

"I don't know," I replied, trying to find stars in the sky but finding them strangely absent. "I just got us to safety."

"Where to?" Wally asked. I scanned the horizon.

"Away from here and not into the desert."

"Lost," Nigel said, provoking a laugh from the kids.

"What we lookin for?" Wally asked.

"I'm not sure, mang," I replied and the kids laughed again at my forced East Bay accent. "You don't feel a pull?" He cocked his head looking at me and looked down to the sand. Nodding, he looked up, his eyes a bit glazed over and rolled up.

"Mmm . . . it pulls like--" he stuttered as he talked himself through it out loud, "a magnet?"

"Me, too," I confirmed.

"Where to then?"

"Find out with me," I answered. Wally nodded and led by example, walking away from the sand into the expanse of the grassy plains. Following suit, Nigel pulled up his pants and waddled to catch up. Corey waited for Candace who was pouring sand out of her shoes and eventually the two trotted off behind Wallace and Nigel. I took the back, making sure to drag my coat behind me to cover our tracks. To boot, I asked the kids to walk single file for the same reason. We trooped for a while. The moon cast wide rays of grayish light across the plains and I was grateful to have the visibility. The kids sang songs to occupy their trudging until their voices ran dry and they ran out of songs. The grass around us had become slightly greener and thick, signaling a proximity to water underground somewhere. Hills in the distance had given way to flats interspersed by a long and wide river. In the distance, I could make out the shape of a giant triangular building, reaching up nearly a mile in height, shadowed by two sequentially smaller buildings of the same design. Recognition sets in, like rediscovering a favorite outfit in a closet you haven't worn in forever but remember why you never got rid of it.

I remembered my trip through the clouds that had brought me here before. The lack of stars disturbed me in a sense of coming home to find one's television missing due to a specialized burglary. You never appreciate how vital some things are until they are taken from you. I barely noticed the stars in the skies above the Bay, but send me to New York for more than three days and the heavens above seem naked without the jewelry that usually hung from the great expanse. Here were three of the oldest buildings in the world, stripped of their morning light, as if part of any metropolitan area. In a place absent of skyscrapers, satellites and jet lines, it seemed wrong that the moon was the only guide we had. Given those buildings, I knew we were in Egypt, but we were nowhere near a North African country you might see on CNN or on a vacation. We had either returned to an earlier time or somewhere close enough to remind us of a clue, a hint. There would be no quick jeep or bus to hop onto.

I slowed our march in a patch of reeds that came to my chest, deciding it would obscure our party as we decided next steps. We had come to a place where four roads met. Perhaps it was the first one that Robert Johnson was connected to. At one time it had been maintained by ceramic lining and some form of sediment laid over tar to give it a shaped quality, but the years not been kind. It was nothing more than a dirt strip, cut into four directions surrounded by untamed brush. In a few places, lily vines stretched across, threatening to bring other foliage with it and swallow the roads altogether. If it wasn't Egypt of the twentieth century, it was a version of that land that certainly was not occupied by many. But what about those huge buildings in the background?

"South," I whispered, pointing at the road leading away from the pyramids, away from the valley, away from the river and the one running parallel along the Nile to the inland.

"North," Wally said, indicating with a head toward the ruins in the valley ahead of us in the opposite direction I was being pulled.

"Really?" I asked Wally, surprised we were not drawn to same source.

"Can we do both," he asked and then chuckled, "startin this way."

"It's possible we're both correct," I replied. "Perhaps it's circular."

"I see light," Nigel croaked, pointing at the east road that led closer to the Nile.

"Something's moving," Corey murmured, looking down Nigel's arm. Wallace turned his eyes that way and squinted.

"I see light," he whispered.

"Down," I hissed and squatted, beckoning the rest down with my hands. They were already moving by the time I finished speaking, crouching and having the sense to hush as we waited. I wasn't even sure crouching was necessary. With the exception of Wally Mac's long frame from too many McChicken's during his mother's pregnancy, causing a freakish height for a young man his age, the reeds came up past the heads of the rest of the band if they stood erect. In the quiet we heard the steady click of hooves in a slow, morbid trot. I also picked up the sound of wheels. They were wooden, turning on axles against the sandy grit of the road. I saw Corey finger the trigger of his pistol and shook my head. Parting a few reeds, I could see past the bramble to the approaching caravan. A young girl, no more than fifteen years of age, stood in chariot driven by a man many years her elder. Their skin was as dark as the shadows across the road with a golden tint that was neither paint nor part of their flesh. The girl looked sad, staring into the night ahead, mumbling as if in prayer. She wore a long white dress; her hands wrapped in some form of lace as she slowly swung a thurible like a pendulum that poofed out sandalwood incense from side to side.

The man leading the reins wore a dented and partially rusted breast plate of coppery material across his chest over a tunic of pale and faded lavender. Judging by his struggle to keep his arm up, I figured his left to be stronger than the right. His face was cracked and sun beaten, giving rich leathery creases to his side profile. His head hung on his neck like a deflated balloon, tied to the bannister of set stairs down to a backyard birthday party. He conveyed a sense of resolve combined with shame.

I tapped Candace on the shoulder and motioned with my head to the stretch of road a few yards north of the travelers. She shrugged with her shoulders and expressive face to show me she didn't get it. I pointed to the direction, walked my fingers through the grass in a loop and then snapped fingers against my thumb, making a hand puppet. The faux mouth wagged uselessly as I switched to tapping my chest, walking my fingers around behind the travelers and pointing to my sword. She opened her mouth for a wide and silent "Oh." Candy crawled through the reeds in the direction I indicated. I watched the chariot carefully.

A few moments later, Candace walked out of the darkness on the road, wiping her face and looking surprised when the light from the rider's lantern caught her face. She began babbling, which only provoked a drawn and rusty short blade from the old man as he chattered back in some thick tongue I couldn't compute. For a moment it sounded like Amharic but it drifted into pronunciations of some version I didn't know. As Candace pulled the chariot to a stop with her blubber, I led the boys through the grass on our bellies behind the old man. Strangely, the closer we got, the more I heard English. In fact, by the time I was crouched on the road, silently drawing my blade, I could swear he was having a full-on argument with our roadblock.

"Who you scarin wit dat?" Candace asked, pointing to the curved and brownish orange fuzz along the rusted blade in the rider's hand. "You need to take dat shit to Home Depot."

"Move, dwarf!" the old man bellowed, rattling off as the loose bits of his garments jingled and he pulled his reins to halt the movement of the horse.

"Dwarf?" her high-pitched squawk cut into his speech. "Oh, no, he didn't. Bring ya ass down here. Bet I'm taller than yo ass." Flabbergasted, he dropped the reins to step off the chariot. The girl stopped her chanting and gasped as I stepped up, lacing the edge of my blade a few inches from the tip at his neck.

"Be easy," I said, making eye contact. I slapped down his sword, which shattered when it hit the ground. I heard Nigel snort his silent disapproving laugh. "Where are you taking the girl?"

"She is my daughter," he said quickly, eyeing the blade at his craw nervously. "She is to be given as tribute so that the tribe might live unharmed from the tyrant."

"What sort of tribute?" I said, horrified at the thought.

"A sacrifice," the girl said, looking off to the road ahead. "Propius Minor demands that a maiden be left once a cycle or he terrorizes our people."

"What's a cycle?" I heard Wallace ask.

"The lord of the land replenishes our livestock and granaries when we are depleted," the old man said. "We cannot grow our own crops since the sun has forgotten us and therefore we cannot raise our own livestock."

"It is an honor to give myself so that my people may live," she said, trying to convince herself. Her eyes still focused on the task ahead. I lowered my blade and sheathed it. The old man followed it with his eyes, taking careful note of the inscriptions on the blade as it passed out of sight into the scabbard.

"You are not of here," he said, looking at all of us.

"No," I replied with a smile.

"Who are your people?" his daughter asked. "Where do you come to us from?"

"The wess," Nigel choked.

"Da town," on top of him Candace added.

"Oakland," Corey gave to the chatter.

"We are pilgrims from the North," I said, almost believing it as I spoke. "Our people came there from lands to the South."

"You are Maati?" the girl inquired, excited.

"What?" Wallace said.

"Colonists who left us long ago to spread the way," the father said proudly. I caught his drift and saw the continent of Africa in my head with arrows rising out of its northeast area aimed into Asia and up.

"Father loves the legends of old," the girl said wistfully, a painful smile following. "A reminder of a gentler time?"

"They shall return!" the old man said emphatically, causing himself a painful cough; his daughter stifled it by placing her hand on his back.

"What changed?" Candace asked.

"The Isfet," the old man growled, waving his hand to the sky, "and soon after the Veil was among us, giving us this night without end." I felt my skin crawl at the mention of the enemy, realizing inadvertently I might have brought us to the heart of their power. I followed his hand to the skyline where my eyes caught for the first time the intricate grid running in the sky. Translucent and crystalline, the lines ran the curvature of the globe defining a large orb around the atmosphere of the Earth. Judging by where the lines intersected, I guessed they were aligned with the longitude and latitude lines I might find on a model globe sitting on my desk back on campus. I was reminded of the viewpoint: seeing the world from Olympus, a view so similar to that from the floor of the Monk's chamber. Both looked down on the earth. I thought of the old man's words about his Isfet master's command and it occurred to me that the absence of the constellations was related not only to the Isfet control but also the presence of these translucent structures lining the sky.

"What are those?" I said, pointing up to the grids reflecting the moon light into pale azure shards before going into prismatic light.

"The Veil," he said. "Our prison"

"Prison," Corey said, concerned and looking around.

"When the Isfet conquered our ancestors," the girl said, "they created the Veil, keeping us from the afterworld."

"And trapping the Isfet Proprius here away from his own as our liege lord," the old man chuckled at the irony. "Even the warden is a prisoner. Hence his misdeeds to the inmates." Isfet had cut off contact, meaning they could neither summon reinforcements nor reveal our whereabouts. *Limited resources, limited capacity, limited production. I also link the orphaned Passenger in my neck to these monsters abusing these people. If I could study the Isfet in their own state cut off from their kin, I could find some chink in the armor of my own passenger away from any from any interference.*

"We will escort you," I said to both the old man and his daughter. "Where you will meet this Minor Proprius?"

"To the north," the girl said pointing down the road. I smiled and winked at Wallace, who smiled back and shrugged, turning his body to the curve into the road headed north.

"Propius?" Candace asked.

"It's Latin," I said.

"Means to own," Nigel said.

"*I love that,*" I felt myself spill out and knew who was speaking through me.

"To take to own," Wallace corrected. Nigel looked over to check and saw Corey nodding.

"Your dad?" Candace asked and Wallace nodded.

"I miss those convos," Candace said with a disappointed glance down. Wallace tightened his lips together, turning his head to scratch above the ear before tying his locks into a ponytail with some black, stretchy material that blended into the color and texture of his hair.

"What's that?" I asked as the old man flicked the reins, signaling the horse to trot forward. As he did, the girl turned to watch Nigel, humming a song under his breath.

"Panty hose," Wallace said. matter of factly pointing to the hose with eye slits hanging from Candace's back pocket. His tone sounded as if I should know better and, after I thought about it, he was absolutely right. I remarked at the ingenuity these little ones exhibited in every aspect of their survival. No one object, raw material or finished good could be limited to one use. Amazing creatures: Wallace, Corey, Nigel and Candace. They might never know how much more they taught me than I influenced them.

I switched my eyes between the giant translucent ribs of the Veil lining the definition of the planet, the road ahead, the pyramids in the not-so-distant background and the kids as they walked along side the chariot. I felt a sense of pride I hadn't known elsewhere. It was a need to brag about the four young people I had met and been impressed with on a continuously increasing basis. I kept shifting my eyes between targets, walking behind the chariot, until I noticed Corey at the rear right staring at me as he plodded along with a half-committed foot drag that I noticed the kids doing. I raised my eyes brows at him, indicating I could tell something was on his mind and I wished to hear it.

"Sup Ro," he said

"Ro?" I asked quietly, making sure my voice did not rise above the conversation at the front of the party.

"They say that in EPA," Corey replied.

"Short for?" I asked.

"Rogue, I heard," Corey replied, rubbing his hands together. "I used to stay there with my daddy before he sent me to my mom's."

"How you feel about that?" I asked genuinely.

"Ay yo . . . why you send her?" he asked in a sort of half whisper that carried just above the sound of the turning wheels on the road but not enough to alert Candace, who walked on the front left of the chariot opposite Wally.

"Made sense at the time," I said honestly, "Don't know why. It just did. Why do you ask?"

"She scary," he said with a slight lisp coming off his lips with a fleck of spit he wasn't aware of. "Send me next time"

"I wasn't scared," Candace said back to us without turning. I found myself smiling at her maturity.

"Why you scream when we started buckin?" Corey said, a mischievous smile on his face, as if knowing he had just laid down the winning hand in a championship poker game.

"I forgot tonight was ABDC," she replied, not missing a beat. "Instead, I'm here fuckin witchall." The kids all began laughing. Candace added a certain gait to her stride at knowing she had adopted some of Nigel's timing before laughing herself. Meanwhile I found myself in my own head, watching the points as I realized I hadn't frozen in the last two encounters with my childhood fear. The itsy not-so-bitsy spider. Still when faced with danger, I held out as long as I could until the odds fed my fear and I ran. I hadn't slept for years over bone-shaking dreams of these talking arachnids and the horrors they'd inflicted on me. When I finally confronted them that night with Horace at the Center, I froze at any real opportunity to send back any fear I had learned. These children saw the horrors everyday in the streets. So what the fuck was a web or two, right? Somewhere between the destruction in their homes, the arms race on their streets and the wars in their communities, they had lost that ability to simply give a fuck, much less be spooked by some razorblade spider mutants. I needed to get like that. To be as in the moment as Candace. To see the universe rear its ugly head and be shocked about one's own small rituals. If her television show got her through life week to week, then that was something valuable indeed when you consider her fearlessness in defense of her loved ones. In hearing Candace speak, my own shame distracted my attention from my watch.

"There," the old man said sadly, "the valley of kings."

I looked up from my own interior monologue to notice the landscape. The air was thick with a pink-tinted light fog that hung with stickiness from the heat of a sun that could not be seen in the darkness. The buildings, monuments, statutes, trees, foothills and anything that stood off the ground by more than six feet was covered by massive spider silk that seemed to ripple. Deeper into the valley I could see a column of padded web, tangled and adhesive like a nest in attic corner. It reached up to the sky, just falling short of the grid of the Veil. I knew my journey with them would end there. Alone. I would face a sleeping and wounded enemy that would fall to my will and unlock the secret to the beastie residing in my neck.

I replayed the rules I had given myself in my head. *You are Sekhem Ka.* Apparently I was. *Your cousin will never leave your side.* Remained to be proven completely. *The child is more important than you or the Carrier you are housed in.* Fair enough; I've made sacrifices. *Trust the Aztec.* That's the easy part. How do I keep her trusting me. *If she uses smoke, you taught her that; just watch people and then feel them.* Athena, next time we meet no okie doke. *Your heart answers to Neith.* The million dollar question: are Neith and Athena one in the same? *The Passenger in your mind will do anything to return you to them.* Yes, I've seen that. *Isfet Propius fears fire.* Thank you, self. Michael Masser's struck chords in my head. *My Hero Is A Gun.* My truth was a sword. The beat picked up. My eyes fell to the small casks of oil and spare torches at the girl's feet in the cab of the chariot. I could light the very nest itself and slay anything that came out, using the narrow mouth of the valley entrance as a stop gap. I would not run. I would be alone but I would not run. My eyes fell on a number of shapes on the ground. Scanning the area, I thought I was making out the remains of several desiccated avian corpses partially wrapped in silk, each the size of a smart car. I poked at one with the tip of my scabbard.

"Peraheru," the old man said, distant and beaten. I caught the translation immediately but looked over at him for clarification.

"A neighboring tribe," the girl explained, "known for their fondness of birds and mastery of husbandry."

"They refused to pay tribute," the old man continued, "and those who survived were driven to the south to the lands at the base of the holy fortress, Gebel Barkal."

"We have not seen them for many a cycle," the girl added. "None are sure they still thrive." I felt eyes on me and found Wallace staring at me with a smile. One for one, so we were both right. I nodded at him and mouthed thank you.

"What is your name, friend?" I asked, staring into the old man's eyes, his silvery white hair reminding me of my Granny.

"I am Werkneh of the Peraaka," he said proudly, almost losing his balance until he was steadied by his daughter. Peraaka was the house of Ka; Peraaheru was house of Heru. "My overly concerned daughter is Wagaye." I held my hands to the reins and guided the horses around to face the way we had come.

"Go home, Werkneh," I said to him, without emotion, "and take your daughter with you."

"But the tribute," Wagaye said, confused. "What will keep the Isfet from grabbing our children in the night and filling our days with their haunting screams?"

"If only they allowed our children to grow," Werkneh added, "they would have nothing to hold us." I smiled at him and drew my hand in front of me. The finger traced a scene before Werkneh, depicting a sun disc, a hillside, an owl, a loaf and a crossroads as glowing sigils in the air. I also noticed that such works came naturally. In Kemet, I found no distance between thought and action in this land. *Intention.* In that recognition, I began to move oil flasks from the chariot without moving a muscle. Werkneh and Wagaye watched, their faces showing a glean and color to their skin that shook off jaundice in the moment as they stared at the phrase hanging before them in golden light.

"The sun shines on Kemet," Wallace said to Corey, who was tracing the glyphs with his hand, trying to discover their meaning. He smiled and nodded.

"What are you?" Wagaye stammered, a quixotic smile and shock on her face. I smiled and looked at Corey, raising my eyebrows. He picked a stick up from the ground and pulled it along the sand, drawing a large, three-sided rectangle in the dirt.

"The Door," I said, returning her gaze as the glyphs faded. "Take your father and return to your people. No more tributes to these beasts." She caught her own relieved, watery eyes much too late to keep me from noticing. Werkneh reached forward, pulling my hand to his face and staring intently at my palm with his tired and aged eyes. He brought his own palm parallel, his disbelief bleeding into his trembling fingers as he ran them along every crease in my grip. They were a parallel image of the lines in his own hands.

"Could it be?" he said, his voice shaking. "Our forbearer has returned in this strange form and cloth?"

"Go home, Werkneh," I said, knowing my voice was a wave of undeniability. "Ready your people, quietly." The last of the oil flasks lay on the ground and I looked to the contents at the side of the road. He nodded and took the reins, roping the horse into a slow trot down the road, watching me with his eyes. Wagaye stared at us from the chariot until the night and distance hid her face.

CHAPTER TWELVE

"I guess . . . that's that."

-Wallace

I picked up a flask, uncorked it and walked to the short pyre on the dais. It originally had been a place for a large replica of a boat to signify the passage of Ra across the waters. This meant day and night. We differentiated day from night by this site. Now it was polluted, a signal built into the valley mouth that summoned the pack to feed. I assumed that would be the sign that a sacrifice was laid for these soul slavers. The pyre was filled with tons of dried branches and fuel, so I barely oiled it. Turning around, I noticed each of the little ones had a flask and looked as if waiting for instructions.

"Draw the pattern on Charlie Brown's t-shirt," I said, using my finger to imitate valley and peaks.

"Who?" Candace asked.

"Think of the sweaters the Fresh Prince used to wear," I replied.

"Oh," Candace shot back, seeing it in her head.

"I want a zigzag across the whole thing. Six feet high, three yards wide and make sure the bottom of the zigzag touches the ground around the web." I studied what I thought I could do without getting entangled in the stuff. I stepped forward and began squirting the sweet-smelling oil upon the cocoon-like structure. My merry band followed in suit, squirting oil in giant, jagged teeth shapes as they walked the periphery of the silk nest. One by one, the oil flasks disappeared until we were out of accelerant. Wallace wandered over to me, his eyebrows looking for the next step.

"Grab the rest," I said, quietly checking my pockets. Excellent. I had remembered to bring my cigarettes and a lighter. "And go catch up to

Werkneh and Wagaye. Get them back safely and then head south. I'll meet you there."

"They'll be fine," Wallace countered. "We good here."

"I didn't know I was asking," I said, examining my pack to find out that only half of the cigarettes broke in the fall. Awesome. I fished one out. "I want you *all* out of here." He pursed his lips, looking away and standing his ground. His practiced defiance was probably so perfected after years of adults making decisions for him. The wheels spun over his head as he balanced being respectful with telling it exactly how he saw it. I watched his hands shift to the middle pocket of his sweatshirt as his shoulders sagged. It was an amazing thing teenagers accomplished in the belief that pretending not to hear by nonverbal communication somehow changed the outcome. While I may have struggled with Desta, I was no stranger to the stubborn moods of young men with a mind to the streets and in fact felt a certain expertise at making my will known.

"Who's in charge here?" I asked calmly.

"My daddy," Wally said, still looking away.

"And who did he tell you to listen to?"

"You."

"Well then," I said putting my hand on his shoulder, "I know you won't let me down." Conflicted and disappointed, Wally Mac tucked his hands in his pockets and walked in defeat toward Nigel. I began to feel guilty to see even ice-cold Nigel was somewhat hurt that he wasn't involved. I understood the extent to which these children had adopted me as their own. I thought I was protecting them and they felt they were protecting me. I found myself working to justify my decision out loud. "You said north, so we did north. Now I do this and you do south," I called after him. I chose not to listen in, just to study body language to see how well they all followed an order. I watched Wallace speak to Nigel, who looked to me, looked back to Wallace and shrugged. He turned on heel to walk to Candace and Corey, who stood a few feet away, arguing. Soon all four trudged along the road, headed back south, watching me with begging eyes like hungry kittens. I watched until their shapes disappeared into the night. Turning, I walked to the dais full of dried bramble and branches. I assumed Werkneh was expected to leave his daughter at the mouth of the cocoon and light the dais. Chuckling to myself, I positioned the lighter in my left hand and rolled the cigarette to my lips. *Hey Xochi, I ain't afraid of spiders no more.*

The steel turned against the flint but no spark ignited. Several more attempts and I tossed the lighter, assuming it was out of fuel. Placing my finger on the tip, I was able to light it and heard the corresponding wet coconut sound from the cocoon. Good. If I was gonna be heard when I played with fire, then I would hear them when they tried to play back. I blew on the cigarette's cherry, sending sparks into the dais that ignited the fuel. Soon the flames roared to life with raw energy as the fire consumed oxygen, growing and spitting out carbon monoxide. Drawing my sword, I stood with the flame between myself and the canopy of silk covering the valley. Then the sound of wet nuts being banged grew louder and the first of them came to investigate. They were the same I first spied on the hillside above Moreland. They were fleshy arachnids with hard crusty exoskeletons that ended in razor spurs, with warped eyes placed into human faces and disgusting spider fangs in their mouths. A swarm of at least a dozen slowly crept from the opening. Typical of their brain, they made the mistake of sticking to the web when their eyes didn't find the easy target in its usual place. I sprang my trap to snare the weaver in its own web.

I kicked the pyre, hard, spraying flaming bits in a wide arc. The branches touched the silk and ignited it. The area was doused by oil and caught fire immediately. Most of the creatures were ablaze in a second. The remainders sprang forward, hissing and cursing me in my head as they felt the agony of their kindred, burning alive. I made sure they knew I was enjoying it, so they only focused on the glowing energy on the other side of the flame from them. Their bestial minds asked how I dared and their answer was dismemberment as soon as they came within an inch of the blaze that masked my presence. I swung through the fire as viciously as I could.

I danced in place, laughing at my ankle without pain, kicking at pieces of the creatures spread in front of me. I picked up my cigarette from where I had dropped it and took a few drags, blowing smoke towards the flame. I felt a breeze shortly after and smiled as the flames jumped around the circumference in a zigzag pattern of burning silk. As the opening burned away I saw deeper into the valley. Thick spirals of tunnels and layers as the awful webs circled in on themselves. The dirt was a nasty green, brownish color, like an overflowing toilet at a beach bathroom. Cocoons hung from long suspended strings, stuck under corners of where columns met arches, doorways and awnings. Crawling along the ceiling of the canopy, upside down as its black eyes beheld me was a tarantula the size of a duplex. Standing on the creature's back, fully upright, naked, and glowing in a liquid chalk white, was a figure. It was human without gender, definition or face. The figure was muscular, tall, toned and carrying a huge cleaver in its phantasmal, human-shaped hand. Slowly it plodded forward, its hissing becoming words in my mind.

I had had dreams about this mental picture my entire life. I have drawn primitive pictures describing my fears. I have withdrawn and hidden in my own head, deep in denial. I have lost entire years of good rest from running from the awful abominations crawling toward me in front of the dais. I have three dust busters: one for the house, one for the office and one for the Center. Each is to vacuum spiders. Even a beetle or a lady bug might get it. Hell, one of the crackheads in the alley might get it too if it has too many legs. Oh, I know you, symbol of terror and corrupting drain to my energies. I know you can hear me, too. I am burning your home. This whole place is going to smell like sundown at a picnic. I'm going to turn your filthy little hidey hole into Duraflame. How fitting it's your home that will be scorched after you have taken mine. To the beastie in my neck, I hope you hear me, too. I'm going to kill your papi and every motherfucker like it until you know it's not safe to chase me. You cannot make me run. Even in corners, I am death. I do not care anymore. My mission is more important than my doubt.

"*Sekhem Ka, son of Ma'at and son of Djeuti,*" I heard in my head, the figure on the spider's back pointing the top edge of the cleaver at me. Its voice was masculine and thin; a wheezing hiss rolled into a demonic growl. "*So good to see you again. I'm afraid you're a bit late for the feast.*" Taunting, calculated, intrigued and overly confident. I start stepping sideways, making sure I kept circling so both rider and mount had difficulty obtaining a solid bead on me. I was being baited away from the fire. I was still steps ahead and completely aware of my opponent's strengths; these creatures trap. Chess not checkers, words as the warning shots. You check the king, then you mate. *I knew to create the hole I wanted them to exploit.* I could use my very intention to force my enemy to commit to my next planned step.

"You know my name," I said, taking a drag again and swinging the sword around in my hand by twirling the wrist so the blade whistled.

"Does that surprise you?"

"Why would that surprise me? We can all name our death, Propius."

"And you know us as well. Excellent."

"But I am surprised."

"Did you really think you had a chance, foolish Neteru?"

"No, I'm surprised you are smart enough to repeat words back."

"Smart enough to hang your people until their juice was right. Every last one of them. When I'm done wrapping you, I'll return to the rest of your family, still untouched."

"Smart enough to know this isn't a toy in my hand? Do I look like some maiden to you?"

"Propius Minor had not tasted fresh Neteru in quite some time," he continued, as its mount extended a cord from its spinneret's and descended to the ground floor. The glowing rider lost no balance or revealed no sense of gravity change at all along the way down. *"How fitting we catch the one who ran."*

"Do you know even know you're speaking in third person?" I asked, tossing my cigarette at its steed's eyes, causing it to back up a few inches. "The third person plural. Xochi would *never* edit your papers." It waited twenty feet in front of me. Who would spring the trap first? Then I heard the click followed by the cursing behind me. I stepped and rolled, hearing a rushing in my ears, just as when I was in the Monk's chamber. Where I had just stood, an Isfet, similar to the species I saw guarded by the swordsman, appeared in mid-leap over my former position. I brought the sword up in a quick loop from seven o'clock to two o'clock back to four o'clock, leaving the creature in three pieces. "I made ya look," I spat out with a smile on my face at the Propius Minor. On the hillside behind me, Wallace stood fiddling with a pistol in frustration.

"Fuckin nuttin," I heard Nigel's voice from the opposite hillock, dropping his shotgun. It was followed by something flying through the air in my periphery, striking the massive tarantula steed in the eye and bouncing to ground. I saw the flung object was a pistol. The tarantula shrieked and flailed its front legs as Propius Minor used his outstretched fingers to quiet it.

"Stupid beast, huh?" I asked. "Well, at least you don't look like your pet." Another firearm sailed through the air toward the rider and was batted away by his blade, ricocheting into the dirt in front of me. The forty-caliber pistol that I saw in Corey's hand earlier lay on the ground. Among the Veil, in a place of pure concept, the machinery and products of its industry have no hold. Neither the steel, the firing pin nor the black star dust inside was a power in a realm where mastery of the underlying principles that shape the universe around us could strafe metal across open space faster than any ballistic explosion. Note to self: the weapons of modern warfare have no effect behind the Veil.

I stepped again, instinct-driven, spinning in a tight circle on half heel with my other foot on toe, bringing my blade up parallel to my back and over my right shoulder. I crossed my right leg in front of my left and unfurled the twist generated in my waist to extend the arm out. The crouch stabbed the vanishing Isfet as it attempted to Shanghai me from behind. The extension hurled its body off my blade to my side, slicing it as I did so. I wished someone was taping so this could go on World Star.

The figure, plan foiled, wasted no time in charging, its mount closing the distance quickly to miss with its first bite. A feint at best, but close enough to worry me as I dodged. The slice came down from the Minor's blade, the speed of which was hard enough to catch on my own blade. But the force bounced my parry so that my own hilt caught me in the left eye. My vision blurred, I jumped on instinct, wheeling to bring the sword up in defense as I realized I only had vision in one eye.

The pain was intense and intrusive: half of my brain reeling at the pain, the other half frantically working to repair my whole excruciated being. What my working right eye revealed was far more troubling. Candace and Corey stood where I just was, ratchet hand knives in their hands, kicking dirt and spitting at the Minor in taunt. Doubting the children, the mount sprang to bite, thinking with its appetite rather than pursuing its goal. As it leapt, Wallace came from behind its left flank, holding his machete at a forty-five degree angle. The monster, not being aware that it had just shorn off its own left legs in the process, landed hard where Candace once stood, sliding haphazardly through a nasty barrel roll. The Minor leapt off before the roll and stepped back to avoid Wallace's weaving machete. Somehow, watching his strokes and steps, I recognized his fighting style, but could not place it exactly. Wallace advanced, being drawn into the retreat, only to barely catch the counter and slice at the last minute. Wally's block was clean, but the Minor's force knocked Wallace back, flipping his body through the air and skidding his face in the dirt. I ran back in, swiping a vanisher with a side cut and burying the tip deep into another. Nigel had planted his knife into the brain of the flailing mount several times. As the glowing figure began to back away, the four kids stood as a perimeter between us.

"Didn't I say no," I snarled at Wallace.

"Huh?" he said, refusing to make eye contact as he rose. I shifted my eyes to Nigel, who shrugged and mouthed to me with a puzzled expression and a dickhead smirk: "Better think of some good music." Don't hear so good. Oh, right?

"*I'm impressed, Neteru,*" Propius said. "*You were deeply underestimated.*"

"Really? I couldn't tell," I said, advancing.

"*Let us make sure your experience is worthy of such merits as yours,*" he said, waving his free hand with its glowing fingers like electric vanilla milk shakes. I heard the rumbling of what sounded like thousands of clicking tongues through a megaphone. Each unique and warped by the amplifier. Then walking down strands at us, numbering in the hundreds was an army of those spurred, jointed spiders. Soon there would be a swarm far greater in number than those children I had deliberately sent away to avoid any harm and to prevent my being sued by some cosmic social worker. More than maybe I alone could handle.

Fear is my friend. *Say it.* Fear is my friend. It is loyal. It's been with me from the start. I once hid in an oven, in off mode, to avoid my parents beating the hope out of one another. Pots flying through air, blood on the floor, yelling through rooms, curses in the night, gargles from chokes, breaking glass shards and shattered ceramic pieces. Even when the tussle turned the gas on, I was smart enough to push the door back open, rush out of the room and find a pocket under my bed to hide in. There was always another way out. Always one more trick. One more route. A new entry to the market. Fear and I were intimate. I was paralyzed by it and freed from it. Fear was a bitch and I was its ho. And so, among the Veil, despite the effortless connection I felt to my surroundings, I was not strong enough. My fear for those children, who in a way shared my reality, made me doubt my ability to fight.

So I would run. I would pass through a door I saw everywhere. I would draw the door of all doors. I would pull my arms in a broad box and trace a grand door without flinching a muscle from my feet to my face. My eyes would be my sketch in stillness as much as my hands moved to grab a large ball I did not see. *The door would lead inside me and through it I would draw the door around me.* Around the children. A giant orb of vibrant energy, pulsing with the silvery translucent color of a frosted windshield, surrounded us like a snow globe. Just as my hands felt a breeze pass over the back of my fingers, so was I aware and connected to the construct surrounding the group inside a toy marble of my creation.

The creatures swarmed, scrambling up the surface of the orb. Ten feet away from the top of my head, they covered the construct, slashing at the surface with their cruel spurs. The kids laughed as the blows bounced back and made the sound of a BART ticket without enough fare being spit back out of a machine. I'm sure I heard what my mind wanted to hear. Frustrated, the fleshy arachnoids began weaving their serrated silk, covering the outside in a chain-link of stingers like a ball of yarn. Once they had covered enough of the orb, the circus began. Each creature retracted its serrated metallic adhesive stingers, pulling the edge across the orb like a chainsaw over wood. There was the sound of metal upon metal, the prolonged clamor of a car crash in front of one's house combined with the whining of troubled gears. Although I could feel them around the surface of the orb, I was neither worried nor daunted by the sensations. My response was much the same as if I handled a snake in hands shielded by protective gloves. Try as they may, their alloy-based webs made no mark on the orb. The connection was apparent; element upon element ended in stalemate and the Isfet disruption could be matched with the disruptive nature of metal itself.

"Har har har, you rusty bishes," I spat out, taunting the scurrying monsters. I could feel the Minor somewhere at the edge of the fray, giving orders and looking for an opening. I said it also as a verbalization of my own surprise, the relief and accomplishment of another breakthrough that had proven invaluable. There was the notion I had found some new application for a very old technique--an innovation those who knew me best such as Xochi or Heru were not aware of. I felt the full weight of hundreds of these creatures upon the orb. Each must have weighed at least four hundred pounds but in such a mass it felt as though an entire city was laid across my back and head. I could feel my focus slipping, just as it had the previous night with the experiments involving Desta, the chair and the gym. Although something about that place allowed me to recharge, the Passenger burning in my neck would work even harder to siphon off my vitality, especially when I worked at subverting its own kind's hold on my home.

As I fought to hold the orb steady, I felt a shift in my temples. The orb grew thick by a foot or so more as it shrunk to a size a few inches larger than the five of us huddled in our half astounded half-prepped group. At that surface size, the orb was still covered by the bodies of creatures while those that had fallen off stood waiting in rank and file. The sheer number disgusted me. The audacity of their presence and unfettered hunger offended me. This had robbed me of sleep and pursued me through countless lifetimes to where I couldn't tell where I began and the fear ended. I finally understood that the Passenger in my neck and the Propius were two pieces of the same being.

Fear became anger, anger became rage, and rage became my hand as it stabbed upward with the blade into the roof of the orb. The construct morphed around the shape of the blade and produced a thin spike that shot through the carapace of one of the creatures. Its blood dropped along the surface of the orb like hot syrup on glass. Corey was first to take notice, letting his teeth bite over his lower lip as he jabbed his knife into the orb's wall right at a creature's knee. The orb followed the forces, sending a razor-sharp porcupine quill into the creature's knee that retracted as he pulled back. Candace followed with a slice from seven to two o'clock, Nigel on the three to eight. The creature's leg was lopped off from the split, causing it to stumble. Wallace lopped its head from its body.

Following my lead, the kids began to wage their attacks on the periphery as I swung at the ceiling of my orb. I sliced through spiders in the tens as the orb matched my intent in razor-sharp fins that rippled through enemies. Bodies dropped to the dirt all around, fetid blood soaking into the nasty dirt, and the surface of the protective marble we stood inside shimmering as it evaporated the blood on it. The kids became more confident and broke from their cluster, diversifying their targets and increasing their attack speed. In that respect, the orb was a living shield, a responsive armor that deflected attacks but also amplified the response. Soon the seemingly impossible happened in front of us; I had cleared all the monsters off the orb itself while the remaining creatures struggled to climb over the dead carcasses of their comrades only to be met by the disturbingly accurate points of the kids.

The clearing of the wave, revealed the Minor in the backdrop, which had reclaimed another massive tarantula-like steed. Its blade was nowhere to be seen; its arms were on either side of its body with its fingers curled as if lifting buckets in each hand. A quartz white smoke curled from its palms, settling on the sterile ground and circling with the pink fog. I began to notice several swirls on the ground both in front and behind the Minor. From the swirl closest to us, I could see a shape rising as if on an elevator to Bobby Brown's My Prerogative video. Standing in the swirl was the shape of a blade male, wearing a uniform that seemed an amalgamation of a Roman centurion, a Forbidden City archer and a Celtic druid. It was taller than the average human, standing near seven feet tall with a girth around three hundred pounds. The being carried a curved sword in each of its massive four arms, its skin translucent like stretchy crystal or spandex made of glass, revealing veins of quartz white leading to organs and muscles of pale cobalt blue. Like their Minor general, their faces were bereft of features or hair.

My eyes counted over a thousand fully emerged and many times that number still growing. As the bulk of them hardened, they formed columns and stood in rank approach. I heard a hiss from the cocoon, knowing something old and wicked was stirring from its sleep. Then raising its hands above, the Minor brought the pink fog closer as I noticed the barking sound coming from the nonexistent mouths of the two armed translucent soldiers.

"*Recluse*," the Minor screamed, "*attack!*" I watched the legion march forward, the vanguard clearing bodies from their path with wide strokes. Everywhere their blades touched, a piece sizzled and decomposed from the inside out, whether inanimate or not. Suddenly, I worried if Cobra Commander wasn't so bad after all.

The Recluse charged to the orb, banging on it in lightning speed. Every blow, although reflected, created a ripple on the surface and a splitting migraine. I struggled to keep my balance and fell to my knees, holding my ears to focus. Their numbers increased as did the attacks and force. Meanwhile the frustrated curses of the kids indicated their knives did little damage. I felt my nose and eyes bleeding, knowing the check I had placed had been responded to with a castle. I was aching, struggling and losing. I saw the ground below me under the canopy of the orb, its sun-deprived color nothing more than a blank palette. The soil turned from an ugly brownish grey to black, the circumference of the orb inscribed as a dome while the lining glowed azure blue. And then . . . we sank, Wallace, Candace, Nigel, Corey and I into the blackness.

On my knees still, I recognized the parking lot of the junior college in the parallel valley behind the county jail. The kids stood before me as they did before. They seemed almost frozen in time. I stepped forward and put my arm on Wally's shoulder, seemingly pulling him from his frozen state. His eyelids fluttered as he looked around. I moved to do the same to the rest, catching myself in my own resistance to moving my eyes from Wallace. Candace was the farthest in front. I could hear her muted whimper as if she were being awakened for Monday morning school. Wally's eyes watched Candace and I followed his sight to hers, which was focused on the hillside we had left. Her mouth was inflated to gasp, but Corey's quick palm over her mouth did the trick to keep our presence unknown and hidden by the shadows under the trees in the parking lot.

The hillside, standing between the parking lot and the valley where Moreland was located, was filled with tiny green men working hard at their tasks. Some walked around with fork and knife, cutting pieces off dead bodies of the long-legged razor Isfet and eating them like a mignon. Others swung whips like a lion tamer at a circus, backing the remaining Isfet into a circle of green midgets who unhooked their jaws with long eviscerating teeth as they took tearing bites from the trapped creatures. Others stood with spray cans, painting a wet grassy green to the patch of lawn still tainted red while their companions stood on large scaffolding bolted against nothing as they used knife and mortar to slap globs of wasabi-looking paste on the corners of the open Isfet strand. Each motion to smooth the paste resulted in the paste changing into the backdrop of the night, blending and flattening out to hard reality.

Across the hole, on the scaffolding's other side, Proxies in overalls hoisted a large patch of night on ropes and pullets to cork off the gap which would be smoothed over by their spackle. Closer to the other side of the hill, a Proxy stood blowing into a doll, which a number of breaths turned into an inflatable sheriff like the one destroyed earlier. Next to him was a Proxy with hair pulled into a bun and wearing a blouse. The Proxy held a stylus and was drawing the outline of a vehicle. A few feet away another green man sat Indian style, with ear buds on that connected to their little black stone, knitting what looked to be a correction's officer's jacket. Farther down the hill and closer to us, green men in brown shirts and shorts opened cardboard boxes with box cutters to spill Styrofoam peanuts onto the grass as they pulled shotguns and radios from the boxes.

I slowly pulled into a crouch, walking on the balls of my feet towards the truck. When I saw my movement was not detected by the cleanup crew, I turned to the kids to signal them to follow in the same way. Creeping in slow methodical steps, I made my way to the truck and slowly opened the door. One by one, the kids slipped in and filled up the cab. I crept into the driver's position. I left the door open to avoid making a sound and pulled the gear into neutral without starting the car. Then, gripping the wheel, finding the subtle layer of Niaw, the truck began to roll forward. I wished I could release the parking brake because the lack of power steering required me to cramp the wheel as we turned out of our space and toward the lot's exit. Once the hillside was well out of sight behind us, I popped on the brake, put the car in park, started the engine with the lights, closed the door, shifted to gear, popped the brake off and sped off as close to seventy miles per hour as I could get. The car was silent but I could hear the relief and chattering of the kids in their own heads.

The car was still silent when I jumped on the freeway and then pulled off quickly to hide the truck behind an abandoned service station to have everyone change clothes. Over the bridge, everything was just as silent. In fact, no one talked until I pulled the truck into the liquor store parking lot across from West Oakland BART and hopped out. Wallace followed me out, but closed the door behind him.

"Back to work tomorrow," I said jokingly.

"I hate Mondays," Wallace said flatly.

"In some parts of the world they call us Mondays" Candy added.

"Some parts of this country they call us that" Wallace corrected,

"Smart kid," I added. He smiled and it faded to a long gaze. I could see the wheels turning over his head as he formed his thoughts.

"He is not going to leave that place, is he?" Wallace asked. I didn't know if he meant his Horace or Propius. The answer was the same for both.

"Not of his own will."

"I guess . . . that's that," Wallace processed out loud.

"Wallace," I said, letting my voice become warm and focused. "Your father loves you."

"I know," he replied, shoving his hands into his pockets. "I'll just have to be patient until he visits soon." He turned and opened the door to return to the truck.

"You should burn the clothes," I said.

"I know," Wally replied quickly as he got in.

"And the truck?"

"Repainted, new plates and on a truck for Detroit in the morning."

"We ain't new at this," Corey added in, leaning over to speak at me from the back seat. "Relax, mang."

"Sleep more?" Wally chimed in joking.

"I'll try," I said. "It's not easy."

"Hit dese trees," Corey countered with a laugh.

"Smack cakes," Nigel groaned and the kids erupted in laughter.

"I don't get it," I said as Wallace closed the door and rolled the window down.

"Get a girlfriend, Doc," Candace said with an annoyed tone and mischievous smile.

"Beatin' em," Nigel fired back and the car returned to laughter as the truck reversed. As the truck pulled away, Nigel rolled down his window to lock his fingers together and pump his palms together so as to make a muted suction clap. His eyes flitted over to a young woman entering the liquor store, his eyes going from her amazingly awesome posterior to my eyes. "Cakes," he said and hooted as the truck pulled off down the street.

CHAPTER THIRTEEN

"Time . . . has not been kind to you."

-Xochi

I n the office, Monday morning after class. Nobody likes Mondays. There is a Black Uhuru song about the subject if you feel like investigating. Undergraduates don't read due to still being drunk from the weekend. Professors don't teach well either, having been drunk themselves or spending most of their evening fighting spiders alongside a West Oakland street gang. So both parties fall on writing assignments, take-home quizzes from the reading and sending classes home early.

I sat at my laptop, my red flash drive in the USB port, my journal pages opened before me as I scrolled through descriptions collected over centuries about the enemy lurking in the corners of my mind: the Isfet. The descriptions were exceptionally detailed. Sometimes the author was quoted and dated, sometimes not. The most useful sections were the summaries of how one might fight each creature. The archive even gave equivalents between human military units and Isfet units. For example, the Passengers were essentially archers while their nasty vanishing counterparts were labeled as "Phantoms" and were generally seen as a charge defense. There were further notes that indicated they held no resistances and their movements could be detected by an Attribute with a minor amount of training in Huh. I added a note about their ability to swing from their silk as well as the medium strength of their venom.

The fleshy melds of both man and arachnid with razor spurs were labeled as Daddy Long Legs. Their venom was the least potent of the bunch but their blades were more than compensation. Although behind the Veil, I had seen bullets cut them down just the same. Among the Veil seemed a whole different case entirely; there the Daddy Long Legs appeared immune to metal. In fact, it was to be noted that I had yet to see where modern warfare worked behind the Veil. These creatures functioned as cavalry with their ability to cover a distance and clear paths. The translucent soldiers were labeled as "Recluses", their blades being lined with necrotic venom that decomposed both organic and inorganic matter in seconds. They were a vicious infantry that knew how to collectively exploit a weakness of a single opponent. There were no listed resistances or strengths to the Recluse.

The little that was left about Isfet leadership, if it could be called that, mentioned a relationship between Minor and Major Isfet. Each Major Isfet ruled an Aspect either adopted from a colonized attribute or developed on its own. They operated in feudalism very similar to the practices of a liege lord. They were named for the aspect under their domain much the same way the names of my family translated to concepts in our native tongue that explained how reality worked. Generally, for every Major Isfet, there were several Minors who acted as enforcers and vassals, doing the maintenance of the fiefdom while the Majors focused on influence and feeding. To date, there was no record of any hierarchy above Majors, though we were still not clear whether the Isfet shared a hive mind or some social structure from which they derived their direction. In outline form appeared a clear warning that Isfet seldom existed in the Veil without invoking paradox. It was suggested that any outnumbered Attribute could flee to the Veil to escape but risked Partisan assault. I made a note to find out more on these Partisans and their leadership.

"Much stronger," I heard a lisping voice whisper and felt warmth on my wrist. Given I wasn't expecting it and I had a screen of creepy spiders on my screen, I jumped in my chair, catching Xochi's eyes in the doorway with a quizzical expression. Looking down, Desta stood at my knee, running his finger along the exposed vein between my palm and wrist. His brow furrowed as he tapped the vein and smiled when it bounced back. "Still," he said with a little boy sigh of relief and climbed up in the chair to cuddle on my lap.

"Yes," Xochi said, eyes slitting as she closed the door to my office, "something is different. Did you do something to your hair?"

"I'm letting it grow," I said. My reply sounded dry as I finished signing off the site, popping out the flash and flipping it into my pocket.

"That's not related to what I meant," Xochi replied, still watching me with some suspicion in the corners of her mouth.

"Still same old Clay," I said, chuckling and opening a folder to select Raphael Saadiq's album from my music collection. Desta chuckled too. I looked downward at his big eyes and shook him with my arm softly. He chuckled more. "Why are you laughing?"

"Cuz you made a joke," he whispered with a sly smile as I shook him a bit more by the arms.

"But you don't get it," I replied.

"I know," he shot back and we both laughed. Raphael was singing now over what might be the greatest Andre Young composition of all time.

"You never came by to pick him up last night," Xochi countered.

"I got delayed," I said, keeping my eyes to the laptop screen. "Didn't want to wake him up."

"Anything I should worry about?"

"Worry? . . . no." I scrolled the mouse, clicking on an address bar in a browser in search of an internet game for Desta. Xochi pushed her hand down on the laptop lid, closing it and holding her hand out. Desta crawled down and grabbed her palm.

"I feel like we're having an awkward parent moment," I said, looking at Xochi. She kept her eyes on Desta, leading over to the doorway.

"Grab his coat. It's cold outside," she said and I looked around for Desta's coat. Then I realized it had been so sunny this weekend I didn't think to buy one for him. When I looked back, he wore a tiny North Face of bright yellow, a gray beanie with yellow Gore-Tex trim to match the jacket with little grey gloves as he wrapped his arms around my overcoat and carried it as best as he could to me. I took it and the hint, knowing full well that the outfit hadn't been there before. Even worse, I had been looking for Desta's jacket and Xochi wasn't even talking to me. I was still thinking too much. Desta skipped off to catch up with Xochi and threw on my coat as I walked out, swinging the door closed behind me. We stepped down the hallway out the doors and on to Golden Gate, Desta far ahead as he got a running start along the driveway up to Lone Mountain. For some reason, Xochi walked between us, keeping herself as some median between extremes. The winter sun was high in the sky, signaling its curl around the globe soon. I told myself I used to work that shift.

We made it to the top of the hill after crossing Turk, Desta standing below the ancient trees in his meditative awe. Xochi looked out to the hills, turning herself so her face was obscured from Desta. I started to fish out a cigarette and received a punch in the arm. That hurt. Her fingers pointed past the valleys to the southwest along the 280 that ran down the Peninsula. I followed her fingertips to the cloud break in the southwest sky. On the hill was a triangular radio tower, flashing its red lights.

"FM Tower," I said calmly. "When I was your age we listened to something called the radio." I felt some thing slap me in the back of the head, right above the hard knob at the back of the skull. Xochi's hand stayed motionless in its point. "Okay, what am I looking at?"

"No," she said quietly and slow like she does when she is pissed, "what are you looking with?" My eyes relaxed, feeling my lids pulls into a subtle squint without strain. The tower was next to a cloud trace, forming an S. What started as white faded to red and I saw the triangle shape left of the cloud turning the same shape but now purple, then blue, green, yellow and back to red.

"Delta S?"

"Change in entropy," Xochi said through her teeth. "It's a caution tape warning Attributes to stay clear of an area that's had heavy paradox activity."

"Wow," I said, leaving my voice calm and low to try to pretend shock. While I wasn't aware that the little green men left caution tape, I would need the information to keep my eyes as bewildered as possible.

"Yes," she said, dropping her hand and putting it her pocket. "Looks like something got very *wild* last night."

"You sure that's recent?"

"Positive. It woke me out of bed. That beacon only flashes for forty-eight hours after an incident. This is only the third in San Francisco."

"Ever?"

"Ever."

"I'll keep an eye out, then," I said, noting to myself that the world I thought was so large last night had become smaller, flatter and hotter.

"You should," Xochi replied, "you really should. Isfet activity on the borders has increased."

"Ugh, that doesn't sound like good news. What exactly constitutes the borders?"

"The radius starts at the center and stretches out to roughly Half Moon Bay."

"How high up or how far deep in the water?"

"Look for yourself. Neither the activity nor the radius is what bothers me."

"No?"

"No, what bothers me is when I went to investigate the caution zone was on a hillside in between Skyline Community College and the San Francisco County Jail."

"You know college kids and their fetishes. I member when I lived in the dorms-"

"The same jail both your cousin and his Carrier were housed in."

"Were?"

"There is always a reaction, Clay," Xochi said looking at me with her intense blue eyes far from my notion of bullshit. "Even now, if I reach out, I'm not sure if I can say I know where he went." Worry starts in the stomach, stress in the temples but abandonment strikes in the temples and spreads to the indentation between the eyebrows on its journey to the base of the spine. Reaching out without moving a finger much less a muscle in the face, I sent my awareness out to the jail. Somehow I knew Xochi would wait until I was done, like a conversation in a house party I knew I could always come back to. My mind covered every inch of the facility; Horace wasn't there. I could neither find the Carrier nor my cousin Heru; I felt like I was locked out of my car. "The equation always balances itself out, Clay. When it does, it leaves logs of *how* and *why*?

"You act like I did something," I said, pouring the guilt syrup over the pissed cakes.

"You know what?" Xochi said, squinting. "You're right. I shouldn't accuse you."

"Thanks," I said, reaching for a cigarette that got blown out of my hand by a powerful gust of wind, a wind strong enough to rip a stogie from your fingers. It carried one more from my pack into the passing day and left as quickly as it came.

"I don't like when my friends are taken advantage of," Xochi said, reaching into her purse to squirt some lotion on her hands. "I tend not to think *rationally*."

"Come on, Xoch," I said, with a chuckle, turning to see Desta completely enamored with a tree and turning back. *"You are a fertility principle."*

"And war," she said, her eyes going cold.

"War with donors?"

"Keep joking. Ever seen a Nazca?"

"No."

"Exactly." A chill ran down my spine and I realized some part of me placed myself near Xochi for protection. "Either you are abusing Clay or Clay is abusing you; either way it stops soon." She laid her boundary thick. *"Very soon."* There was so much I wanted to tell Xochi but had decided she would be safer uninvolved. She was trying to position herself to buffer me but I thought she would be safer if it was I who was the buffer. I wasn't sure if it was Xochi or the being inside her who was upset. Maybe it was both. I knew somehow there was a trust eroding between Xochi and me that I tiptoed around. Instinctively I knew I had done something wrong. I was pretty sure I would continue to as long as I could find the happy medium between the conditions of Xochi's love and completing whatever the hell I had set myself on.

"Why do you assume it's abuse?" I heard myself say.

"Look," Xochi said with the voice I knew was a step away from an ultimatum. "Whichever of you is driving. You asked for my help wiping your memory. I did. You asked for help with recovery. I did. Why? Because I am friends with *both* of you. The least I have asked in return was a respect for the cost of this sanctuary as well as the cost of *citizenship*. Not because I want the Concord but because there has to be somewhere to for those who do not want it . The failure to do has larger costs." She let her voice come to a firm stop. Her head tilted slightly to the left and her face appeared as if she was responding to another speaker.

"Do *you* really think you can . . ." she struck out and paused again, wringing her fingers before both hands into fists and bringing her palm together, resting the back of her thumbs against where her nose met the top of her upper lip. "This is new territory to all of *us*," she began again, slow and present. "Which is why I am giving you liberties, but you shouldn't just take them. You are staring at five hundreds. Over five centuries by a Roman solar calendar that those who live among these hills might *never* know what waits for them just outside that fog. A fog you built for the very reason that there should be *someplace* that we don't have to run from those blood suckers."

"Time . . . has not been kind to you" she continued. "That is not a quarrel any *one of us* would make with you. By that token, we understand your need to try new paths, even in light of prior knowledge, but never mistake our compassion for *pity*. Pity will lead you stepping on boundaries. You will even step on your own boundaries, but more often mine. *Respect my time,* if not your own time. I have invested my essence in keeping this a pocket free from Isfet. It is my efforts in this city that prevent the enemy from snatching mortals like wet meat like in Food Co. If you want a set of rules for yourself and a set of rules for everyone else, so be it. Go find where that is. Have the vigor and frankly the *nuts* to walk away and follow that path. This place exists because of rules. We take no followers, we commit no works in the eyes of the mortals and we enjoy a sanctuary away from Concordian politics and Isfet law at the discretion of the Proxy Lord."

"Entropy," I said recognizing the reference. "Freedom from imposed democracy, under a tyrant no less. More compromise . . . "

"That," Xochi interrupted, grabbing my head and turning my eyes back to the caution sign. "That tyrant keeps spiders out of your tree house, *fool!* Perhaps like these children you are so gifted in reaching, you also cannot picture it until it's laid out before you. Except we can't afford you learning the hard way."

"I still feel I'm being harangued over an accusation. It's not like you can say that out there," I motioned with my hand at the sigil, "is my doing."

"No," Xochi said, taking her hands away from the sides of my skull, "but I'm right to be suspicious. Entropy may have wronged your cousin but it's right to look for you."

"Oh yeah?" I said, pulling my hand over my face to grab a cigarette away from Xochi's temper, "and why is that?"

"If I was there when it started, I might say the two of you were formed to foil one another," Xochi replied. The cigarette lit on its own and I took a deep breath. "Paradox is the function of the universe that limits humanity's imagination. It is largely a reaction of how people see their place in the world."

"No," I argued, "Entropy is a feudalism imposed upon the imagination."

"Chicken or egg, right?" Xochi hucked back at me. "But when you strip it down, it is very dependent on perception. I could run down the street naked on fire and no one would think twice."

"It's San Francisco-"

"Same reaction if I was walking? Breathing fire? Naked? With the paws of a jaguar for feet?"

"People would wig out! Shit like that doesn't happen every day"

"For some reason, you seem to think it does. In fact, you'll make flyers and encourage people to demand a fire-breathing Mexican cat bitch in their neighborhood." I laughed hard.

"Far fetched, don't you think?"

"*I've seen you do it,*" she countered.

"You're exaggerating"

"Pet rock."

"Really? No, why would I?"

"To prove it could be done. Same with that smiley face and have a nice day. Same as always. You seem to think it's your job to cause paradox and then contradict it."

"For sake of argument, what if it is, Xochi?"

"Memory or none," she said and then laughed, "I still don't have an answer for that."

"Except it has a cost, right?"

"Yes, unless you are a citizen like your friend, Dina."

"Somewhere that *had* to come up . . . " I exhaled.

"My feelings aside. She pays her taxes. That makes her a citizen. A citizen who gets warnings when Paradox comes knocking."

"So why don't we just pay taxes?"

"Because none of us are citizens. Any belief collected is by donation."

"Ah, a nonprofit."

"Something close." Xochi poked her finger into my chest. "So stop spending like we're . . ."

"Or we'll get audited?"

"Yes. Plus I'm not sure your carrier can handle any more . . ."

"I found a way to stop the Passenger. I'll be fine," I said with confidence.

"So that was you."

"No," I said, slowing her roll, "but if pushed I know how to regenerate now."

"I'm going to continue with the good faith you won't make an ass of me."

"Of course not."

"Itch code," I heard Desta say and looked down at the little peanut M&M pulling on my coat.

"Is that one of those cute ways of asking for hot chocolate?" I asked, putting my hand over his gloved paw. Desta looked off into the distance and then back to me blankly. "All right, walk a bit ahead and we'll go."

Desta started to say something, looked over to Xochi's expression and let his child instincts kick in, which told him to respect grown folks' business. Soon as he had a bit of leader space, I crushed the cigarette under my shoe and started following.

"Maybe it would be best if we placed someone to watch the Concord," I said at the bottom of Turk, as we crossed the street toward the main campus.

"Who says we don't?" Xochi replied, "You seem to be the only one without a frame of reference."

"Maybe I should do something about that."

"Maybe you should call your *friend*."

"Here we go again," I chided, crossing Golden Gate. "You really don't like her, do you?"

"Even if I did," Xochi said, holding Desta back so a car could pass, "I wouldn't trust her."

"*Who do you trust at this point?*" I asked on the other side of Golden Gate, walking through campus by the library.

"Those who trust themselves."

"Awesome! More fucking riddles. Gee, Xochi, thanks for laying into me and following with urban surreal cryptology."

"Well, since you aren't forgetting as much, I don't have to explain everything any more now, do I?" We walked around the grass, through the plaza, up its steps, into the stairwell and down to the student café. I smirked at the title as I passed under the sign reading Crossroads Café.

"Crossroads," I said, pointing at the sign. "It's the symbol used to denote a city or country."

"Relevance?" Xochi asked.

"Not sure yet, I'll see what happens" I replied. I stood in line behind the other four students waiting for coffee. The line moved slower than a minivan full of older women in the right lane of 101 South between the airport and the San Mateo Bridge. It amazed me how it could be the same student working there for a semester or more, but they worked the register and counter like it was their very first day. I remembered working at a bagel shop in undergrad, waking up at five in the morning to get to that stupid café just to be told how to slice bread and make smoothies from a manager who hadn't lifted her finger past anything but a register button. Do that for five days a week, plus class, plus homework, plus minimum wage and that's a reason to work slow. iPod playing, television on in viewing distance, shifts that start at noon and a lifestyle paid for by parents did not seem to merit seven minutes per customer to pour a single cup of coffee and grab a muffin. With effort like this, it was a wonder why the economy was feeling shudders in the labor curve.

A few centuries later, I was at the counter, and held his little majesty up to eye level with the girl working the counter. Given the fact I taught at such a global school, I was shocked to note that all the girls behind the counter were Filipina with accents that sounded straight out of Huntington Beach. Of course the benefit was I didn't have to lift him very high in the air. I laughed as he stuttered through ordering a hot chocolate, despite his excitement at all the attention. I wished I still had the mischievous streak that had me lie to say he was my son. Instead, we made our order and I put him back on his feet. I led him over to the delivery counter and out of the way of the stomping feet of clueless Millennials yapping on their phones. Xochi stood a few paces away from us, waving at Desta with her fingers, which made him smile shyly and wave back in an attempt to imitate her. Her smile froze and her hands dug into the pockets of her burgundy quarter length to pull out the smart phone which made my inner gadget geek jealous. She typed in something with her fingers, nostrils flaring as she covered her mouth with her hand.

"Hot chocolate," I heard the counter call. Desta became jumpy and I aimed him over to Xochi with my hand, grabbing the cup to check its temperature. Far too hot for his young tongue. My fingers on the cup dropped about twenty degrees off the temperature.

"Clay," I heard Xochi call my name, disappointed and worried.

"Coming," I said, still working the cup over with my thoughts.

"*Oh no*," I heard Xochi's voice sound in my head, causing me to look for her without using my eyes. Across from the café counter, clustered in a rough semi-circle of rolling love seats and plush chairs, students huddled between classes watching soccer, talk-show paternity tests and replays of reality shows. Today it was the local news, broadcast by a mid-thirties African American with a box cut that made me miss Dennis Richmond.

The footage showed the exterior of the San Francisco County Jail. In the right corner of the screen, the on-the-location Asian woman reporter responded to questions while keeping her hand on the ear piece receiver in her right ear. The teletype read "BART Police Killer Murdered In Jail Riot" and I felt a cold grip seize as well as shrink my stomach. My ears shut off the hum of conversation, tinny iPod-generated digital music, cell phone ring tones and cash register sound bytes. All I heard and knew was the sound of the anchorman as he made morbidity sell advertising space.

"Good afternoon. I am Truman White, with KRON breaking news. San Francisco's Sheriff Department is reporting a riot broke out at the county jail early this morning, injuring several officers and inmates. Cleanup crews are still reporting casualities, with over twenty inmates murdered." The screen flashed an image that shook my feet. Wallace. Wallace in twenty years. Elongated frame, bright eyes, sunken sockets, broad nose, rounded chin and a kind smirking mouth contorted into a sneer of a mug shot. "Horace 'Mack' Marshall, who was held under suspicion of murdering two BART police . . ." The video feed showed the visuals of EMTs pulling bodies out of the Powell Street station, "was found murdered in the aftermath of the incident. Marshall, a repudiated cartel leader," back to the mug shot of a man I knew with a look to his eyes I did not, "was wanted in connection with numerous drug-related murders spanning from West Oakland to East Palo Alto to his own local San Francisco Bayview neighborhood. So far investigators have not released details as to suspects in his murder."

"*Clay?*" I heard Xochi's voice say with a shake.

"*I think I need some hot chocolate now.*"

⨍

"I don't think this is our field cousin," I hear myself saying, staring out at the mix of marsh, sand and plains stretching in front of the city.

"You would prefer where?" responds Heru's voice, coming from the body of a man who has his back turned to me. I can tell it is not the Heru I am accustomed to seeing. He is in some condensed form, the original before bootleg, yet not as gritty and therefore less real than the Heru I know. I realize we are both shorter, our skin like a golden coal, like Wagaye's, and his head is bare except for a single bunched lock pulled to the side of his skull. The wind picks up and I am forced to push my own locks away from my face. It is impractical to wear my hair down but I know war is also impractical.

"South to the fortress at Gebel Barkal," I said in response. "It's far more defensible."

"You would bring weapons," Heru says, turning to knock his knuckles against the familiar and welcome blade at my side, "into the rest of our ancestors?"

"I leave the superstition to you," I say. "I am about surviving a war."

"And you believe we can move an entire city to a fortress and defend the rear?"

"Not as one unit," I said, "but we could send the people ahead and catch up when we've minimized the assaults and delayed any pursuers."

"Who would you have?"

"Khonsu. Anpu as scout. Ba can circle the flanks." Heru walked in small circle, grumbling with his fingers poking at each other.

"Leaves me with only one general in the field."

"You uncle is still waiting with the surprise reinforcements." A groan and then a sharp intake of breath. Then he clears one of his nose by holding down one nostril with a finger and exhaling hard on to the sand; a small crater the diameter of my foot forms where the projectile lands.

"Trust is a slow process, my prince," I reassure him.

"So is vengeance."

"You both gave your word," I corrected. "That means something."

"Not to him. He is without words and his wife is all lies. Those two are--" he spat out before stopping himself. I looked to the small gravel under my feet while shielding my face. "I apologize." I heard his voice restructure, tender and concerned. "I do not wish to strain relations between you and your inlaws."

"Thank you," I reply, looking up and meeting his eyes. "I am more concerned about your oath to my father. Your oath to the land as a whole."

"That would be unfortunate," Heru says, rubbing his head with his palm.

"And your word to yourself. If you cannot keep your own word, how are you better than your uncle?"

"Ah," Heru says with a bright, rebellious smile. "We have returned to class, have we now, master?"

"No my prince," I say calmly, "but you retained me as your advisor, so what am I if not advisory?"

"Your loyalty despite turbulent moods," Heru says, placing a hand on my shoulder, "humbles me cousin. Your father's treaty does not soothe me the way it might for you."

"And your vengeance in your father's name was too long a war, Heru. Now we have a new invader at our realm's edge. A wise king would not fight at his borders as well as in his own court."

"And if I am not a *wise* king?"

"Then I want my old job back."

"Playing spearmen for him so he can languish is some delusional credit that he is Ra's protector? Your wife would love hearing you are stealing her spot so you can spend more time with her father."

"Are you son of Ausar or a brat with a sword?" I queried. Heru purses his lips and flares his nostrils. He paces.

"I discourse with you because you are often closer to correct than I am," Heru explains. He looks out into the dark night, in expectation of the coming dawn, scanning his eyes over the campfires of our troops camped below. "Send the city forces south with Khonsu, absorb his troops and send the city guard with him instead. Instruct the rest to hold the city should we need to fall back. We will follow after the engagement and the opportunity has been presented."

"Good man," I reply watching the horizon. I reach into my armor and feel under the fabric of my tunic for the stone. It is a square-cut piece of obsidian, with sanded edges to avoid the stone's vicissitude-like nature. It was obtained by Khonsu during his visits to the lands of the next world west. Licking the tips, I place my fingers on the surface. The stone takes on a lavender smoke look, like burning pastels, before it clears and I stare at the face. Ebon and glowing, the head was proportional to that of a small giant. His huge eyes followed me as I made out the signs of campfire in the background. "Khonsu," I say finally.

"Lord," his deep booming voice replies.

"Leave your troops with me and return to Memphis." His lip curls and I can tell he was not pleased.

"M'lord?" he asks, looking for clarity.

"We want you to evacuate the city. Bring the people south to the fortress at Gebel Barkel."

"And the Narmer?" he asks. I look to Heru who stood watching the distance, listening silently.

"They won't budge from the throne," I say to Heru, "not until Ra is done raising the sun and their Veil is up as a result." Heru nods and plays with the skin under his nose, as he always did when he was thinking.

"Inform Neith she is now responsible for the Narmer. Move Anpu and Serekh Ba to the city gates to take on our rear guard," Heru sends silently.

"Without troops?" Khonsu asks. "She will not be pleased"

"Tell her I asked," I add, "and she will acquiesce."

"And the city guard?" Khonsu asked with an urgency to his growl.

"No," I say, "take them with you. I just want the people to be well insulated against any assault."

"You leave your ranks thin," he comes back.

"Do as I say."

"Yes, general," he replies. "The sun shines on Kemet."

"Indeed," Heru sends through the stone. I smile and wave off the connection. We are silent as Heru walks down the ridge towards his troops. I follow in tow. Time passes as Heru walks by as every single man, making a mental count of their size, weapons, how they sleep, what they eat and what family waits for them at home. Heru cares about victory but his passion is the lives of those who are willing to die for their homeland. They are the details that add up to our grand cause. Finally, he says, "you ask her to step out of a battle the same week as you tell her you will not give her children. Bold."

"Oh, you were just waiting to say that one, eh?" I ask.

"I fear for you. Your wife is not much for denial"

"She'll live."

"Will you?" Heru says with a chuckle.

"You are being dramatic. What makes you so sure this will be a problem?"

"It is her nature. When she pursues, she completes. Push comes to shove, and Neith finds a way to be involved after being *uninvolved*."

"That is any warrior hungry for glory," I say to dismiss him.

"That is her aspect. I hope it serves the people as well as it has her."

"I would think the honor would be in protecting the royals and our government."

"Is that why you two married? So convergent and yet identical. Ma'at be praised," Heru says with a sarcasm thick in his smile.

"You are teasing me now with that joke at the end about my mother."

"Touchy. Who's the role model here?"

"A role model for a self-made deity? You do realize I do not buy into that worship nonsense. I leave the nonsense for those of you who find it worth debating."

"Whether you like it or not, the people look to Heru for inspiration. Heru looks to you for guidance."

"I wish to be dismissed from my post," I say, chuckling.

"Denied." He replies through a laugh. We walked the length of the field before he stopped. "Dawn is late." I look around noticing the night seemed unnaturally prolonged. On the edge of the sky a faint pink mist was forming.

"Field Marshal!" I bellow, stepping in front of Heru and circling to see how quickly I was responded to. The delay is longer than I am comfortable with. I turned to see a half-dressed sergeant standing at attention. "Find me the field marshal. Now. Any soldier who is not dressed and ready by the time I blink will be fighting me." He turns a shade of pale that was easy to see amongst his dark skin and scurried off. Heru pulls a shield from off the rack, drawing his sword and banging the two together as he rolled his shoulders in a slow pulse. *Doom. Doom. Doom.* Yells and shouts erupted from the camp as men call to action. The marshal arrives shortly after, informing me that scouts had not returned from patrol and there was no word from Anpu. Anpu, silent on his feet, is the leader of that patrol. My heart feels a sense of chill at the notion that the aspect that could bend shadows around his body might have been toppled by a foe we only knew by the desiccated carnage it had left at the villages to the border near the deep desert. These Isfet had appeared out of the night, far more vicious than any thing that desert had sent at us before. I told the marshal to add the scouts as our first casualities. It wasn't long before the camp had transformed into formations. Infantry, spearmen, archers, chariots and both Heru as well as my own special units within the benefits of our individual aspects were assembled.

"I'm worried, Cousin," Heru says, standing in front of the line, watching the thick pink fog which had hidden the sky from us.

"What does your heart say?" I reply.

"Our right flank will be weak."

"On purpose. It is where Uncle will surprise them in a pincer."

"Mmmm."

"I'll cover it if need be."

"Need be," he replies and I nod to acknowledge I will cover that flank. Heru draws his sword, holding it high above his head. The valley echoes with the war cries of thousands ready to lay down their life for the land of the black. The fog swirled without wind, invoking the sounds of barking with millions of glowing eyes. The wind dies. leaving us with the smell of sticky sweet fermented death. Then from the fog, shapes emerge, arachnids the size of work ponies, crawling in mass. Behind them walked a medley of men of the world, the black Nubians of tribes that worshipped fire spirits in the caves, the brown from the west with their animal tongues, the yellow from the lands north with their thick eye lids and the red desert princes with their curved blades. Each stood naked except for the guttural paint on their face and the red hour glasses on their chests.

"If anything should happen--" Heru starts.

"It won't," I cut him off.

"I won't leave you, Ka."

"You won't have to, my prince," I answer. With that, Heru steps forward, spearmen marching behind him. "Good hunting, cousin," I hear him say in my mind. I step with the left foot, the right bringing me to the other side of the field with our exposed flank. Heru would engage at the vanguard, drawing them along the line and baiting a surge on the right. Set, our master of war, would wait until the enemy was committed and bring his ruthless Partisan units to crush the enemy with the element of surprise. Heru's grudge was hard killed; it was only a century ago these two had had warred for the throne and blemished the land with their conflict, Heru for his father's murder and Set for his wife's respect. What was time to those born of the universe itself, though? The wound might as well been yesterday, but my father's foresight and threat of war from the Isfet would be enough to unite us, or so my faith told me.

The first wave fell quickly. The spearmen, mostly conscripted villagers, were unprepared for the dexterity of the Isfet spiders that disappeared before one could strike and appeared right behind for the kill. Between that and the murmuring zealots with their wicked magics raining down the elements with clouds of poisonous gas and illusions to confound the mind, it was a slow slaughter ramping up into a massacre. Heru, relentless, stood his ground and continued to cut bodies like a scythe through tall grass. We lost over thirty percent of our troops in the first charge but had established a front line closer to the border than to our own gates. Heru is forced to bring in the infantry to hold the line. His blade swings and cuts multiple targets. Pulses of blue white flame burst from him when he is surrounded and pressured for space. Soon after, Heru regains position and I hear the horn sound.

Signal given, the right flank folds in toward the middle, making a hole in the line that we hoped would bait the enemy. There is the sound of wet nut shells banged together, increasing in volume. They spring from the very ground; it seemed as fleshy carapace hybrids of arachnid and man rushed us. Each of their eight legs ended in a sharp bone spur at the highest joint which they each used to perforate the men around me. Unlike the spiders at the front who bit and dragged bodies back into the fog, these creatures punctured and drained the men from a sickly stinger that came from their wicked asses. I order the archers to release, the volleys arching through the sky above our heads, connecting with deadly accuracy but barely penetrating the armor of the foe. It is enough to push them back a bit, cluster and regroup. I call my horse, uttering words asking for the *Nun* to give me the power; I had no problem with superstition when I was in distress. As I mount, the cavalry known to the house of Ma'at formed behind me. My mind draws a rung in the field, circling the foe with a tall cylinder. Drawing my sword, I ordered the charge, letting the ring erupt. Fire consumes the creatures, which are surprisingly flammable, just before we sweep through. Looking behind me, the rest of my column had not been so successful. Most of the horses have been cut from under the riders, leaving them to crash to the field with their steeds falling on top. In some cases, both rider and steed had been shorn in pieces, left for the slimy tubes protruding from the back of the creatures to puncture and drain of their blood.

We were being slaughtered efficiently as if these creatures were spawned to counter every single unit with which we had established our military superiority. Out of respect for my steed, I jump off, slapping its hindquarters to send it away. As it gallops off, I dropped my shield in favor of picking up another blade. My mind reaches out to the vanguard where Heru fares much better, maintaining at least half of his troops, with minimal contact to himself. I catch his arm, swinging his massive blade that spits bodies back like a plough through the pernicious grasses that clogged the back of crack houses. In the thick of it all, I recognize a divine entity that could heal his comrades with a gaze from one eye and melt its enemies with the other. I find Heru's mind and connect. He knows no fear, not since birth, not ever. I silently relay to him the results of my charge and my suspicions. In agreement, he asks me to work towards him and reaches for the horn that would sound the second wave. The horn echoes through the valley, invoking a cheer from our remaining troops. They swell and hold, as they fight in expectation of reinforcements. The prince's will was clear: "stand with me."

Positioning, I know the plan. If I was unable to deflate this flank, I should turn their attention. Backing slowly, I felt my protective Orb rise around me. I used this orb as Set's spearman against the serpents who sought to swallow the sun. I pull it just around the circumference of my body as a set of armor instead of a barrier. The blade-like creatures, bouncing on their joints clustered on all sides of me, cut me off from Heru's force. Forward I push, more in my mind than anywhere else, looking to cut a path on the diagonal. My blades wave in front of me, I cut with steps in a zig, then a zag and then a zig through bodies. I swing to the right over my head in a slash while stabbing behind with the left, hopping over a leg shot, crossing both blades in front, twisting the right wrist to chop left, and pushing in for the thrust. I even kicked bodies into each other, speaking the words that would ignite their carcasses as they flew. In due time, with a fourth of these Daddy Long Legs still standing and cautiously following me away from Heru's flank, I bounce on the balls of my feet, ready for the next episode. Instead, the horn's companion sounded from behind. I wheel, protecting my side to view the hill crest where the horn sounded.

High in the sky, projected against the back drop of a pink fog, hangs a flag without suspension or ties, a red beast's head, flapping in the wind on a pole that did not exist. Then I see him. Tall, gaunt, ferocious and awesome. Standing nearly seven feet, his armor did not conceal enough of his massive rippling muscles along his arms and legs. I saw the head of a terrible typhonic creature with a curved snout and square ears that resembled an aardvark, jackal and donkey but was none at the same time. His blood-red eyes scanned the field and found no comfort in anything except the grip of his black- handled spear with its wicked tip, an extension of his very arm.

"Kemet," his voice rumbles and the clouds roll above. His throat was the coming thunder, his timing with the words the crackling of lightning. The lord of storms had made his presence known. "Hold your weapons a while longer." His flag evaporated, replaced by the image of his giant typhoon head viewing the field. "Look at us. Beasts at the whim of a dream. A dream of a coward. Once these men you stand by ruled from the southern mines to the jade mountains of the north, confident in the power of our will. *Our will.* Now look at us: bickering with a foe that should be our ally against any whimper of a tribe who would oppose us. For what, I ask? The sickening hope that our way can be diluted as our solar blood has become in pursuit of a royal elite who would rather hide from their birthright than rule the people as it was meant to do."

"And what would that be?" I hear across the field. We all knew the source--Heru.

"Worship. Worship of Kemet as the divine, above all else." Set back by this chiding, I was annoyed. "All they see is due to us." I found myself shaking my head again. This reasoning had brought us to war amongst our own once before, ending in a conflict between prince and uncle that land nearly did not recover from. Still in the pit of disbelief and horror, I notice our arachnid foes had paused their assault while he spoke. This suggested an intelligence to the bugs I had not seen before, a pre-ordered recognition. This was part of a plan. I could smell it as sick as the sticky rot coming from the pink mist. The scent of betrayal. Opening my mind to Heru, I felt myself walking involuntarily toward Set's position. I notice I am not the only one; in fact, over eighty percent of our forces seemed in trance stepping toward the lord of the desert. "The era of the weak has ended. The king has returned to his throne."

A silhouette appears at his right shoulder, nearly as tall but far more compact: a black jackal's head atop the body of a muscular man in his early twenties. He moves like smoke, slippery and weightless, down the slope. He pulls his long curved knives as his eyes lock onto mine. Anpu, the embalmer, is stealth itself. As the masses of our troops flow into Set's ranks, I hear Heru's words from earlier. Surprise folds into betrayal and wrath, as I reconcile our own war master has turned against us, when needed most. To add insult, the very strategy he persuaded us to pursue was nothing more than a ruse to destroy us all.

The Isfet are unconcerned as their target is clear; the swarm scurrying to surround Heru and his forces confirms this. A more calculating mind might have realized that I had a better chance against the millions of the beasties with their back completely turned to me as they focused their attack on my cousin. I was not in reflection then; I was passion, engorged and blinded. Passion at my own family member's ability to slaughter thousands for his own pursuit, shame at defending Set against Heru's better judgment and rage at being returned to war I did not want. It was what led to my slow, steady advance at Set. I waved with each blade, signaling that any of my former men who did not wish to die should show no opposition as I aimed at my uncle. One made the mistake and was rewarded with a disemboweling, his torso split in two pieces and his legs clove at the knees.

"Sekhem," Set rumbled with a deep laugh in the back of my brain, "have you come to pledge fealty once again? I accept." Mockingly, sarcastic and caustic, Set was aware I wouldn't align with anyone who instigated such rivalry between us. I kept my thoughts shielded from him; there was no need to give him the means of my next step. I focused on the bee line between Set and myself. The shadows formed between us, the smoke collapsing into the shape of a man, half crouched with its canine eyes locked on me as he it swirled its carving knives in each hand. Anpu sneers as I close in on the few steps between us, few for us but running distance for the mortal men who had formed the column for us to meet. I could also feel Anpu's hatred of me. It was old and infantile resentment, smelling of mildew that pushed past the nose to the tongue so it could be tasted. I paid it no mind despite his foolish notion that we were peers in any form of prowess.

My slow walk turns from a jog to a leap, my arms wide with a blade to parallel each of his knives. Anpu, leaps to meet me, stubborn and feral as the domesticated canines he chose to lead. I slap him to the earth with flat of my left blade that he barely blocked with both of his knives in a clumsy cross. I follow with a stab from the right into the sand by his head, which I knew would cause him to roll away from into a crouch. I follow with a quick side blow to the side of his head from the hilt of my left sword. He sprawls on to all fours to catch his bearings and I kick him hard in the stomach to flatten him with his face in the sand.

"Yield," I say non-emotionally, in a matter of fact tone. As far as I was concerned, this conflict was over the minute it started. I wait for his answer as I yank my blade from the sand to refill my right hand. Anpu shutters blood, moving his mouth to begin an invocation and to let me know he still believed he stood a chance. I knew the words and knew this ended in paralysis of his target--me. My patience thin, I kick him again in the same place as he rose which flipped him on his side and send him skidding forward towards his uncle. I lock eyes with Set, take two steps forward starting with the left to stamp away the wickedness in the air, walk quickly through the air, land with my left blade piercing through Anpu's thighs and pin him to the earth. He screams as I lean into it. I watch Set flinch out of the top of my eyes and fight his urge to rush me. He has failed in his attachment to this small pet of his who hadn't spent nearly enough time to be considered a fair combatant. "Good puppy," I say, stroking Anpu's shoulder and smiling at Set. "Sit." Anpu screams curses at me and I shrug as if to say he had indeed revealed me as someone who slept with their mother before I brought my fist down like an effortless hammer onto his jaw to knock him silent and unconscious. I look up at the disoriented crowd; some appear shaken from their trance, the rest unsure if they fared better by my blade or Set's wrath.

"None will stand between us," I say, making sure Set could see the intent in my eyes. "I was wrong to stay uninvolved last time. When I am master of war for Kemet, I will ensure--"

"When *you?*" Set boomed, his giant projected head mocking and curt. "Take my essence and absorb my aspect, will you? You? The wet nurse?" He swings his spear to rest the haft on his shoulder, with the tip pointed behind him. "I look forward to seeing this accomplished," he smiled. "If you are the victor, then I will know I trained you well." I had been there in the Darkness when Set had driven the great Serpent from us, together locking it in a place without time or space. I had heard my father speak of other creatures of dangerous power and eternal hunger that existed beyond my reach, bubbling in chaotic atomic combustion with the will to consume existence itself if allowed access. It had been Set who had faced these terrors before I was born, not alone, but it had been he who had bore the full brunt of the attacks. Mortals, foot soldier to generals came to our schools that he built where they could learn strategy and warfare from its founder. Here I was blade in hand, positive I would be victor due to my cause.

I close cautiously, not the least bit fooled by his passively laid weapon. In fact, the closer I got to him, the less risk I felt I wanted to incur by relying on my blade alone that was a quarter the length of his spear. My beeline turned into a circling as I moved my awareness into my sword, feeling it stretch and lose the coolness of steel. Set must have sensed my distribution, for his arm telescoped out, just nicking my face with the edge of the spearhead when I dodged back. He nods to note my timing and counter circles against me. I twist my arm, bringing the staff behind me and the other hand in front as a guard. I was inside his range now, with a distance weapon to match his own. Set would attack faster; I knew him my better there but I would respond quicker as I had just proven. The danger would be in falling into trading blow for blow with him. His power was insurmountable and lethal with blunt objects, eviscerating with blades and crippling with that piercing spear tipped with a silvery metal that looked suspiciously similar to the kind I had brought back from the Middle. I, on the other hand, hold a long staff of the same metal that could match his range but would do little or no damage to any areas covered by his armor.

He sweeps in with the back haft, striking to the body, which I easily parry with a flicker up, which he reverses into and sends the head forward with a thrust. I bat it to the side with another parry and then the storm came. His thrusts were like rice rain on the horizontal, the spearhead darting at me thousands of times per second. I step, twist, circle, spin, and am able to catch most of them; those I did not left cuts in my armpit, arms, neck and legs. I begin backing up, knowing I was being positioned but unable to defend and hold the terrain. Set leaves the last thrust out too long; I counter by wrapping my left arm around the spear, trapping it against my body. I bring my right arm across low, the staff reverberating when it hit his knees and sweeps him. As he falls, he pulls up on his spear, launching me into the air and slamming me on my back behind him. The maneuver breaks the ribs on my left side where I land but I still hold his weapon pushed against my injured side. I drag myself up and allow the staff to revert to its blade form, hacking his spear into five pieces and kicking the head out of sight.

"Good show, Sekhem!," Set announces excitedly, his feral teeth showing against his black gums. "I was foolish to ignore my own pupil who has now mastered the master." My breathing is labored and it hurts to walk, but the blood in my mouth pushes me to walk forward to the unarmed Set. It was the same blood as Ma'at, the judgment of humanity's heart, my mother. It was the same blood as Djeuti, wisdom in reflection, my father. The same blood as Set, the elder brother of Djeuti and younger brother of Ausar, whom Set had slain in treachery and a thirst for power. This feud had lasted far too long and had become far too personal.

"I didn't learn that from you, fool," I spit, trying to conceal my bloodied gums and invoke his emotions to break his concentration.

"Then it is also good fortune that I did not instruct you on how to kill a lord of Kemet," Set mocks. "Surely you are still curious if you even can."

"No, I leave the murder of my own family to you the expert," I reply, jabbing at his pride. "I am only here to remove one last serpent in our grass." I continue my slow stalk towards him, gripping tight to the hilt of my blade. This was the same blade that had been forged in the green mountains of the north by those who called themselves the Middle. It was there that Heru and I had fled when our home in a cave overlooking the sea was discovered by Set and his Partisans that had been dispatched to remove us. As talented as Heru was, I was not sure my ward was ready for a conflict and had taken him to safety at his mother's request. We had sought allies among the Maati we had sent forward from Kemet to colonize the rest of unexplored world to the south and the north so many eras before. We were surprised to find a thriving new culture that cherished the way just outside the jungles to the north of Memphis.

These people informed us of Maati they had sent even farther north over the cold mountains that seems to touch the sky and through the deserts that burned the air from one's lungs. In transversing both of these elements, we found our way to the land of the Middle as well as a further continuation of the Way. What we saw as our ancestors, the Nun, the people of the Middle, measured reality in trigrams that could be cast to reveal what tomorrow held, similar to the way my father spoke to the tree in the center of our home. Heru revealed my arrogance in thinking all life must be uniform to Kemet and showed me how our relatives abroad must be celebrated for their adaptation to their new conditions. Therein, the people of the Middle's eyelids had grown thick and slanted to better protect their eyes against the harsh rays that Ra cast down from being so close. Their immortals spawned from the very hope of the people as it melded with the raw essence of the land much the same way mist is drawn from the ground in the morning and much the same way my entire family was born. We relearned from one another, trading our symbol-based writing for the art of body mechanics and martial prowess based on studying nature itself. Heru and I were schooled in new forms of conditioning and combat by melding ourselves with the sciences the people of the Middle used to answer their purpose. As a pledge between our enlightened sponsor and our exiled faction, the Middle kingdom crafted my blade from the strange metal buried within each of its hills. The same blade had cut through the copper swords of Set's Partisans upon our return to Kemet with claims to the throne. There was comfort and confidence in the interlocking of characters by brush and symbols by picture engraved into the blade that caught my eye as I walked forward.

"I am not out to slay you, uncle," I say through my teeth. "I am just going to hold you here until Heru arrives. If mercy prevails, he will only cut you into as many pieces as you left his father."

"Oh, is that all?" Set counters. "I was looking forward to my end at *your* hand. Perhaps I was naïve to think you could ever learn to finish that which you undertake." He knew that would set me off enough to let passion lead where caution was far more useful. I flinched to telegraph the blow, bringing his hands up to defend with a side step. Set was neither a fool nor an amateur. His ability to pluck a moving blade from the hands of an opponent was a skill he had eons to perfect before my birth. I swing again, looking to lop off his hands where the bracers on his arms ended to expose his flesh at the wrists.

The blow falls short as I felt the sharp sting in my back, just at the shoulder blade. I drop to one knee, my blade hanging from its strap about my wrist. Reaching with my left hand, my fingers found the shape of the blade in my back, a knife best suited for butchering game and poultry. I hear the laughter of Anpu in my head, realizing I had allowed him a clear line to throw from. Set steps forward, his hand breaking through the armor of my breast plate, fingers piercing into my torso and lifting me off the ground with a grip around my rib cage. The pain is beyond excruciating and I screamed as the world dangled below me through a haze.

"Tis a shame, Sekhem," Set whispered in my ear, his bloody eyes meeting mine. "While it would have pained me to bring your body back home to your mother, I was looking forward to describing how you fell to your cousin's treacherous blade. Now, imagine my disappointment. Yes, that's the word, at explaining how my pupil had become an accomplice to the hand of doom."

"Witnesses," I say, unable to prevent the blood from dripping from my mouth as I spoke, my lungs feeling both dry and filled with water. "Your betrayal shall be uttered for eternity from the lips of my men." Set lets out a long laugh, his head rolling back on his shoulders. He holds it long, each shake within his chest bringing me closer to the reality that I was going to die. I thought of Neith and whether she would care that her father had killed her husband.

"Dead men tell no lies," he both hisses and whispers with a burst of sobriety, his eyes burning into my face with the intent of bloody slaughter to any male wearing my coat of arms.

"Children, flee! Come no closer," is all I can gasp into the air, my broken face projected above the field next to Set's. Set had not expected me to use my powers and therefore had not prepared. Loyal to a fault, I heard the agony of defeat in cries of retreat from my men, their numbers scattering to the four winds. I smile one last time, watching myself fade away from a third person perspective.

Only I did not fade. The shape of Anpu flies across my vision, slamming into Set's knees and knocking him on his ass. When he falls again, he releases my crumpled body to the sand. Anpu's body had flown screaming by, almost a soccer ball being kicked at a goalie screaming in terror at its trajectory. My sight in this state catches the source of the flight. Heru stands where Anpu had once lay, sword hilt gripped in both hands, a crater in the ground where his catalytic legs had flung his younger half brother. He rushes forward, checking the pulse on my corpse and looking to the dazed traitors. The wheels turn in his head; he debates in seconds, which for him feels like an eternity. Decided, he lifts my body over his shoulder, reaching up with other arm to extend his fist. Magnetic, my perception is drawn back into my body and I feel the weight of my own flesh struggling for life. Grappling toward existence is pain; fleeing from the pain will mean the end of Sekhem Ka. There is a screech of a large bird and we are gone, my forearm clasped by the talons of the building-sized hawk flying away.

"Wherever you run, I shall chase," are Set's final words in our ear.

CHAPTER FOURTEEN

"Not on my life."

-Clay

I rolled out of bed onto the floor. I was crouched, covered in sweat, aware, and frightened. Awake. Just when I had grown accustomed to sleeping again, the nightmares return as full memories to reveal what I wish I did not know so clearly. The sheets on my bed were torn and shredded, spread across the room in pieces. The bottom sheet was soaked and kicked up at the corners. The bed frame was broken in several places. Had I thrashed so fiercely that so much damage could be done in the unconscious state? Perhaps it had been more than a dream, a looping reliving that my mind chose not to abandon? Xochi's words echoed in my head, *"time has not been kind to you."* What would be the time to the attribute hiding within the recesses of my very dna? What would be time to a being who had been born before measurement and had taught humanity the very points of reference it used to differentiate now from then? Thinking back to my linguistic studies, I remember that Mdw Ntr was without verb tense. One could read a hieroglyph and transliterate "was", "is" and "will be" all in one. Chinese and many of the Semitic languages required a determinative by the verb itself to predict tense; however, the language written on the back of my eyes had no such linguistic signals. What is time to those who do not believe in it or are the measurement itself? Memories millions of years ago might as well have been last night.

There was no sense in fronting as if I was going back to sleep any time soon. I pulled the sheets from the bed and dropped them in the trash, pulling my bath robe on and walking down the hall to check on Desta. He slept soundly, unmoving, breathing steadily like a ship at dock with a look of peace upon his little face. I whispered the eye into existence, a small

233

invisible cloud of lavender in the corner of his room that would allow me to watch him sleep in my mind. Then I returned to my room to shower and make up the bed. In the linen closet, I found over fifty different sets of sheets, some of which were still in their package, which led me to believe these nightmares were consistently hard on my bedding.

I made myself a quick snack out of a bowl of hot cereal and some sausages I grilled. I also included a tall glass of orange juice to replenish the electrolytes I had lost from sweating. I took my meal upstairs to the office. Flicking on the computer, I logged into Paper Thrones to start searching the archives. My brain swimming with new knowledge, I tried to focus on what stood out from seconds ago. Instead, I found myself sitting back, watching three duplicates of myself sitting in the same chair. One sat transcribing the night's dreams into my black, hard-backed moleskin journal while another simultaneously typed it into the archives. The third used key word searches to see what was already catalogued into the journals. There was also one watching the other, making what I guess was a total of four. Talk about multi-tasking.

I remembered Xochi's warning about such liberal uses of power but figured in the safety of my second home and at such a low level I risked no Paradox. My initial searches turned up blank until I crossed referenced "The Veil" with "Kemet." It would be the only reference and I thought it odd that the Veil was not more explicitly explained. The entry was a journal, apparently my own hand again, signed by me at the bottom. There was no date, but a note mentioned it had been recovered from a wealthy aristocrat of Greek origin who claimed his family had been descended from the philosopher Aristotle. Apparently the entry was translated from a scroll brought out of the library that would later be dubbed Alexandria (wasn't on my watch) before its consumption in flames at the accidental hands of Caesar. I read the text aloud to make sure I was gaining comprehension.

"Father met me at the small lake behind our home. To call it a lake would be ambitious. It was a pond with that was fed from a subterranean creek bed and bled into the ocean through an underground stream. The elders of the Narmer met and went to a resolution. Although no longer Pharaoh, through his son Ausar had seen to a group process. Those of my generation were asked to depart the throne room while our elders debated beyond what we could comprehend, and we obeyed dutifully. The arguments were clear but as flawed on either side as

the messengers who championed them. Set, held no secret in his desire to return to military conquest as the means to guide our wardens. Only through dominion and trepidation would the strongest arise in the mortals to uphold our Way and defend it against the serpents swimming in the bottom of creation. No one us would refute Kemet's military prowess under Set but who would dare point out the myopia of Set's vision when it was in direct opposition to his brother's vision. No one but I was ejected from the chamber. Not even wise Ausar, speaking through his son's brutal wisdom, would confirm his suspicions of the brother who had shredded his body to the four winds. No acknowledgement would be given to the messenger, only that military conquest had come at a savage and feral price in the development of the humans we were entrusted to protect.

Instead, Ausar restated his position that as the very Earth spread apart, splitting the land into massive islands too far to ride across, the distance between East and West became too far to treat as one kingdom. The world Ausar spoke to us from was Western, past the harvest, while his son dwelled with us in the land of the East, before the Flood. Therefore, it would be necessary to construct a bridge between the two lands. It would be a thinly layered construct that would not only allow passage from our lands but prevent the humans from crossing over to our realm before abandoning the feral nature of their mortal physicality. The Veil, as my father named it, would also summon the very thoughts and feelings of the populations of this world, sending them to our very throne for the Narmer to shape and guide at one central location. As I left the chamber, our elders excused the remainder of my generation, save for Heru who spoke for Ausar.

Leaving the chamber, I waited for Neith at the steps down to the road. She caught my gaze and held it as she walked by emotionlessly. Though she would not speak out against her husband, her distance signaled her displeasure. I bowed low as she passed, paying face to her temper in front of her relatives and the humans in the city watching us. There would be little to discuss as it would take time for her icy hot anger to subside at the notion of her husband directly opposing her father. Face must be paid to her family as much my face must be to my own. Yet my objection had not come as the duty to my father, his loyalty to Ausar, or my loyalty to his son and my disciple Heru. Instead, my loyalty was to my mother, Ma'at, who had taught me to always match my discipline against the voices in the heart. My heart had told me that sending a horde to the four winds would be the end of Kemet.

So I sit alone, stirring the layers of the lake with a twig, watching the ripples. I saw his reflection in the waters, standing behind me. His tall, lithe frame is matched by the Ibis head on his next and his scrolls under his arm pushed against his torso. As he cleared the fabric of the linen away from his legs, he simultaneously squatted at the water's edge and allowed his head to shift to its human aspect. I felt his hand on my shoulder and I was surprised at my age how relieved his touch could be for me.

"Back to stirring the waters," *I hear the rumble of his low and raspy voice in my ear. I watch his warm brown eyes on either side of his long bird-like nose symmetrical to his long black locks that fell from his head. Legend tells he was born with them, a sign of full knowledge as a child. I nodded silently, continuing to poke at the water, avoiding impaling any of the local fish.* "You always came here when you were troubled as a child. You dig at the bottom and watch how the dirt settles. I wonder if you think you are the stick or the soil?"

"The water itself," *I replied, sullen and quiet.* "Have I really not changed so much since I was child?" *He smiled and tapped me on the shoulder before placing his hand on his lap.*

"No, you have grown into quite the fine young man. Your mother and I often discuss how wonderful it is to have met the adult you. However, our comforts seldom change."

"I apologize if I spoke out of turn at the chamber," *I say, frustrated.*

"While you have always been more outspoken than your siblings," *Djeuti continued,* "we have always treasured your passion regarding your values."

"We?" *I asked.*

"Your mother and I. You always make us proud"

"I returned with the prince with war at my heels."

"But you served your lord with duty. Heru's will was no small matter. I am more pleased by your honor than offended by your hand in the conflict." *There was silence for a long while as we both watched the settling of the mud to the bottom of the lake.*

"Are we to go to war again, Father? Who will burn this time for Kemet's way? I will not serve under Set--"

"That will not be necessary. The Narmer has decided upon the construction of the Veil," *my father answers.*

"That does not quiet my heart anymore than the alternative. Who are we to shape the growing world? To decide between the civilized and those who are not."

"*You ask penetrating questions. Questions I do not know the answer to, Sekhem. Do you know what was before us? Before my brothers and sisters?*"

"*The humans ate their dead. They roamed, killing animals without utility, fighting even amongst themselves for the smallest seed of the earth,*" I reply.

"*Yes, and Ausar, being the first, still remembers. I suspect the memory chills his being far worse than his own murder. Now with the sight of the next world, he has seen a future where the humans will treat our father Geb with a savagery surpassing any the humans showed one another at their beginning. This vision terrifies him in proportion to his adoration of the development of the humans.*"

"*So you believe the Veil will prevent this future? A redirection away from a land where the human itself is not in oppression of the land?*" I ask.

"*I am not certain, my son. I trust Ausar. He is not only my elder but my brother. His insight is something of virtue that I place my trust in.*" He studied the water's surface for a time and then dipped his feet in. "*I also rest easier in focusing Set's ambition elsewhere, away from the throne.*"

"*And where will that be?*" I ask.

"*The southern kings have informed us of something that fell from Nut in the desert. It has buried itself deep beneath the sand, leaving a trail of some new metal we have not seen before.*" The great Djeuti cocks his head to look around and studies me for a moment. He extended his arm around my shoulder to pull me closer. "*In confidence I tell you this. Do not make it public knowledge. Khpr tells me it is the same metal as that you wear on your hip, the blade you brought back from the Middle.*" He stood and walked deeper into the pond, the hem of his lower garments shrinking up to avoid the water. "*I do not remember this lake being this cool.*"

"*Tell me of the new metal,*" I queried.

"*You tell me,*" he said with a smile, reminding me I was not as passive in this exchange as I made myself out to be.

"*It is unlike our copper, much stronger. Silvery in color, but it does not bend and takes far more to heat to melt than silver. Heru's blade is made of the same metal as mine, although far denser.*"

"*The yellow men of the north must have fancied his two-handed grip,*" Djeuti mused.

"*The Middle,*" I corrected.

"*Forgive me,*" Djeuti whispered, "*I have neither travelled to the lengths my son has nor have I committed his journals to memory as of yet.*"

"I see, Father. If Set is to head the excavations, who will man our defenses?" I ask.

"Neith," he replies, looking off into the distance at the city toward the East. "As we speak, she is on route to pay tribute to our ancestors at Gebel Barkal and ask for their guidance."

"Really? Her father's idea?"

"Mine. We require Set's works for construction of the Veil."

"Who could object to a father castrating his own son," I murmur, disappointed.

"It would be wise for you to focus on the task at hand, Sekhem. The prince has requested you as his vizier."

"I will want Khonsu and Serekh Ba near me to help administrate if I am to work on infrastructure."

"Khonsu you will have. Your younger brother we will send to Indus Kush as representative of our priests to encourage the Maati."

"You have robbed me of all my faculties. I suppose I am to be all things to all people?"

"Anpu shall answer to you in all things," my father responds.

"And you place a thorn in my boot to add insult. I was wrong to think you were not displeased with me, Father."

"Sekhem, you are defeatist and negative. Your people named you for your will to overcome not for the holes you seem to poke in the very fabric of all plans." Djeuti returned to the shore, looking down upon me. "I will trust you to uphold the vision. One of a Kemet that is greater than the divisions of our family. What hope is there for our children in the villages and by the river's edge, if we ourselves cannot see past our old wounds?"

"I will do as you ask, Father," I say, looking past him into the water. "I wish to be alone again." He nods with approval but his eyes showed his disappointment and hurt. Once again, being a good son in public, had made us more distant at home. I dropped my stick in the lake and produced a parchment on which to write.

I trailed off the last words, feeling the sadness of the moment as if it were new. Something told me father and son had not spoken since that day. It was an empty place in my chest that gnawed and fed the burned feelings of my own abandonment. My hands found there way to the keyboard, pulling up a browser to view a link. Cat Steven's "Father and Son" played softly on the computer speakers. I had accurately fooled myself into not feeling any sense of loss at my murdered parents. I had failed at fooling myself I did not need any guidance or familial allegiance to call my own. Granny only softened the blow and meeting Horace stripped me of my illusion of isolation. Then there was an ancient sense of duty and need for validation from a man, if he could be called that, I did not know. I found old hatred buried under guilt. It united Sekhem Ka and me. We both sought to serve justice for a traitor's punishment; we both shared hatred of the Isfet satisfied only by obliteration and we both ached for our missing fathers.

I cross-referenced a few more things that stood out in my mind. No leads. I also admitted there were new terms I was afraid to use; in fact, I decided I would use my uncle's name in my head sparingly. From that moment on the word for a pair would be used to describe two of anything as opposed to a set. *Breathe.* Think. I stared out the window at the city, wondering if Granny was able to sleep without nightmares. Wouldn't that be a fair tradeoff? I wondered how deep the mystery went. Would Granny tell me I was crazy or would she make me a cup of coffee, stroke the small of my back and let me know she knew this day would come eventually. "Baby, sometimes we just gon accept we got an Egyptian god inside us. What chu gon do? Run from it? Don't have me pull out the strap and whip you into shape, boy!" I missed her counsel. I missed Djeuti. I wondered if Heru and I were not the only ones free and roaming the earth in human costumes. Perhaps Djeuti had been Clay's father, murdered by foul play rather than the accident of a narcotic induced madness. I no longer trusted my past.

I could not be certain about who I was or if the many haphazard coincidences that culminated Clay's personal history were nothing more than a design in some elaborate scheme meant to out-think my own subconscious. I would have to explore my pain, my own, as well as the entity I carried within, in order to find out what was being hidden. It would suck harder than the penises Dewayne Carter placed in his mouth in order to get his check from an older male who called himself Baby but claimed to be his father. This was going to ache like no other. Walking barefoot across nails while drinking broken glass would feel more comforting compared to this work. This was going to floor me. I shook up the mud in my pool from a restful stability I had constructed though years of applying my schooling to myself. In that pain, I knew I would break through my own Veil in my mind. There it was. I typed in "Veil", "pain", "father", and "loss." The entry was there.

Our stay here will shortly come to an end. We have learned we can from the Dogon and their intricate charts depict the war between Apep and the Isfet. There is no comfort in their knowledge, only the inevitability that soon the western coast of this continent will soon be subject to the Isfet dominion. We assumed that remaining invisible and unknown to the people in the great city north of these caves would keep them free of our pursuers. Khonsu informs me the enemy is on the march, his brutal Partisans leading the charge. Who knows what he will do to that gorgeous place of learning. Preserve it? Pervert it as he did Greece, Rome and Indus Kush? Burn it as he ordered my father's library in Memphis? The pain still haunts me to know every scroll Djeuti meticulously wrote for the humans is no more. For what? Spite? Would Set chase us all over the corners of the Earth? Maybe it was futile to continue our flight, for standing was equally useless. For all we knew, Djeuti could be one of the turned, helping to dog our steps, allowing us no more than a hundred years in one location before the nightmare fog showed itself on the horizon.

Heru assures me such thoughts are defeatist and my father is bound like the rest of our family in that disgusting Nest adhered to the sky above Kemet. Fearless as always, Heru used his discipline over the Kwk works to change his form into a simulacra of those horrid crawlers, penetrating deep into their cocoon. There he found the rest of our family who were neither aligned to Set nor free like us. In process, the creatures moved our family in bound cocoons to other points along the Veil, galvanizing their hold and influence upon the very reality of humans. Ausar would not be moved, his form bound to the Essence itself. There the weakness was exposed as they broke Ausar's form back into its pieces and struggled to move him each at a time. Heru is convinced with time we can revive his father into a carrier body.

With Ausar risen, we would have the throne and therefore have direct control over the very Veil the enemy uses to spread its empire. Although the process of doing a Reconciliation in an adult can kill a Carrier, Heru is convinced a small child could survive the process, provided the child was close to our blood line. Unfortunately, none of the Nehesy made the voyage outside of the Veil. Time suggests we wait; patience and subtlety will resolve the answer. Although my ego would suffer, it has occurred to me that the Olympian Athena is more swayed by my mastery of the Imnt works than her own father's thunder. She could be persuaded that a child of Kemet and Greece could hold the traits necessary for the Reconciliation. Soon we will sail west on the black current, leaving this conti-

nent forever. Access to Kemet will become for more difficult. Perhaps I will barter with her, playing weak to her guiles, if she can be used to see what we cannot. Ultimately the Greek is enticed by playing both sides against one another. Aggravating this circumstance could prove useful until it turns ugly.

Time is up. The first of the enemy's scouts have been sent to meet the lords of Timbuktu. We will need to sail shortly. Father, if you can hear me, I am not leaving you. I will just take longer to get this right for you. Neith, why are you not at my side?

I logged off the computer and checked on Desta. He slept soundly as I watched him from my mind's eye. I stretched out in the newly redressed bed, wondering how sound my sleep would be. I decided I'd leave a piece of me in the room to monitor him in case he stirred. As I felt my awareness shift, changing from Huh's control over to actually being in the room to Imnt's range over the mind. I began to notice my own mind playing tricks with me. If I looked through a Huh lens, I saw a small boy curled in a ball, peacefully asleep. Through the Imnt lens, a grown man of green complexion sat at the edge of the bed reading from the world Atlas I had placed in the room for Desta. I bolted upright in bed, taking a few steps before arriving in the bedroom. There slept Desta unmoved. I switched to the Imnt lens, flooding the room with lavender shades of either deep purple or light pastel, depending on how close I was to the other occupant. The green man stood naked before me. The bags under his eyes seeming nearly fifty years old, his physique no more than thirty but his tired smile being timeless. I knew him well. He was my father's elder and my uncle. Ausar, the lord of the day. I felt my mouth curling to squawk in sheer reactionary disbelief, but his green finger over my lips prevented it. Then he motioned with his head to the bed where a sleeping boy lay. I nodded in recognition. His smile grew less tired and he walked out of the room, beckoning me to follow.

I followed him to my bedroom, where his hand motioned like a conductor's. Lying on the bed, motionless on his back except for his closed and fluttering eyelids was me; Clay. Ausar made a motion as if suggesting I should sit on the bed and walked through me to return to Desta's room. His body language expected his gracious request to be fulfilled. I wasn't done inquiring due to so much new information but found it impossible to follow him to Desta's room. In fact, I was exhausted and felt pulled toward myself like a bit of spinach from a plate spiraling down the kitchen sink toward the garbage compactor. Pulled now, I can't think. Clay's eyelids are magnetic.

Ausar is dead and the people have mourned through the flood. Our queen is missing as well. Set has assumed the throne as vizier until the status of the kingship can be determined. Anpu, son of Ausar and Neb-het, is expected to be named heir. In a few hours, Neith, Set's only blood heir, will pick her husband, aligning any suitor's house with her own. Gossip, if one paid attention to such chatter, puts Neith with Anpu, locking in Set's hold over the kingdom both by dominion and inheritance. My morning has been troubled. Quietly, away from any ears of those who work in our house, my mother shared with me that she has evidence it was Set who in fact murdered Ausar and not the Kushites to the south. If such things were repeated aloud, one might disappear in the night at the hands of the storm lord's Partisans. For most of my life, I have trained under Set, his chief spearman in the boat that leads across the waters bringing light to the world. Many a time, we were confronted by the serpents who slept in the depths, led by their progenitor, Apep, whose hunger led to our boat time and time again.

When my spear failed, my uncle's was true, goring the beast and coloring the sky with its blood. There came a certainty of his purpose that I relied on. In fact, I had abandoned my father's ways of the law and scribe as dogmatic and soft, wishing privately I had been born of the house of Set with claims to his nobility and strength at the end of a weapon. Now I felt sick with shame and regret. I had been cruel and disrespectful to my father's warning, only to hear my mother's cool words as her mastery over works replayed the scene in detail of our king's murder. Disgusted by my naivety, I secluded myself to our concentration chamber, an indoor garden at the center of our ancestral home built around an enormous cedar tree.

I wished so hard I was a man, treated with and given the respect of adulthood. Now at its cusp, I found it hard to swallow and clinched my stomach with grief. Unable to eat or sleep, I burnt incense and stared at the tree. To think it was I who built the box for my uncle, thinking it would trap and hold a serpent. Hubris, my own selfish quest for recognition that had been the instrument that led to Ausar's death. In the morning, when Ra returned to the sky, I would watch another travesty as Neith picked her husband.

Though it was easy to hide my feelings about her as a child, this would only make my world uglier and somehow darker. She had been the tag-along I was expected to play with as a child, but who wants to be slowed down by a girl? Not just any girl, but one who can run faster, kick harder, climb higher and received only praise for her acts. Maybe I should have told my mother I chose not to continue her school in lieu of Set's academy just to gain some form of recognition from his daughter. A lot of good it did.

I feel now I am not alone; eyes watch me. Scanning the area, my ears detect masked, heavy breathing from above. There in the tree, high in the branches, sitting quietly in observation, are my watchers. They do not know I have spotted them with their foolish grin, enjoying the false sense of blindness I am projecting. I stand as if heading to the door to leave the garden, only to run up one of the support columns to the roof and spring off to the tree. I land on a branch and climb easily as any time before to sit myself next to one of my spectators. Her smile widens as I pretend not to see her and stare at where her eyes were directed before. Her eyes glow in the darkness, emphatic green spirals that contrast against her ebon and gilded skin. She is barely clothed, wearing only a cloth over her genitals, her chest bare and glistening. The tree was no exertion for her. That must be water on her skin; she started her days swimming in the ocean.

"I looked for you at the lake, but you were not there," she says, smiling wide and burning holes into the side of my face with her eyes.

"I was not there," I reply, staring down at the garden.

"Of course not," she chimes, "so I came here. You are predictable like that." She giggled and kissed my cheek. I pulled away at the last moment. Her smiled faded. "Have I offended you?"

"Respect for my cousin, Anpu," I murmur, still unable to make contact with those eyes and be betrayed by their spell. "Your future husband," I finish.

"I see," she said, locking her ankles under the next lower branch and leaning forward. "And pray tell, when is this to happen?"

"You tell me," I said, finally making eye contact. "You are the one getting married at the day's beginning."

"It is an announcement, nothing more," she says. "Politics and performance to support my father. As far as whom I chose at my side, it will not be as easily surmised by the likes of courtesans and throne room gossip." She let her eyebrows droop, watching me with a pierce to her gaze. "You are not attending, are you?"

"No," I reply, swinging my feet slightly against the branch. "I will wait here until it is over. By the morning after festivities, I'll begin my mother's school with the goal of being moved to one of the colonies."

"As an initiate?"

"If need be. I want no extra consideration."

"My father expects you in his . . . "

"I am no Partisan nor will I take any part in any further plots to divide this family." Her cheeks flush and her eyes became cold. She attempted to look through me and found only the mirror she had. The same mirror she had held up to me most of my life. They had paired us from birth, having both emerged from our parents on the same day. Neith from Set and Neb-het. I from Djeuti and Ma'at. It was expected that Set's successor would be male and Ma'at's successor would be female. Irony ran deep in this family and so Neith became my childhood friend.

Twins, they titled us, although our demeanors pulled us farther from the birth date that pegged us together. As a child, I resented her finding a way into any activity I found for myself outside of school or my duties to my parents. Damned if she wasn't better at it too, shoving me out of the way in the minds of those giving praise. When we both began adolescence, she became my friend and confidant. We shared secrets in the dark via the balcony outside her bedroom window or the tree in the center of my ancestral home. Somewhere from there, she became my mirror, showing me what I did not want to see, keeping me from inflating myself too much, and listening near the breaking points. Now, prepared to lose it all, I found no hesitation in reflecting it back. In fact, I found myself processing all the moments I had bit my tongue about to seem nobler than I was or my fear of her rejection to something I saw.

"You are just full of rumors tonight, aren't you?" she sulks through silted eyes and teeth. "Anything to stay out of a position that pushes your potential, eh?"

"Potential," I say nodding, "this is about me? Me? You were an untamable storm free from any lasting bond until your father came into power. Now you sit next to me swinging your legs like a travelling performer, playing coy and clueless, as you flirt with me the night before your sham of a marriage?"

"If it is such a sham," she growls, "you will support me and be there when I make my decision."

"I will not, Neith. You mistake me for one of your noblemen easily swayed by your empty promises." She struck out, the speed of a stab with the force of a hook. I stopped her hand at the wrist. "You, Neith, daughter of Neb-het, will be the first to stop telling me what I should be doing." I release her hand and pushed off the branch, falling a few stories below and landing in a crouch. I stand, walking toward the exit from the garden, expecting the conversation to end. The rushing in my ears, the heat added to my skin, the change in breathing and the detail to my vision told me someone was invoking works in my presence. I stepped in a *shuffle to the side and turned forty-five degrees to my right, kicking the back of her legs as she passed. Neith is furious and holds back no force from her blows as she misses with her kick, skids through the dirt and launches back at me from the ground. Punch, punch, palm, knee, duck, kick, predictable and wild. Negated at every attempt, it only fuels her aggression.*

"Stop, Neith," I say, after her last swing had her arm wrapped behind her head and my right leg behind both of hers.

"Are you coming to the ceremony?" she asks, panting and sniffling through her tearful frustration. Her sweat smells like the ocean, clean and full of movement.

"Not on my life," I say through clenched teeth. "Now go home and get ready for your cousin." She nods and lets her shoulders shrug as if submitting. Then, her body drops to her knees, her frame a blur as it bends over before me. She rises with the other arm, elbow connecting to my chin and I see white pinholes in a black tunnel. I focus and see I am flying through the air, elevated by her blow and aware she was hitting with force meant to kill. I curl my body and direct the spin, landing on my feet in the midst of the lake behind my parent's house. The waters do not splash when I land; they are silently spreading and reforming around my waist. I hold myself there, calling a light orb, translucent and close, expecting her at any moment. Neith is talented but arrogant. She assumes I have never studied her or am unaware of her tactics. When the watery form appears from my blind side, throwing its full weight behind its attack, I am not surprised. Neith is thorough and the velocity of her assault repels her back along the water like a dart. Her body hits a rock the pond's edge where it dips to feed out to the sea by underground current and produces a shriek as she is laid out on the shore, losing her liquid form. It is one step to appear next to her, grabbing her head by the hair and posing my fist so her fluttering eyelids could see it.

"Beaten," I say, feeling tears pour from my face. "You are no longer here to one-up me or push me." I shake her head until her eyes focus and she regains consciousness. "It stops tonight, Neith. No more competing. Leave me be. I'm done, Neith." I drop her head to the soil and walk back toward the house.

"Get some sleep," I hear Neith call after me, groggy and slurring. "You will need it for tomorrow."

My eyes open. The sheets were wet and shredded.

Chapter Fifteen

"Develop competitive advantage. A sustainable one at that."

-Harrison

They were serving roast chicken with gravy, green beans and cinnamon apple compote for dinner. You can smell it in the elevator as it permeates everything crack in the sterile metallic box. The doors opened and I stepped on to the first floor into the hallway. Most residents were in the dining common to my right, either chewing with open mouths, enjoying conversations of half-finished sentences or being spoon fed by an attending nurse. I wanted to be greeted but was invisible to the caregiver and resident alike as I walked the hallway toward the loneliest room in the world.

The radio was on, a small boom box that played a burnt CD of Ella and Louie on repeat. The curtains were drawn shut. The room was dark except for the bed side lamp with one bulb lit by its pull chain. She lay in bed, gray straight hair brushed to either side of her face, cheeks shallower than the last time I remembered; she was eating less. Her eyes were glassy and lacked a focus you generally got with people when you talked to them. She stared at the ceiling, cute and adorable in her powder blue bathrobe and matching wool gloves. Top sheet, a thin blanket and a comforter all layered across her neck. It was one of the rare times she was awake and I was glad.

I pulled up a chair from her desk, where I hear she paints in watercolors whenever I am not around. Convenient. I placed the chair by the bed and sat so she could easily see my face; eye contact was everything.

"Granny?" I whispered, soft and questioning. Who knew what would come out. It had been so long since we both talked. I rubbed my hand along the area of her forearm between her perfect gloves and sleeve of the bathrobe, counting on the warmth of my touch to notify her I was in proximity. She blinked slowly and turned her head to face me as I repeated her name. Her eyes found me and her mind cycled like roulette to match my face, voice, touch, name and memory so that she could determine if I was safe. Children do the same thing when some one calls their name with urgency. Then connecting all points, she lost some of the glass to her stare and smiled warmly at me. *Contact.*

"Roland," she said, moving her hand to grip mine. "Oh, I missed you, sweetie." She pulled me forward slowly for her embrace and kissed my forehead. I smelled denture adhesive and gingivitis on her breath, but made no indication to her. The hug felt good, better than Xochi's or Heru's, but it was not for me. It belonged to my father, Roland Durward.

"How are you?" I found difficult to say and keep in character with a man I didn't know enough to talk to, much less imitate or impersonate.

"Good . . . okay," she said in a soft voice, stroking my face.

"They treatin' you okay in here," I asked earnestly.

"Yes, baby. Momma can take care of herself," she said with pride. "Besides, they are very nice people here."

"That's good to hear," I replied, noting the shake in my tone and attempting to mask it; she must have noted it because her head cocked slowly and her palm rested on my chin.

"You look worried," she said softly.

"Tired but not worried," I quipped back, making sure I was neither brusque or somber.

"Your boy," she said, not hearing me, moving her hand to scratch one furry palm with the fuzzy fingers of her other hand. "I worry too, you know. I watch him when he sleeps. So restless--" she pauses trying to form words. "You don't think he skipped the bug, do you?" Hold on to your seats, we've encountered some turbulence and are raising altitude to adjust.

"The bug?" I said, trying to sound informed while genuinely needing clarification. "I don't remember him being sick."

"No," she said with a chuckle that sounded more like chiding than being humored. "The bug we're trying to kill." I didn't even notice the gloves had been removed when her hand reached past my ear, under my sweatshirt and on to my neck between the shoulders. Then, as I felt the weak twinge of malevolent life there, her hands returned to her lap where she began working her fingers into her gloves again. It was confirmation on the most painful of platters. The captain has activated the seat belt sign above the head rest. Please assist us by remaining in your seats until we are given the indication of your safety.

"What did we try already?" I asked. "Are you sure it didn't work?"

"You never give me too many details, Roland. Secretive. That is your father in you."

"I see. So what makes you believe the bug is in him."

"He's got the walking sleep like you and your father. The crib is enough for now but I worry when he gets older and starts walking."

"Well, we'll just keep up with the plan--"

"What plan? You and that wife of yours were so sure it would end. Don't think I don't hear the arguments. That baby hears it. too. Probably knows that he's the reason you twp aren't having any more kids"

"I didn't realize you were so aware," I said with a fading smile, strangely intrigued by Granny's juicy tidbits. However, in that moment of glee, I broke character. Granny's eyes became glassy as I talked.

"Clay?" she asked, feeling around on my arm and disoriented.

"Yes, Granny, it's me."

"I had a dream I was talking to your daddy." She seemed alarmed and lost.

"That sounds nice. What did you talk about?" I was trying to steer this to pleasant.

"I can't tell you that, baby. A mother has to keep some of her son's secrets." Her head slowly pressed back to the pillow. "I'm so tired," she mumbled as her eyes closed. Just like that, she was asleep, leaving me alone again. Alone in knowing that like two generations before me I carried a spider in my spine and a kingdom in my blood stream. I waited another half hour at her bedside before accepting that she wouldn't be waking up. It was a sad and somber walk out her room into an empty lobby. I felt a sense of defeat and a temptation to go lie in my own bed, pull the covers over my head and well wish the world from my brain. Then I felt the eyes on me and turned to see Mr. Wobogo smiling at me from his open doorway. I smelled myrrh incense and could make out Roy Ayers and Ubiquity's "The Memory" playing from his background. He walked back into his room and out of sight, leaving his door open behind. I looked around to make sure no other pair of eyes were on me and walked into Mr. Wobogo's room.

I closed the door behind me to find him at his desk. There were large sheets of drafting paper on the desk and measuring tools such as a slide rule, compass and a large eraser. I could see on his wall various drafts of his previous renditions which he was working to improve. Seated at his table, he was going over his pencil lines in a blue pen to finish each blue print. From the looks of it, it was a massive throne that looked tribal yet Victorian steam age. I pulled up a stool next to him and debated how much attention it would attract to communicate with him. I decided I was sick of living in my head and far too lonely for the normal world. I reached my hand over to touch my palm to the back of Harrison's head where his skull curved down his shoulders. His shoulders raised some and I got a look of concern. I looked back into his eyes and tried my best to indicate he should have no worries from me. Then I swam through my mind's eye, down my neck, into the shoulders, past my wrist, into the palm, and inside to Harrison's blood stream.

He jumped and his back became taut as we were joined. I was heat pushing through his circulatory system until I found the back of his brain. I could feel the dark cloak of venom pumped upward from where his Passenger lay wrapped around his spine. I wasn't sure what confronting the creature directly would do. Even if I killed it, I might kill Harrison in the process. Instead, I drew an Orb around myself and swam closer to his brain. There it was, a wet coral reef of plaque enveloping the surface area of his brain which seemed like a covering or a mesh of sinuous spider webs, depending on the angle you examine it from. It covered more than half of his brain, spiraling down to his spine, where I suspected his passenger had begun weaving it. I remember the Isfet webs as being nearly imperious to cutting but highly flammable. How did one create a blaze within liquid? Would it even be possible? What would Heru do? I focused and tried to call the fire to my hands.

Back in the stool, staring off into space, my palm on Harrison's skull. That was a miserable fail; the Chinese would call it sut bai. The attempt must have been too much, bringing me back to basics. I focused again on my palm, feeling myself breathe and being in the moment. Relaxing the vision in my eyes, I was aware of Harrison's breathing as I aligned my own to it. I swam through my mind's eye into his, appearing in an empty theater full of dust and decay. Strung from the corners and ceilings were glistening cobwebs, empty of inhabitants but making me nervous for my blade nonetheless. The stagecraft was leaned against the walls, the paint looking diminished and reduced under the layer of dust. I thought I stood under a single spotlight only to realize it was a beam from the sunlight channeled through a single open skylight. My entrance and my exit. I looked out into the gloom and made out no surprises waiting in the orchestra pit or the stands of pews.

That established, I hopped down to ground floor from the stage. There were no stairs down to the grand hall. My shoes brought up a small cloud of dust. I was tempted to cough until I realized I was in Harrison's mind; breathing wasn't actually happening. Before me in the dust were footprints, small and barefoot. I guessed them no bigger than four inches and male by the flatness of the step. My heart leapt to my throat almost expecting to find Desta here, but logic and the reassurance I needed pushed that from my mind. Carefully, I tracked them to their first stop: a shallow alcove on the stage right aisle, slanted upward to the other entrance. There were numerous burnt-out matches and marks in the dust as if some small body had spilled several drops of liquid on the floor. I bent to touch them and rubbed it in my fingers. Slippery with a hint of bubble. Soap suds.

The footprints led from that spot down a row. I stood again, reaching my hand up to the candle-style lantern mounted in the alcove. My fingers found the wick and I uttered the words necessary to begin the spark. The lantern lit to life but didn't just stop there. One by one the wicks of each of the lamps in the alcoves along the circumference of the hall birthed flame. They illuminated the room. I could now see the theater was two stories high--a main hall and a balcony. Seated in the row parallel to me sat a boy, back erect and pushed against the chair he sat in. His legs came over the lip by a bit, wearing a pair of work pants that had been cut at the knees to imitate shorts. They were hung on his body by a set of small red suspenders with painted clasps that that were exceptionally shiny compared to the grease on his faded blue shirt near his shoulders. His hair was high off his brown skin and was neither unkempt nor shaped. The child's tiny hands patted his thighs rhythmically without making a sound. Watching the way the frames of his glasses moved on his ears as he inhaled and exhaled, I saw the man he would grow to one day be in his detailed mannerisms.

Cautiously, mindful not to disturb the bucket of sudsy water on the floor of the row by his right foot, I walked towards him and took a seat with a space between us. His gaze didn't shift when the weight of my body made the chair squeak; his eyes remained focused forward.

"Harrison," I whispered slowly, not sure if it would get his attention.

"Grandson," he replied in the whisper of a young boy deep with Southern accents and a high pitched rasp I hadn't expected. "You are right on time."

"For what, Grandpa?" I queried.

"The Magician," he said excitedly, pushing the big Coke bottles onto his face with his nimble fingers that were rightly sized for his body despite his lenses being too large for the shape of his face. I suspect there was no Lens Crafters in the 1940's, at least none that allowed Negroes to patronize it.

"When does the performance start?"

"They can't perform in here," he fired back, indicating with an arm at the hall and the stage props. "Not like this. Too much mess." He was annoyed at me.

"Why don't we clean it?" I said, reaching my hand down to the pail's handle and starting to lift my body from the seat.

"No," Harrison replied, putting his hand on my forearm and his eyes quaking behind the glasses. "Don't wake the monster."

"Monster?" I said, rather arrogantly with too much doubt in my voice for my family, let alone for the small child sitting worried before me.

"The monster," Harrison replied, taking his hand off my arm and pointing upward. I followed his gaze toward the ceiling covered with shimmering cob webs. The closer the ceiling got to the balcony and the entrance, the thicker and larger the web got until I realized the entrance was wrapped in a silk tunnel. "The monster is sick," he continued, "so it sleeps now. If you wake it up, it will hurt me." I nodded and looked back to his face.

"Harrison," I said calmly, but with a firm tone.

"Yes, Grandson," he replied, causing me to pause. There was a hint of a smile on his face which led me to believe he enjoyed the roles of being both my elder as well as my ward. I laughed a bit to break the tension and he played with my hair.

"I beat up monsters now," I said, with a growl and a crinkle on the skin of my nose. "And I'm going to beat the living shit out of this one"

"Really?" he said excitedly.

"No," I replied, his shoulders dropping. "But I am going to keep it from hurting you while we clean, okay?" His energy changed immediately, hopeful but still not comprehending. I wasn't sure I understood either. I stood and studied the problem once more. The balcony entrance was a quarter of the size of the tunnel on the ground floor entrance. It was an assumption but I figured the lack of webbing of the upstairs portal meant whatever creepy crawly that was hiding in the lobby couldn't fit through the balcony opening and the only access it had was through the ground floor. I reached my hand out, feeling the energy swirl in my palms, the right a positive charge, the left a negative charge; a sphere of dynamics between the two hands. *Niaw*, the meter of motion, principle of the universe without rest was summoned to my mind. I pictured everything I could that reminded me of my goal: MAC trucks barreling down 880 South, fire crackers exploding on strings at New Year's Parades along Market St., corks on champagne bottles flying from the mouth into the air, the flash as a round leaves the nozzle of a four pound in Marin City and Bonds slamming a fast ball over the Virgin America billboard into McCovey Cove. My hands surged, the room turns a pink tint that I cannot decide if only I see or the actual scene has changed as I impose my will upon it. The more I pushed, the deeper the shade becomes until my vision is swimming in a crimson hue and the balcony doors yank from the wall and slam shut. Then my hands drain as the heaps of trash and random building materials fly from the floor to block the closed balcony door.

I heard a tingle-like bells and wet coconuts being knocked together. I wished it was a Monty Python skit but knew better. I ran over to one of the props and pull a loose two by eight from the construct, holding it near the lantern and begin uttering. As I waited, the board's tip ignites and I pull it back, letting the flame reach the first two feet before I calm it. Holding the burning board, I turn my gaze upon the little Wobogo.

"Harrison."

"Yes?"

"Stand by the stage, in the middle," I instructed him. The motion in my periphery told me he is complying. I walked up the aisle toward the main entrance, gauging my approach against the sounds and vibrations on the strands connected to the ceiling down the hallway. The closer I stepped, I could hear numerous whispers. Familiar. Not my Passenger but a similar voice. I was next to the left door, my left, which is covered in strong cable-like webbing. Among the Veil, Isfet strands are highly combustible and contained. I have no idea how physics works in the subconscious of Harrison Wobogo but I found my works to be more effortless than outside of the Veil. I touch the burning board to the webbing and it ignites immediately releasing the smell of sticky sweetness I hate but appreciated for its symbolic victory. I knew better than to walk in front of the door as I heard the sounds down the portal increase in volume.

"Harrison, what are you doing?" It seduces with a echo I don't like at all.

"Don't answer!" I yell to Harrison and his head snaps to attention at the sound of my voice.

"Who is that, Harrison? Did I not tell you about guests? Must we bite you yet again?" God, can you hear me? You know the same god who made me and created the universe? Can you please stop that echoing? This fucking thing is creepier than seeing Killa Mike in drag.

"It's your Momma, bitch," I respond, after using my Huh works to place myself on the other side of the door with out walking past the opening.

"That voice. I know thee, though I cannot name," I heard as I saw the strands shaking with movement. The Passenger is closer now. A second is all it takes to ignite the web around the door. I stepped out of the door's arch, holding the board in two hands behind me to prep as I remember Heru's death stroke: *Be Heru. Be brave, Clay. Face the pain. Face it.* The moment was at hand as the first legs of its hideous form show themselves. Surprisingly, this was like no other crawly I have seen. Its legs seemed synthetic, made of a plastic or a polymer resembling Tupperware, maybe even Legos. The farther its body emerged from the silk tunnel, the more I noticed its body looked assembled from a painted black model set. Each piece seemed built and assembled, painted with stencils of day glow-colored symbols the same language as the argot painted on the walls of the apartment I found Desta in. Its head came into view and I expected to see the familiar visage of multiple eyes and fangs. Instead, it wore a head pieces like a tragedy and comedy affixed by small bolts that seemed locked into its head. The mask was white and eerie, multiple eye slits and a cut for its fangs in lieu of either a frown or a smile.

"Harrison," I heard it hiss, "*surely thou did not set afire my web alone. We smell the works of Neteru.*"

It continues to advance, focused on intimidating Harrison, who shook in place, a pool of urine forming under his feet as he was unable to look away from the creature. Its arrogance brought it forward, with its front legs exposed. I noted its carapace was neither organic nor the plastic of the rest of its body. Its body was almost clear, filled with a bubbling, viscous liquid that steamed as it dropped out of the wet and mucus-covered gland into the rest of the beaker. Its eyes shifted to the right and scanned the hole in the ceiling where the sun dropped down into the room to remind of the way home. It turned back to Harrison and began to approach him, hissing "*Sekhem Ka. The rogue is here.*"

"Yeah, yeah!" I yelled in its direction, causing it to pivot and find the source of the sound. I gave it just enough time to focus on me before the upswing landed, crashing into its mask and cracking it. I whipped the board back down in a curve, throwing all my weight behind the stroke as it connected with the Passenger's front leg and bounced back. It squealed in pain and reared on its back legs. I stepped in a circle, expecting it to either leap or crash down with its fangs. It paced with me and dropped down to level again. I waited until just before it front legs touched floor before I stabbed forward, landing square on its forehead, causing a piece of its mask to fall to the ground. Stunned, the spider legs wobbled and I swung the board like a bat. Here's another hit, Barry Bonds. We outta here, baby. The Passenger flew back some, tipped over and on its back. I silently thanked Hacksaw Jim Duggan and swung again as hard as I could, pouring Niaw works into the blow. I launched it in the air and down the tunnel, followed by the board I hurled at the silk. I spoke the word and watched the tunnel ignite in an exploding blaze, laughing out loud as the Passenger cursed. I slammed both doors with my hands, pushing my back against it and smiling at the heat of the blaze seeping through.

"Harrison!"

"Yes!"

"Find me lots of long boards. A hammer and some long nails, too."

"Okay!" He ran from his puddle and disappeared behind the stage.

"*Thou cannot slay me by such means,*" I heard behind the door.

"I don't need to, but you ain't comin in here again," I yelled back, taunting. I smelled melting plastic and felt a rock against the door.

"Dead race of heathens."

"Yeah, that's us. Tell me, though," I growled through my nose, lowering my legs to put my full stance against the door, "who just got knocked out, bitch?"

Harrison returned and ran up the aisle carrying a long board, a hammer and some nails. He was taller now, a lanky bean sprout, maybe his natural age of twelve.

"Start at the bottom," I said, "against the floor, wall to wall."

"Got it, jack," he replied, his voice deeper and flirting with a scratchy tone. I dropped my back more and tried to push the door in some, shifting my weight from my legs to my back as Harrison placed the first board against the door and floor, nailing the foundation of the barricade into the left wall. I coaxed the flames in my mind, heard another squeal and assumed the Isfet would be back away from the door. For every time Harrison returned with a board, I could almost see his form grow. Finally, when the final board was nailed, I stepped back to inspect the work. I folded my arms triumphantly and screamed taunts at the door. The Passenger responded with a nudge that caused me to jump back and scramble to find another board. The door held and I relaxed, looking to Harrison who stood amazed and relieved. He looked over to me and smiled, then scratched near his widow's peak as if to say "I don't know how, but thank you."

"Okay," I said, leaning against the back of the last row of seats. "I beat up the monsters so you can clean up now, right?"

"Yeah," Harrison said and half walked, half ran toward his aisle which held the bucket. I slumped over to the nearest lantern, which had been broken in igniting the board. Holding my hand close, I found myself whispering to the flame like a small gurgling baby. It seemed to sway with my words and then spread to my palm as well as forearm; I felt no heat and the lantern was extinguished. I walked back to the center where the ceiling still held remnants of the Harrison's passenger's webs. I extended my arm. The flames shot up to the webs. I watched the fire and held it with my attention before slowly releasing it do its work. I gazed as it danced, burning each strand in turn and staying away from the wood of the structure. *It is the natural state of fire to consume the works of Isfet.* I would remember that.

The flames died as the room was cleansed of the last web, proving to me I had a web of my own for the crawlers. *My sticky flame.*

Strangely, when my eyes found Harrison, he was on stage pulling the ropes to close the curtains. The theater was immaculate once it had been cleaned. The wood was polished, the bronze shiny, pillars reflected, and there was a warm glow to the room. As I walked to find a seat, I studied the ceiling to find an amazing mural stretching to the expanse. It was surprisingly well maintained, given the decay in the rest of the theater and the vibrancy of the mural's colors. A blue-paned background, it was the color of the sky at three am as the winter gave way to spring. Peppering the outer rims and the borders of the mural's top portion were a number of symmetrical twinkles that shone and faded as models of the original, stars of yellowing appearances and white disappearances. In the center of the pane was a bronze-skinned woman, stretching in a yoga posture across the entire length of the painting. Performing an iron bridge, her feet stayed firmly planted on the left side of the painting so she could stretch backwards, place her hands behind her and look at her knees. Below her, three rows of figures were painted in azure and sea green panels to demonstrate the process going along the assembly line in the cosmos. I knew her, Nut, wife of Geb, the planet Earth, mother of Ausar, Auset, Set, Neb-het and Djeuti. My grandmother, the sky.

I watched Harrison return to his seat and placed myself next to him. He swung his legs in the seat expectantly, slapping his little palm on my knee and looking back to the stage. I chuckled and let my back drop into the seat which was surprisingly uncomfortable. There was the sound of instruments being tuned from an undisclosed location and the curtain rippled, signaling movement on stage.

"If you are out here," I whispered, "who's handling the curtain?"

"Shhhh," he returned louder than I had been, "they are starting." I chuckled to myself and nodded dramatically, indulging the little person. As the curtain was withdrawn, the lights dimmed, leaving us in darkness. Then the stars above glowed and swirled, seeming to spin us with them. Where a stage had once been was a nebula of colors and gaseous bodies, the distinct notion of being underwater.

"When we began, creation was unformed in the waters, unmoved other than by the will of the creator. Then the Word stirred the waters and the

Nun was brought to engineer the Creator's will." Shapes formed in the gas and the water, one more prominent than the others. "The first of the Nun took on the force of the waters, Nwn, followed by his mate, Nwnt, ensuring that there must be a decay to his primeval aspect." The shape was lit by a mustard hue, joined by its feminine counterpart in a quartz-like white outline. "From these two, Huh, the principles of space were joined by Hht, the principle of time." Two more shapes were outlines, each drawn together to sit side by side. Then they were placed like icons behind the first two shapes. "Understanding creation and its decay brought forth space and time, but the combination of these four brought forth Kwk and his mate Kwt, light and darkness."

Two more shapes materialized in the waters as male and female statues, outlined in their respective green and blue, opposed on either side of the stage. "Drawn together by the forces before them, their union brought forth the next two of the Nun. Niaw, creation in motion and Niawt, the universe at rest." Two more shapes appeared, outlined in their colors and on either side of the stage. Niaw took on a red outline while Niawt was emboldened by silver. The pattern was clear: every one of the Nun principles was a principle of the universe and therefore had a male and female quality that ensured balance. However, by the nature of their attraction, conflict was mitigated by their need for each other to exist. "The last of the Nun, Imn and Imnt arose, bringing the known that can be seen and the unknown that cannot." There were two more statuesque icons highlighted in their unique colors and aligned in the column. I counted a total of ten now.

"Given the parameters of the universe, it was the Creator's will that an architecture be applied to its Creation. Inspired by the Creator's will rose Ra, the materials in which to build." A number of gases flowed and spiraled around the ten figurines. The mass pulled into a small orb. The orb collapsed in on itself and exploded in a blinding light that forced me to shut my eyelids and cover my face with my forearm. When the light died away I peeked to see the Nun figurines had disappeared. The orb was burning as it rose, boiling the waters around it, ascending as it both spun and rotated. The higher it scaled, I was able to make out the beetle under it, using its pincers to roll the orb. The orb broke from the waters and continued to climb, propelled by the beetle until its final ascent sent it into a spin and then hung near the ceiling of the room by the skylight. In fact, I noted that orb had moved and was synonymous with the sun in the sky I had seen earlier through the skylight. I felt the warmth on my face, and turned to watch the beetle make its way to stage left and fade from sight as emphasis was on the sun. The lights faded and there was darkness for a moment but when the spotlight cut through it, the beam focused on one spot. Standing where the beetle had last been seen, I recognized the smiling form of Harrison Wobogo. He stood tall, his hand holding a long top hat, the other palm over his belly, which was under a flawless black velvet vest with a chain attached to a time piece. He wore a white shirt under that with an appropriate black bow tie under his tuxedo jacket with long tails. His shoes had an immaculate shine that almost reflected as much light as the lenses on his glasses. Impressed, I turned to point the sight to my young companion but he had disappeared without notice.

"Among the materials Ra supplied, a catalyst was needed to add value to the process. Therein, Ra's companion Khpr was up for the challenge." Harrison spoke with a smile and charisma I had not seen before, which was rewarded with laughter from the audience. Looking around, I saw the seats were filled with people: men clapping as they chuckled, women covering their mouth to giggle, small children with their eyes dancing in expectant supplication of the magician's trick. When I turned back to the narrator, he was bowing, earning a loud round of applause from the audience.

"Thank you," Khpr boomed, "you are too kind." He began backing up as the curtain was drawn to a close. The lights grew brighter and the stands full of people rose to standing applause. As the room became less dark, I noticed the ceiling was not the only mural in that chamber. To my left, painted in a lavender font, the wall was covered in mathematical equations, formulas and conversions that reminded me of brushed spray paint. To my right, the same color and handwriting spelled out one sentence: "Thank you, grandchild."

I looked back to the stage but the magician was gone with an empty stage and closed curtains that were unmoved. I scanned the room only to see the audience discussing amongst themselves as if I was not there. Maybe I wasn't. I felt the sunlight on my face once again and the temptation to sleep like a cat. Looking up, the skylight was brighter than I remembered when I first entered, filling my eyes with so much radiance that it filled my vision until white balanced. I remembered my father lifting me from the crib and burying my face in his neck. I couldn't remember if it was Clay sharing Sekhem's memories or the reverse, but I remembered. Then I opened my eyes to look and stared at the street light across from Harrison Wobogo's room.

I heard the sound of humming coming from the bathroom in the suite accompanied by the running of water in the sink. I was alone in the room, awake and almost still somewhere else in my mind. The world got *clearer* and I got near realizing I hadn't left at all. I rode the train in my head, racing by a few stations of truth in the truth as my family saw it. It was all so convenient as far as each one's individual value system allowed. Truth is who we are when the door locks on its own. It was a few seconds before I listened again. So I stood and headed toward the bathroom. The door swung open slowly with the ridge of my hand along the edge, my pinky slightly pushing it open. Harrison Wobogo was shirtless. His glasses on a face were covered in a pie swirl of a blue gel and foamy lather. I figured out the humming was originating from the electric razor. He was moving in concentric rings on his cheek. His face was two-thirds shaven, his forehead beading with sweat from the water's steam. The toilet was trickling water on a refill to compliment the towel wrapped around his faded but lean frame. He'd been a wiry and muscular man in his youth, his body made up of repetitive labor in sequential difficulty to make his physique that dimension. Probably a farmer.

"Remarkable instrument," he said, inspecting himself in the mirror as he worked. The precision was remarkable for a man who required a hand up and off the toilet weeks ago. The shaving was distracting me from the fact his speech was unrestricted, sharp and pointed. "From the second I touched it," he said pausing to stare at the titanium blue Norelco in his hand, "I knew its design." He looked over to me to smile and nod, including me in the discovery. He turned to the mirror again, pressing the razor to his face.

"This is going to attract a Paradox," I said, unsure and worried from Xochi's warning that afternoon.

"You will find a back story and I will follow," Harrison replied, continuing to shave. "Just convince a nurse you shaved me."

"I am more than concerned about drawing a connection between us"

"Then convince her that she did the shaving. It is all just the same; I will be leaving soon."

"How will I explain that?" I asked.

"You don't honestly expect me to stay here forever, do you?"

"No, but I get so tired of saying this. It's all so new to me as well. I need time to come up with some plans."

"I will give the appearance of death. Eventually. I can feel my works are far easier accessed since you quieted the Passenger."

"I can't say I'm sure how I did that exactly" I admitted.

"Strange." He paused and examined his neck, rubbing his finger tips under his chin. "You were quite certain of your method the last time."

"Last time?"

"Your last Carrier," he said, eyeballing me from head to toe in the mirror. He moved the razor to his neck. "I thought you took care of the details for the transfer."

"I keep surprising myself. I almost know the plan and then I lose it or I'm unsure, so I'd rather forget. I get the feeling like someone or something is pressuring me to forget."

"You are reclaiming your works, yes?"

"Some, but to what end?"

"Reuniting with your . . . " He moved the razor to the other side of his neck. "Our ancestors bring us closer to who we are and what we are." He chuckled and moved the razor away to snort a laugh. "I might more accurately say what we will become."

"I say names in my head or out loud," I almost stuttered out but turned to a stagnant moan. "I watch and make things happen, but not sure what exactly it is. How it fits. How I fit?"

"That is the underlying magic of the plan, it would seem," he said with a focus as he worked the area directly below his chin. "The discovery of learning what you already knew."

"I am going to need more than that. One might think, for a family member, you enjoy keeping me in the dark more than our enemies."

"What does one do when their family is the enemy, right?"

"Yes!" I said with more relief in my own voice than I had expected.

"Develop competitive advantage. A sustainable one at that."

"Still don't follow and you missed a spot. Here, let me." I reached out and grabbed the razor, working over the areas by his lymph nodes that seemed to resist the one brush of a razor on the necks of men since the beginning of time. When I was done he flicked on the stream at the washbasin and motioned toward a damp wash cloth hanging on the bar outside the walk in shower. I turned off the razor and placed it on the basin near its charger, passing him the clothes, which he followed with by dropping it into the bowl.

"Our works were once the management tools we used to add value to our wards."

"The humans?" I asked.

"Primarily, but beast and plant fell under secondary duties. As a whole it was our family's domain to improve cooperation between all three. Given the attribute of the individual, the more specialized the works became." He pulled the steaming wash cloth from the water, his hands seemingly unharmed by the heat and washed the entirety of his face.

"What about potency? Is there a hierarchy?"

"What do you think?" he asked.

"I can't tell. Is it generational?"

"One would think so. The closer to the source, the greater the works accomplished. For example, Set's--"

"Don't say the name," I cut in cold and brutal. Harrison paused and looked at me with condescension. "That was rude; forgive me," I added. He nodded and hung up the wash cloth, replacing it with a finger nail clipper.

"The traitor's works are generally more powerful than any of your generation or below." He continued. "There are, of course, exceptions."

"Heru and I."

"The first that come to mind. Certainly not the only outliers."

"Why do you suppose that is?"

"Ah, the passion of my research! The last thirty years was spent on precisely this subject." He was excited, almost delighted.

"So what have you found?"

"Nothing!" he said, stopping his clippings with a wide smile and bright eyes. "That's why it is a passion. What is the use of chasing something when the answers are obvious?" His smile was even wider and I was reminded of Sir Didymus from the Jim Henson movie with David Bowie in Lita Ford's wig and Jennifer Connelly before we realized she had enormously luscious tatas.

"So what can you tell me about Nwn and Nwnt?"

"Same as before. You didn't write it down?"

"If I did, I can't find it."

"The diagram I drew you is posted on my wall as poster. I made it look like a rock concert. Can you visualize it?" My mind reaches from the bathroom to wall space between his bed and his desk to find the poster. I walk out of the bathroom to stare at it.

"Okay," I say from the bedroom of the facility suite, "I'm looking at it."

"Well," he started, cantankerous and bored at teaching the same one hundred level course. To Harrison, the material he was covering for me was the most basic level while to the average person it was shit that would make Lucasfilm say "wow, I want some of that there, boy!" He would much rather tackle the graduate seminar on why you can walk through walls and pull atoms apart like popcorn balls. "It all started in the waters. Nwn was asleep and alone. He was awakened when the creator gave him a partner in Nwnt.

"You know this Carrier isn't exactly a sheep. You can skip the cosmology and get to the practical. I saw your show earlier." He looked me up and down through his glasses with his head poked out from the bathroom like he was ready to yell at some neighborhood children stepping on the lawn he just watered. "The cosmology is the practicum, isn't it?" I said, defeated, folding my arms in front of my chest and leaning against the wall to stare at the poster.

"Nwn then," he said, turning back to filing his nails and disappearing from view into the bathroom, "became the framework of the universe, the underlying influence that allows multiple possibilities to exist. Counter and yet complimented by Nwnt."

"Essentially she is Decay?"

"Not essentially as Nwn is the essence and Nwnt is its absence."

"But why?"

"Things must fail, Sekhem. How else can there be progress?"

"I see. And their union bore Kwk and Kwkt?"

"Birth is a term needed for human comprehension. Nwn and Nwnt communicated a need and the creator built a solution."

"Kwk being light and Kwkt being dark."

"Kwk we call growth. Imagine watching the cycle of photosynthesis happening all at once."

"I've seen Heru use it to heal."

"Precisely. The minutiae of organic matter."

"I tried using it to block your Passenger and failed miserably."

"How's Harvard's football team doing this season?"

"What? They have a football team? How is that relevant?"

"Each school has their own focus?"

"And mine isn't Kwk."

"Not yet."

"But Kwkt I seem to get."

"Of course, she rules the psyche. The depth of the possibilities that one's spirit can learn. No surprise, considering your parents."

"We have spirits?"

"We started as that--perhaps pure energy is a better description. These carriers were never meant to be permanent."

"Was it the Veil that changed that?"

"No, but it made it far more difficult to do without"

"Because of?"

"Collect more data for me and we will find out," he said, walking out of the bathroom. I turned to follow him with my eyes but shifted away when he began disrobing in front of his dresser. I began to detect that Harrison, unlike the rest of the attributes I had encountered, did not favor tangents. He seemed ruffled when we veered to new topics and almost became disconnected. I decided I would need to focus on one set of data points to get the most out of him without being deferred to "go find out."

"Imn and Imnt I know as seen and unseen," I started, attempting to keep my voice humble and inquisitive. "How are those applied?"

"Imn," Khpr said, shaking his head at a drawer full of onesies and sweat pants, "was brought forth from the need to measure past light and dark. You can conceive of Imn as the domain of non-organic material, the micro environment in building block form."

"Wouldn't that be the same as Nwn then?"

"No. Nwn is the primal state, encouraging *all* matter to take form; whereas Kwk is organic, Imn inorganic."

"I want to change that dresser into a standing wardrobe. I invoke Kwk?"

"You are basing that query on the fact the furniture is made of wood?"

"Precisely."

"Precisely wrong. The wood is dead; trees are not. You would invoke Imn, understanding that the wood before you is composed of molecules. Those molecules are composed of inanimate objects such as protons, neutrons and electrons--"

"Always cause explosions" I interrupted.

"Excuse me?"

"Never mind. So if I heard you correctly, Imnt is unseen, which means?"

"The mind."

"Why would that not be Kwk as well; the brain is part of the living body."

"The mind is a state of perception constructed by an organ in your skull. Under the lens of perception alone, your brain is just meat, but show me your mind."

"As opposed to within the Veil, Kwkt replaces the mind."

"Replace is too clumsy a term. I would prefer you view it as a compass as well as velocity within the Veil." He had finally found some slacks he liked and began trying them on.

"I would prefer you wear some underwear before you put on those pants."

"You think this old man can't slap you?" he teased me.

"Can he put on some boxers at least?" I asked, teasing him back. He rolled his eyes and searched through the drawers for undergarments, took off the pants and replaced them once he had on a pair of yellow boxers with the Cal Bear logo on them.

"Additionally, you can think of it as a spray nozzle on a yard hose for the other works you perform while within the Veil."

"An amplifier?"

"Precisely. Take special note of the difference. You have one of the best disciplines in Kwkt of all of us. I look to you for discovery."

"Niaw and Niawt are motion and friction, as a product of the need placed by Kwk and Kwkt?"

"You are understanding the causality of the need which spawns their creation, but the friction definition is inaccurate. I would like you to consider Niawt as rest."

"Absence of motion."

"As well as absorption. Gravity, to put it grossly."

"So theoretically a Niawt master could absorb any other work performed against them," I dug at him.

"I have yet to see it done, but theoretically yes" he answered.

"Thank you. I got an idea to try. You need help finding a belt?"

"I prefer not. The waist on these slacks is a tad bit snug."

"Hh and Hht are space and time. Once Niaw and Niawt saw a need for spatial and temporal differentiation?"

"That is an excellent way to put it. I'm quite pleased with your mind for this topic."

"How would you put it?"

"Hh is spatial--where things are. Hht is temporal--how long things take."

"That's far less convoluted than my version," I pointed out.

"It's easier for me to grasp. To you these are abstract concepts. From where I stand, these are my parents."

"Do you remember your childhood?"

"Yes, but not in a way I could verbalize that would clarify the subject for you to further your understanding."

"Fair. Can we back up?"

"Let's then."

"I get Hh. In fact, I find it the easiest to invoke."

"You should. It is one of your specializations."

"That makes sense. How would one use Hht, then?"

"Perhaps you would like to correct a mistake from this morning or delay the amount of degrees it takes for two cars to collide near you in traffic."

"Ah, so I might be able to go back--"

"Be warned, nephew," he said cold and somber, "the equation *must* balance. Potency in one means deficiency in another. Therefore time has not been kind to you. Hht has the most potential to attract paradox."

"I keep hearing that! Xochi told me the same thing."

"The Aztec?"

"Yes."

"It is good they are still among us. Perhaps we can meet soon."

"You haven't met?" I asked.

"No, I only know the extent to which you and your cousin keep me informed."

"I have a better picture of the game now. How would you suggest we approach this competitive advantage?"

"I have some ideas," Harrison started, "and with this new freedom of thought I can begin doing some analysis. I will require more data on every confrontation you have with other attributes."

"Well, I'm fairly new to this but if I can figure out an internet connection, I can get you into the database."

"That would be excellent. I also require everything you know about countering the influence of these passengers," he said sternly.

"I can't say you will get any more insight there as well. I've sorta stumbled into it."

"Yet you have achieved the most success of any of us Rogues. Even now, though in control of my own faculties, I can feel my own parasite's confusion over its inability to communicate with yours."

"I hear nothing."

"All the more reason for you to take the lead on this project. Retrace your steps, look at things with new eyes."

"Got it. One last thing. Heru is no more. That Entropy thing murdered him."

"Bleak indeed," Khpr said, removing his glasses and closing his eyes to squeeze the bridge of his nose. "So we are the last."

"Not necessarily," I said, looking around as if someone was watching us. *Ausar is risen.*" His eyes shot open with an intensity I had not seen before.

"The child?" he hissed. "The Reconciliation was successful?"

"I believe so, but I'd like a second opinion."

"Then we must move expeditiously. With the key returned, we must place him on the throne before anyone detects we are brokering a spot in the game."

"We will need more than some coronation if we are going--"

"No, stubborn boy! I speak of more than similes and metaphors! We must literally place the child on the throne in order to exert our control on the Veil itself." John Madden says, "Ah, there is our running game."

"I've been to Kemet. There's a fat, nasty, talking spider there."

"When the time is ours, I shall return with you and we shall see how fierce this spider is."

"And if that's not enough?"

"Then we didn't have much of a plan to begin with."

CHAPTER SIXTEEN

"All the details count when perception is everything."

-Xochi

Xochi's text was precise with directions as well as the warning about parking. One would think that South Van Ness south of Mission would be desolate in the evenings. The whole of 16th from Valencia down to Potrero was a notorious with underage sex sales and the cottage industries that came with it, such as heroin, stolen goods and new identities. While the gentrifying hipsters in their apartments and skinny jean, fixed gear bike fiends stayed within their comfort zoned of the invisible border down Valencia, a related world bubbled to existence a few blocks down. I turned off the engine in front of a meter in a long string of empty parking spots reflective of the class war. Meanwhile, whether immigrant day laborers or out-of-state art student transplants, both parties were in better psychological health not being aware of the war being fought for their belief. Just as the line that divided the forcedly vulgar from the feigned holy along Valencia, a line separated the freedom of choice from the imposition of devotion along the perimeter of the city of San Francisco.

I locked the car and scanned the street for eyes that shouldn't be watching. The night was empty except for the shopping cart full of bottles and rugs which covered the homeless man sleeping under it adjacent to the car dealership's glass doors. The Dodge logo on the side of the building near the roof was the only remaining sign of activity for the business, as the inventory had been removed. Papers continued to forecast shaky ground in the housing market and bubbles were showing signs of a pop in the credit markets. You can feel the storm brewing even without a sign of moisture in the air.

The restaurant was titled "Kenny's" with lettering indicating it also served as a bar. I noted it because when I walked in it was the last English I would see. It was dark, lit by the neon Coors sign in the window and the sparse bulbs over the bar. There was some reflection off the mirror behind the bar from the two video poker machines attached to the bar and dusted by the salts of various aged drinking snacks but it only served as a guide to separate one booth from another. I let my eyes adjust and found a booth in the middle of the row, facing the door but keeping the door to the bathroom as well as the kitchen in my periphery via the mirror behind the bar. I looked over the menu waiting at the table noting again that everything was in Cantonese. I heard a cough and looked up in surprise at the tiny Chinese man who stood eye level with me in the walk way. His mouth held a half smoked Parliament with red, tired eyes and a mouth that might have never known a smile. His hands rose to hold a small server pad, which he posed a golf pencil at in expectation of an order. I ran my finger down the list of options and pointed at a rice plate. The server made a sound that was indistinguishable between cough, throat clearing and a negatory grunt. I studied his eyes and saw a blank stare. I moved my hand down the list and pointed at a second option--some fried rice with egg. Again, the sound was produced and his face was blank.

"I'll just have some tea," I said. The face stayed blank for a while and emotionless. The pad and pencil disappeared into the pocket of an apron around his waist I hadn't thought to notice before. He produced a folded wax paper hat, unfolded it like a note and placed it on his head. I took that as a sign that my order had been approved and watched him from the periphery as he left the room. I looked to my watch; ten minutes had gone by and no sign from the messenger. I scanned the room for details, something I had missed that would have brought me closer to my meeting. The delay and inherent waiting was doing nothing for my anxiety.

Reliving the conversation with Harrison brought a sense of urgency to my cause. I not only had a parasite dwelling in my neck but a bug tracking mechanism. Somehow naming it for what it was gave me the feeling of temporary control over it: an organic metaphysical spy that had been unhooked from its broadcast capabilities for some time. If reactivated it had the potential to pinpoint my whereabouts if not my innermost schemes. To add further to injury, if allowed in strength, the bug could exert its will to turn me against my own intentions without my knowledge. It seemed our investments of generations of trial and error was near to a futile close or a bountiful fruition, which opened a new hope. It was up to the Monk to relay the message that would turn the tide for us all.

Lost in my thoughts again the return of the Chef with a small pot and cup was not in my awareness until after he had placed the teacup on the table. I nodded my head to say thank you, careful not to make eye contact. My strategy was an attempt at ingratiating myself to place him as my superior. He grumbled and waved me off with the right hand as if to say, "Don't give me that shit." His hand was not as steady as we had both hoped and a cup of steaming hot oolong made its way along the glass table into my lap. It was only a few moment before the temperature burned through my garments and touched my thighs. I jumped up in pain, nearly falling, as I panicked my way out of the booth and into the walkway. The Chef grumbled several apologies and dusted my pants with a towel.

"Bathroom?" I asked as over-annunciated as possible to get this awkward moment done and behind us. He mumbled something in Chinese and pointed hurriedly to the door to the kitchen. I nodded and walked along the aisle until I hit the door. I didn't look for many details such as a sign that indicated whether it was a little boys or little girls room. No luck in that department; just a slightly ajar door with an out-of-order message written in light blue crayola marker on the back of a menu taped over the doorknob. Even someone without my heightened senses could pick up the smell of cured urine and residual boo boo rolling around in the air between me and the door. I decided I didn't have time to ask why I had been sent to an inoperable lavatory and decided I could clean up out of sight and risk of Paradox.

I pushed the door open with the toe of my footwear, careful to keep any germs off my hands. It was a simple step inside; unfortunately, I hadn't counted on the spring- loaded mechanism attached to the top. The door slammed shut behind me, leaving me in the dark. Forgetting hygiene, my hands fumbled for a light switch. After more than a minute, I decided there was no hope and I should probably open the door to let in some light to my search. When I pulled on the knob, I discovered it locked, from multiple places besides the lock on the knob. This heightened my panic and I switched on my vision.

Looking through the Veil can often be as revealing as it is disconcerting. I was learning not to use it in open space to save myself from the sight of huge spider webs just outside the city limits. In this small compartment of a bathroom, it gave a duality the naked eye just didn't allow for. Parallel in my vision was a gloomy dark room of damp and musty clouds as well as grey tiles enclosing the minimum of appliance. A bare ceiling had been slapped with a few coats of white primer long ago. Written on the ceiling in a brush stroke of an ink I was sure was only viewable by trained eye was a single Chinese character: Humility. My eye followed the ceiling to the wall, then the mirror above the sink and then the small statue on the lip below the mirror.

Next to the mini-Buddha were a few sticks of incense and an ash pot. I lit the stick and placed it in the pot without picking it up, keeping my hands free to see what might be next. The smoke drifted off the stick and changed the color the room to a hazy red. Then I felt movement and got the notion I was descending. I looked through my lenses to see red arrows of force indicating I was in fact moving downward as was the room, although nothing I tried with Huh could tell me where I was in relation to the restaurant. I felt the motion stop just around the same time as I heard a sound like bolts being removed from a gate. The door swung up and I swiveled in reaction.

My foot found stone when I stepped out. It was polished white marble in which one could see their reflection. Long and wide, the floor stretched down an expansive corridor. The walls were an intricacy of polished and treated copper squares rimmed by a finished wood that ran as beams from the floor well above my head to the marshmallow- like material that constituted a ceiling. My shoes clicked as I walked the hallway, passing a bronze plate or two to catch a glimpse in it for a brief second. I followed the hallway for a period until ending at a doorway that looked out on to a mountaintop. Crested with new snow, the temperature of the wind told me the garments I had worn in preparation for San Francisco rain would be no help, although better than being naked. Sitting cross-legged in the snow, I recognized the back profile of the Monk's assistant.

I stepped lightly, hoping not to disturb the meditation he appeared to be enraptured by. The crunch of my weight against the snow made me wince and I saw no movement to indicate I shouldn't proceed. I tried walking on the balls of my feet which reduced the sound but gave an unbalanced feeling as I looked below to realize there were clouds below this peak. Then I began to wonder why I had experienced the shortness of breath I had always been told existed at the top of the world. It was enough to wonder if one juicy green menthol laden loogie spit from this height could be enough to put a hole in concrete at the bottom.

"Sekhem Ka," I heard from Wukong's direction but realized I hadn't heard him speak enough to recognize his voice.

"I was given word the Monk wished to see me," I replied.

"In trusted company, there is no need for deception," he said and rose to his feet; his body lifted in the air and he dropped his legs to stand upon them. It was there I realized he stood barefoot in the snow without shivering. His face was calm but his eyes burned with a restless, unrelenting passion I somehow identified with, but also felt uneasy with when his eyes fixed on me. "Was it not you, Sekhem Ka, who requested to see my master?"

"Yes," I said, "I suppose that is a more accurate statement. The message back brought me here somehow."

"And so you are here," Wukong said back to me with a sarcastic smile.

"Where exactly is here?"

"A pocket, an unknown pouch hidden on the garment of creation. Away from the eyes of those with too many." *Away from the eyes of too many: Isfet.*

"This is not in the Veil, is it," I probed. He shook his head, sucked his teeth and waved his hand like a small child, unsure if they actually liked the candy their mother had forced them to eat. "Somewhere in between?" I continued and received his response in the form of his wiping one hand over the palm of the other: *something like.* I sensed an annoyance I could not place; he was impatient with me and almost condescending. "You don't like me much, do you?"

Wukong ground his foot into the snow as if extinguishing a cigarette, seeming to cock his head to listen to the sound, the same sound I found abrasive and disturbing just a few moments ago. Hopefully it was moments ago. For all I knew, as I stood atop this summit, looking down into some hidden vent between worlds, San Francisco had been moved to the moon as a byproduct of the year 2050.

"Moreover," Wukong said in an accent somewhere between natural and ridicule, "it is you who do not like yourself. Much like this frozen water," he said grinding his heel, "you will have to endure if you are to move forward."

"Endure?" I asked, "I find that term is becoming a clever substitute for suffering."

"I don't like the snow much," Wukong replied, "but I own it as part of this peak, as I own this land."

"This land?"

"Yes. The Mountain of Flowers and Fruit," he moved his hand like plucking a tablecloth from a dining set and the clouds moved to reveal a lively valley filled with high shoots of bamboo pushing up from jungles fed from rivers in a hatch-work pattern. Perhaps through my imagination, perhaps I wanted to see it, perhaps by Wukong's will, I could see the snow melt in droplets that trickled down the mountainside and collected into streams that gave comfort to the rivers, which in turn inevitably ended at the blue green ocean surrounding us on all sides. Atop the trees, blending in with the bird calls, buzz of flying insects and creaking of the wood in the wind, sat the burbling chatter of thousands of monkeys communicating among themselves. For short periods, I could actually make out conversations ranging from what the next meal would be to the delight one would take in bathing in the ocean. Then again it was the chirping staccato of monkeys living among bamboo shoots. As the sounds bounced among the walls of the very walls of my ears, I accepted that these were the hopes and dreams of a people. However I chose to define people, I was bearing witness to the evolution of a community.

From every thought, a chemical release facilitated an electric reaction. Such flashes could be seen snapping into sparks through the mind of each smiling primate face. In all, there might be over a million of such beings on this hidden island and that would be a conservative estimate. Those million or so thoughts drifted into the air the way the heat from the morning sun lifts mist from a road. The thoughts thicken when in proximity and rise to the cloud below me as a manifestation of these collective thoughts. It was impossible to decide if the clouds were purely condensation, a symbol of these creatures' hopes or some hybrid of both. These clouds spiraled one atop another and were coalesced into intended form: Wukong. There on that I summit, with Khpr's lessons still ringing in my head, I stumbled upon the obvious truth.

"You draw in their thoughts," I mumbled, looking to Wukong. "You are their *magnet*."

"I am sustained," Wukong confirmed, casually stepping from the snow into the air as if walking from the lawn on to the driveway. "I am but a focus point for my people's reality but I cannot exist without input."

"So you are in fact an attribute," I said making the connection, "a principle like the rest of us."

"If that helps your understanding, I will agree."

"What would you call it?"

"I am but one facet of my children's ability to know themselves."

I thought back to the webs covering the temples of my homeland. The daughters sent to appease the bloodsuckers' cycle after cycle so that the survivors of my kin might struggle on another day. I thought of the smiling and cynical expressions of four teenagers I found that I missed. I thought back to the lonely and missing love expressions in the eyes of my neighbors on the T train. Somehow there was a cause and effect relationship with Wukong and the inhabitants of the island. Somehow there was also a connection between Granny, the four smelly rug rats who helped me break into jail to save Horace and myself. That is and was my people, the ones I could recognize and perceive. I understood that Heru and I remained obscure symbols for a people in hiding hi from themselves. To continue to see obscurity was to continue to hide from those who needed us most and received us best.

"I feel I owe my own people something," I said, prodding the open sky between Wukong and me with the understanding that a step would mean a long, painful fall.

"What would you give them?," Wukong queried, "since you yourself cannot receive?"

"You really think that is the key, eh? A confidence boost and Clay will start dancing again?"

"I enjoy your humor. I find it quite effective at defusing the disappointments of the ages," Wukong said quietly. "I wonder if you remember to laugh along or can you only laugh at yourself?"

"I've got a bug in my neck. I find no humor there."

"Nor should you. Take comfort in that you are closer to its removal than any of us."

"Soon as your Master gets here," I said, lighting a cigarette and finding the taste less potent than I was expecting. "I'm looking forward to moving on with my day without carrying this burden."

"Then I hate to further your burden with such news," Wukong said, taking light steps back toward me.

"What? That this is light rather than just a menthol? You really need to clean that bathroom then."

"Again, I have always enjoyed your humor," Wukong said, touching his finger tip to my cigarette and not showing the slightest bit of shock when it turned to pure ash less than a second after. I scrunched my lips as the particles took flight in the wind a moment after that. "It has been your timing and wit that has made me the student," Wukong said, bowing his head. And for the first time through Clay's eyes, I saw him smile.

"The Monk isn't coming, is he?" I asked, beginning to deflate.

"No. He asked me to bear this message to you."

"Which is?"

"While we are passionate about your work in removing the Passenger, he can longer aid you."

"Did I offend him in some way?" I stammered. "Let me make amends. I am sure--"

"No, nothing of the sort or so simple. I assure you the master is not as easy to offend to as one might think. I have been the beneficiary of his mercy more times than I believed possible."

"The why the change?"

"Change is a fact we have to accept, even in realms without much alteration such as the goal of the Isfet. You should know this. It is your own change that spurred a response in our relationship. My Master cannot honor his purpose and your friendship with your recent pursuits."

"I don't understand."

"It is one thing to carve out a haven far in the West, free of Isfet rule. It is another to pool our faculties toward removing the Passengers from our neck. That has been the way of things for hundreds of years. My master could serve both his people and his bond with you. However, the Sekhem

Ka who stands before me would not stop at freedom for himself. He will continue until his people are free and the oppressors are removed."

"Is that so wrong?" I asked.

"That is not for me to decide. The Monk serves the Middle and therein its people."

"If he helps me it would put China in direct conflict with Isfet law. which his people cannot survive" I guessed.

"I am truly sorry," Wukong said with a head bow, "but we cannot be sure as to your intentions in this matter. This is the much safer option." I pictured my evening by Moreland San Francisco County jail, the fight in Kemet, Xochi's warning, Harrison's dream and the unknown glyph I had gotten from Contadina. Yes. Some form of scale at some level was tipping beyond preservation of the Sanctuary. I was at the middle of it without a clear sense of what the end goal was. With Heru gone, it called into question if I wasn't triggering events that would have irrevocable damage. A more hallowing thought was if I was truly directing the course of things to come or was an unwitting pawn of the enemy. What if I had done this before? What if the Monk's response was the pitied disengagement of a sibling? He could feel like establishing distance from a family member, the avoiding of a cousin who can't stop breaking your possessions. Far more unsettling was the possibility that I was moved by another invisible hand unseen to the conflict. Maybe it was another player to the game that swore allegiance to neither the Isfet nor the Concord, all too happy to see combatants tear each asunder with the least amount of involvement as possible. Disappointed as Wukong's recent news made me, I was still obsessed with my own goal.

"And what of the procedure? I came here to remove a bug." Wukong stared at me for a while before answering.

"I heard nothing further on the matter from our last session."

"I didn't come for a hand off or some diffusion. Find out."

"Would you like to ask for yourself?" Wukong interrupted with an urgent irreverence in his tone. "Go quickly," he said pointing toward the horizon, "the Middle lies that way. I suspect it is not the China you remember."

"Is that a threat I hear?" Wukong stepped forward, eye level, nose inches from one another. He smiled, I smiled back.

"Do you know what the world is outside of the Sanctuary? Go find out. Go peek into the corners where Entropy cannot intervene."

"I think I'll do that," I said nodding, controlling the enveloping fear I felt in my stomach at the notion of what it could be like. "Would you like a report? Single spaced and twelve point font? I'll whip that up for you, but I want my answer." I stepped to the edge of the peak, away from Wukong, leaving my back to him.

"I will honor your request because of our bond. However, the exit is behind you."

"No," I said, drawing my fingers in front as the lines pulled to front. "I may be slow but one thing I am getting is that the door is wherever we choose." With the frame aligned, I stepped through and into the dark patch under the eave of the dealership on 16th. Not a person in sight.

"You have a point there," I heard Wukong's voice in my head and then the feeling of being watched vanished.

I could probably retrace my steps and barge my way back into the bathroom, hoping for a repeat visit. I found myself lucky to have avoided Paradox as it was and knew my sound-off with Wukong could border on respect for only so long. It became about cartography at some point: mapping in my brain where there was a connection through the Veil. I would put a marker here to signal what was Wukong's and where the Veil was porous enough to leap through. A crack in the screen, a hole in the web, a space between strands. *Aztec.* I strode to my car, pumping hands under my jacket to fish out my phone. Intent upon texting, I have to change hands to grab my keys. I unlock the door as I finish the message and send it immediately.

Me: Coming by to check on him
Xochi: Perfect timing! I have some leads for you
Me: That was quick
Xochi: Just got a message for your ears and was preparing phone as you texted.
Me: See you soon

Down South Van Ness and a left onto 16th Street. It was a straight shot from there. I kept my pace tame due to the moisture in the air, which seemed to make drivers in the city skittish. By skittish, I am not only referring to the nervousness in which they handle behind-the-wheel decision-making but also the skits they play out which always seem new to them despite how many times both of us have witnessed the performance. I released my hand from the stick shift, which truly served no purpose given that the automobile was an automatic, to massage the air with my fingers. I knew electricity, timers, and a basic computer ran each of these traffic signals. You could almost smell the connections like the scent of freshly laid tar even though the eyes saw no road work. If I could only dig into that smell, I could make every light green for my journey. Alas, my hold on such Works was not to the liking of my cousin who I missed even more with the Monk turning away. Had I been among the Veil, I would probably have performed the feat with ease but the need for a car would have been a non sequitor. Note to self: probably best not to experiment with magic while operating a vehicle in the Mission district traffic; other drivers were more of a threat than Paradox.

Up the slope past Florida, around the nonsense at the shopping center before Potrero, though the thought of Boston Market's cinnamon apples did make me consider stopping. Across Potrero, ignoring the crowd in the McDonald's drive-through, down the slope wondering why no ever entered the Real Audio building from the street entrance. Past Il Pirata and the UPS facility; yes, you can always count on brown to pay brown people low wages. Further down the slope and stop sign under the 280, to watch the cops leave Starbucks as they stare at married women carrying children and groceries out of Whole Foods. Still moving to the structure of glass and metal that was Xochi's loft on top of the Sally's building. The parking lot was usually reserved for the patrons of the breakfast spot, the overpriced yoga studio or the home decorations store. Distractions. All detours of the sense to give the appearance of normalcy and disguise Xochi's natural brilliance.

I parked on the street and walked briskly toward the door, which was opened by a intimate call box. After punching in the code, there was a buzz and a click which indicated the door could be pulled open. I walked through and began climbing the stairs. Gone was the smell of fresh paint which I had remembered over the years. Instead, I smelled hot cooking oil and spices I couldn't put a finger on. By the top of the stairs the door to her loft was already cracked open. I pushed it slightly to enter and found that

I did not recognize the place. When I last dropped by, forgetting exactly when, the décor had always reminded of the semblance of the hipster gone domestic: pale orange-brown walls, wooden cabinets, white deco storage, brass light fixtures and sprinkles of technology viewable from the street so the resident appeared as hip as those around. The walls were now a wash of white, cabinets had become darker, stained brownish red, the furniture was vibrant blues, the appliances were black and most of the wall space was cleared of items to emphasize the large, picturesque rugs that were in each room.

Xochi kneeled in the middle of the foyer, focused on a cactus in a large pot before her. Desta stood next to her, holding a sippy cup that his two arms held high, pouring a delicate stream into the succulent's pot. As the water dropped and splashed back on his shirt, he moved closer, mesmer- ized--too close so that one of the quills poked his tiny forearm, just above the elbow. He yelped in pain, dropping his alternative water jug and step- ping back. His hand shot to his arm with his brown cherubim face still stuck in a frozen twist of pain. Upon seeing a prickle of blood on his palm, he stood firm, leaning back, hands down in the air, staring at the cactus. I watched its aloe-like green shimmer momentarily and start to fade to yellow.

"*Desta!*" Xochi forcefully, "*is that you?*" Her voice dripped with disap- pointment, a tone I had to come know far too well. Her voice broke his concentration and he even turned to object, moving his head first, which spun his shoulders first and almost obligated his waist to follow. "*Even if you can hear the cacti's voice,*" Xochi continued. "*You cannot assume it meant to hurt you. Who moved closer to whom, Desta?*"

Desta relaxed his eyebrows and looked to Xochi's gaze, then to the cac- tus and back. There was a struggle in his yes--the mind of a child grasping the reconciliation of the classic dispute between who started it and one of mankind's foremost ancestors explaining thousands of arguments as to why blame was irrelevant. "Desta--" Xochi pushed, bringing him closer to a decision as well as closer to her by wrapping her arm around the back of his knees. At a loss, his eyes shifted to me for guidance. "*Desta,*" Xochi perse- vered, turning his head at the chin to meet her gaze, "*I asked you a question.*" He met her gaze for what must have seemed like hours in a child's eye only to shrug as a sign of acceptance.

"I did," he said finally and sad, perhaps even embarrassed.

"Should I lash out because you spilled water?"

"No," he said in the long drawn tone, hoping she wouldn't.

"Why not?"

"Because I didn't mean to."

"You didn't mean to. So many living things may hurt us, when we only want to help. They too do not mean to hurt us, okay?" She got a sheepish yes and smiled, releasing his head. His gaze returned to the cactus, a softer, sadder light to his eyes. The air in front of the cactus shimmered again and the plant began to turn green. Within a moment, the color of a bottle of Reed's Ginger Beer returned to the succulent. I watched in a frozen sense of real time until I saw the bud of a flower poke from one of the tallest stalks. It opened and spread its petals; the air between us became still and Desta placed his palm over its pistil. With a giggle he placed his hand over his hip. He looked to me and jogged out of the room to gather his stuff.

"You make a good mother," I said, half joking.

"Not really," Xochi countered, "I find I get too attached."

"Yeah, but those are someone else's" I said, thinking she meant the kids at the center.

"Those are easy, Clay," Xochi said, standing up from her kneel. "It's watching the ones you made with your own womb die that leaves the bad taste. Enough to make you want to quit having any." I could see how watching thousands of Aztecs decimated by disease, slavery and flat-out tyranny could change her attitude to the whole maternity thing. For the first time, I understood that Xochi and I shared a bitterness she seldom spoke about openly.

"But you maintain your bloodline." She chuckled at me as if I had stated the obvious.

"In California? How hard is that? Mexicans don't indulge in extinction." It took me a bit to realize she was being humorous, so I waited until she laughed first. "Here, let me get you what you came for." Xochi walked toward her kitchen, out of sight except for her hands picking up cans of teas on her counter.

"I like what you've done with the place," I said, trying to break the silence. "A lot more space." I heard her second chuckle from afar.

"You always were fascinated with distance and dimension," she replied. "But to be honest, I haven't changed a damn thing in several decades."

"Quit playing," I spat out. "There was a couch where I'm standing less than a month ago."

"You decided I needed a couch, so your imagination put one here."

"Bullshit."

"No?"

"Fuck no, Xoch."

"Come in here. I want to show you something" she said, laughing.

I turned on heel, heading for the kitchen with the solemn oath that I was done with mind games for the day. I remember stepping off the carpet and expecting tile. I got pebbles instead. Pebbles that led to a cobblestone road. It was evening and the sun was setting outside, playing games with the waters of the lake surrounding the island we stood on. There was a massive fire in the center of the peak, which seemed be some ceremonial cooking site connected to the homes made of brick, white stucco and lime green plaster ringing the coast of the island in a modern village-type pattern. I gathered this spot would probably be where Xochi met with worshippers centuries ago. I looked over to her and saw she held a scroll in her hand.

"Whoa," I stuttered, "you changed it again with works."

"I never changed it, Clay," she said with a tired smile. "Most days I let you see what you choose to see. Today I decided you should see my home as it is."

"It's about choice?"

"I removed your choice just now. What does that tell you?"

"Most of what I know about the world is what one chooses to see."

"For the most part, you have a much more enforceable choice due to your lineage."

"Why?" I asked.

"Because the reality is too difficult to accept. This . . . what is this?"

"A haven. A pocket away from the eyes of those with too many," I replied, happy to quote Wukong.

"This area should have been built centuries ago so their conscious mind applies a layer they can accept."

"Who is they?"

"The couple in the parking lot right now leaving yoga."

"Does their mind shape their view with assistance?"

"Paradox."

"Yes. All the details count when perception is everything. It wouldn't make sense to have an island in the middle of the Mission. Have you been to my haven? Do I have one?"

"That is one of the few secrets Sekhem has never shared. I have heard you refer to somewhere as the Workshop"

"I'll look into it. I did, however, get an invite to what I believe to be Wukong's haven."

"Do tell."

"An island, much like this, I'm pretty sure that doesn't exist any where on the map."

"His mountain. I've heard him talk of it but I have never been there myself. Shows a huge sense of faith in you on his part."

"Why? Because he let me into his tree house? He has so much faith that the Monk took a vacation"

"What?"

"Yeah. Back on the mainland. I'm still chasing him for a solution." I chose not to bring up his warnings about conflict but thought I would probe Xochi some. "I would have thought he would have told you. You seem surprised."

"I am. When this arrived without a message," she said, brandishing the scroll, "I expected an update to follow."

"So this is not a part of the all-encompassing recovery plan you had worked out with him for me."

"No and I think we should see what this says as soon as possible. I don't know that I like where my mind is going in worrying."

"Okay. How do I turn that one?" I said, motioning at the scroll in her hand.

"You can read it or toss it in the fire," she said, referring to the fire pit.

"Does it spark and do cool colors?"

"If you like--"

"Let's do the fire, then. Also, this the great outdoors, so can I--"

"Smoke? Yes, but I don't want the second-hand in my face." I smiled and flicked my wrist a bit, finding a menthol in my hand. There was only a thought for the ignition which told me Xochi's haven existed as deep behind the Veil as Wukong's peak. It also meant I would have plenty of ease exerting my works if need be. To keep Xochi from zapping me, I opened a Ka door, six by six. It led to the intake vent in San Francisco General. It pulled the cigarette smoke away from both Xochi and me, through the vent, and into the square ventilation piping. Feeling myself, I opened a second door just behind the first at SF General, this one leading to a wall behind the desk where both of Avalos's monitors were parked in their cubicles attempting to make a career by building a case on me. Yay for me.

I nodded at Xochi and she dropped the parchment into the flames, curling her fingers as if drizzling a spice into a pot as the scroll fell. The scroll twirled as it drifted down, invulnerable to the heat in retaining its shape yet evaporating once it touched the coals at the bottom of the pot. The effect sent a plume of smoke the color of thick jade high into the sky, undeterred by the vent I had created. As the green smoke thickened, it choked the light from the fire pit, leaving us in darkness except for a spectral glow shaping into a monochrome outline. I heard the Monk's familiar voice as his face came into view, though the sound seemed distant.

"Can you turn up the sound or--" I started to ask until Xochi's frown silenced me toward patience.

"I cannot hear myself," the Monk said, looking behind himself, his classic frown playing upon his forehead. "I told you to figure this out before you turned it on, not talk back to me, Wukon. Oh, it is?" With that, the Monk turned his body to face me, a ringing appearing in my ears as if the volume on the television had been turned up past the level its meager speakers could handle.

"I expect this message to find you in sound mind and body. Regarding your request, I am disappointed to tell you that I have done everything to the extent of my knowledge. Our efforts have weakened the parasite and stifled its ability to communicate with its kind. This has been a huge step forward and has allowed for new strategies that were not conceivable until steps were taken for security. Now that we are afforded a greater deal of privacy, your sacrifice will not go unnoticed. It saddens me to tell you that I cannot find a method to remove it without killing your Carrier and possibly damaging your attribute irreparably."

"As I am sure Wukong has made you aware, I can longer support your endeavors in a public fashion. To do so would bring retribution upon my people that I cannot justify. Surely if our roles were reversed, you would put the needs of Kemet above mine. One could even suggest that has occurred already and it would be unethical to blame you for doing so. This is not to say I have not enjoyed our friendship nor do I wish to abandon it. As proof, I will leave Wukong here in my stead, as he is already posted as a fixture within the Resonance upon the Peaks. My laboratory as well as the Chamber is at your disposal should you wish further experimentation, though I ask you to continue to use discretion in addition to seeking Wukong's supervision. It is my hope our paths cross again under more favorable conditions."

He turned his back and walked out of sight, the smoke compressing his image, dismissing itself in much the same way it came. I took the remaining drags off what was left of my cigarette, noting that my throat was beginning to burn. My whole life I have had this habit. I could tell the onset of a cold by the tightening of my nostrils and a burning in my throat. The constriction was followed by the snot in my nose drying into hard boogers, a coating similar to the plaque on my teeth. I was coming down with something, obviously. I believe the layman's term is "I caught a bug." I'm emotionally intelligent and I have dealt with the sound the heart makes when hope is punctured like a big red balloon by the bullies of pragmatism. Imagine what the eggs says as it is hurled at a house. Just before its shell breaks it must discard the possibility it entertained where its shell is strong enough to withstand the impact. As it touches the wall, it is consumed with disappointment that its survival will not be continued. Experience had taught me the connection between disappointment and the onset of a weakening immune system. The symptoms were identical from the dropped shoulders to the clamminess on the fingertips to the tightening in the chest followed by the added difficulty breathing.

Loss, lies, frustration, dementia, disorientation, regret, imprisonment, exile, reunification, abandonment, hope and disappointment--I was losing any sense of purpose. Pushing forward toward what, exactly? A futile acceptance that I was the remaining survivor of a fruitless cold war that could not be won? Something inside me, though weak and paralyzed, knew it too.

"On second thought," I said, walking out of the kitchen, "keep the kid here tonight."

"I can't. The Parchicks are hosting a fundraiser for us," I heard Xochi reply, the strength gone from her voice. She was visibly shaken and wrong. "One of us should show up."

"I'll go," I said, twisting the front door knob open. "Would be good to get back to my real job. Fuck, maybe I'll even shake a hand or two."

"Clay, I know you hate selling funders."

"No, Xoch. They hate me and I don't blame them. I hate drinking alone even more, though."

As I walked down the stairs, something told me to watch the windows. Across the asphalt as well as the parking lot, from where I stood on the street, I couldn't decide whether I was looking back at a window on a loft or a limestone bench on the edge of a hill's crest atop an island at the center of a lake. A little boy stood animated, waving his hands excitedly and crying. I shrugged my shoulders and got in the car.

Chapter Seventeen

"Least I'll be lookin righ even wen I'm buried"

-Icks

Get your black tux on, pull your fake smile out, the taste of philan-thropy's gonna move ya. Take some hors d'oeuvres. The taste of catering is gonna move you when you pop it in your mouth. Chair-a-tee! (sing along you know you know the tune). Its gonna move you, the cash is soft, and it gets right to you. Chair-a-tee, the sob, the sob, the sob story is gonna move ya!

Melted chocolate pours from a chamber looking more like a hookah than a serving device and drips the fondue down into a small molten pool. Selections of fruits, vegetables and short breads were laid out for dipping. I stuck to the strawberries, positioning my body between the fondue maker and the wall where the shadow of an indoor palm masks my form against the wall. High in the hills above Belmont, at the home the Parchicks, we assembled the wealthy elite of the Peninsula to grunge their heart strings so they would donate to keep our Center growing.

I had been there two hours and could not finish a conversation. That was largely due to Alexandra, who has been allowed to play assistant host-ess to her Mom by walking around with a slitted box for donation enve-lopes. She introduced me frequently as not just her "Doc Durward" but the "best for kids ever." Yeah, she added the pause between kids and "ever," not me. Her GPA was climbing, she is active around the house, and her piss has been clear for months. Alexandra was losing weight, has lost her taste for junk food, needs no assistance waking up in the morning and she even has a boyfriend. She met him at a SAT prep class that a friend of her mother's suggested so it's in the family. She was the clone her mother had hoped for but walks by every once in a while to wink just enough to let me know she is resilient enough to know how to play the game. In return for her daughter's stability, the Parchick matriarch set herself to the task of helping to grow our donor base. Generally, Xochi would be there to answer questions, dazzle folks with her supernatural intellect and deflect the probes of bored housewives who want to dish about that doctor that the kids love. Instead, I was there so the potential donors could stare without interaction, going into some private place in their fantasy world. They think I can't see as they imagine me naked and slightly sweaty chopping some wood like a damn hick stranded on a tropical island in some television drama. I continued to eat strawberries, leaving the stems in the soil of the potted palm to satisfy some troubled little boy inside of me. The chocolate was so hot that I seared off any taste buds I have left. The wound was cauterized by the champagne chaser and the occasion conversation seems to heal them back.

The smell of hair products masked the scent of self absorption and insecurity based on status, but I easily dissected it. The separation between intention and smell was losing its width. Competition smelled like sweat, obsession like liquor and nostalgia had the hint of talcum powder. The Parchicks began ushering guests into a home theatre where they have a slide show of photos depicting the activities of residents and drop in clients at the Center in what we labeled transition. The various rooms were emptying in lieu of the main attraction. I looked to my right at the bored face of the young woman who writes grants for us. I caught her eyes in the hand mirror she pulled out for the sixth time in fifteen minutes to do her eyebrows and check her pressed hair. She realized I was watching and looked up. I remember her when she hid her body in baggy, hooded sweatshirts and kept her hair to long cornrows--better to be a boy than a girl where she came from. Now having been with our program long enough, Cynthia had completed two years of general education at City College followed by two more years at SF State, coming to work for us in our fundraising and development department. She climbed the ranks from client to service provider. I motioned with my head and right eyebrow toward the door. She looked to the collection box and then to me as if to say she is supposed to stay to collect. I frowned, smirked and nodded my head to the door again: *Get out of here. I got it.* Her smile was big and bright, she seemed to be packed up and out the door quicker than my eyes could perceive. I decided to interest myself by putting all nonessential marketing materials away. I lost myself in stacking and rubber banding brochures.

I was lost in packing until the hair on the back of my neck bristled. A small electrified comb was run down my spine, brushing my awareness. *Eat.* There were pyres being played in a distant valley of my psyche. I suddenly had a longing to eat at a restaurant in Queens; $20 a head and you can go fat with all the fish, wine and salad made of spinach, feta, onions and olives your stomach can hold. I smelled the way olive oil makes a crack in the air when its been heated and combed through hair. It was mixing with a sweet perfume I am both drawn to and hate. *Careful.* I knew I shouldn't leave my back to the room, but to turn around seems too late. Then before a word was exchanged I already know who, what and where.

"Ya know," I heard the familiar voice start, "I took you serious the last time you said you were out." I kept my eyes to the table, trying to calm myself in the midst of the strongest urge to both kick the speaker as well as embrace her. More importantly, she was referred to something I wanted to know about. More information was needed. How to get what I wanted without giving away anything I needed. Whatever we were talking about, it was clear I held the upper hand as the object of her attention.

"You should try expanding your imagination more," I squeezed out of my lips. "I haven't the desire to babystep it for you, Constandina, so consider my status unchanged."

"Gee, you are really sexy when you hate me," Constadina says, positioning her body to stand behind the booth so that she was in my direct line of sight. She wore a jacket, appropriate for the affair but over-designed for my tastes. It had probably never been washed nor would it when she was done with it. I knew that she was the type to live out of the package and the bag, probably only purchased clothes to be waited on by sales personnel. The blouse under her coat was a clumsy, shiny material that was not appropriate, nor were the three buttons down from the collar that gave too much insight into her cleavage. She topped off the ensemble with a skirt the same color as the jacket. I was positive the stockings and heels were to make her fit in with the other women in the room as well as entice the husbands of the unlucky ones who brought them.

There was no good reason for her hand to be extended and touching her fingertips to my chin. I released the stack of brochures in my hand and gripped her fingers, yanking them away as I crushed her fingers together. She yanked her arm back into place with a speed and force that surprised me.

"Careful, Neteru," she replied coolly, her ice-perfect discs of light blue without pupils. "You are not in your beloved sanctuary. The rules apply here." There was sarcasm in her tone and it hung in the air when she said Neteru and Sanctuary. I got the sense I was being mocked: she found me some cute and ignorant immigrant she could sell a bridge in New York to.

"There are no rules," I said moving my hand to her hand to her wrist, "that you adhere to that I want to follow." It was a quick movement that rippled her arm and stepped her back a foot. Her eyes shifted and she smiled.

"Well, then," she said in low, drooling tones, "that would make you sovereign over yourself."

"Pretty fucking much," I said, frustrated with the table and walking a few steps from it. "Anything else might bring me closer to kissing your ass."

"Can I just say . . . what a great ass it is," she said, turning and doing a fake curtsy with a smile as if showing jewelry for QVC, "though it never stopped you before. So, I'm delighted to see you try your hand at the *Thrones*." What was that word again—the context of some game or strategy? I remembered Khpr referring to Desta as being critical to activating our throne, but the result thereafter was still unclear. I was in no position to inquire from Constadina; I could neither trust her with my ignorance nor the validity of any information she gave while assuming I was half-informed. I also knew that my database was named Paper Thrones.

"Don't worry, we're not in the same league. You go play with yours and leave me to my stone thrones."

"*Stone!*" I heard her announce. "That Aztec pulled you over, didn't she? Very smart to put roots in that continent, what with its population growth and migration. What did she offer you?"

"I have no idea what--" I started in earnest. Her interruption was a relief.

"I'll double it. Bring me in and I'll give you a one to one ratio. That's a robust market."

"You're insane. Clinically and criminally." Her ego. Her crack was the ego. She couldn't stand be told what she could not do. Exploit. Playing into attacking her faculties only opened the floodgate of information.

"For you? A fair split? No, a split at all? I wouldn't share half a ciga-rette with you, not worth it," I fired back. Red filled her cheeks and she scrunched her nose, placing a hand on her left hip.

"I want a piece of those followers when you take a throne. I'll give you three to my one if you cut me in."

"Ha!" I said, walking away, deciding a bathroom trip was in order to keep her following. You can make any child spill the beans if you take a possession and walk away with it. "Share followers with you?" Then something about the interaction poked its ugly tip out. *"Remember, Greek, I taught you this game. You wouldn't even know a throne if not for me."* There it was. Playing the Thrones resonated deep within me between both voices. The wounded spider and the hunted cosmic body both valued playing the Thrones at a high level. We had consensus.

"Is the idea so foreign to you, Sekhem?" she said, stepping lightly in pursuit down the hallway. She was one heel click against hard wood upon another some where behind me by five feet or so. I pivoted my head so she could see my profile and swung my arms as I walked. I would run out of momentum on this goad streak if I didn't keep up. Running out of time, I scrutinized her with a cocky smile out of the corner of my mouth.

"Share with you? Anything I have become . . . it certainly isn't desper-ate."

"So a child does not count?" she countered, sticking her chin at me with her apple head as if standing up to a school yard bully. I knew she was breaking and a few more volleys would crack her open. What I didn't know is if by child, she meant that Desta was mine as well.

"You like making things up still?" I said quietly, stopping in my tracks and turning away. "That child could be anyone's, given your appetite."

"Whore of a man," she said, the color drained from her face, giving it the appearance of moving alabaster and eyes that were the hillsides of Mace-donia. *"I have ripped apart nations for questioning my vision. On a whim--on a whim, Sekhem. I am the virgin daughter of Olympus and to think I stand in front of the likes of a man afraid to embrace his very divinity. What exactly will history know you for? I kill Titans and shattered the Persian empire, twice. How many seek counsel from the greatest warrior to run from battle?"*

"Well, thank you for that Princess Pop Off." I appreciated her as sar-castically as possible. "Might I add that, despite alleged omnipotence, you still don't know who the father of your child is." We were inches from each other by then, sneering and ready to spit like cats warding fences. "In the end Persia got the oil and Greece got light cigarettes. You failed."

"So cocky," she said, studying me, "sure of what is and what is not. How did that work out for you last time? Or the time before that? Or how about when--"

"You are still in tow like the puppy I took you for at the time so to answer your question. Pretty much so it's a good type of thing so far."

"Oh, that's it, asshole," she said, scrunching her nose and stepping closer. Her hands came up quickly. I saw their movements in blurs of Xeno freeze frames and was somehow unable to move fast enough. Her palm touched my chest hard and solid. The impact felt as if it disintegrated my ribcage. I kept my feet under me but was knocked backwards. I expected to slam into the hallway behind me, bringing down the painting mounted behind me. Instead, I felt the stucco absorb me and the whirl of colors as I passed through paint, wood, canvas, plaster, lathe, ceramics and metal. The natural reaction was to sprawl my arms in order to break velocity but by the time I did, I was only knocking her arms away. She stood exactly the same distance from me within a brand new room.

It was more of a chamber. Dim, lit only by candles, the smell of aged saw dust and scented oils; the sounds began buzzing in my ears. Somewhere, between the traces of forty years of incense or the voices of every visitor to this room, there was the dull hum in the back of my head making my inner ears itch. Horrified, I didn't need my eyes or her voice to tell me how important this chamber was or how unimportant I needed to make it. In the drone of the voices in collective supplication, in the selfishness of the human need, a room full of expectants cry out in the darkness for guidance, solutions and hands-on deliverance. Whether it was the statue of her in full regalia, spear held in position, blue light from a neon bulb hidden in the alcove in the wall, with a three foot white stone portrait or her in that fucking Erin Brockevich jacket standing with her arms ready to hurl me by the ear, I understood that Athena was the answer to somebody in this house--the same somebody who was currently hosting a fundraiser party to benefit the Center, the place that made me sane. There was a second alcove with the crossbar and dual rounded beams up, the figurine below of some black, stone, faceless statuette without features turned at a forty-five angle, with its locks falling on a bowed head, arms upraised to create the bracket turned in same angle as the metallic one above. I lived in that alcove and in the body where I stood. I too was important to someone in this house. Not just one, but many generations had come to this room to throw their dreams into the arms of their living god by self-appointment. In this room, human beings came to pray to the visage of Ka and Athena in the privacy afforded away from the world of criticism and public perception. For some reason, these visages were as approachable as the cross atop a building every four blocks as one drove down El Camino Real or the prayer center at Civic Center that was open for all five of the daily prayers.

I knew I wanted no part of this room. I was both surprised that it existed and disappointed that this was the not the first time I had found some piece of myself comingled with the Greek. On top of which I felt outrage. A sense of integration to the duality of Constadina and Athena, utterly disgusted and unable to forget. I knew that this was not the first offense, she had certainly been warned before. Dire consequences had been promised should she associate any likeness of myself or my aspect with her offering in idol form. For some reason, I would have to investigate later, the word "Syria" came to mind. There was a familiar smirk to her supple and natural pink lips as she studied my face, sure she had won her hand.

"What does the Door say now?" she goaded me, most likely detecting some middle ground between surprise and horror in my face. She reached her hand up to stroke my face, a few inches shy of my cheek. I closed my eyes, lost in her perfume and jambalaya of emotions that came too intense to be sorted. "Are you so sure that there isn't a single thing we share?"

"You will need to hurry," I said, clearing my throat and removing my jacket.

"We need the Aztec," she said, victorious. "No Resonance built with two aspects alone has ever lasted. We will need this as soon as you can get her here."

"We are not hurrying for that," I replied, placing my jacket behind me across the back of one of the pews. I followed by unbuttoning my shirt at the wrists, loosening my tie and starting on the buttons from the collar down.

"Well, I do want to get back to the party," she said with a giggle and headed toward the door I hadn't enjoyed the pleasure of being able to enter through. "Why are you disrobing?"

"So I don't tear my clothes," I replied, placing my shirt over the jacket on the pew. "I don't want any of your blood on my clothing." She stepped away, cocking her head and giving me on of those open mouth stares that white girls do when they want you to know they can't believe you. Then I watched her lose a few inches of height as she stepped out of her high heels and tickled her fingers in front of her in the air.

"Right now is the worst moment for a duel," she said, stepping backwards and dropping her weight into her legs. Her words attempted to dissuade; her body was prepping and her eyes showed fear. "Stay focused, Sekhem; we have something here to build upon."

"*I don't want your domain*," I heard myself say, "*not yet, at least. I'm just quite tired of the multitude. It's time to lessen the denominator.*" With that I balled up my hands and brought them up in front of me in a boxing stance.

"You know what it will cost if you lose?" she said with a smile, "*I'll break you, old man.*"

"I won't lose," I said without moving my lips and stepped with the right jab. *It will cost more if we don't.* My vision returned to third person then. My perspective shifted to watch Athena step back out of hand's reach but catch my leg in her stomach. She bent over at the impact, clamped her hands on to my leg and swung. I watched my body hurl into the wall and bounce back on to the floor with blood forming in my mouth as I rose. She reached her arm out as if waiting for a bird of prey to land on the forearm, summoning a clothing rack mounted on a pole from the other side of the room to her hand. It flew through the air lopsided and crashed into my back, splintering off one of the prongs. I watched my facial expression change from pain to surprise when the impact blew my body forward to where I had touched the floor with my finger tips to keep from falling on my face. Then I knew I had picked a fight I expected to win and would not.

Her arms, looking as if they have never seen a day of labor other than the barking orders of a physical trainer in a gym, ripped off the prongs of the clothing pole and cracked the base with her palm. *She hadn't been deadly then; her speech a symbol of sheepherders and farmers and focused on the rewards of hard work and self-education. In my gratitude for fishing me out of the ocean's soup, I taught her how the spear could overcome the blade or club of her neighbors. Naïve then, I thought the title of Titan was a compliment. A title of respect. It was also naivete that told me the invaders who had colonized my home had won by the element of surprise and superior arms, blinding myself to the fact that we were our own worst enemy. In the company the matron of western wisdom, I alluded to the treasures of the mind left behind in Kemet. Men seeking enlightenment through her guidance would trek south in togas and return in our native tunics with the stories of their mastery within the schools of Kemet. How were they to know they only received a kernel of the true beauty that had been lost. Through our many days together, she hoped I would forget that I was an exile, that I had been a husband, a son and that my prince was lost to me.*

In a daze, overlooking waterfalls that fed a quiet lagoon, she and I traded blows from spears as well as swords. Over the progression, the crude scrawlings on cave walls below us matched with smoky walls from far too many offerings took the form of an Oracle. That was one of my first of what would prove to be my future mistakes: leaving the nature of belief to shape the believer. As much as I dodged and spun from each spear thrust, she was consistent in her pursuit, able to follow up with every moment. Time would catch on to us and by the time Heru had found me among the pride of the Western world, it would be only after the first of the Partisans had made Olympus an offer. The pattern would begin again as Olympian fought Olympian by bringing in their respective factions of Titan and Gorgon. Athena, the consummate archetype of a daughter in search of detached father's affection, would play both sides. Blood from the arteries of human Greeks would saturate the soil and serve as the primer for Greek unification from a group of city-states to a nation.

The best I could do in the meanwhile was to hold my guard near my head as best as possible. My hands groped and found a shank of wood from one of the shattered pews, my body had eviscerated with its velocity. I used it as a prop to regain my standing, seeing Athena in her aspect twirling her weapon with a smile I would have love to have knocked off her face. Pride and ego fought with good judgment and restraint. I hadn't loss my temper, but the thought of losing a contest to her after being the victor countless times before did not sit well.

I moved at her again, closing my left eye as blood from a forehead wound dripped into my vision, coloring my sight and stinging my eyes. Ignoring the pain, I thrust the jagged edge toward her chest. It was a feint, as

I knew she would go for it, allowing me to change it into an upward swipe. She lowered her center and crouched to avoid, opening the door for me to bring my hand down and pummel the back of her head with the blunt edge of the wood fragment. It knocked her on to all fours and I followed with a kick that flipped her onto her back, skidding through more pews. Damn if she didn't keep a grip on that pole. She was up in less than a second, a broken piece of wood in her free hand to simulate a shield. As a spear maiden, she was just a problem. But as a Phalanx, she was a fucking monster. I got through a few slashes, but every impact against her shield made my arm freeze more and more. I tried one last swipe and spun hoping she wouldn't remember. I remembered . . . .

We all had our price. Her price was not only her father's love but the knowledge that no woman would ever embody her ability to learn and demonstrate knowledge. She would later be infuriated when the surge of monotheism out of Canaan banned her name, her temples and her worship along with Ishtar, Auset and any feminine principle related to literacy. She would revel in the superficial; no woman would match her education which she found more sustainable than even Aphrodite's beauty. Foolishly, it would be a woman or a principle wearing the body of a mortal woman who would prevent her gender's development across the globe for the next several thousand years. Even when I found her at the bedside of the dying nobility of Venice, promising immortality through the annals of history for devotion in Athena's way, I knew. I knew she would never stand in the wind, only pivot to which stance kept it at her back. No matter the Carrier she took, as long as a spider lived in her neck she wouldn't pick a side. For that, I knew the next time we met I would show her why even the losing side was better than playing both sides against one another.

As I came out of the spin and planted my weight to swing, I knew she had not fallen for it. She was accurate, the thrust already planned and executed before I had finished. In the before the butt end of her spear met my forehead, I was able to mutter: "Well done." Then I knew darkness.

Half here but half away, I saw without opening my eyes. She stood over me, poking at me with her spearhead. "This is all you brought?" she said with venom and disapproval. "You'll never stay in the game with such low-level glyphs." I felt hands rifling through my pockets, searching for something, like a looter over the dead. "We have moved on, but I'll take your burial rites for my trouble." Then occurred the sacrifice that opened the door. I saw my clothes being removed, hers as well. Unable to protest, I felt a familiar and sick paralysis as her naked form straddled me. "We should have done this long ago," she whispered in my ear and I knew darkness again.

It could be said academics were created to give a template for people to model themselves after, needing an explanation to an unexplainable event. Naked and cold, I woke up, curled into a little ball on a stone floor. Breathing regularly, my eyes focused and I realized I was still the temple, hopefully somewhere on the Parchick's property. I checked my body to find several scrapes, bruises and what looked like bite marks from either canine or sapien jaws. The residue on my lower regions combined with the aches in my lower back told a disappointing but clear narrative. I used the survivor in me to get standing and scan the room for my clothes. They were folded neatly and placed on the pew closest to where I had been lying. Methodically and with several groans, I was able to place my garments back on, promising myself I could burn them at home. This was the survivor at its best, a planned response for any crisis I lived through. I first became acquainted with it in my early teens, picking myself off the ground at the gas station on Third and Evans. The boys has said they wanted my jacket but they were each wearing more than triple my lunch money over a whole year on the their shoes alone. What they wanted was dominance. I was too stupid and too proud to hand over my power. So after the blows, the kicks, the spitting and the name-calling, they left my limp form to lie at the bus stop in front of the Shell sign.

There was a sense of success when I got standing, waved off the crackled calls of the Korean woman behind the glass of the gas station's booth and dragged my back pack to a pole which signaled a MUNI stop. When the 15 Third Street bus arrived, I climbed on, happy to show my Fastpass with blood-crusted fingers. I kept riding until I got to Granny's. She greeted me at the door with a hug, telling me to shower and dinner would be waiting. Before I fell asleep, I heard her voice on the phone from the other room, proud that I "didn't run and didn't die." That night, my survivor and I became best friends.

I was also an academic. I spent a lot of time in school. I had gone from high school to college to graduate school, chasing a doctorate. That was over fourteen years of school back to back without break. I made the transition from recording lectures to designing them. I also treated children along with my partner who specialized in recovery for abuse. The academic thought I should call Xochi immediately and ask to be picked up. What do I say exactly? *Xochi, you warned me and I got raped? Oh by the way, she's got it out for you. In addition, I haven't been as straight up as I could be.* Wait. Did I just admit that? Yes, the academic would win one battle but not both. I had been raped. I would not report this. I would get even.

Turning my attention to the alcove that served as an altar, I noted that any images related to my aspect had been removed. In its place was a larger porcelain bust, staring at me with almost the same expression as its flesh counterpart had when I was last conscious. I noticed the banner above the alcove, white writing on an azure field, in Greek. I couldn't tell you the dialect but I can assure you that this form of Greek hadn't been spoken in more than a thousand years. My hands took their own will and pulled the tapestry from its perch, trying my best to rip it as it came down. I crumpled it in my hands, only to hear her voice in my head, "I watch for their passing." I shoved the cloth into my pocket and made my way to the door.

The other side led to a hide-away panel in between rows of shelving in what appeared to be a disaster shelter. There were boxes of rations, gallons of water, entire cupboards of Kirkland brand batteries of all sizes, flashlights, sleeping bags, first aid kits and gasoline. The room itself looked like it could safely shelter ten to twelve people for well over a year. I made my way to the loading hatch doors and the pool house they led into. This brought me to the rear of the Parchick's property with a great view down the hill past downtown San Mateo and onto the San Mateo bridge.

From the darkness of the tree line that rimmed the acreage, I could make out movement in the well-lit house. Serving staff were in the process of cleaning up and packing materials for transport back to the catering truck. I pulled out my phone, waited for the signal to transform from roaming to a few reception bars and determined it was about a quarter before two in the morning. I lit a cigarette and walked toward the house, putting together my cover story in my head. I had lost five hours and would need to account for them. Coming over the ridge of the hill that over-looked the pool and was being used for parking lot, I scanned the terrain. There were very few cars left in the lot the one closest to mine had silhouettes sitting on the hood. I was down wind so I can smell the combination of the marijuana and tobacco leaf from a sub par cigar; I rhymed again, yay for me! As I got closer, I can make out the giggles of teenage girls mixed with the sounds coming from a battery-powered radio. The Gorillaz warned anyone who would listen about kids with guns. I was listening unfortunately those who should have been listening as well were too enthralled in the giggles of tongue kisses to notice. Closer with each step and I know. My feet made no sound in the gravel. My eyes told me the soles of my shoes left no tracks. I lost no weight but felt immensely lighter in weight. Another step closer and I could make out Alexandra's facial contours being stroked by the hand of the other girl leaning against the car right next to her. Her companion whispers in her ear, causing her to smile big and blush. They stay in stasis for a few moments longer until something perks her fear.

"What, baby?" her friend asked and I detect a lisp she hides with a false throat gravel.

"Why do I feel like someone is watching us?" Alexandra asks almost rhetorically.

"Because they often are," I said dead plan, standing off to the side of the two with my back to my car.

"Oh fuckin Doc!" she shrieked, dropping the joint and scrambling on the trunk of the car as her friend freezes with a pale shimmer to her face. "I'm so glad it's just you. You scared the shit out of me." I shrugged and sniffed the air as if to say, it's some good shit but it don't smell like shit that came out of you. I glanced between the girl and the remains of what was still smoking in the gravel.

"Event over?' I asked.

"It's been done," Alexandra's friend spits out. "They been getting drunk since the check!" Alex nudges her girlfriend in the stomach, giving her a glare.

"What are you doing out here, Doc?" Alexandra asks, trying to change the subject.

"You know how much I hate being called Doc?"

"Sorry, Clay," she replied. I shrugged to say thank you.

"What are you doing out here?" I replied back with a quick and indignant smile. I get the stoned deer in headlights reaction, so I take the lead. "Thought not. What check?"

"Oh, one of mom's friends dumped a big check on her for the center."

"How big is big?" I asked

"I think she said two million"

"Two million for four years," her friend corrected.

"He wasn't talking to you, Lucia," Alexandra snapped back.

"I was," I corrected. "Which friend was it?"

"I don't know," Alexandra said. "I've never seen her before."

"My mom didn't know her either," Lucia added, "but she said her name was old money."

"What name?"

"What is this? A police interrogation?" Lucia quipped, her eyes flashing.

"Fucking right," I said, folding my arms in front of me and trying to appear as if I had meant to knock the cherry off my cigarette on my coat.

"It's okay," Alexandra said in my defense. "The Doc--I mean Clay--is cool. He listens, ya know?" Alexandra stroked Lucia's arm, an attempt at cooling her need to protect. It was a moment that reminds you of all the secrets you hold but also the secrets you protect.

"Nagging bitch," Lucia said, cross.

"But you love me," Alexandra shot back with a smile. Lucia flumped her mouth and looked between me and Alexandra. She reached into the back pocket of her jeans and pulled out a business card, handing it to me as if I was taking out her house keys.

"She gave me her business card," Lucia added, looking away into the dark. "Told me to call her if I needed help with my portfolio." I read it as soon as it touched my hand, not taking my eyes off of Lucia. Constandina Kephalos, Gallery Owner and Art Buyer. Marin address, office phone, cell number and email. *Lucia enters the room, looking for the source of the commotion. Her mother is glazed over--a woman who has just handed the eldest Parchick a check. Her mother's eyes show reverence and jealousy over how a woman of that age could hold the confidence of a fifty-year-old with a body in her midtwenties. Lucia attempts to retrace her steps out of the room, alarmed by the squawks and coos of wealthy women when they have been drinking. Instead her mother's hand finds her wrist and she is led to the stranger to wait in line as the rest of the adorers put in their two cents. Lucia's mother introduces herself and then her daughter, explaining that Lucia is in the process of applying to art school for the fall. Lucia finds this strange, due to her last argument with her mother, clearly stating that unless it was a four-year university, she would be paying for school herself. Then the woman asks Lucia about her portfolio and Lucia finds herself talking without wanting to. She takes the business card and looks to her mother's mesmerized face as this woman talks. She feels the grip on the wrist loosen and knows she was only an icebreaker. Slinking out of the room, she meets Alexandra at her bedroom and the two keep up best appearance of good friends as they sneak out the backyard.*

"Thank you," I said, handing the card back to Lucia and shoving my hands in my pocket. I flicked the alarm off to unlock the doors to my car and walked to the driver's side door. I debate whether I should return to the house and pack up the informational table. If she was still in there, it would be another confrontation. If she wasn't, it would be another group of people I would have to whom I would have to explain my whereabouts. I decided I would tell Xochi about the visit and have someone sent to pick up the table. Sitting in the driver's seat brought back the ache to my lower back. I pulled down the window and turned the air conditioning on full to clean out the smell of the sun- heated car.

"Clay," Alexandra inquired, coming up to my window, as I backed past her location.

"Yeah?" I replied, stopping the car, shifting to drive and holding my foot on the brake.

"That lady's money. It's bad news, huh?"

"How many trips to Europe can your mother's money buy you to date a boy?" I asked.

"But this is who I am," Alexandra pleaded.

"Better to keep her distracted then?"

"Yeah, until she accepts me as my own person"

"Well, sometimes I guess we take the bribe and still do what comes natural," I answered.

"I guess this is a bit of a letdown, huh? I just want you to know I really do feel better after our sessions."

"Not a letdown at all; in fact, it's a relief. Hey, if she were my mother, I'd be stoned all the time too," I replied.

The rain was too hard to take 280 home. Too quick, too violent and too much gust to the wind. I didn't trust drivers to do the right thing in conditions like that, even with six lanes. To keep with the irony, the water only stayed vitrulent as I worked my way out of the hills and through downtown San Mateo. By the time I could see the 101 north entrance, the only hints of rain were the surviving drops rolling off the windshield to the hood. I smirked and just filed it under "figures" along with my palm pat determining I had two cigarettes left to the pack. I predicted it would take one cigarette to get home if the 101 was empty, two if there was a crowd, and pure panic if it was bumper to bumper.

Driving along the stretch, I counted signs to keep my sanity and pot holes to save the suspension. Nothing on the radio seemed to stick; I could stay with five seconds of any given song before searching the band for another selection. The CDs in the changer either ground on my nerves or reminded me of a time I couldn't bring back. That is where the mind can go--dangerous. The search for a replacement obsession to avoid all the topics one did not want to think about. Going down the list like a shopping trip: do I need to worry about Granny? No. Grading papers before next Monday? No. Putting another meal in my system before bed? Yes, but only if I follow it with a six-pack. I lit the first of my remaining cigarettes, debating in my head if anything said by this woman could be trusted. Then the replays kicked off in my head, some compromise between a past I couldn't decipher and a compensation for the previous hours.

We are looking out a window, down toward construction below us in streets. Las Vegas is being built. Not the Vegas of the movies but the modern marvel of indulgence we all know it for. Judging by the placement, I'm in the upper floor of the Flamingo, one of the first high rises on the strip. She sits across the room at the table, smoking a cigarette to go along with the drink she has poured herself from the inlay bar. Her back to me, the body language is confrontational and dejected. I notice the white bathrobe wrapped loosely around her body while assessing the discarded women's clothing on the floor by her bedroom.

"You can stop checking," Constandina whines. "My people are placed throughout the entire building."

"Your people don't work with me," I watch myself reply.

"But they work for me," she flashes back, "and I work for you."

"You work for yourself," I counter, "and sometimes that works for me."

"And you work for your fucking cats," she says with a repugnance and frustration.

"I take care of those who take care of me." She laughed then, not that she thought it was funny; it was the need to dismiss me.

"He's right; you are as archaic as you are idealistic. How is that possible? To be innovation itself and yet afraid of new systems? Nobody uses the felines to Reconcile anymore."

"Yeah, rogue me and put my faith in an Isfet system. That sounds wise," I attack sarcastically.

"Just because it's theirs doesn't mean you can't build you own"

"So they know the ins and outs better than me? Just because it's new doesn't make it better."

"That's ridiculous, Sekhem. New is better," she throws back at me.

"No, pudgy spearmaid." I watch myself turn from the window with eyes so full of depth they lack pupils. She is alert in her chair, the long black hair falling on her shoulders that had been tanned from a life near the south of France. A different era, a different face, a different body, the same lost girl. *"After these buildings fall to the sheer arrogance of your statement, I'll find you, show you Giza and remind you about the old that is better."*

"You are being spiteful for the sake of it!" she spits at me. I looked back to the window, watching the workmen in the lot at their task. It was nearly a hundred degrees of desert heat, which surprised me considering the pace. I was reminded of the laborers toiling in the sands of work sites near my home, which later became the very temples my name was placed on. The watchful eye ignores nothing, including the potent raw clouds moving to give a few workmen shade in this region. The hard hats should tip so they can wipe their foreheads in relief afforded from the blotter between their skins and the Nevada sun. Those who notice this cloud should not be there at this place and this time, take no comfort, continuing to dig at the earth while their eyes lift to scan the worksite in search of anyone else suddenly unsettled. Out of every ten workmen in the site, only two seem unnerved but sadly unaware that a ratio is forming around them. There are also six out of every ten working that hit the earth more diligently, grinding away at their task. They are ants in a colony who never ask the queen why the leaf must be cut. Watching them, are two more loosening up in how they toil. They stiffen

the back and slow in their pace, somehow delighted that the sweat covered backs in front of them are troubled and the grunting pick axe to their right is chucking harder than them. 2:6:2

My eyes are pulled to the roof, two blocks away from the work site but higher by six stories and twice as wide. On a building that should be bare except for ventilation and elevator shacks sits a dog glaring down into the lunch tray of labor and flying earth. I know this canine enjoys the false assumption of a mixed breed corner hound but I know it better. A narrow head down to small thin snout, looking more like a rabbit than a dog, loves to hide is history. On Malta they would properly name it but it has taken a falsely noble hint in its current incarnation being named after the kings of our home. I see right through the red and tan skin to the jackal. The two scars along its front legs always identify it. He can't hide that from me because I put them there. I know when the hound leaves these men returning to their lives will shrink the ratio to .05:8.5:1. It is due to the items being built into the foundation of the building that nobody but myself, the woman in the hotel room with me and the hound would know are there. To the work men, they are pieces of a puzzle firing away at a plan pulled from an architect's map. We see the blueprint before us. The building might as well be built to us.

"Then at least you know I am dependable," I say and move away from the window heading into the bathroom. There is a pink leather make up case I pack up and carry out of the bathroom to the room service cart in the hallway just before the door leading out of the suite. I lift the fold of the white tablecloth and place the make up case on the second shelf next to the four mason jars with glyphs written on each. Moving my arm makes me recognize the all white monkey suit extending from the jacket sleeve on my arm matching the white gloves on my hands in stark contrast to the deep shade of brown of my skin tone. My hair is a slick conk pushed down on to my head and my face shaved clean. Different body, different era, same purpose. I push the cart out of the room and into the hallway, buttoning the front of my tuxedo jacket at the stomach to cover the hunting knife I have tucked in the waistline.

I push the cart down the hallway and wait for the elevator. The first two were full of people. I keep my eyes low waiting for an empty car; black men didn't make eye contact with the white patrons. It came eventually, quiet and spacious, smelling of cigars and meat with heavy gravy. I step inside, pressing the button to send it to the top most floor of the building. The doors take ages to close, but once they did, the car jerked upward towards the rest of the penthouses. It is the haze of the Veil, breaking the building into its specific architecture. My mind shoots through the hallway, across the worksite and into the elevator shaft of the building where the dog sat. There is a sound like a rubberband being snapped against a rolled-up newspaper. The haze faded and I waited, the elevator's doors opening upon the roof of the building I had just spied from Constandina's window. I push the cart into the doorway, stepping backwards through the solid rear wall of the elevator housing. I move quickly to its west corner, watching through the very structure as the dog turned its head at the sound of the cart in the door track. It pads over to the end of the cart protruding on to the rooftop, its nose catching a drawing scent. Its ears flatten on its head, shaping effortlessly into that of a man crouching in front of the door.

It didn't occur to me until after I edge around and step right through the elevator shaft on a long diagonal that I hold the hunting knife and am stalking forward in a low crouch myself. The knife cuts into his neck right under the chin, making a line of over-fill from a Kelly Moore can across the stained wood of his larynx. He jerks backwards gurgling, his hand reaching up to grasp at his throat. "Yes," I reassure him. I seize this opportunity to kick his frozen body in the chest, lifting him in the air and twirling him onto his belly. He continues to panic and swivel his shoulders, to both raise his body and get a grip on his bleeding throat. I lay my weight on his lumbar, pulling at his shoulders with my white gloves hands until the snap stopped his struggles. It is messy work from there, plunging the knife into his back and cutting along the rear of his rib cage. I place his liver, his kidneys, his lungs and his spleen in each of the mason jars. I find myself debating whether to leave his heart or not, deciding taking it was the level of viciousness I wanted to communicate. With his heart cut out, I place it in the makeup case, lifting his neck to fill the bottom of the case with a small puddle of blood.

By this time, the evening has arrived with the sun dipping behind the horizon along with the rain clouds forming sprinkles across the city. I can hear the thoughts and conversations of the dwellers in the streets below, questioning the strength of the rain in the desert during a Vegas summer. It didn't matter where but that storm would make its presence known. Grabbing what I came for, I stuff the jars and make up case in the second shelf of the cart. There are two bottles of Glen Fiddich on the cart, over half a century old. I douse the mangled cadaver in the liquid. I stare at the body, knowing that while it didn't draw breath it certainly wasn't done watching me. Sharing my thoughts, I remind it that though I had losses on my record, I was in the lead without any draws. I'm not just going to discard this body you hid within; I am going to scar you this time for how they associate my name with you. These thoughts burn, and his corpse, lit afire, smells of the burning flesh, telling me there was a short time for the blaze without attracting attention or being put down by the increasing water. I knew that storm would bring him, the hound always preceded the storm which marked his arrival. I'd let him have his water fit and picked up the wind to balance back against him, pushing the drops away from me and away from his fallen scout. The oxygen fed the flames but it wouldn't go unnoticed for too much longer; the rain increased to fight the wind and began pull away the blood. Pushing the cart inside the elevator, I let the doors close and the car begin its descent.

Across the street, facing the worksite was a supply truck parked with its back doors open. It was unmanned the writing on the side suggesting its driver was inside a building either delivering clean or picking up soiled linen. Another snap and I push the dining cart out of the back of the truck, down the slope into the work site. It was empty, the laborers gone for today with the promise of concrete being poured in the morning. Moving quickly, I bury a mason jar in its upper left corner, followed with another in the upper right. Two more jars at each lower corner. I return with the make up case, tilting so the blood dripped in lines. Soon after, I have written the shape of the beetle into the very dirt and sand, commanding that location to transfer the kinetic energy of the mind of anything on the building's grounds into fuel that made the rules. I leave the makeup case in the center of the foundation of what would one day be Caesar's Palace, its placement being the center of the shell on the beetle's back. The site becomes fused with words, thoughts, intent and action. I also place a door. As the entire resort, casino and shopping plaza rose before me into a three dimensional mock up of what would take the next four years to become Caesar's, I push the ratio to 3: 6: 1. For every ten in this place, three would have the remarkable notion that the world before them was not to be taken at face value and could been through for the Veil that lies under, six would go about their lives easily misled and one would thank the woman in the hotel room for their ability to manipulate the six to whatever end served their purpose; human and sponsor. The next time I walked into this building, neither she nor my family could harm me.

I take the cart with me as I left, ensuring the lack of suspicion in the hold that been placed on the ground themselves. I snatched minor works from the hands of my enemies and gave it to a competitor they could not harry; both answered to the same venomous masters' greed. Athena could pay more. I ditch the *cart two alleys over. Four more blocks away, I decide to cast off my blood-stained clothes in lieu of a discarded set of coveralls and boots left out near a clothesline. I didn't actually recognize it was a trap, of course, until my pants were off one leg and I was working on the standing leg. It was the fire escape, the bolting against the building pulling away from the mortar and toppling down. As it collided, snapping my ribs and rushing their sharp pieces into my heart, I sense a smile on my face, knowing I had won some round of the game. I stare into the last sights I would know, a small, malnourished cat licking my face before running off at the sound of the foot steps. Then from the view of the cat, I watch the lord of storms check the pulse on the body I had just vacated. He had been outrun again, just as he had been every time before.*

"Fuck," I said, passing the Oyster Point road exit and overshooting the way home. If I hadn't been in remembrance I would have been watching the signs better. I realized at that late hour I would probably have better success heading north than trying to back track. Silver Avenue was showing its face after both the Third Street and the 280 junction had tempted me. I turned on an early signal and cruised down the far right lane toward the off ramp. The signage of the Union 76 station and its overbearing four soda machines put it in perspective: what ever was done in Vegas in my memory of the sixties permanently left a mark on that city. Not just a mark but a title, a deed of ownership. As long as the Palace stood, with pieces of an attribute's chosen Carrier's organs embedded to its foundation, Athena would have a voting membership of the city of Las Vegas. There was the essence of why I was offended. She owed us! How dare she steal from me! As hopeless as this war was, I was energized by the possibility of revenge; I still had her son.

I parked across the street on San Bruno, sauntering to the late night-spot called the Pizza Joint. I ordered two slices and a soda, walking over to the gas station for a pack of smokes. Surprisingly the door to the mini-mart was unlocked and open to the mini-mart with no window service. I bought two packs, waiting at the door for the two kids to pass by. They walked in front of me by four feet, leaving the scent of burnt weed and spilled cognac in their wake. I smirked at their constant limp from sagged pants that made it harder to run from police and even harder to hold a pistol concealed securely. The black hoodies they sported for anonymity contrasted against the dyed tips of their dreadlocks, making them that much easier to pick out of a lineup. I believe it was my sarcasm and judgmental cynicism that tuned me into their conversation.

"Nahh," the taller one chides, "it don't even work that way."

"What chu mean?" the shorter and more lithe one replied.

"My nga, this shit ain't even real," he says as he pulls at the shorter one's clothes and hair. "The fits, dem cars, clothes and dis hair. Dat shit don't mean nothing cuz it was nothing to begin with."

"Least I'll be lookin righ even wen I'm buried."

"Nga, we already dead. Ain't matta how you look," D'Anthony argues.

"I ain't see how some dood gon change all dat. Ngas still gon hustle shoot kill all dat shit. Dats how it's been."

"Not foreva, dats jus what we expect. The door, doe. If ngas gon beef, shit gotta be for something, not dis fucked shit my nga." The taller, fatter one reaches into the pocket of his sweatshirt, pulling out a CD and hurling it across Bayshore into the freeway in frustration.

"Dee, that's yo mixtape!" says the taller one, who I realize by the squawk in his voice is the younger of the pair.

"Icks," D'Anthony says, reminding me of the coffee he bought for me weeks ago, "that shit ain't real. The Hawk is real, nga. I'm ridin for them." D'Anthony rushed forward to the street to check the oncoming traffic. "C'mon. Icks," he yells and the companion follows, both of them making it across the street, before the 9X pulls up at the stop. I walk into the restaurant, getting the nonverbal cue that my food was ready. I gave the counter person my card, waiting for the debit transaction to be approved. I let my eyes drift over to the mounted television, which I expected to being playing a soccer game or at least some music videos. Instead, the cable was tuned to CNBC, a special expose on a new social media site called Twitter.

"I've got 100 followers so far," the young kid behind the counter says, looking between my face for approval and his Blackberry. I felt I was being baited in some kind of juvenile competition.

"That's one follower too many in my world," I replied.

CHAPTER EIGHTEEN

"The better the idea, the more it has to be sold. Especially to those it benefits most."

-Joyce

The next morning was a bitch, harsh with cold symptoms. I dosed up, eating a full breakfast to chase the thousands of milligrams of Vitamin C, Vitamin B and cleansers such as Echinacea. I found the drive to school easier than I expected, with a ton of nose-blowing and phlegm shots out the window into on coming traffic. I parked in the faculty lot, fabricating a parking pass out of an empty pack of cigarettes, my pen and a few spoken glyphs. When I wrote it, it appeared as the most ghetto shit I ever pulled, but walking away from the car toward my building, it had morphed into the real deal along with an officiating sticker.

My mailbox was full. Full of shit I wouldn't use, full of shit I shouldn't use and full of shit I couldn't use. I shoved the entire stack into my backpack and headed to the cafeteria to get coffee. It was still a mystery to me why the undergraduates got a better brewed cup than the faculty, but overall it was just nasty stuff. I had learned that free trade coffee was a buzz word for muddy outhouse back-run with caffeine. I needed the kick after the cold meds had taken their affect. There was an hour before I would need to walk across the street and set up for the day's lecture. I spent the time clicking on emails to pretend I had read them while sorting my mail into three piles: notify to never notify me again, recycling after shred, and should read these. The envelope was heavy, thicker than standard postage, but certainly not a manila.

I used a letter opener on it, probably one of the few times. The smell alone explained that this item was a pile of its own. It was intoxicating, a perfume, someplace between a sweet ceremonial oil and the scent of room service breakfast. The envelope contained two items, a folded paper and a small plastic bag, the size used to package tinctures and medications. I dug out the letter, sipping my coffee, unfolding it. Checking it for a moment, I starred at the envelope. Neither the letter nor the envelope had a single marking on them. Could it be that an envelope was misplaced in my inbox containing a single sheet of paper that was bereft of writing? Was it an analogy? Was the blank white paper being a code for a new direction? A flag of surrender?

My phone at the desk rang, startling me and then stopping. The jolt caused a bit of coffee to drip out of my retarded jaw and onto the sheet before. Precision defeated, I shook the paper to roll the droplets off the sheet, dripping it over the garbage can. Can I do anything right today? Perhaps I can if it involves a cigarette. Then again maybe the accident is the solution. I noticed after the brown stain of the caffeinated bilge water turns the sheet black as carbon. Black as the land my soul hails from. The stain dried nearly instantly, reducing the paper to a sea of white with a mis-shaped streak of flimsy dark. Being the stupid advanced monkey I am, I dip a Kleenex in my cup and lightly brush it across the paper, converting it to a landscape of ebon. It now looks like charcoal tablet covered in tiny letters etched into the paper and painted in blood red. I put on my glasses from their tomb in my middle desk drawer, hidden away the fear that that wearing them might encourage my perpetual singledom. The prescription is strong but helpful, revealing letters that are actually glyphs--hieroglyphs of the Old Kingdom dating to the earliest days of the BC era.

At one point, free will was the lead-in to every discussion we held. Every decision we made. Making your own choices might even be clichéd when presented with the facts that will only lead to a specific outcome. Patience has never been my strong suit. I found I rely on you for that. I honored your request in allowing the abilities you needed to enact the solution. I am also burdened with your removal should you be wrong. This is not the beginning of a threat; do not make that mistake. I only wish to tell you that you have to be right, Sekhem. This must work because I cannot repeat this again. It is impossible to endure. My faith, a notion you have often wrestled with, is placed in that you do indeed know what will end this bitter game. Know then that should you have forgotten too much and remembered too little, I will be the last thing your existence knows. Remember what is right, not what is easy, my Sekhem. One of us will lead you to their hold over you forever; one of us will return you to yourself. When it is your day to know which is which, remember that I am still a woman. I need you to pick me.

I heard the voice in my head as I read the words, second nature as intrinsic as my breath but unknown and distant. No face nor name could be placed, although I found myself smiling despite the strong threats embedded in the language. I folded the letter back along its creases, returned it to its envelope and placed the envelope in my breast pocket. I debated a long time in my head the possible meanings. Xochi was obviously not in the running as she was married and we had more sibling relationship than anything. I did happen to remember it was not uncommon for both Egyptian and Aztec deities to marry their siblings. With Xochi out of the running that left two unnamed feminine energies with claims to my attention; some guys have all the luck, right? Was Athena the piece to be mindful of and misled by? As much history as we had or I remembered, that just wasn't the one my gut told me. Beyond all prejudices I held, I knew her to be too opportunistic to match myself too. Then I remembered the warnings to myself. Number Six: Your heart answers to Neith. *Neith.* I did a quick internet search with a silent self-criticism amounting to a statement that I should know this. Somehow I didn't like what I read: inaccurate, prepared for viewing and with such a sense of innocent naivete that I wondered how it could be applied to a huntress. Then there were the dreams of Neith. My hands massaged my jaw where her fists had landed. Could it be that the letter was from Neith? I tried to probe that question, piecing together what I could remember with what was in archive. It only produced a splitting headache that caused me to hold my head and take a cat nap on the cool. The appointment notification went off on my phone, signaling I needed to pack up to go prep my classroom. It was perhaps fortuitous that I hadn't unpacked my laptop so transition to the next building was that much easier.

I placed my pack on the desk in the classroom, pulling my laptop out with a flicker on the power switch. While the computer started, I booted up the smart board and came back to pull out my lecture notes. I was supposed to have papers back that I didn't feel like correcting so I made a mental note to make an announcement regarding the delay. Looking through my notes, the reading for the week had to do with the necessity of symbols. I wasn't enamored with the text as a whole, but I found that Sandstrom struck a balance between psychological theories I agree with and had the gift for teaching woven into the writing. Today, I found the title of the text as whole particularly ironic: Symbols, Selves, and Social Reality: A Symbolic Interactionist Approach to Social Psychology and Sociology. I smiled to myself, happy that I uploaded additional articles electronically to the Blackboard platform for student download rather than compile a hundred-plus dollar reader that would use about four pages. Such amenities were the privilege of the information technology age that also blinded these kids from appreciating how truly good that had they had it.

They filed into the classroom one by one, then in clumps and then back to the soloists as they found their seats. A few, only the young women, asked about my weekend and how I was doing in general. I made up a story about having friends from out of town visiting, cooking dinner at home and listening to jazz vocalists on Pandora while drinking wine as we played Cranium. So I'm a good liar, but it isn't all necessarily fabricated. I knew this was a guaranteed tactic to put me into the "safe and boring" category in the minds of these young women. It worked at faculty meetings to keep me politically neutral and it worked in the classroom to make me socially sterile since I was an unmarried straight male academician who didn't sleep with female research assistants and worked with kids. It worked a little too well, drawing a number of inquiries as to my favorite jazz artists. I threw out some names I'd either seen online or heard referred to in the most obscure of terms in order to throw off the interviewer; I was good at keeping people out of my head so I could stay in theirs.

Instead, she began to tell me how many live shows she had attended of the artists and how upset that their latest performance this weekend was an invite only. Some other meathead named Noah who always wore earphones to class mentioned his girlfriend's mother was going to the event, tickets being made available by a sizable donation to a political organization. He went on to wax poetic about how his mother didn't know shit about politics but was doing it because there was a chance to meet some high profile Marin art gallery owner who was hosting it. My antennas perked up as I waited for the class to settle. As they found their seats and fell silent at the sight of my dead-faced gaze out to the world, I made sure I reached into Noah's memories, finding images of his mother. His mother Ronnie wasn't hard to find after that, as she was currently up the street doing laps at Koret gym. Ronnie gave me an address for the art gallery which matched exactly with the address of the business card that had been given to Lucia. I decided to begin researching the performer, since I planned on seeing her performance.

"Your papers will be ready by next class," I led with, noting the medley of relief and concern in the eyes of the sea of social-networking zombies seated before me. "For those of you worried, we are going to do an assignment today that will tack on some points to the paper."

I didn't want it to happen but it was involuntary. I suppose it was to be expected by tempting fate via Noah and Ronnie's memories. *Shades of silence in the library, highlighting notes and recopying into college-ruled personal index. Drafting, revising, sending out and redoing with a heavy emphasis on stress and perfection. The night before, still hung over from the previous weekend, cursing my name for assigning homework, putting anything that will work into the blood to stay awake. Texting furiously, calling like a maniac, offering any price a black American Express card can buy, promising the world if only the sucker on the other end would write their paper for Professor Durward's class. Thought for thought, I knew every single member of my class like the back of my hand.*

I loaded up the Powerpoint I prepared and walked through my opening monologue in my head. It seemed to make sense so I let loose verbally. I related a story to the class of when I was in graduate school I was required to attend a retreat the first week of school. There I was, Clay Durward, a child of buses and block parties, sitting in a cabin in the remote wilderness on the eastern seaboard with thirty-nine other candidates who not only didn't look like me but were absolutely more comfortable in rustic settings than I was. This earned me some laughs out of the group, which was a good sign. The opportunity was there. On one hand, I could sense a true moment of empathy, gauging the facial responses of our audience with the memories that drifted from their minds like bubbles off the stem held by a small child at a parade. On the other hand, I was more comfortable being the only person who had never sat around a campfire in the company of a room of evolving personalities who replied with the nonverbal recognition of their own moments of isolation.

I clicked to my first slide, which was a table of participant names. "As you can see, I've assigned you to work groups." I went on to describe their specific team learning tasks. Warren, the ultimate problem student, sat huddled in the back. My problem with Warren was this was the second time he had come to class stoned. The first I suspected, the second I heard his guilty inner monologue. On top of which he had taken my class because he was told I was "cool" and assumed that meant I would let him do little. His goal for today was to keep his head low, glance at his phone and not say a word. By the time I made my way to his team and requested Warren be the spokesperson to present out to the class as a whole, his paranoia led him down the walk way to deciding I really did hate him.

"Actually I like you a lot, Warren," I said out loud walking away as he smirked. "Just wished you felt the same way about yourself." He licked his lips and stared at me, feeling exposed, wanting to scream at me and thank me, but deciding on nothing. Had Wukong's words sunk so deep into my psyche that I had to say the phrase to defend my own subconscious? Then perhaps Warren was one of my people, no different from Xochi's farmers or Wukong's monkeys, who reflected the values of their sponsors. For all I knew, any member of the class could be one of my people by following the genetic gravy train from migration patterns back to Kemet. No, fuck that. I wanted no part of those people claiming me or follower notions that would only grow if I let it. I thought back to the two young men by the Pizza Joint the night before. What if there was no opt in? What if I couldn't deny or fire a customer? The thought had not even occurred to me that I might not be not be able to reject followers. Even if I whispered to each and every one of my self-appointed followers, stating my objections, if they followed my instructions to abandon my worship, they were still following. This is a problem I decided. This was Paradox.

I figured out I had been staring out at the traffic on Turk by the sound of the door closing. It was another professor, walking in for prep and fighting the urge to take ownership of a room. He was reassigned a new room each semester while attempting to do what educators encourage as "filling the room with your presence." I vaguely remember class ending, hearing the distant goodbyes of my students and the silence of an empty room. I walked over and began my shutdown, using my body language to apologize to the other professor while my eyes took me to what to needed to be packed up. Five minutes and I walking back across Turk to my office. I grabbed four bottles of water from the faculty lounge and made my back to the office. Closing the door and locking it, I found I had polished off three bottles without thinking about it. My headache had returned and kept it impossible to keep my eyes open. I popped two Advil out of a bottle I kept in the desk drawer and chased them with what remained in the last bottle of water. Waiting for the effect seemed too long, so I lay out on the couch.

My phone alarm woke me up. Groping in my pocket bleary-eyed, I saw a notification for a board meeting prep at the Center was happening in fifteen minutes. The Center was in the Tenderloin, thirty minutes by car, even longer by cab and pointless by bus. In addition, my breath smelled like slap-boxing midgets and my eyes looked as if I had just left a dust storm. I considered sending the "can't make it" text to Xochi but knew the group couldn't move on if I wasn't there. Swinging my feet off the couch, I drew a small door, peering into the bathroom on the first floor nearest to the conference room at the Center. It was empty but to be safe I did a quick scan of the hallway outside of the bathroom. Cynthia, our up-and-coming professional, was a heart beat away, looking intent at the door to the bathroom. I made the jump quickly, locking the door as soon as I was inside. The tug from the other side came just a second later. There was two tugs and a pause. I started to question why people do that until I realized the light was off inside. I heard Cynthia click her heels against the floor as she walked away.

"Hello Cynthia," I heard Xochi's bright voice say from down the hallway. "See you in there?"

"Yes," Cynthia replied, "just needed to freshen up before, but the door's locked."

"I know," Xochi answered loudly, "I always have to pee in the middle of a meeting and feel bad for leaving. Locked? Weird." I hear the click of her shoes coming closer to the door. She tugs and then pauses. "One of the kids must have locked it. I have a spare key on my desk." Two sets of foot falls walking away. I turn on the light and push the faucet on to a full blast from the left, waiting for the stream to turn hot and steamy. By the time it does, I hear the footfalls approaching. I flush the toilet in hopes that the combined sound of running water would send a message; it doesn't. Placing my hand on the handle, I pull against it with all my weight as the key enters the lock. First tug is easy to negate; the second one gets about half a millimeter before it's yanked back.

"Hm," Xochi says with suspicion, "think this *door* is acting up. Why don't you use one of the restrooms upstairs in the dorms."

"I don't want to hold up the meeting," Cynthia replied with a lot of worry and even more concern.

"I'll cover for you," Xochi says softly and I can almost imagine her putting her arm around the kid's shoulder. Kid in the respect that either Xochi or my own body was much older than Cynthia, but not so young that she was the client we found hanging out in our computer labs years ago. I heard footfalls walking away and up the stairs. I finished washing my face, making sure the hot water had run through my eyelids three times. I turned off the water and stared at the light under the crack of the door.

"*Open this door,*" Xochi growled low and focused at me. I unbuckled my pants, dropped through and waddled over to the toilet. Sitting on a throne of a whole different nature, I put my chin on my palm and sat.

"Little busy in here," I moaned dramatically, catching my own smile in the mirror.

"*Three minutes, Durward,*" I heard through the door.

"You can't push this stuff, Cervantes," I replied back and covered my mouth with my palm to keep from laughing. "Get roids that way. You know fundraiser food is worse than beer and chocolate."

"*Two minutes forty three seconds,*" I heard in my head and saw the light under the door had turned a loading zone yellow with shades of carnelian. I smirked and watched the light fade, moving my hands like a percussionist as the foot falls took her away from the door. I had half a mind to stay there too but I've never been one to delay an absolution.

I was in my chair shortly after having completely awakened and reviewed meeting documents. Cynthia came in just after I had greeted Samuel, our silver-haired CFO, Joyce, our development director, and gave a non-committed headnod to Xochi.

"Hello, Clay," Cynthia said with surprise, "I didn't see you come in." Cynthia hadn't meant to make me explain but her office was near the front door. I usually walked by her when entering and caught up with her as I mixed the first of several cups of coffee in the kitchen across from her office.

"Heya, Cynthia," I replied, losing no time despite the milky-blue orbs above Xochi's nosecork screwing their wall into the side of my head. "I came in the back today. Needed a change of routine." I glanced at Xochi and got a dead stare of non-amusement. I pulled out a pen, biting my mouth down on the cap as I locked my fingers behind my head and stared at the documents I pulled from my bag to lay on the table before me.

"Thank you, everyone, for your punctuality," Xochi started as she handed us all a sheet of paper. "As I mentioned in my email, I've moved some items up on the agenda in the interest of meeting our deadline." I waited until the packets went around, taking one for myself and passing it down. The agenda alone was enough to say that the time I spent skimming the documents on the toilet was lost to futility as the new versions touched my hands. It wasn't hard through I kept a slow pace of turning pages, knowing I had memorized the contents soon as I touched the first page. "Sam, would you like to lead us off?" Xochi asked rhetorically with a smile.

"Of course," Sam replied taking the glasses off of his face, placing them on the table and folding his hands in front of him. Samuel has a slow tone, aggravated by deep nostrils that bring out a almost congested sediment to his words. New Jersey, Pennsylvania, maybe even Virginia. This rock back and forth between the harsh accents of the East Coast was the affectation of being educated outside of New York. He stares at us before he speaks, large brown eyes with the hints of yellow that only come from being on the planet long enough to see a county win a world war and lose a conflict in Vietnam. There's a slight pop at the corners of his mouth as he begins to speak, the signal to say you better listen. Samuel isn't even aware that he does this. It was those years at Merrill Lynch that taught him to make sure everything counts, but it was a forced retirement due to his age that brought him to the Center.

"Our year began in June with a projected fiscal operating budget of $756,000, seventy-three percent of funds for this year already allocated to close the gap of the $250,000 we would need to complete the year as well as build up for programs next year. There was an estimated window of four to five months for us to raise funds." He paused to sip from a paper cup of water that he was never far from. "$175K of those restricted funds were raised by grant awards and sponsorships leaving us close to $75,000 to meet our target."

"Which is why we held the fundraiser last night," Cynthia chimed in with a smile. I smiled back, happy to see she could keep up with the discourse, whereas Sam starred until he determined she was finished speaking and he could continue. "Although a third of our gap was closed, we were still well below the mark." Sam laid his palms flat on the table and looked from face to face. "A conservative projection of last night's event had us prepared to ask for voluntary salary reductions. However, due to the generous network of Chloe Parchick, we were awarded with a philanthropic gift of two million dollars." The silence afterward was deafening in its permanence.

"Why aren't we clapping?" I asked, not seeing the need for histronical somber face.

"Two million dollars closes the gap," Sam answers, "but also creates a surplus we hadn't anticipated nor does that bode well with funders or the board."

"Problem solved," I chirped. "Pay the bills for next year and split what's left over among us." Sam was making the sound of laughter in his throat well before his head shaking and he replaced his glasses on his face.

"That is not going to happen."

"Why not?" I pushed. "Hell, if anything you all can take my piece. I have money coming in from teaching. You could pay off the new house and take your wife to the Florida Keys, Sam."

"I highly doubt--"

"We have extra money and are supposed to live as humbly as we sew people back together again?"

"It's an abuse," Xochi said cold and direct. "The tax structure of a nonprofit foregoes taxes in lieu of distribution of profit."

"So don't call it that--"

"No. Surplus funds can only be reinvested into the organization for operational capacity." It was then through meeting Xochi's eyes that I realized more than one conversation was taking place. "We also have to think how it would look, shooting around asking for donation, begging for contributions for this Center's youth only to reap the rewards with new cars and material gain? There are limits and consequences to every act."

"How also does it look?" I cut in, generally unwilling to argue with Xochi in a public setting but feeling a necessary debate coming. "How does it look to provide a service to a population when you can't provide for yourself? Cynthia shares an apartment with three other women. Joyce is being eaten alive by student loans. Sam supplements his pension with what we can pay him. I teach and you haven't had a car in four years because of the cost of gas."

"And carbon footprints," she added.

"But mostly the cost of gas." I was spitting as I talked, incensed and didn't care. "Meanwhile--"

"Clay," Xochi tried to interrupt.

"Meanwhile we are putting in over eighty hours a week, weekends too, impressing upon young people that they cannot check out–they must buy in. The message is that even if they get to a place where they can make a change in their community, they do so at the sake of things in life they want because--"

"Clay . . . ," Xochi charged.

"Because! Because why? I'll tell you: the goods guys are pussies. Yeah, I said it. Fucking pussies. That's what we're telling them. The pimp who molested you since you were a child gets a caddy because we expect his wicked ass to have it nice because that's why people exploit to have nice shit. However, you and anyone else who helps that child will struggle for a bloody fast pass, because in this story, standing up to oppression means you have to *suffer*. You know why the new Superman movie tanked? Because who wants to idolize a dude in tights who can fly around the fucking globe but has to dress like an introverted stereotypical spaz with stalker pedophile tendencies in order to get close to the woman he loves. He can't just tell her 'my fulltime job is being from Krypton but I'll be home for dinner'. No. Fuck no. He has to act like a bumbling high school chemistry club president to share her space until one day she realizes the caped hero she's in love with is the same as the guy at the office she hates car pooling with."

"What is this about, Clay?" Xochi asked with a slight head nod to remind me of who was in the room.

"So isn't this more about how women value strength in men?" Cynthia asks, intrigued.

"No, it's about making sure that rules work for us and not against us," I answered Xochi but directed my response to Cynthia.

"Personally, I enjoyed the Batman movie more," Samuel added with a playful tone and an emotionless face. "But rules are rules so you tell us how to make this work for you, Clay."

"Raise salaries excluding mine, starting with Cynthia," I shot back to Sam. "Hire more case managers, double the amount of beds upstairs and put aside cash for every kid who walks through our program who wants to finish school has the money to do so."

"Can we afford that?" Joyce asked. Samuel pulled out a pen and scribbled some things on the back of his report. He crossed out a few lines, added a few more and ran his finger over the items a couple times. "We can afford it," Sam concluded. "If we kept fundraising at current rate, these new programs should keep flowing into another four years."

"Problem solved," I said with an exhale and began stacking the paperwork over the old.

"Until it creates new problems," Xochi said with a counter grin. "For all the new programs we have to make sure it meets the mission and produces fruit."

"An optimist," I replied, "always good to have one on the team."

"Well, you can't change the rules," Sam added, "and expect the game to end on its own."

"Well put," Xochi interjected. "Cynthia, can you take lead on how we program this?"

"Of course," Cynthia smiled at new task.

"Joyce, after you get the language from Cynthia," Xochi asked, looking through her calendar and motioning at Cynthia, "can you--"

"Figure out how to sell it to the kids and then the board?," Joyce asked.

"Read my mind," Xochi said with a girlish chuckle. "Well, I think we're done here unless else one else has pressing business?" She looked around the room and was met with silent smiles. I found my eyes fixed on the map stretched on the wall. It was of California with an unfortunate emphasis on counties, I ran my eyes along the border connected Alameda to Contra Costa, trying to find something that didn't exist. In the low light I swore I even saw a small creature of red body and orange legs crawling legs along the borderlines I was currently studying. One blink and my eyes told me I had made that up as a way of avoiding the visit to Granny today.

"Joyce," I said still unable to look away from the map, "sell free money to the kids?" Joyce had risen by then and was packing materials in front of her on the table. She smiled sadly and shrugged, giving me her full gaze.

"I know it sounds ridiculous, Clay," Joyce replied, "but the better the idea, the more it has to be sold. Especially to those it benefits most."

"Ironic," I said. "Why do you suspect that is?"

"Because we work with kids--" Joyce started before Xochi cut in.

"And children are skeptical about making contracts that will challenge what's their sense of comfortable," Xochi laid out.

"What if comfortable is bad for the kids?" I asked Xochi directly.

"Doesn't matter," Cynthia answered. "At least you know bad. Change has guarantees on paper but not in real life." We were all silent then, the room emptying one by one. I was left alone with my thoughts, that as well as Cynthia packing away her bag.

"Ugh. I so hate going home," she said out loud, surprised that she had said it so abruptly.

"You'd rather stay at work," I asked.

"No," she replied, "I just hate walking to BART. It's all bad." I thought about the six-block walk down the hill to the Civic Center BART station. I had never had an issue myself in the Tenderloin, insulated by my own skin being neither Southeast Asian or Central American, survivors and victors of jungle wars who had found a transference to the heroin trade. Given the dominance of the junkies, I had never seen the area as exceedingly violent. Who can rob you when they are in mid-nod off and holding a shit bag? The rules were pretty clear: drugs and sex sold here, violence erodes sales.

"I'll walk with you," I offered. "Would that be safer?"

"Oh, I never worry about safety," Cynthia replied. "It's just sad seeing so many who have given up."

"Well, maybe a little company will fight the despair," I suggested.

"Oh, I don't want you to go out of your way."

"It's not. I need to go to the East Bay to visit Granny. The walk will keep me honest."

"How is she doing, by the way?" Cynthia asked, grabbing her stack in an armful and nearly dropping it. I moved quickly and lessened the load by half, motioning toward the door with my head.

"She sleeps a lot," I answered, following Cynthia out toward her office. "We barely talk."

"That's gotta be really hard," Cynthia replied with a sad shrug. "I guess it ruins my what-if." She placed her materials on her desk; I put the stack I was carrying next to it. She pulled a notebook from the stack and placed it into her large bag with handles that double as shoulder straps.

"What do you mean?" I asked, walking out of her office as she turned out the light and followed me back to the conference room.

"I don't have family," she said, checking her phone with a headshake at something she saw. I grabbed my own bag and slung it over my shoulder. "Well, I have my sister but that's it. I always wondered what it would be like to have a Dad or Mom around."

"Me too," I replied, walking out of the conference room a second time. "My parents killed each other when I was really young. All I know is Granny."

"Oh no," Cynthia says, covering her mouth with her hand. "I didn't know that." She stops in her tracks to stare at me, eyes debating if they want to react to the horror. "I'm sorry."

"Don't apologize," I say. "Not your fault."

"Sorry for bringing it up."

"Since when does the doctor dislike talking?"

"True," she says, walking at my side past the security booth, waving at the attendant and following me past the doors out to the street. The first thing that hit me was the cold in the air on the streets; the smell followed right after. It was as if someone had taken a piss in a walk-in refrigerator and fragrant puddles had formed icicles. "I thought never knowing was hard. but I think losing my sister or her not remembering me would be harder."

"It's easy to look at another's pain and think you have it better," I said as we started down the hill. "Truth is, pain is not competitive."

"What do you mean?" she asked as we waited for the light to cross.

"Well, for all purposes that matter, you and I are black. Black Americans. A term used for descendants of African slaves. As horrible as slavery was, would you rather be in a German concentration camp?"

"No," Cynthia said shaking her head, "how about neither?"

"That's been my thought. I don't think it's a good idea to compare the pain of either of those tragedies. Nobody had exclusive rights to suffering."

"That makes a lot of sense to me. To say Jews in Germany or Africans in America suffered more is kinda missing the point," she agreed.

"Yeah, it almost takes the blame off who's at fault," I said, my eyes catching the monstrosity of a sculpture ahead of us at Civic Center plaza.

"Might be better to focus on what you do have," Cynthia replied, "rather than what you lost."

"I'm only now starting to see that," I said back to her as we crossed McAllister and started into Civic Center plaza. The lights from the street posts seemed dwarfed by the light pouring from the Venetian blinds hanging in the Scientology center. Strange that they would be open at that hour but then again I wasn't sure what they actually did inside. Our conversation slumped in the presence of homelessness, Carl's Jr patrons, aimless tourists, and roaming dealers looking for a sale. I watched the sculpture, daring there to be a web I could light on fire. With nowhere to turn my spite, I yawned as we entered the station, drawing in a full lung of the foul swamp gas the city emits at night.

Walking down the stairs, my thoughts drifted to my lost comrade. Irony seemed to be God's sense of humor; I learned of a spiritual cousin, bonded by a millennium of generational heredity, residing in the body of SFPD's most hunted criminal only to lose them to an ill-fated BART trip. How does that happen? Then again, wasn't the possibility of a savior left to subjectivity? Who's to say that Horace Marshall was not a savior to those he fed, employed, protected and kept from jail? I would never know. The tunnels beneath both city and water had robbed me of his answers.

I let Cynthia go through the stiles first, fishing through my wallet for a BART card with a large value. I was not sure why I kept so many cards with values under a quarter that would get me a twentieth of a stop. Maybe it was a fear of letting go or a belief that one day I would use it again. We made our way to the escalator and down to the platform. I was surprised when she stood waiting on the outbound side of the tube.

"Thought you lived in the city," I pried.

"I do," Cynthia replied. "I visiting my sister in Pittsburg. Spend the night and get a ride into the city the next morning."

"Ah," I replied, "just being nosy me." The last words of my sentence were compromised by the digital horns of the oncoming Pittsburg/Concord BART train. I smiled and snapped my jaw closed, the wind through the tunnels pushing air into the nostrils. As expected, the train passed and slowed in alignment between door and black mark on yellow coding. I noted the absence of people crowding to circumvent our position in line. Could be the time of night or the station, maybe a combination. The train finally stopped and opened its doors to one of the older cars from the nineties with the hard seats designed for commuters with no ass. It was blue canvas over padding for seats; I was old enough to remember when they were all hard plastic identical to the bus seats of MUNI or AC Transit. The car was relatively empty, no more than nine people total on the train. Cynthia hooked the hard right and grabbed a row of two seats perpendicular to the pull downs for seniors and riders with disabilities. I grabbed the seats across the aisle from her, taking no time in positioning myself near the window so I could rest my head. The car gave its digital gong signaling the doors were closing. I should have been alarmed at the familiarity of those sounds but I was too happy to close my eyes and breathe.

The BART continues its path, making stops every two minutes. Cynthia is oblivious to the ins and outs of passengers; she is engrossed in the notebook on her lap where her mechanical pencil transcribes against paper furiously. She is oblivious to one of her bosses snoring loudly in the seats parallel to hers just as she is to a duplicate of her boss sitting behind her with a boyish grin on his face as she writes. Asleep, I am somehow also able to watch myself, unconscious, across the aisle as well as behind Cynthia, pushing her to find the bright ideas within her own heart. If she lifts her pencil with a pause to think, I see my chin raise in anticipation. That's it, you are close, keep asking the penetrating questions. When her pencil drops again to capture into the page, my forehead drops with it, eyes gleaming into the lines separating each of her fragments or sentences. There is no disappointment when she erases or crosses out as long as she writes something new seconds after.

There isn't a single word on the page that comes directly from me. Whether I am sound asleep or watching over her shoulder, I am there to add safety. The safety that comes from ideas without judgment, creativity without limits and passion without critics. What is left is ownership, with Cynthia's intellectual capital contributing to the greater whole of the project. A sketch became revision and then became finalization. The pencil strokes lessen in the presence of Cynthia digging into her handbag for her laptop.

The digital bell of BART alerted me to the fact someone was standing over me. I cranked an eyelid open to see Cynthia standing less than a foot away, bag over shoulder, arm reaching half the distance between us with a concerned expression.

"What's wrong?" I said, far more groggy than I had intended.

"You missed your stop," she replied. I sat up in a bolt, looking around. The car was completely empty except for the two of us, doors posted open in stationary fixed position. The platform was outside, long and recently built, a look of cleanliness with escalators up to the entrance or exit. To my left out the window was an empty track before the high chain link fence that ran along a stretch of highway. Past the highway, I could make out the expanse of water which I knew to be the Bay cut across by the Carquinez Bridge. Directly opposite of the water, through the window to my right was the parking lot and the empty green rolling hills. The sign hanging above the tracks on either side read Pittsburg Baypoint. "I would have awakened you," Cynthia said with a guiltier tone than was needed, "but I got so engrossed in the project that I zoned out."

"Good stuff," I said with a smile, standing up to stretch. I held my ass cheek taut to keep from letting out an old-man post-nap fart. My eyes caught the train operator through the doors two cars down, walking to inspect that the entire train was vacant before turning around.

"Yes," Cynthia replied, still worried. "I can't believe I got it all finished."

"Good," I said, smiling again and slinging my bag over my shoulder. I motioned to the platform with my head. She followed carefully, looking around.

"It will still need Joyce's eyes," Cynthia said as we went up the escalator. I moved to stand behind her so I could let out a silent one that wouldn't slap her nostrils.

"Yeah, but not by much. I'm sure you got it right the first time."

"Wow, I really appreciate the faith you have in me," Cynthia said as we hit the top of the platform, leading to a view of bathrooms, station agent booth and exit stiles.

"It's not really a faith thing. It has to do with the vision that others may be blind to."

"Gosh, I still feel horrible--" she started before I cut her off as I let her pass through the stiles first.

"Don't," I said, stopping her train of thought and exiting myself. "You didn't even know what stop I would need to transfer at. I needed the nap. Now I am going to walk to the lot," I said pointing down the gangplank to another set of stairs that led to the lot. "Smoke a cigarette and ride back home. It's not an issue."

I got an "if you say so" shrug for my trouble, but we walked in silence; the air out in the Delta mouth was much warmer but dry. At the bottom of the stairs, the sidewalk led to bus stops on the right and a pickup cul de sac on the left. A light blue Honda Civic parked in the half circle flashed its lights in our general direction. I saw a woman in the driver's seat with a little one in a child seat's securely mounted in the back seat. I immediately saw the resemblance in facial features between the passengers and my companion. "Your chariot awaits," I said with an arm to the car.

"Thanks," Cynthia said back with a giggle. "You in the office tomorrow?"

"Maybe," I replied, "if not certainly this weekend."

"Okay, see you then. I'll buy you some coffee?"

"Ballin now?"

"Hey," she said getting in the car, "my boss demanded I get a raise." I laughed hard and loudly until the car pulled off, feeling pretty good about myself. Dropping my narrow ass down on the circular planter filled with litter and sandy plants, I lit a cigarette, watching the tracks for signs of movement of a train to carry me home. The train I had awakened from pulled off into the night, probably headed to a turn-around point further down in the gloom. Alone smoking in the lot, it was me, a few empty cars and the buzz of insects.

Until the buzz stopped. Being a city kid, I couldn't tell you I knew the consistency of sonic wild life. It just seemed odd that the chirp of crickets, static pulse of bugs and birdcalls would disappear all at once. Then I lost the smell of my cigarettes. Mind you, my nose was congested, but I still taste the dirty tobacco cut by the menthol in my nostrils. Not then. The harsh burning of the American Spirit that remind me of a dirt cloud was gone. In its place was a sticky sweet smell somewhere between hangover farts and cotton candy. My skin began to tingle. Not the pins and needles of numbness, but something crawling on me. Maybe more than one something. A sharp glance to my arm revealed nothing, but the periphery told me another story all together. Minute and nearly invisible, a tiny spider crawled along the sidewalk in the direction of the hills. My eyes shot over to a white one, slightly larger crawling along the darkness of the black asphalt that constituted the parking lot.

The cloud of pink fog had begun forming on the hillside by the time I heard the screams. My eyes scanned the world in front of me critically for the source, finding some blurred movement from the fog ahead of me. Off my ass, I began running toward the hillside, noting the sounds of crunching under my shoes as I smashed the lines of arachnids with my soles. This section of the lot was empty--not a sign of life anywhere except for the woman running. Brown hair, slightly overweight, a work blouse and pencil skirt. She broke a heel as she ran in terror. Behind her, for unknown reasons, chased a man in a tuxedo and red bow tie. I needed no refresher nor did I need a face. Hate took over. I pumped my legs to sprint an intercept course, my left hand curving to cut the air and my right locked in a kung fu death grip around my cigarette. I hadn't thought of the consequences and they dawned suddenly on me right before my shoulder-led charge barreled into the midsection of the Stranger. The impact almost took my balance, but the sound of El Michel's Mystery somehow stabilized me enough to scramble with my hands on the grass and to keep moving forward without toppling over. The woman, hearing the sound of the collision, foolishly stopped to scream warnings at me. I pointed back to the train station, moving to place my body between her and the Stranger.

"*Run and don't stop until you are inside the gates,*" I barked. I could tell by the sounds that she had not fled but something less ideal was happening behind me. I sidestepped to watch the Stranger and scan the woman in my left periphery; she was frozen in place with her eyes fixed on me. Then I watched her posture begin to change as the legs, eight, began sprouting from her back. A trap.

"*We know thee,*" it hissed taking a step back for either retreat or prep.

"We know each other well," I replied, feeling a weight in my right hand. A refingering of my grip told me my cigarette was gone, replaced by the familiar cold metal of the blade that had befriended me in both dreams and county jail hillsides alike. I smiled and brought the tip of the blade up between us, revealing that this time I apparently had an advantage. The first Stranger returned my smile and made no motion when I pushed the thrust forward, burying the good half of the blade in the groove just to the left of his right ribcage. He dropped to his knees, his smile concrete, although his eyes rolled in the back of his sockets to show me the pure black orbs. Too easy. There had been pink fog pouring out of his palms the whole time, creating a U-shaped cloud around our position. I noticed it when I spun with a top cut to catch the leaping woman who had fully converted to her spider self, catching her in the side and dropping her in two barely connected pieces.

The original bodies of two slain Strangers pulled away from their skeletons as if a giant vacuum pulled at their beings and sucked tissue from bone. Muscles, blood and skin all flew behind each of them, splattering against the cloud-like water flung from a wet dog, flattening the very dimensions of the cloud. The pieces congealed, forming three discs that hollowed and formed tunnel mouths--silk tunnels. I began backing up, holding my blade overhead in a guard position. Out of the threads poured Daddy Long Legs, one after a bony motherfucking another. They swarmed out directly at me. I began swinging as I retreated, cleaving chunks off the front lines. If I had ignored progress and stuck to just my plan, I probably would have hung in there. I didn't, though. I got excited at my marginal success, lost focus and was rewarded with knicks on the fingers and a cut along the belly. Behind the legions of Daddy Long Legs, the first waves of Recluse began to appear along with the first of Entropy's gongs sounding shortly after.

It was a backpedal at first that turned into a full-tilt run. I ran a good thirty yards before attempting to cut right back to the BART station. I was foiled by the fog wall that had grown to pace me. I leaped back as thread appeared right where I had considered running through it. The Recluse leapt out. I parried several stabs from their multiple arms, cutting at both their arms and the webs that had appeared from the flight path to restrain me. Swarming and circling, they continued to pour in as I tried my best to counter. I saw the blade come at my neck a bit too late and knew it wouldn't be able to counter as I was blocking a head cut. Instead, my mind prepared itself to take the inevitable chest thrust and I continued to fight. Just fight. The blade came within inches of my chest before it was intercepted by the dark wood of a maquahuitl. The weapon threw the blade back and cut hard in a swipe, combining both a slash and impact blow to knock back several Recluse. Xochi, glowing in her carnelian, swung again, causing the Recluse to pause, using her other hand to point to the flank she wasn't protecting. There was a small channel between the flanks, leading to an incline up the hill. Swinging, stabbing and thrusting, I began cleaving along the channel, Xochi following to watch the rear as we paced our way up the hill. At the top of the crest, I could look down to the valley below full of tiny green men standing expectantly as if waiting for a band to begin playing at the

Shoreline. Spiders to the sides and behind, Paradox to the front. A very well-done trap. *A trap works on the willingness of the prey to fight within the snare.* The fly who fights in the web becomes more tangled and alerts the arachnid. *Find the holes between threads.*

"*Sekhem,*" Xochi screamed up at me from the hillside a few steps below me.

"*Door,*" I screamed at the ground below me. The grass opened up in a pool of black with brown ripples. I fell through darkness for a time, sprawling my arms the whole time. Then I landed, hard face first on gravel, feeling the impact on my belly cut. I lay there for a very long time before picking up my head to see the fire pit. A few feet away, Xochi kneeled with her back to me, facing out to the waters of the lake in meditation. I crawled to the rim of the fire pit closest to her, propping myself up on my back against the fire pit's rim.

"Thirsty," Xochi asked without moving. I nodded and watched the clay pitcher appear in front of me. I poured it into my mouth with both hands, not caring how much I spilled on my torn shirt. After my breathing calmed, I lit a cigarette and stared at the waters.

"The check is from the Greek," I said finally. She slowly nods, still not facing me. "She also stole Burial Rites." I saw her back stiffen.

"Against your will?" she asked. Then I nodded. "I'm sorry. That must have been that Carrier's first time." Silence.

"Why aren't you mad at me?" I asked.

"Because that glyph was a bugged replica," she replied "and now we can track her."

"You knew this would happen?"

"I made an educated guess."

"Why didn't you warn me?"

"Oh, so we are sharing again, are we?" I asked.

Long silence.

"So I was sent a text from some kids the other night," I started.

CHAPTER NINETEEN

"Try living through a depression."

--Harrison

I tapped on the door with my knuckles. It opened on its own. Music was playing--James Brown's "Payback." Harrison stood over his desk, rolling up a long paper that had been stretched across the workstation. My eyes caught blue lines on a grey thick paper of schematics before Harrison let out a synchronized "Revenge!" to the music.

"Shush," I said, closing the door quickly, "one of the nurses will hear you."

"Let them," he smiled back. "I'll be leaving soon enough"

"Grandpa, we talked about this." I let out with extra worry.

"Did you know he hated this song?"

"Who?"

"James. Every instrument was recorded in separate sessions without his supervision. When he came in to lay the vocals, it sounded *off* to him."

"Weren't his vocals impromptu? Almost a freestyle?"

"Yes."

"I somehow remember hearing that," I said, believing it after I said it.

"You should. You helped him indirectly. Instead of taking it seriously, he spoke about what was challenging him at the moment of betrayal." Harrison could tell I didn't follow, so he continued for my benefit. "His wife left him for his manager. Double the pain."

"I would have thrown it out--saved it for a B side."

"Me too. Then when he heard everything together he discovered not only a hit but a formula."

"There's a lesson in there somewhere, isn't there?"

"Certainly. Decant it out loud, please," Harrison asked. I thought hard for a few moments.

"Being human is pain management. We can find moments of beauty--timeless beauty for others to benefit from if we embrace our pain"

"I would agree with that. Too bad it is really difficult to remember that at the time."

"It brings us back to the reminders about being in the moment," I added.

"Yes. So if all we have to do is master the moment, why do you think that is so hard to enact?"

"I don't know."

"I don't either. It was truly a question I'm asking you, and not a rhetorical one. I find you far better versed with the human experience than I." I waited for the idea to tumble in my mind a few times, considering the story for what juicy gravy drops might fall off the spigot.

"Control," I said with relief. James hated the song because he experienced a loss of control. Both in the production of the track as well as his own personal life. Fear of having or losing control directly competes with being in the moment."

"Is being in the moment the same as removing the idea of control?"

"I don't know that it is possible to remove ideas but certainly suspending the necessity for control is the quickest path to being in the moment."

"I would agree," Harrison smiled, "though I am curious about why you think ideas cannot be removed."

"Probably my own arrogance or ignorance, or both. I'm curious if you could answer something for me."

"I thought that was my purpose here, not that I don't enjoy prune dishes and adult diapers."

"Just a bit longer, Grandpa, until I can figure out where to move you," I replied. I pulled a scrap of paper from his desk and scribbled down some glyphs I'd seen in my head during my ordeal the night of Athena's attack. When I was done I looked for Harrison's reaction, which was very matter of fact and almost bored.

"Burial rites," he said flatly, "owned by Kemet"

"Owned."

"Meaning only the owners have permission for the concept's use. Think of owned as being the same as a patent."

"Okay," I said, probing his face with my eyes. "How about these?" I scribbled down the Greek that was on the banner over Athena's shrine under the Parchick's pool house.

"Burial rights taken from Kemet," he replied. "This must be very old"

"Why do you say that?" I asked, trying to feign all ignorance on the subject.

"We never conducted trade of soft works with other attributes or pantheons."

"Why not?"

"A combination of opportunity and approach. Ausar always held to the path that rather than trading fish we should trading fish poles. The other attributes and pantheons should be taught and then adapt their own. We inherited the rules that came when the Isfet conquered us and deactivated our throne."

"Soft works?"

"Stored and tangible ideas," Harrison said, tapping his fingers against the two sets of writing on the sheet of paper. "Before us, there were no written instructions on how to bury the deal to prepare the soul for the next world."

"As opposed to hard works," I said, hoping I was following, "which would be me inside your head."

"Something to that effect. If these had dates we could see the transfer of ownership."

"So these are patents? What's to enforce their proper usage?" I waited for Harrison's answer, but he just stared at me, fighting a smirk in the corner of his mouth. "Entropy, right?" Harrison looked back to the glyphs.

"The more important question is deciding why the Isfet would allow such works."

"Why wouldn't they?"

"Suppose you invented the idea that the Isfet had to be removed and perfected a process for doing so. Isn't that risky?"

"It is," I said nodding, "so something must be happening that causes the benefits to outweigh the risk to the Isfet."

"Maybe we should map out the Isfet as a structure rather than just an enemy."

"Okay, you lead."

Kphr began sketching on a piece of paper, starting another circular flow diagram. He kept some constants such as Firms and Households. He added two destinations between two in the form of a resource market and a product market in between Firms and Households.

"Do you know these?" Harrison said, pointing at the markets.

"Product markets being stuff like televisions, house cleaning and web searches, right?"

"Yes," Harrison agreed, "the goods and services flowing from the firms."

"Resources are what they need to create these goods and services?"

"Drill down more. Televisions require steel and steel comes from ore. There is a finite amount of ore on this planet."

"Therefore, it has a worth because the more that is purchased, the less there is. Resources markets are commodities, then? Oranges and timber."

"Precisely. They are purchased and sold for manufacturing in the product market, but they have value in of themselves outside the product market."

"Just as the product market can be purchased from, in order to cut down a tree to make timber. Now the dollar signs are where money is coming into the economy along the arrows. I don't get the M and X."

"M is a notation for imports. What's X?"

"Exports. There are influxes of imported goods and services that the economy exchanges currency for. In addition, there are goods and services we export to other countries that they exchange currency for. Same rules apply to importing and exporting resources."

"Yes, you follow," Harrison said, reaching over for another piece of paper, "now try this one." Kphr began sketching the same diagram, changing the labels to fit his discussion. Once again the Firms became replaced by "Aspects" and "Pantheons." The Households were replaced by "Person." The product market had become "People" and the resource market had become "Environment (Earth)."

"What's the difference between a Person, People and Other People?" I asked.

"A Person speaks about the individual where as People is what happens with a community."

"I'm not sure what to make of the exchanges."

"How about if I explain the first two and we see where we are from there?" Harrison asked. I nodded and he patted me on the head. "Before you moved too slow; now you are ahead of yourself." I smiled and he smiled back. "When humans interact as a community, they have a greater access to ideas and approaches. Take our discussion on burial rites. There were tribes who didn't even bury or burn their dead before Ausar's instruction. When burial rites are introduced to a community it is no different than a product or service from a firm for sale to a household. When another tribe, outside of the influence of Ausar, hears of such practices and adopts it into their community, it has been *Expanded*."

"Imported by the other tribe, exported by Ausar's?"

"Yes," Harrison said, holding the syllable for a long time. "How does that affect Ausar's economy?"

"It grows it because he can charge more to another tribe than his own. What is the currency, though." Harrison stared at me in a frozen position, refusing to respond or answer. Then it came to me. "Belief. Ausar becomes a legend to the foreign community."

"As the trade between Ausar and a foreign tribe's attribute continues, a Resonance is created. The people of both tribes begin to understand the relationship between Ausar and the foreign tribe's attribute."

"So a Resonance is fairly binding. For instance, most people don't even know that Mexico and Canada are better trade partners to the United States than China or Europe."

"Would that explain why we don't go to war with Mexico or Canada?"

"Yes, because there would be no more Toyota engines and BlackBerry smart phones. That's a North American Resonance, a trade agreement that is very resilient."

"Yet if the foreign tribe was exporting more to us than it imported from Ausar, it brings us to a place of *Irrelevance*."

"The community become less independent and begins to believe it is an offshoot of this foreign tribe. Meanwhile, the foreign tribe begins absorbing who they are exporting to as a part of the exchange."

"The Romans stand with their thumbs in the back of the Greeks."

"Which forces the Greeks to take risk to remain as the progenitor of the culture, although they are not considered as massive or sustainable through history."

"When it comes to the freedom of government, whether democracy or a republic, all educated eyes in this country look to Greece and Rome as the center of governmental perfection."

"So these exchanges are works, both soft and hard?"

"Yes! Now, explain the environmental exchanges."

"Well, the resource market is comprised of commodities. So the *Environment* is how both Attribute and humanity interacts with the very planet itself."

"Yes, keep going."

"Distilling would be importing. Therefore, an Attribute can bring in resources such as wood or stone from another Attribute's part of the planet."

"No, there are not two Attributes involved in this exchange," he corrected.

"Ah, the planet itself. As so-called forces of nature, each Attribute must exchange with the planet itself."

"Why?"

"Because Earth is finite. There is a given and set amount of wood at any given time. To some Pantheons, there is an Attribute for the Earth. Ours is Geb and ancestor."

"Did your parent let you help yourself to pantry?" I asked.

"For the most part, but anything taken had to be written on the shopping list."

"Why?" I asked, continuing the metaphor.

"So it is replaced?"

"So what is Distilling?"

"Distilling is taking from the earth itself but the cost is Holding. The Attribute trades belief in the earth for use of finite material at the risk of less of a domain on the Earth."

"And *Passing*?"

"The Attribute is adding resources to the Earth itself, replacing a crater with a lake. Infusing expands the Attribute's domain because a piece of itself is in fact infused to the Earth itself."

"Give me an example."

"Stonehenge?"

"Stonehenge is a structure and therefore?"

"A minor work, perhaps with a soft work placed in there?"

"Yes. So let your mind fly east of Stonehenge to England in the region of Somerset."

"Of course, the hot spring at Bath. Cold country with a natural hot geyser union with the planet. I'm sure if you were to research it, you would find someone spent ample time equating her to Minerva."

"Absorption."

"Precisely." Harrison proceeded to flip over both sheets. "Let's pretend what we just saw was the structure and flow before the Isfet. I would like to say it was never that exact, but it would be the closest to the goal we were aiming for before the Split."

"Between our family?"

"Yes, before the betrayal and the invasion. Give me a second to set this up." The page disappeared from the stack of white paper and appeared before us. A sketch of another circular flow began without Harrison moving a hand at all.

"You are getting stronger, Grandpa," I said excitedly.

"Not with you talking," he growled at me, waving his hands, frustrated as if I had just stopped him from sneezing. I mouthed sorry and he continued. The same template form began with a circular flow between Firms and Households, with a Product and Resource market on either side. This time he placed a new factor in the dead middle, which he labeled Financial Institutions. This model had no exchanges for the markets but focused on the exchanges between the parties involved.

"You may speak now," Harrison said to me without looking over. "Walk me through what you see."

"Financial institutions, although outside of the flow, have very much to do with keeping or siphoning the flow. These institutions, better yet, banks take savings from households in the form of monthly deposits to savings accounts. They pay back to households a growth on the money in the form of interest or a growth on a stock in the form of dividends."

"And stocks are?"

"Ownership in firms."

"Continue."

"Firms have a very similar relationship to banks as households, the difference being a larger volume. Firms can make much larger deposits or investments, so they earn larger returns on interest or dividends. They also take huge loans out to build their businesses and pay the bank back with large returns from the interest. Households could do that too, but in a much smaller amount."

"What about these?" Harrison said, pointing to the lines leaving the financial institutions toward the lower right corners of the diagram.

"Foreign countries?"

"What specifically?"

"I keep skipping details. You hate that, I'm sorry. Foreign governments, banks, firms and households"

"So what is happening?"

"The governments, banks, firms and households borrow from the banks and pay the bank in interest. The bank also takes money from them for investments and deposits so they can return interest returns and dividends."

"Excellent. Does that explain why the financial institutions are in the center of the diagram?" he queried.

"Yes, I was thinking about that as you drew and now I have the answer. Although essential to the flow, the banks are not locked down to any one focal point the way a household or firm or the markets are." Harrison smiled mischievously and nodded his head.

"One would say 'lawless' while making the law"

"Why are old black people so suspicious of banks?"

"Try living through a depression," Harrison answered with a sarcastic quip and a murmur about young people.

"Okay, let's apply it to the Thrones."

Harrison set about sketching again, first flipping the page without moving and then bringing over another. The same diagram began to take shape but labels were being replaced. Firms were still Attributes, Households were Person, the Product market was People and Resource market was Environment. Now the exchanges were labeled between the four parties. In addition, there was no label for the banks but the exchanges were labeled. Kphr held his finger to the exchanges between People and Other People. "Explain," he said more instructionally than by way of a request.

"We are still using a currency of belief?"

"Of course."

"Okay. As the individual places belief in their community, they are paid in Hope. As the community places their belief in an individual that individual becomes a leader. A leader they see as a pathway for enlightenment in the form of what you have called Ascension."

"Give me an example."

"Ausar was born a hybrid, part Attribute and part human. His appearance was suited to associate with humans and aid them. As he taught, they practiced and learned cooperation, thereby abandoning the hunter-gatherer lifestyle for that of civilization. Civilization requires a belief in collective intelligence. When that showed results he became an example of Ascension. He was a man to them at that time and therefore a leader. It was only until his Carrier was killed that they made the mistake of calling him a god."

"Excellent," Harrison responded and moved his hand to the exchanges between People and Attributes. "Explain these."

"The community places belief in the form of their entire Civilization in an Attribute or a group of them, being repaid in Order. Order in the sense of how work collectively with the Attribute. Even a chaos Attribute has a structure preferring how they like to operate."

"I would agree. What about here?" Harrison moved his hand over the exchanges between Attributes and Environment. I needed to study it for a bit before I took it for its meaning.

"Attributes as individuals or groups can affect or even determine the conditions of a landscape if they are willing to invest their own vital energies into the given terrain. As Attributes we can raise the profile of the real estate and make it a place of Power. The deserts outside our cities were always more hospitable to the Traitor."

"He claimed the desert had more life than any field of crops and our cities. From his perspective that's what he saw. Now, any area that resembles a desert could be his."

"Like a housing project," I said sadly.

"Oh that's good. Yes, I guess that why your kids call their gangs his name."

"I just said that recently. I'm glad you feel me. What do you think about this. They are also cities, though."

"Which means they are shared by Heru. Cities are collective acts of protection."

"We are on to something."

"Yes, yes, yes, keeping going. Perhaps we will pull off more layers. What is the exchange for investing one's self too much in real estate, as you put it?"

"The very earth absorbs you; it would invoke too much Paradox to be that connected to the planet and that connected to a physical body. The exchange is Destruction, the loss of the physical body."

"Yes, and precedent would also suggest the essence of the Attribute is tethered to a location."

"Is Sulis part of Bath?"

"You should check as discreetly as possible."

"Noted. I can do the rest on my own, as cool as your hand is over a self-documenting piece of paper, highlighting areas. I can follow a circle." He chuckled long and hard, happy see the turn of my mouth as I spoke.

"That's a good thing. I do have to point out to you: adapt how you perceive and I will teach differently. Remember that, professor."

"Also noted," I said and decided to try that in class. My eyes moved over to the area between Environment and People. *Limited Resources* and *Exploitation*. These are works I have to realize. There is an exchange. Why is this here? How is this helpful? I thought long and hard before it came to me. "The individual is still an individual. A beast with intellect. Evolved monkey or genetic hybrid. It must have a response to collective wisdom.

"*It is selfish.*"

"*It is indeed selfish, thereby needing both guidance and collectivity.*"

"But when its selfishness affects collectivity?"

"A leader can aim the tribe to being selfish. In the individual pursuit of mastery over the resources abound, the realization of Limited Resources leads to the tendency to covet and hoard."

"The exchange for limited resources is Exploitation. Ultimately the power of the one can destroy the ability of all to function. What of the exchanges to the center?"

"The individual draws in the authority for Dominance from the Attribute through the center piece. The exchange, through the center, is a payment of Fear--fear to run, fear to freeze and fear to follow. The Attribute is given access to Bloodlines for Carriers that are compatible with an Attribute residing within, the ability to have Followers and the use of regulated Works by which to gain more. The center, the banks of the system, are paid in human sacrifices. When Attributes go to war it is reflected in conflict between humans. This ensures that Attributes will compete within Pantheons and no one Pantheon will be allowed to rise too far above the rest."

"What about the foreign governments, banks, and so forth?"

"Those are foreign Attributes or Pantheons. They use the center to either import Cult members or export Converts."

"Hence the importance of the center."

I leaned back against the wall, arms folded in front of me, watching the swirling images projected before me. I could know my enemy with a certainty of definition. This wasn't the initial guess of a conservative soldier. I understood my opponent's function. Harrison had provided the perfect analogy. It was one thing to fear the power of the financial industry; it was an easy scapegoat. It was another to be aware of the financiers taking over the very institution built to counter their influence as well as their fall.

"In the older models we focused on the government being at the center. However, this is a different model?" I asked.

"Well, what would cross-reference the government and the banks?" Harrison asked flatly.

Thomas Jefferson had always warned against it and Aaron Burr had to kill Hamilton to get history to hear him. I wondered who had sponsored that and then decided I didn't want to answer that. As much as I accepted that business and economics wasn't my thing, I was a social scientist in my heart. Economics was a social science. How ironic during a period of what was shaping up to be the biggest financial crisis in sixty years I could name the core instigators of an ancient spiritual war as pieces of a supply and demand puzzle. The Grand Concord was the current government operating on both sides of the Veil. The government of the county I lived in used a series of Federal Banks along with an outside system called the Federal Reserve to ensure the system was too big to fail. The helping hand becomes just the hand. The federal banks and reserve of the Veil was the Isfet. As long as the sponsors within fought for control, they would be oblivious and apathetic to the abuses within the structure. Dependency kept them blind; as long as slaves keep a competition they never question the plantation owner. Nor do they question if they have been inserted into a structure that is flawed from inception. The Isfet were not as simple as the box Monotheism had built around its greatest adversary. All things not

God must be the Devil. Easy box. Insidious, preying on the very blind spots within free will, the Isfet worked to confuse the issue altogether: chaos. "The Isfet are the Central bank, and each of the major Isfet are separate Federal Banks."

"And therefore banks . . . ," Harrison hinted.

"Do nothing," I said, "and they will crash the markets every century or so to expand their control."

"Century?" he asked sarcastically.

"Right. The timeline is much faster now. Half of that."

"Every 54.5 years, but who is counting?"

"Confront them and you crash the system. It's a loser scenario" I blurted outloud.

"What about creative destruction?"

"I don't follow."

"Crafting new markets outside of their control that replace previous markets."

"New works, you mean?"

"If possible. Try to find what's missing and jump ahead."

"I don't know enough. I take it I also have a bad track record. What if we've tried this before and it--"

"Failed? Got some other alternatives?"

"No." I enjoyed another long pause as the lights returned to the room with the same velocity as the projected diagrams vanished to shadowy memories before my eyes. "I'll need some time to get my hands dirty with this."

"What are you thinking?" Harrison asked.

"I should see the Concord up close. Get a temperature check."

"You are aware of the risks?"

"An assembly of every demi-god or principle all vying for a one-up in a central location."

"Worse. The Partisan will certainly be there."

"I've beaten him up before."

"He was alone then and less potent. Now the numbers are on his side and he has had plenty of opportunities to study your might."

"I've got a plan for that. Won't say what, though. Any souvenir requests?"

"As a matter of fact, yes. Your cousin has told me the Concord assembles in a structure that replicates our own courtroom for the Narmer. That would mean the room has a direct access to the appliances the Isfet added to our original Veil design."

"You want to see it?"

"If you get see it and return, then I will have seen it."

"Okay, I will make an attempt." I rubbed his shoulder to say goodbye and began to walk out. I opened the door quickly and walked through it even faster, making sure my body obscured a view into the room. In front of me, nurses were assembling residents in walkers, wheelchairs and rolling chairs in front of the large television. It was movie night.

"Oh, meester Durward," the young nurse named Diana with a thick Bolivian accent said, making eye contact. "Are you staying for da moobie?" My eyes scanned the room. A lot of familiar faces but none of them was Granny.

"What are you watching?" I asked with feigned interest.

"Har ree Pot Tear." Diana replied, "is berry pop you lar." My smile locked in as a silent no thank you but it was really the only way I could avoid asking if that should have been Senor Geraldo Potter. I walked to the elevator using my card to call the car.

"*Here that old man,*" I sent to Harrison, "*Har Ree Pot Tear on the tele.*"

"*If you want me to stay here a moment longer, you will keep such information to yourself,*" I heard back in my head as cranky and gruff as I had hoped for. I laughed out loud and stepped into the opening doors.

CHAPTER TWENTY

"We were never one of you nor will we ever be."

- Clay

The tickets were Xochi's, the lead was mine, and the plan was ours. We entered separately, each in formal attire having waited in the park across from city hall for our signal. She was anything but subtle, arriving in a long limousine with several entourage members following. I snickered when the doorman greeted her as Ms. Kephalos. Xochi just exhaled silently. The message was clear enough, though: *Don't make it personal.* We waited an hour after she entered, posted in our position. Xochi worked on getting Constandina's drinks strong and refilled frequently, while I fed Xochi information on room locations and how people were feeling. When Ms. Kephalos was the center of attention and sloshy enough to let her focus go, we walked slowly from the Civic Center parking structure which was covered by empty park to the doors of the Bill Graham auditorium. Our tickets approved, we strolled into the anteroom where another usher stood before the double doors leading into the event. We were pleasantly surprised to learn that the event was comprised of two floors: the ground floor a costume party and the second floor a masquerade affair with masks required. We passed through the doors and into where the magic began, or perhaps the appearance thereof.

Painting a picture for you wouldn't do justice to the images we witnessed. Downstairs, the local athletes, actors, district supervisors, new money and socialites surfed the room, eating hor d'oeuvres chased by wine to the sounds of a live brass band. You could watch the actor from Mork and Mindy enjoy deep belly laughs as the black actor from Lethal Weapon cracked jokes to him. Given that we hadn't brought our own masks, the usher greeted us as we made our way up the stairs to the second floor. He rang a bell that summoned another server, this one holding a collection of masks on a satin pillow. I took the lavender mask and Xochi the yellow, figuring the one with hieroglyphs might be a give-away. We made our way through small crowds of franchise owners, studio executives, senators, tech founders, angel investors, old money and power brokers. Despite all being hidden behind masks, they wore their status on their sleeves from the conversations they held to their champagne flutes to the thoughts they let leak from their heads. This was the human pursuit of power, not the personal aspect that develops one's being. This was the hunt for dominion over others. We were surrounded by a step beyond making history; this was that core elite obsessed with defying the future while denying much of the past.

Xochi stuck to the shadows on the other side of the room, masking her presence behind the Latin American actor who played the narcotics cop in "Blood In, Blood Out." I took to the shadows on the other side from Xochi, eavesdropping on an interaction between the Chief of Police and the controller for the city of San Francisco. I was able to stay out of trouble for twenty minutes before the perfume caught me. She seemed to float as she walked across the floor, picking the path of most human obstacles for her retinue to clear ahead of her steps and allowing her to stop for seconds at a time to promise quick chat some time in the future. Then Ms. Kephalos made it to the stage, her azure blue gown being held from behind by one of her sycophants as she ascended the stage and took her place at the podium.

At first I was intrigued; the invitation hadn't said anything about an auction. I watched from behind a mask as she introduced herself, thanked everyone for coming and gave a little wave to someone unnamed in the crowd. As I tried to understand why she was the only unmasked guest in the room, she explained the mission of her organization and how much fundraisers such as the one currently being endured benefitted the greater "good." The Sisters of Wisdom. Cute Greek . . . real fucking cute. The first photo on the screen should have been the tip off but it wasn't until the third that I got the hint. Constandina Kephalos was auctioning off her collection of pre-dynastic Egyptian artifacts. As she introduced each piece, she emphasized the messaging on each artifact, taking extra time to pinpoint the after life themes.

I caught Xochi's eyes blazing at me from behind her mask. My mind swam past the chief, around the server with the platter of champagne flutes, around the neck of the jewelry wholesaler, under the leg of the social media site founder and pausing directly in front of Xochi.

"*These replicas, too?*" I asked her silently.

"*As phony as the glyph,*" she sent back.

"*Why auction them?*"

"*She has to distribute the soft works to her followers – wait, this is important.*" I followed her eyes to the photo over the stage of an ancient and tattered broom. Its bristles came from the hairs of some animal, bound with sinew and mounted on along cedar pole. Due to decay, I could barely make out the glyphs on it.

"*What's that?*" I sent.

"*Not sure. I see your name on it but also what looks like Chinese.*"

"*Should we bid on it?*"

"*No, but do you know the original's purpose?*"

"*I don't.*"

"*Let see how it plays out.*" I made a mental note to investigate the broom provided I could find where I had hidden the original burial glyph. There was only a few more items auctioned after that. Xochi took inventory of the amount of money raised. When it was over, Ms. Kephalos brought the woman of the hour or minute, depending on who was asking, the candidate she was endorsing for district attorney. The candidate was home grown, locally educated, a person of color, semi-progressive and had a kindness to her eyes. She was also Constandina's prospect as well as fairly high profile as far as the assistant district attorneys were concerned inside of San Francisco.

"*The DA appears to be quite well received tonight,*" Xochi sent.

"*Any idea on her track record?*" I sent back.

"*None, but I know she has worked Avalos's squad for two years.*"

"*Trickle down?*" I sent in inquiry.

"*Look at her sponsor,*" she sent.

"*Of course. You think Avalos is under the thumb too?*"

"*Yes, but I know that's not an argument you would hear me on.*"

"*You would be correct there,*" I sent back.

With the auction over, the music returned. Harps, strings, piano, woodwinds and a few chimes. The sounds of high civilization at its most sardonic. With the auction over, the swell of the crowd seemed to increase, people clustered to use up more space and the amount of people tipped toward occupancy. I kept my eyes locked on Constandina, watching her work the crowd, especially as she was able to engage in each conversation as the center of importance while fading away seamlessly. There was no one to call her on it or suspect what she was up to. There were no bells of entropy to regulate her transactions. I studied and resented.

The one time I looked away to find Xochi, I lost her in the human bubble bath. Adjusting my eyes showed no trace of wisp trail. She must have walked off. Resisting the urge to panic, I showed my hands in my pockets and found Constandina with my eyes again. She had gathered her original sycophantic vapor trail that had followed her into the event, whispering instructions in a hushed tone to one of the women in the group. Judging by her similarity in hair, skin tone and stature to her sponsor, I guessed she was some form of lieutenant or chamberlain. Constandina began her exit, heading to a door near the stairs up to the stage, I hadn't seen before. Her retinue began to follow, I made a move to cross the room without notice and felt my shoulder collide with something solid and grounded. Looking over, I saw no pillar or person that might have rocked me as such. Turning back to the mark, the last trail of the Greek's private party was exiting through the door in a total of thirty people; Xochi was at the tail walking as if she belonged. I skirted the edge of the room my shoulder scraping the walls to make as much time as possible without attracting attention to myself. I was able to slink into the opening just before it closed on its own.

We were in a hallway slightly inclined, pitch black except for the azure glow emitted from Constandina's big ole water head. I was surprised at the slope aiming upwards rather than the expected down turn, the hallway going for what seemed a city block straight and then beginning a winding circular ramp for what might have been three stories up. My feet picked up no dust as the walkway was immaculately clean although the corners of the ceiling became increasingly covered in webs. I suspected I was experiencing what a shell would feel like if it had to walk its own insides. At the top of the circular ramp was a circular antechamber full of alcoves cut into the wall with a rounded portal exit. By the time I arrived, Constandina was waning, having completely disrobed to stand before the portal. In her place was Athena in full aspect, taking a spear in one hand with an owl resting on her left shoulder. Her followers were also disrobing, replacing their garments with robes of low hanging hoods in powerful azure. They made no eye contact, no sign of life in their faces, just the slow drugged expression of an Oxycontin-friendly family watching the fourth of July fireworks through a haze. Athena opened the portal, revealing a long tunnel of finely spun silk, moved by a breeze I couldn't see. I felt a chill go through my body, under standing the connection between a deeply intrinsic hatred and embedded attraction. Time gave the appearance of suspension, having the belief I had been at this moment before and would keep coming back to it. The loop in its esoteric superfluous cycle, never fairly explaining if it was sending or receiving.

Athena walked forward, both stepping as lithe as a ballet dancer and floating, rolling on the very air as if on a Costco cart. Her hooded train began to follow, filing through the thread to its end destination. Xochi waited until the last of the train was posed to enter before she began to fit into the robe, opting to throw it on over her clothes. Signaled by Xochi's crushing her masquerade mask in her hand, she shook her palm open to let the breeze catch the dust and lift it from her skin. If the previous encounter in Pittsburg hadn't been the metric, I was certainly persuaded that Xochiquetzal was as strong as she was smart.

I followed her example, pulling the robe over my head, assuming she would watch the thread's opening as I had while my vision was momentarily obscured. Once I had the hood low I pulled the mask off my face, snapping the nylon cord and handing it to Xochi. She crushed the evidence, pulling on the shoulders of the garment like a mother straightening her son's prom corsage.

"You sure you want to do this?" Xochi sent, a look of concern in her eyes and in the vocal quality I heard in my head.

"I'm here, aren't I?" I sent back.

"Yes. That's not enough for me."

"What would be?"

"Clay often does what's right when nobody else will. I want this to be a choice."

"And I choose to move forward."

"*Many of your nightmares you have shared are memories of what they did to you in there. I am worried about you.*"

"*We'll be okay,*" I say, tapping my side to feel the pen that I knew could be a sharp, engraved blade when I needed it.

"*You should be clear. The rules are different in there.*"

"*Not so different that I can't adapt.*"

"*Maybe so. Just remember, this leads to the Nest, into the Veil. There is no paradox to limit other attributes, no entropy to keep things fair. This is their chessboard, where the Isfet are in control.*"

"*We did pretty good in Pittsburg.*"

"*We had the Sanctuary to run back to. As I told you before, where we stand now is a protected zone that we decide parameters for. It is still a zone. A zone has borders that you have just begun to see the lengths we must go to in order to prevent infiltration. We have no such tactics in there. If you follow this thread, we are the mercy of the Concord and their Isfet masters.*"

"*I understand.*"

"*I will go alone if you feel . . .*"

"*No. We do this together.*"

She smiled at me and squeezed my hand, her way of saying she was better suited for this adventure with a partner. Then she turned and stepped into the tunnel. I noticed as she walked she never let her feet touch the silk, a fraction of an inch between the soles of her feet and the silk of the tunnel. I wasn't sure how she did it, so I reasoned out what I had at my disposal. *Huh.* I felt a lift to my legs, almost as if on planet with less gravity. Trying my first step, I found a thin brown line shooting along the z-axis into the tube. Placing my weight on it, I found it held my mass, a bit higher than Xochi but it kept me off the silk. A second and parallel line appeared I placed my other foot, stepping along train track rails in slow pursuit of Xochi. She moved quickly at first, catching up with the end of Athena's entourage then slowing to match their pace. Whether a reflection of their arrogance or their own limited mortal conception, none of her followers even noticed two members of their party had been lagging.

The tunnel was almost transparent, a dull cloudy white with hints of pink, cylindrical, and eight feet in diameter. I could see through to its exterior numerous other similar tunnels leading to a woven orb at the center. Crawling along the outside of the knotted ball at the center as well as every thread were Isfet, small to large. Tiny spiders the size of pinheads, tarantulas with the wingspan of cantaloupes and the ever friendly smart car sized Daddy Long Legs. Back and forth, they moved along the network, carrying operations through the Veil regarding their nefarious deeds. My skin crawled and I felt my nose crinkle, finding my mind returning to memories of the first night I fought the Isfet. They were a rumor then, an alien force that had appeared in the desert. Arrogance, denying ourselves the possibility of defeat, had led us right into the hands of the Isfet. Efficient and storage-based. All forms of arachnid carried cocoons away from threads leading out of the Nest; each bundle ranged from person, to dream, to idea, to fear, or to newly-born Attribute. I felt my non-corporeal teeth clench, wanting to find a fire brighter than a thousand hydrogen bombs and nineteen suns to purge this place clean. Something inside of me stirred, calling up images of the Unnamed who we had fought before the serpents, bubbling hungry masses of atomic chaos that would love nothing more than to eat this Nest whole.

"*Mind your thoughts,*" Xochi sent. "*This place is pure intent. Each of these threads is an antenna.*"

I nodded my head a slight amount to signal I understood without making any obvious movements. We were nearing the Nest, the leads in the train speeding their pace. I tried to mirror their intent: quests for power and status, narcotic expectations rested in the hands of their sponsor. Larger breasts, box seats at the Giants games, an interview on KQED, the largest house in Laurel Village. I didn't dare delve into my own real desires, both for fear of revealing myself as well as finding out what that part of me looked like. Athena led her crowd through another portal and into a room that seemed both an open dais and the segmented tier of an agora. Athena stood near the rim, each of us kneeling behind her. There were multiple others in concentric circles, elevated vertically along the chamber the farther each circular dais got from the center. Shifting my eyes across the expanse I saw similar parties to ours, either arriving through their threads or waiting behind their sponsor. Each sponsor stood at the edge of their segment both staring at the center of the room and each other. Lifting my eyes again, I noticed the sponsors in our proximity all carried a binding thread. Hera, Zeus, Dionysus, Apollo, Artemis, Poseidon, Hephaestus, and

Hades. The lords and ladies of Olympus, gods and demigods, each had their own segmented dais with a number of followers present.

Below us I saw face on bodies I did not recognize, but knew them for their aspect. Anpu, Menthu, Neb-het, Qebui, Aken and Nefetem. Half of my family. The lord of storms was nowhere to be found, only his bloody hound. Behind us on a higher tier were the Babylonians, and to the right of them were the Assyrians. I continued to swirl. Tier ordering becoming less valuable than accurate naming. Asgard, Zulu, Celt, Pict, Hopi, Dravidian, Mayan, Yoruba and maybe Shinto. I prided myself in having an open mind that had respected as many mythologies, stories and spiritual journeys I could get my hands on. I loved reading as much about both ancient and modern cultures as I could. For as many pantheons and groups as I could cluster, each missed a few characters I was familiar with. Those I could name awed me in their ability to be both antiquated and current. Each of the attending Attributes came with a cadre of believers clothed in a colored robe respective to their sponsor and in some form of worship.

As I studied the tiers I got the sense it was drifting in rotation at the same time that it was stationary. My eyes, veiled or not, could not mistake the shape. Concentric circles going from small to large, connected by a patch work of spokes originating at the center and moving outward. A web. A horrible spider web woven with pure energy and whatever else deludes the aspirations of humans. What came next should have been expected, almost predictable if you assume all that has been wrong started from the beginning to now. A light appeared below the center of the web, spilling out small plumes of pink fog that fought gravity and hovered near the top. A shape ascended from the light, elevated on a platform that did not exist. It was humanoid but remained covered by a robe the same color as spoiled milk. I resisted the urged to rip the Amazon forest out of the ground, push it through a processing plant, create a sheet of paper the dimensions of the state of Montana, roll up a newspaper the size of the Transamerica pyramid and smack the creature against the wall. It was just a given response: see a spider, smack to wall.

As the figure got closer to the center platform, I recognized the face but nor the garb. I made sure I made no eye contact, but it was certainly the Stranger or some form of it. It was taller than the ones I had encountered with an elongated skull, much thinner hands, with a wider frame and thicker hair. I was reminded of the bad wizard from the Aladdin movie that Granny had taken me to on Thanksgiving night when I was in sixth grade. The closer the Stranger got, the more I picked up on the swirling nature of its clothing, looking like quarry acid woven into clothing. Upon reaching the platform, it passed through it as if the platform were porous, and stood on legs I could not see. It stared at the assembly, showing multiple sets of pink eyes from under its hood, scattered across its face like gun shots. It was that which made me realize it had no nose or anything on its face with which to draw breath. Though its mouth was human, I looked away when it spoke, for fear of its teeth. That was when the flashbacks started again and I found the horrible truth of why I could not sleep. I could feel the fangs pierce my skin, helpless and bound, pulling at my very being. I had been a prisoner here once, perhaps twice, maybe more than my mind would let me know. Below us I knew lay only desolation, millions of disgusting Isfet and the remains of all that had fed them over the centuries to this point. *Never run down, never fly down; down is where they get bigger.*

"I call to order this session of the Grand Concord," I heard the creature say. "I trust all members are in attendance." It lifted its chin and folded one seat of arms in front of itself, the other reaching upward as if lifting a heavy stone. Its wicked eyes began to flow with a smoky quartz that turned back to its feigned pink. I felt my vision fade away, feeling as if my very body had been ripped away. *Certainly among the Veil now.* Everything had the blue outline appearance of an architect's design. The followers before us in the tier were gone in lieu of luminous egg shapes, either composed of or filled with swirling patterns of multicolored light. In front of us, Athena had risen off her tier and stood suspended, her flesh made of glass. She hung there like all the attributes in attendance, plucked into the air by a pink quartzy beam, emanating from the hands of the Stranger at the center. The beam connected to all every attribute in the chamber. All of their bodies had the look of blue glass save for tiny but unmistakable black spiders crawling in place within their necks where the skull meets the spine. All of them locked into a web of energy, all of their followers, nothing more than a microcosms of works that sustained their egg like beings. All of the attributes, except for Xochi and I. The beams seemed to lessen in potency as each attribute began to descend back to their tier, the world taking on its dirtiest illusion. The Stranger dropped its arms and swept its vision across the chamber.

"Hotu Matu'a of the Rapa Nui stand forth," it commanded, an impatience and cruelty to its words. We all searched the chamber, eyes looking for the attribute in particular. Finally we heard the resounding "I am here."

Hotu was moving forward on his tier, strangely behind his followers rather than in front. Both simultaneously in an Armani suit and strapping loin cloth as his only garment. In the traditions of his aspect, he stepped forward. I noticed his followers to be thin compared to the other attributes, numbering in the four to five as opposed to Athena's thirty.

"Hotu Matu'a, this great council has assembled for the fourth time this solar cycle," the Stranger addressed him. "How say you?"

"This is true," Hotu replied.

"Each of these sessions," the congressional Stranger continued, "you have been without the belief needed to enjoy the privilege of membership within our great Concord." There was something sinister and inflictive about how he said the word privilege; a moisture to his mouth that was without saliva. "Liens were placed upon your aspect and domains; still you have not made payment. How say you?"

Hotu Matu'a looked to the few warriors he had brought, both those in rugby uniforms and grass skirts. Their faces did not show the need for guidance I had expected but instead a fearless support I remembered. This "man" before me, Hotu Matu'a, had been a boat builder, crafting with papyrus as easily as the Phoenicians would later find making their wood vessels. A humble and kind soul, I remembered him as a fierce athlete and tested warrior. He looked back from his men to the speaker.

"Prefect, that has been your will," Hotu replied.

"Tell me then," the Stranger said more excitedly, an almost vicious smile crossing his face as he cocked his head and moved forward to aim his eyes at Hotu, "why does your Lictor report that you collected tithe from your followers, yet you are here in debt."

"It is simple," Hotu replied, his accent or my imagination produced a slight lisp when he spoke. "I paid my tithe to the Hollow Lord so that my islands would be free of the storms." I almost didn't catch it at first, but when Hotu said storms he looked Anpu's way with an implied snarl. My cousin the Jackal only smiled and blinked as if to say "and?"

"You paid tithe to the Hollow Lord?" the Stranger repeated, spitting as it talked if only it could. "Surely this cannot be the case since such acts are tantamount to betrayal." The Stranger folded all of its hands before it on its chest. "We shall assume you are lying in order to save face, which among the Enlightened," he motioned with his arms toward the assembled attributes before returning his hands to their folded position, "is unnecessary and wasteful. Let us verify with the Hollow Lord himself. Entropy, stand forth."

The name. The reality. Even as the plumes of burning hot plasma mixed with freezing cold gasses circled in the air between the Stranger and Hotu's tier, I worked my hardest not to know what was next. The shapes billowed, collapsed, expanded and pulled into a vacuum taking no committed form. Then it both imploded and exploded, forming a gateway into the unknown. The first green man climbed out of the gateway and jumped down, hanging in the air about six inches below the lower lip of the portal. Two more followed and were stationery next to the first. The little green man hung six inches below the initial three entrants. One after one, the little green men fell in line, forming a perfect staircase from the portal down to the center dais. Then he came into view just as gnarly as I had remembered and somehow diminished. He walked into view. His body was a pure exoskeleton of armor, blades and hooks. His head looked like the top of a Bic lighter, a mechanical gorilla with the face of anguish torn in iron and misery. Though I hated the visage, I couldn't keep my eyes off the gaunt figure. I felt I was watching the carnage of a four car crash as I sped by.

"Imperator," Entropy's wheezing and booming whisper echoed out from his death mask, "we have not begun domain approvals. Why have you summoned me early?"

"My apologies, grand judicator," the Imperator said with feigned posterity, "a matter involving your own domain is before our esteemed collective."

"I highly doubt such matters," Entropy replied back and I noted the layers of etiquette drizzled over disdain the two shared. "But please continue."

"The attribute Hotu Matu'a has been delinquent in tributary payment for some four cycles. His domain has been placed into covenant and we are just to learn he has transferred his latest round of currency to you. Do you refute this?"

"The attribute did in fact pay me," Entropy replied.

"So are we to understand the Judicator is now collecting payments in replacement of this elected body of representatives?"

"The payment was to keep my islands from sinking due to the storms sent by that Egyptian dog and his shadowy father," Hotu interrupted, directing a pointed hand at Anpu who replied with a smile. It was moments like this that reminded me of why I distrusted dogs and enjoying beating on the Jackal.

"Never the less," the Imperator interjected, "the attribute's account is still left for wanting. Shall Lord Entropy cover the rest of the debt?"

"You know that I will not," Entropy said with neither disappointment nor affirmation. The sound of his voice echoed through the chamber and I found myself realizing this was the hollow behind his title. The Imperator nodded and moved its arms in a wiping motion turning away from both speakers. I heard the wet knocking sound and watched as the thread behind Hotu's retinue closed.

"Hotu Matu'a," the Imperator to the assembly, choosing not to face the man as he spoke, "you have been found guilty of attempting to defraud the Grand Concord and delinquency of payment. Your domain shall be stripped from you until such time as you can pay your debt. What say you?"

"Far more than two hundred years and three carriers, I have met with the Concord and paid its cost," Hotu spoke, moving his head to address everyone. "For what exactly? My people were not spared the diseases the Europeans brought to our islands. They were not sparred from the storms. They were never given the protections I was assured would come with my membership. The very hypocrisy we were all guaranteed we would be free of by opposing the Monotheists is precisely what we are left with. Nothing. I am an immortal who can only hope the one true God can restore the grace of those of you who remember why we were sent to this planet."

"You words are both heretical and bordering treason," the Imperator spoke to the attribute who now seemed segmented and distant from the rest of the groups of pantheons and figures of speech. I felt my sight change as if looking through a fishbowl. Hotu was isolated, his dais away from the rest of the attendants stood watching. I got the sense that the sequence of events had happened for my digestion, broken into smaller more tactical widgets in which my own mind could toss around. Whether I caught the other glances from other participating attributes or the lean over followed by cover the mouth messaging, before or after Hotu's speech, it did not matter there was unrest growing in the edges of the Grand Concord like dark mold in neglected showers. I caught the entertainment of those who expected the very least of us all. Anpu was a good example, although he wore the body of a black Colombian by way of Greece. He stood in humiliating defiance at Hotu from his own dais while somehow also in the dais with the Greeks receiving their leaned whispers and smiles. Anpu could be found in most of the daises like echoes in cavern, sticky to the ear if one was tuned.

"I have seen the truth of it," Hotu spoke out, his voice directed at Entropy.

"Have you?" replied the Imperator, "show us this path."

"Once I was skeptical," Hotu stated, "now I am convinced. The Door was correct. There can be no balance as long as the Isfet here. No more than can you kill the Door can you remove from me this truth."

"Such heresy is the end goal and futile struggle of a dead race. Our laws are clear," the Imperator said with a cold and wicked satisfaction. "From this day forth, Hotu Matu'a shall be banned from utterance, his presence forgotten and his essence locked away in obsolescence for eternity." I watched Entropy's reaction to the verdict with great confusion, trying to intuit why a figure of such soulless authority would turn away from what occurred next. Hotu was ready for the first one; I was not. It came from behind, mid-leap from out of the very air, flying with a velocity meant for his back. He spun and back fisted it, sending the Phantom in a vector off of the dais and flailing its flagitious ass into the darkness below. His honor guard had not been of the same fortune, leaving Hotu alone. The second gave no warning; it was on him with a bite without any time between its appearance and Hotu's deflection.

From some black hole in the fabric that formed that chamber, the Phantom leapt out with terminal velocity, knocking Hotu off his feet and into an identical hole. Then in echoes that followed to a silence was all that was left of the legendary king and his retinue. "Do not ever forget this Concord exists to protect us all. There are worse things than obsolescence." In the murmurs that followed through the chamber, I recorded the talking points used to justify and rationalize such tyranny. In my mind, the best answer I could give was there were things even the Isfet feared, none of them including the name of God and that's what worried me more. "If we are quite done with that display of reckless self-destruction," the Imperator continued, "we can move on to Appropriations." It looked from side to side, blankly expecting a response. When one came, it nodded its head and stepped back a bit. There were the sounds of the digital gongs, higher pitch and more delay than reverb than ones I previously heard. Entropy stepped forward in its place, folding his hands in front of his armored waist.

"Elatha," Entropy announced, "present your collateral for approval." When Entropy spoke, an outline formed before him in mercurial blue, gridlines on the horizontal and then vertical. As it filled in and became solidified, I felt what my mind registered as my eyes creating a pattern into shape. A rising set of cylinders that were both a tapestry on a roll and a loading giant LCD came from the ceiling to meet its other half raising from the platform. Angles and vectors became impossible to predict in lieu of the emotion involved in interpreting the images. Even as my eyes processed the visages, I reminded myself they were orchestrated from my consumption. None of this existed beyond a few flashes of light in liquid chemical form inside my brain.

Ramps from each ring of the daises extended to the center showing the sinister shape of the web. A sole figure walked one of the gangplanks to the center, talking slow, plodding steps that rippled through his imagine from footfall to the top of his head. He walked to the pedestal construct, throwing back his hood to address Entropy with his eyes. One glance was a luminous egg blob with a circlet about its upper region. The second glance was a cloak the color of steamy breath in a cold morning. A well-built man of medium height appeared, dark blonde hair that fell on his head slicked back; shiny in some places while appearing wet in others. His eyes were a dull brown color with a brightness behind the pupils. He wore well-trimmed facial hair, a lighter shade than his head hair, reminding me of a swashbuckler. The circlet appeared of silver, contrasting with the whiteness of his teeth. He arranged his jaw to give an empty stare into Entropy.

It was the movement of his cheeks that revealed his slight dimples camouflaged into his small mouth. Something told me not to let thoughts drift too close to his in a place such as this. Elatha reached into the folds of his robe, producing a stone with a carving upon it. My eyes focused on the runes, Gaelic in nature, as he placed the stone on the pedestal. The mind works in overtime to connect the dots. Two runes each with separate meanings. The first was for a tree that no longer grows that was the equivalent of giving back. The second was the equivalent of tying a rope upon itself over and over again. Both were in Ogham. How to put together the concepts into ones congruent meaning, I am not sure. My imagination found the answer shortly before Entropy's announcement.

"Elatha of the Tuatha Dé Danann has submitted the semi-conductor to the Concord," Entropy's voice croaked.

"Objection," cried out a voice and the dais holding the Norse delegation was highlighted.

"The Concord recognizes Loki of Asgard," the Imperator stated.

Somehow he was taller than you would expect, most typical depictions having him as a shorter yelp sort of younger brother figure. In fact he reminded me of the vengeful German terrorist who loses his brother in the first Die Hard movie. Blonde, euro trash hair hang, a sweater, designer jeans and some furry shoes he should have been slapped for wearing. Then he was also in browns and greens, his clothes reminding me of the stereotypes of Europe's old candy makers. He pushed past his haughty-faced relatives, standing with hands on his hip in the direct center of the spotlight without any visible source.

"These aspects are duplicates," Loki called out, "Elatha already has submitted these works."

"The gentleman from Asgard is correct," Elatha replied, quiet and sullen. "An objection is indeed in order. I am a Fomorian in origin, though it is also true I married one of the Tuatha De'. A further objection might be with associating Loki with Asgard." This generated a number of laughs, mostly from the female attributes. Loki looked around protest to his original complaint, found none and folded his arms behind his back before beginning his proud march back to obscuring shapes of his pantheon assembled in the front of their dais. "To the untrained eye this is in fact a duplicate. Upon further inquiry, I believe it becomes obvious that the glyph in question is an improvement upon previous concepts. The organic semiconductor is not the same as the semiconductor or the element of silicon which are used for manufacturing microchips." There was a turbulent rumble of voices in the hall as the ramifications spread.

"Entropy, is this true?" Loki screamed, outraged. Entropy held his gruesome adorned hand, lifting his palm to aim at the anvil-shaped pedestal. The glyph rose to eye level and turned the color of blueprint, matching my vision within the Veil.

"Let the record show," Entropy's voice rang out from his obliterating helm, "Elatha of the Celts has added the organic semiconductor to his domain as an addition to the original semiconductor and silicon. Any attributes wishing to use such works must gain permission from Elatha himself including the Celts. Violations are enforceable by this gathering." I gathered that some prior incident had occurred involving Elatha and the Celts over some new works that hadn't gone through proper channels. Elatha smiled and nodded, placing his hands within the cuffs of each of the robe's arms. His eyes never left the glyph as it changed to red outlines with black fill, suspended in a column of mercurial blue light filled by gray. The column spun like a drill bit, torqued by the base and signaling an opening in the ceiling of the chamber. Exactly like the doors Xochi and I entered through, the opening in the ceiling spun to allow access to another party of the chamber. My view didn't allow me a full view but I could see a lip to the opening like looking at the edge of a hot tube after raising your head from being submerged. A hot tub of blue outlines and gray fills. I caught a few hints of glints of the same pattern as the red and black glyph that was rising to the top of the column. I turned my eyes back to the center dais before the glyph had ascended to its destination to ensure my own anonymity. Elatha was half way along the cat walk back to the Celtic dais. As he walked I saw another catwalk extend from what appeared from the other side of the chamber.

A linear path between the center and where a group of dark-skinned individuals stood, each with brightly colored hair. One in particular, the one with an assortment of ribbon like and thick cord dread locks the color of the Target logo, was disrobing. He had a fat, friendly face that seemed to fit his long and lithe frame. As he stood, removing his robe, I studied the print of his suit. He wore a jacket and pants of a translucent material that moved with images of newsreel type footage. Men sitting by trees in cloths, women in markets speaking with animated jaw movements, over the exchange of shells, marching youth in tattered clothes holding rifles and large ships leaving beaches full of imprisoned Africans all decorated his clothes. The suit was countered against the crisp white button up and red tie he wore. He strode barefoot, after passing his robe to a man behind him with white hair with similar facial features. Across the catwalk with the life of the people through time splashed across his clothes. I let my eyes fall to the floor as I wrestled with my thoughts. I liked this man. I knew him before he was named.

"Oba Koso," Entropy called out as the man neared his destination. "Orisha of the Yoruba on behalf of the Ife." I loved this man; his smile lit my heart. *Quiet.* Oba stood on the center dais as the catwalks out to the Celts disappeared and I could no longer make out their dais from any others, only the Orishas. When I looked back to the center, Oba Koso had placed a briefcase on to the anvil and was reaching in its open lid. He pulled a glyph into plain view, placed it on the anvil, closed the briefcase, set the briefcase on the floor and took a step back.

The writings on this glyph were not in Gaelic. It was Yoruba, used currently only in scattered records of what was left of the arcane practitioners of Southern Nigeria. The language of potent and wise men of Igbo, the unifying written language of Nigeria's first people was gone almost entirely gone. I picked through each symbol: energy, plant, water.

"Oba Koso has submitted blue algae. Explain this work."

"An alternative fuel," Oba Koso replied. He held none of Elatha's restraint. Proud, defiant and aloof. Oba was no fan of the Concord and too powerful to be disposed of. "This will replace petroleum usage in my domain by sixty percent over the next ten years." There was a murmuring laughter throughout the chamber as if Oba's statement was too preposterous to openly challenge. Oba was used to the doubt; it showed in how he nodded and kept eyes on Entropy though his jaw rolled with clenched teeth. His gaze almost spelled out that he expected public ridicule and was in baited breath until it arrived to justify the response he had been looking for just this very moment. I recalled a story around Henry Ford's flagship invention, how he returned to the place and audience of humiliation for six years in a row before unveiling his grand prestige. What it must have been like on Ford's final trip to the World Fair, knowing he would have his day to dream out loud and a lifetime of history to record his response. There were padded voices, but nobody challenged Oba in the same manner as Elatha.

"Let the record show that Oba Koso, Shango of the Orishas, has submitted the hard works of blue algae giving him domain of this form of energy," Paradox itself announced.

"Let the record also show, as the primary source of resources for both Shell Oil and Exxon Mobil, Nigeria will be the blue algae Saudi Arabia by 2014," Oba added. There were sneers then and the riptide of jealousy across faces as Oba's announcement echoed out. Then the glyph like the one before it changed color and levitated up to the column, which had grown the size of the opening in the ceiling by another foot in diameter. There were other attributes ready to submit as Oba walked back to his dais, invoking the nods of his people and others. Some of the attributes who submitted during the Appropriation session were rejected, some accepted and some were told further research was required. It was a long arduous process on the mind that I had fast tracked through the majority of until an announcement brought me into focus.

"If there are no other submissions," Entropy rang out, "then this concludes our session."

"Master adjudicator," the woman's voice sounded out. "There is one last submission." The catwalk was extending toward the dais where I kneeled.

"Athena of Olympus," Entropy stated, "it has been some time since you last came before us." Her cheeks got a bit more rosy at the mention of her name. I felt bad when I wished cherried smile points would drop off her face. I wished it had been her and not Hotu that been swallowed by the Nest. She began her step forward, leaving her owl to her lieutenant to hold and her spear as well. Her toga was interchangeable with the outfit she had worn to the Gala. No different or same from the first time I met her in the ocean's froth. Athena.

She was close to the center of everyone's attention. I wrestled with my thoughts as I drifted to a bird's eye view, still focused on the intent behind it all. It was the umbrella turned on its top to drain the storm off. The very word brought it home to reality. Looking down an open umbrella on a sun porch, the eye catches the hilt, down the stem to the base and its eight arms out folded to make the canopy. *The hilt.*

She neatly pranced to the center, bold in her intent, holding the glyph in her hand and leaving her robe to trail behind her like a bird on a leash.

No introductions would suit her as Athena placed the glyph she had stolen from me on the pedestal with force, standing back with her arms folded.

"I've brought a foundation glyph and I expect its full rights," Athena stated, her voice cold and assured. The response from the chamber was deafening. Imagine a million voices all yelling in your head at once, none of them in agreeing or disagreeing quite the same. Stretches of the imagination from "how dare she" to "praise Athena, you have a friend in us" rang in my head. Entropy's eyes flashed and I felt a sharp ringing that was painful to the point of blinding me. It was the sound of five hundred billion year-old fluorescent light bulbs plugged into their sockets about to shatter. Then there was silence.

"I do not expect to gain this assembly's attention again," the Imperator whispered like an angry parent warning a child in a grocery store that an ass whooping was imminent.

"Daughter of Zeus, no attribute had ever submitted a foundation glyph," Entropy spoke. "They are both rare and potent in that the glyphs are the source of our works."

"You are correct, my hollow lord," Athena replied with a disgusting sweetness to her voice "It is rare that one of our attributes should have contact with such cosmic architecture. However, the grace of Olympus is as formidable as it is old. Were my people not of the first to form this Concord? Then let Athena stand honored where others have failed, for this glyph was obtained in duel." Thousands of whispers in my head led to inquisitive thoughts. *Who had she beaten? Not us. Which one of you here broke?*

"There are very few attributes," the Imperator added, "who contributed foundation glyphs to our formation. It is unlikely that any would hold back to lose them in duel to you."

"That is because this glyph was taken from a rogue," Athena replied. "Although I was unable to capture him for the reward, this glyph was won in combat from the Door of the Kemet." Another ruckus arose from the Concord, this time out loud. Above the center dais appeared thousands of portraits, all of different men from different eras across time. The newest portrait remained a cloudy silhouette but shared the same glyphs as the rest: Sekhem Ka, Neteru Rogue. The second to last picture was a face I knew too well: my father.

"That is most opportune," the Imperator stated, revealing something it considered a smile. "Let us process her submission immediately so we can reward such loyalty." Athena smiled and stepped back when the glyph lifted off the pedestal along the column. It lifted half way and froze in place, turning to a black and yellow pattern instead of the black and red. The column disappeared and the top was neither able to expand or contract.

"Judicator," the Stranger hissed, "what is the problem?" Entropy strode below the glyph, holding his palm beneath it.

"This is no glyph," he stated. "It is a forgery, but not by her hand." Entropy motioned to Athena with his head. "Daughter of Olympus, you have been fooled." His arm extended to well over twelve feet, grabbing onto the glyph, which caused a spilling of yellow light. It formed like an arrow and shot toward our dais.

"*I got this, Xoch,*" I sent to my companion as I stood, reaching my hand out to slap down the arrow.

"There are traitors among us," the Imperator screamed out. I stood out of my kneel, using my hands to pull my cloak's hood farther down to hide my face while Xochi set about knocking out each of Athena's followers in less than a second.

"Traitor requires a lost sense of loyalty," I yelled out, aware that the thread behind us had closed. "You stole our land. Then you stole our culture. Then you stole our way and perverted it, calling it some sick form." I stared down at Anpu, who remained shocked in his boots to hear my voice. I picked up Athena's spear and hurled it at him, breaking his stride as he had to jump back to avoid where the tip lodged in the dais where his leg had just been. "We were never one of you nor will we ever be. Hide in the convenience of your bubble, manipulating humanity from afar and satisfying your own vanity if you like. There is but one God and you all are an extension of it." I pointed my hand at the Imperator. "Accept your beasts of chaos and all those who love you." I turned my attention to the Concord again, speaking to the group from someplace within. "Your free will has led you astray. Know then, the day will come when even this place will not save you. Hotu was correct, you cannot kill me. I am Sekhem Ka, son of Ma'at, servant to the true lord of Kemet." By the last phrase, I had grabbed Xochi's hand and sent *discs*! Below us, millions of red eyes had become the shapes of hordes of spider legions crawling up near our dais. I ignored the reverberating, wet knocking sound coming from every corner of the chamber.

I laughed when Xochi's first disc, yellow in color with flickers of red trim, hung in the air near where the column was like a sun red tea saucer. I jumped from the ledge, pulling Xochi with me. *Huh.* We appeared on the disc; a second appeared across the chamber higher than the first. Still holding on to Xochi, I leapt again. *Huh.* On to the second disc, watching Isfet clamor on to the first disc and then topple down as it disappeared. We continued this; each time a new disc appeared it was farther away from us and higher up than one before it, the previous disc evaporating when the newest appeared. Finally, the disc was just below the opening in the ceiling, which Xochi used like an elevator platform to bring us up to. Once inside the new chamber, the disc beveled and created a dome over the entrance, which sounded like a wooden spoon against a bowl as the spiders began to bang against the opening.

"I can't hold them for long," Xochi said. "Get what you need so we can go."

The chamber was red outlined with black fill, resembling a U-Haul storage more than a room. Walls were filled with translucent boxes, labeled in Isfet script and networked. Each box had a series of cables and tubes running out of them and into the floor.

"He's this way," I heard a familiar voice call in my head. I turned to Xochi, who must have heard it too because she seemed alarmed.

"Careful," Xochi warned, "we don't know what tricks they can pull in here."

I walked forward, following my instincts in a place of ideas through several rooms into a large chamber. The first thing to catch my eyes was the sight of a large mummy, floating in a tank of viscous and clear liquid. There were thousands of tubes coming out of the tank, running up the wall into the midsection of woman fastened there. She was pinned to the wall like a butterfly in case, her wings outstretched across the wall. Beautiful and wise, her dark skin was contrasted by her silvery hair that hung off her head.

"Mother?" I said, feeling the emotions well and the water hit my eyes. *"Mother!"*

"Yes, beloved Sekhem," she sent back to me, *"I knew you would come."*

"How?"

"You have always kept your promises to me. It is why you are my child." I began to run forward, building strength to find a way up the wall. "Do not waste your focus on me, there is little time. Take what is left of Ausar with you. Without him, they will not be able to function as well and would be required to shift me to a less restrictive prison." Conflicted being a momma's boy, I followed directions and approached Ausar's prison. The lock wouldn't budge and the tubes were immovable.

"Clay!" I heard Xochi yell before she dropped to her knees and put fingers to her temples. My eyes looked down the hallways to Xochi's barrier, which was filled with eight-legged shapes battering against it. Frustrated, I searched the room. My eyes found a figure, the body of a circus strongman with the face of a teenager. He was kneeling on one knee, pinned in place by several large needles with opaque quartz colored heads. I pulled one from each of his shoulders, holding one in each hand by the shaft. A mace in each hand, I banged against the glass like structure holding Ausar. The first blows didn't impact its integrity; I screamed and flurried the result, being a number of cracks spidering their way through the glass. I kicked with a stomp and shattered the container, liquid spilling out. I reached inside, freeing the mummy and throwing it over my shoulder.

I knew I would have to return some day. I moved to the other side of the room farthest away from the hallway back to Xochi's barrier. There stood two empty containers. One bore my name on it and the other with Khpr's. Choosing not to be so obvious, I drew a door on the floor in the corner. Then I dropped the mummy through the door and ran near my mother.

"M'lord," I heard turned to see the eyes of the kneeling giant were open and staring at me. "Some assistance?"

"Of course," I said and removed the rest of the pins to watch him stand, all seven feet of him. "Take the Aztec and exit." Khonsu lifted Xochi and walked to the door, dropping through. I walked to stand below Ma'at. "When I return, you are coming with me." She gave me a tired smile.

"Of course, my heart," Ma'at replied.

"Where is father?" I asked.

"I have not seen him here. I cannot sense him," she replied sadly. "I do not know if Djeuti exists at all."

"He does," I said out more desperation than fact. "I will be back, mother. I am sorry. I wished I had listened to you."

"Hush," she chided. "Leave me before they put you in a box under me again." I nodded and ran to the door, stepping down to waist level and pulling the Harrison container back in its place over the door. On the other side, I locked the door to the attic in my house on San Bruno mountain and starred at the three guests sprawled on the stairs below me. Xochi lay on the ground, rubbing her eyes before looking at me.

"So an Aztec, a mummy and a guy with a scythe walk into a bar," I say.

CHAPTER TWENTY-ONE

"Imagine how often someone throws garbage at a person because no one else is watching."

-Avalos

Normally the cafe is full, brimming with all form of Potrero Hill and Dog Patch media workers enjoying a weekend meal among the peasants. Today it is emptier than the bridges the day they raise tolls. They raise them yearly the day after rapid transit and running for seats holding a mocha isn't so sexy anymore so the bridges fill up again. That is the nature of life in San Francisco, a flock of seagulls scared away from one piece of bread by a pedestrian and scared back to it by a car horn. I was glad the spot was near closing, there would be little chance of the flock returning.

I had finished my meal a while ago and musing to myself over a cup of coffee. Despite the events of the masquerade ball, one voice inside me seemed at peace. I guessed the sight of his mother renewed his purpose and quelled any guilt he may have felt. There was an empathy I shared: Granny was a prisoner of her own mind and Sekhem's mother was prisoner of her own people. There wasn't anything either of us could do at the moment to change that.

I was debating leaving a giant tip as an incentive to let me back into the restaurant after a cigarette when I heard the front door open. I matched the time on my phone to the head waiter greeting the detective as he walked by the register. Today I kept my eyes off him, watching him through the lens as he stepped down the hallway and pulled up a seat across from me. I kept my eyes to the newspaper I was pretending to read, while extending the lens to the street, then a couple block radius around the cafe. There were no familiar faces so I greeted him.

"Detective," I said, sipping my coffee while keeping the appearance of being engrossed in an article on foreclosures in the Bayview.

"Doctor," he replied, taking off his hat and placing it on the seat next to him.

"You came alone," I said with a smile. "I feel less important."

"You are," Avalos replied, his eyes flashing, "for right now."

"How long will it last?" I asked, looking past Avalos to make eye contact with the waiter to summon a menu.

"Depends how much time it takes for you to connect the dots for me with this," Avalos replied.

Reaching under the table for something as he moved, his trench coat opened to show me the revolver in his holster. Old school and regimented, Avalos kept a gun because it came with the badge rather than a double-digit death-dealer that gave him power. When his hands reappeared, they carried a manila folder with the string post tie off in red. He placed it on his side of the table and pushed it across to me just before his menu arrived on the table. He examined the breakfast side, leaving me time to open the folder and pretend to read. One finger on the envelope was all I needed to scan all sixty pages into my brain, an amalgamation of police reports, witness testimonials, cold cases, shipping records, accounting files and custom agent findings.

"What's good here?" Avalos asked, staying locked on the menu.

"Any of the meats that come with two eggs," I replied, keeping pace with his bluff. "Though I usually substitute the starch for vegetables."

"That's probably the bright choice," Avalos replied. "My wife will thank me for it."

"I don't see any notations from you," I started. "New cases?"

"Case you started me down," Avalos replied, "a collection of bread crumbs." He paused when the waiter came over, gave his order and leaned back in the chair to allow menu removal. He wasted no time once we were alone at our table. "I see you hinting at something. A far cry from the local kid fresh out of school with a shrink degree looking to volunteer with any juvenile squad who would have him."

"I don't know that I'm even hinting," I replied, continuing to read through the packet. "I'm not the cop at the table." I made sure I looked up after I said that so Avalos could see my eyes. I saw his as well. Avalos was a straight shooter; that much was clear. He would do his job whether it went along with the rule book. He had not survived this long by being naive about the top-down policies that affected promotions, assignments and squads but certainly not pensions. He needed to be sure if he went down an alley it wouldn't be blind and if it was going to get him political heat there had to be a payoff for his morality.

"Just tell me what I'm missing," Avalos replied.

"You have customs violations, shipping tons of exotic spiders from South America and Africa into SFO. For every one arrest, you are left with either a fake visa worker you send to INS or a perp who doesn't talk. They do five to seven at most, discharge and disappear off the grid upon release. Still you catch what, two, three a year and wonder where's the demand. It isn't Florida where exotic pets fill the Star Island mansion and the black market doesn't chirp at bugs the way it would for human organs or Russian prostitutes."

"Keep going," Avalos said, starting with his eggs.

"So for every small number you catch, you know more is coming and wonder about the ones you don't. So let's say each one of these customs files represents about six more who slipped through the crack. These are customs issues focused on terrorism and narcotics, not importing poisonous bugs. Then we factor in this isn't your cup of tea either. Your squad deals with children and families, which despite San Francisco leading the nation in child pornography production, does a very good job of closing convictions. Where are the links?" I asked.

"Each of these customs violations matches with an indictment or investigation on my board," Avalos replied. "Some are cold going back to when I was a rookie. Most we have everything short of a witness testimony to go to court."

"And that's where the statements come in," I replied. "You can't get these kids to testify."

"No. It doesn't matter if they are 13 or 31 now. Got over 40 assault victims terrified to show their face on record."

"Did they mention why?"

"Not a one. There was one kid, now a mother of three living in Marin City. In 2001 she was brought in for an interview under hypnosis." I sucked my teeth. Avalos shook his head and defended. "This was 2001, well before you became an ace in the hole."

"You admit I'm an ace."

"I admit you get mute kids to turn into motor mouths" he replied.

"What did the hypnosis produce?"

"Nothing more than bad dreams. I have a daughter. A couple of years ago she got a bad fever. The wife was on call so I stayed home with the kid. She would just sweat in bed and murmur through her sleep. No more than five words at a time. When the fever broke she couldn't remember a single dream."

"The interview reminded you of that?"

"Nearly identical except my daughter's words were incomprehensible. The interview is full of broken meaning." I watched Avalos take more bites and scrolled my mind into the transcripts of the interview. Somewhere after eight minutes came the messages Avalos referred to:

-You can't protect me

-They keep biting

-It hurts and they are laughing

-Weavers

-If I tell anyone they will bite them too.

"I caught that," I replied. "What does your squad actually have on any of these suspects?"

"A disgusting jambalaya," Avalos replied. "Laptops full of kiddy porn, a few prior assault charges, statutory rape and in one case attempting to purchase sex with a minor in a sting operation. Over all, these same importers have a thing for hurting kids." I felt my jaw tighten and my nose crinkle. I needed someone to pay and there wasn't a clear target. It was clear that there had been a ten-year effort to feed my enemy with the terror of children living in our sanctuary.

"Any common links?," I asked

"It varies wildly. You couldn't pin down an ethnicity, religion or any demographic. I'm looking for this group you keep aiming me at, but I don't see it. If it exists, it's too well hidden. The church of Satan was sloppy; these monsters are not."

I sat back in my chair and sipped my coffee. It wasn't coming to me, not as easily as previous attempts. I found myself becoming distracted at how ironic things had become. There was an image in my mind of a younger Avalos, well before the gray streaks and the good suits, a wise and hip beat cop looking down on me as I slept on the bench. I was cuffed to the inside bars of the police station on Williams. My first and only offense--a fifteen-year-old semblance of myself, who had blacked out in a Walgreens. When I awoke, other teens had been beaten within an inch of their lives. Witness testimonies reported the youngsters were assaulting an elderly gentleman in attempts to steal his newly-cashed SS check when another teen, who watched from the candy aisle, passed out, crashed through the cosmetics counter as a result, rose again with his eyes rolled back in his head and proceeded to attack the mob in defense of the elderly man.

The first officer on the scene was a foot patrolman by the name of John Avalos, who reported the assault. The assailant had sent six boys to the ER with his bare hands and now lay convulsing on the floor suffering from what appeared to be an epileptic seizure. The scene must not have added up to the patrolman because after the EMTs declared the assailant safe to move, he ended up on a bench instead of a holding cell. Over the next few months, the case went to trial. The assailant, thought by all accounts to have been acting in defense of a vulnerable citizen, had put at least one attacker in a coma for a number of weeks. The result was a reassignment to a group home, as it was determined his grandmother was too old to properly care for him. His only visitor was the patrolman who often brought him books, snacks and science journals. Perhaps it was the combination of the incident, the readings and the visits that led the boy to apply for a scholarship which carried him to the East Coast to pursue studies on the human mind.

Eight years later the boy returned to San Francisco, a doctorate in tow, showing up at the patrolman's favorite grocery store. The patrolman was an inspector now, running a squad of detectives investigating crimes against youth. The boy, now a man, believed he could get any child to talk.

"Did I see a map in there?" I asked.

"Yes," Avalos said, finishing his breakfast with the last fork scrape and starting on his orange juice that I hadn't notice before. "It was a blind alley. I was lost on any demographic connections so I made a stab at locations. Each of the black dots is where a victim was either abducted from or propositioned. The red dots are where the assaults were conducted. The orange dots are where the victims currently live." I nodded and reached over to the file, pulling out the black and white copy of a map Avalos had marked up. It was mostly of San Francisco County, but it was pieced together with surrounding locales of Marin, San Mateo and Alameda county. My pupils studied every red dot as I reached down to the floor next to my chair to find my satchel. Reaching inside I knew there were no pencils, only pens. What my hand placed on the table was certainly a number two pencil. A second pause and there was no digital gongs, so I began drawing lines. First, the red dots to each of the black dots, point A to point B.

"Are you telling me out of pool of victims, none of them left the area after the assault?" I asked.

"Yeah," Avalos responded. "That's what threw me for a loop. Not a single one moved away more than forty-five minutes from the scene. They relocate from one county to another county but none of them left Northern California or the state."

"Do you have the original residencies at the time of abduction?"

"I hadn't thought of that," Avalos said, "but yes." He turned the files to him and began flipping through. "Read them out to you?"

"Yes, please." We began, and for each address I made a gray lead dot. When he read of the last address, I placed a dot, then I connected the orange dots to the gray. Thin isosceles triangles, long in height, short in width, etched along the length with their apexes starting a radial pattern. What's missing, Clay? Something is here. What is it? What could it be? *What do you call several pyramids laid flat and connected at the tips?*

I felt my hand move without my volition. It started at the apexes and connected each to make a rough octagon shape. Then it moved in toward the first set of points along the nearest triangle, drew a line between and connected them to their equivalent in the triangle to the right. The pattern continued creating a second and larger octagon. Then my hand went wild, connecting, connecting, *connecting*. With an arthritic ache, I stopped, dropping the pencil and clutching at my hand. Avalos stared at me through slatted eyes, although the curve of his jaw said pity.

"You still have those?" He asked.

"Have what?" I snapped, clutching at my wrist to where the pain had spread.

"Your eyes rolled back in your head after you drew the second line." I pursed my lips and looked away embarrassed, staring at the shape that had taken place. I shouldn't be surprised that I was staring at yet another upside down umbrella. If the San Francisco Bay Area was a right hand with the thumb curled towards the index finger, then San Francisco and its peninsula was the thumb. Oakland would be the knuckle of my index finger and Marin would be the nail of the same finger. The web was built around Marin.

"That look familiar?" I said, tapping my finger at the center of the web on the page. Avalos removed his plate from our table and placed it at the table behind us. He reached into his breast pocket and produced his glasses, once again reminding me that he was packing. As he flipped out the frames in preparation to place the horns over his ears he picked the paper containing the map up so he could view it in front of his face. The paper was thin and my handwriting was dense, I could see the shape etched into the pages from across the table. Avalos nodded his head and placed the map back on the table between us.

"I remember the night this started." He said low and calm, tapping his finger against the page. "It didn't bother me until a few days later that your cigarette shouldn't have stuck to the silk." Avalos took his glasses off and returned them to the case. "You know, I was going to be a zoologist once."

"Oh yeah?" I asked.

"Yeah. I loved animals ever since I was a kid."

"Yes, you joined SFPD."

"You know, for the first time in a long period, I would like a cigarette," Avalos said looking at his hands in his lap. I dug into the breast pocked of my jacket and dropped the pack on the table with my lighter. He shook his head and continued. "Wanting something and doing something are very different. It's what separates us from the beasts." He paused. "I worked an internship at the zoo in college."

"SF . . . by the lake?"

"Right there. I worked nine months on applying and interviews, they were unsure about me due to my age, what with me being a sophomore."

"Can you commit?"

"Something to that effect."

"I'm sure you played the working class Chicano at State card?"

"No. I was a Bear."

"Cal, heartbreaking. Such treachery," I teased.

"I know, I was trying to make my parents proud."

"Dad liked college football?"

"Never missed a game."

"I forgive you . . . hustlin' just ain't you." Avalos laughed.

"That's a Jay-Z line right?" he asked.

"I'm impressed."

"I listened to the tapes you sent. Never understood why the DJ screamed on them, though."

"It's a regional thing they do back East."

"I should have told you to apply to Southern Cal. You could have sent me some decent weather."

"With a touch of pollution?"

"Right."

"Being a zookeeper didn't weird you out?" I asked.

"Did worse. I spent three months there monitoring cages. Are they locked? Is it safe? Have we followed every step? Those months of observation led me to believe the animals were fine; it was the humans we need to be safe from."

"How so?"

"My Dad came to this country with one English phrase written on a piece of paper: I work hard. It didn't matter if it was construction, painting, line cook, wood cutter or janitor--he spent most of his time earning and the rest with family. The first Sunday of the month, we would visit the zoo. He had friends who were city employees who would donate their passes to him. Admission was free but you had to buy a box of pink popcorn. He loved the lions. He would spend hours at the pit, smiling wide when they roared. On those free days, the staff ratio was low, especially security. It would be amazing to see the other families who would attend from Marin to the Marina on the same day."

"Well, the wealthy stay that way somehow."

"If it was them alone I wouldn't keep the memory. It was how they influenced others."

"What do you mean?"

"There was a father and his sons. They came to gawk at the lions. They started by dangling hot dogs. Then it transformed into taunts and throwing garbage."

"Security didn't get involved? Oh right, they were off duty. What did you do?"

"I joined in. I started throwing the popcorn like all the other poor kids, yet I was sad. It seemed wrong. However, I didn't want to seem like I didn't fit in. Then my father grabbed me and dragged me out of there. We never spoke about it again, but we also never went to the zoo again, either."

"So zoology was a way of redeeming yourself with your father?"

"No, I loved animals. I have two dogs and a bird. My internship was to protect the humans from the animals. I came to a point where I saw that the animals needed protection from the humans."

"So you became a cop?"

"Imagine how often someone throws garbage at a person because no one else is watching."

"So you expect to be that eye?"

"Among others . . . ."

"You're a good man, John." His cell phone rang. I waited for him as he checked the number, signaled with his face he recognized it and picked up. His voice was soft and bright when he answered which led me to believe it was either his wife or children. He pointed out to the street and I nodded as he rose to walk outside. My eyes fell back to the printed amalgamation of the Bay Area county map. I put my finger on the paper and pulled it on the table closer to me. My fingers continued to walk and stop at the center of the web. *Where are you?*

I saw the Golden Gate Bridge below me like a chalk painting on the sidewalk. I walked along the bridge to the bay by Tiburon. Still following highway 1, I traveled over the hill, past the tunnel and over the metropolitan area that could loosely be defined as Marin. I scanned rooftops not exactly sure what I was looking for. I almost moved on until I caught the single strand from the sky aimed at one particular roof. I stepped closer to inspect each foot fall covering a quarter of a mile while each home was the size of a match box. I came closer to the building, squatting to improve my view of the details. I don't know if I was surprised or not to find the blue flag on the corner of the structure signifying a member of Olympus frequented the building. I take that back: the flag surprised me, but the address did not. The building was a two-story affair, in fact an art gallery owned by a Constandina Kefalos. I memorized the street address.

"Not sleeping well?" I heard Avalos say and opened my eyes. I placed my right hand on my left in my lap and stretched my neck so I could meet his eyes. I shrugged.

"What makes you say that?" I asked.

"Aside from the color of your eyelids" Avalos replied, "the map you were making."

"I was just resting my eyes. I hear it's a prerogative of old men." Avalos chuckled and shrugged back as if to say point well taken. "I have an address for you."

"Oh?"

"Yes." I said, rifling off the Marin address I remembered from Constandina's business card. I pointed my eyes to the center of the web on the map before Avalos. "Nothing you can start an investigation with."

"I see." Avalos said with a mix of disappointment and boredom. "I don't think you were being clever. You did as asked but I don't have anything to make a case with." I pulled out my pen, copied down the address, and slid it across the table to him.

"Watch the house and see what you get." I suggested. "The best leverage you're going to get is to attempt a sting on the customs end or what you're not going to like. The customs piece is too much of a stretch. It's not like there's a plethora of exotic spiders available in the evidence room down at 850. It's too delicious to these sickos to get a chance at a second try."

"You're right, I don't like it. But it makes sense. A victim and a child would sweeten the smell."

"Like flies to a web."

"I will have to sit with it before I make a final decision."

"I like it the less we talk about it. Thought it's probably got the best chance of making a case for you. "

"I'll put a car on the address for now and hope that gives us something." Avalos reached for his wallet. I waved it off when I realized what he was up to. He folded his bottom lip, agreed with his shoulders and grabbed his hat. Avalos rose from the table, placed his hat upon his head, threw on his jacket and clasped up the files. He turned on heel and walked away. "Thank you," he said as he got near the door.

"For what?"

"For talking me out of it." Then he was back into the rain. It was then I realized he hadn't been wet when he came back from the call.

The front door is always the problem. As Granny had aged, she had become more isolated and it tended to give her a hermetic lifestyle; she began showing acute signs of paranoia. The front door had six dead bolts total. At one time each of the bolts had their own key and that was after you got through the security gate. Coming home for breaks to visit, I was given one new key to add to the ammunition-like ring she had developed on my keychain. When I moved back to care for her, I was able to negotiate a key for all six. It had started as trying to replace the door with fewer bolts but that had only invoked her wrath and accusations that another male was trying to control her destiny. I bet you think you are a smarty-pants. You would have pointed out there is already a security gate. Tried that too. This house wasn't built on logic; it was constructed from drama and glued together with guilt.

Through the door there is a collection of heaters. Let's pretend Target released a space heater once a year in updated, buzz-worthy and brag-heavy designs. Let's also pretend there is a penalty for not upgrading them. You begin to understand why every room in the house has at least three space heaters. Had Granny been allowed, she would have brought home the heater with GPS and Wi-Fi, not that such a thing exists. But if it did, it would be staring at me from the outlet. Do something! You ain't nobody! Who is Clay? I dare you to move me!

I stepped past the pile of mail accruing on the floor by the front door under the mail slot. A new door was supposed to remove the need for her to bend over to grab mail, but we covered that already. Try as I might, my limp from my leg dragged a few magazines along from the stack on the floor to stare at Maya Angelou on the cover of AARP. I flopped my satchel on the couch which had the protective blankets removed and was covered it cat hair. There was a smell in the air. It resembled the combination of seafood lying in the sun for a full day and burning dust from the heater. It was so potent you couldn't identify one independent contributor. The easiest place was the kitchen, which consisted of stacked up dishes and full garbage sitting for two weeks I had left with every intention of cleaning when I got home. I'm pretty sure if I hadn't gone to Oakland I would have come home to a cupboard full of dishes. Further discovery into the adjoining sun porch revealed two brimming cat boxes and a number of dying plants. Walking back into the kitchen, I opened the fridge to see the shining gem in a canyon of spoiled food. There were two six packs of beer and two bottles left in a third.

Walking back into the living room with an open beer, I made my way to the entertainment center. On a set of shelves in an alcove that I am sure was once a fireplace judging by the ceramic tiles under it was a record player, a tuner, an eight track, and a cassette deck. The six-disc CD changer had been my addition when I grew tired of having to flip a record after three or four songs. The speakers, perhaps over twenty years old, were mounted in the corners of the room, so the wires had no chance to trip her when she walked through. I opened the plastic lid of the phonograph and removed the Sam Cooke that had been the night Avalos called me to the apartment with Desta. I turned off the power on everything, as it had been on for a few weeks, starting with the tuner that acted as a faux amp. Powering everything up again, I replaced the Sam Cooke into its sleeve and dug through the stacks of records until I found something with staying power. Though there were a number of albums, a quick look around the room meant I was going to need a selection.

Last year I traveled to New York for a conference I vaguely remember. I would remember better if I hadn't been drinking so heavily while there. I was waiting to meet with some friends from school who lived in Alphabet City on the island. Stumbling hung over and chain smoking to get that all powerful relief. It was three hours after my first diner breakfast of the day designed to soak up most of the pain from my stomach. I found myself standing outside of a record store. It was a Granny moment. Sometimes when you travel, you see things that connect you to people you are hurrying to rush back to yet you are relieved you can get a break from. Seeing a record store for vinyl in a time when the laserdisc was killed by the plague and the CD had HIV, there was something reassuring about vinyl. It reminded me of something endearing and sweet. "We used to watch it spin and sing to the lines," Granny would say. "Your father couldn't hold a tune, but it didn't matter. He meant the words deeper than the sanger." Granny's accent slipped out during the progressive tense words built with e-r suffix. The sign above the door read Good Records. The good memory took me inside. I didn't buy anything, but the stuff the owner was playing stuck with me for a while. *We have it.* I sliced my eyes through the records stack by the entertainment center, my pupils punching the scenery like a typewriter head recording artists and names. It was then I realized I had enjoyed the music at that store because they owner had a collection that matched my Granny's.

Placing the record on the spindle, I put the needle on the first groove and walked into the kitchen. I used Art Farmer's "Mau Mau" to start unloading the dish washer. I got to Dorothy Ashby's "Soul Vibrations" when I had finished the cups and plates. Too many cups, a clear sign I had started drinking heavier again. The large pots and pans got the business, and I was finishing the silverware when The Afro Blues Quintet Plus One rolled into "South Side Habit" with a blend into their "Mirror Image." I began loading again when Roy Ayers and Ubiquity started "The Memory." I thought about summer time and Spice 1 tapes while I waited for the water out of the sink to get hot enough to put the bucket under it to fill it up. I thought about Harrison with his records. Gary Bartz's "Music Is My Sanctuary" got me through the kitchen floors and I was almost done with the bathroom as a whole by the time Donald Byrd's "Dominoes" played its way out. I kept everything mundane, reserving my works for removing records, placing them in their sleeve, then case, pulling out a new record, putting it on the turntable and placing the needle.

The living room was all together much harder. Maybe it was the sheer number of different categories needed. I suspect it was actually the amount of empty bottles and cans I was accruing in the blue recycling bins on the sun porch. I could almost cope as I worked thanks to James Mason's "Sweet Power Your Embrace" It was easy to have a kindly view of a loved one losing their mind. You need that when the going gets tough in your head and you believe you have lost your connection to who you truly care for. I took a minute to stare of into space when Leon Ware's "Why I Came To California" came on but I was able to sniff the thoughts of Granny back into my chest and ignore the hints of tears in my eyes.

When I looked across the room, I no longer saw chaos. I saw my grandmother's mind during the disease: a collection of priceless items by sentimental value but useless in one's realistic utility when they couldn't be used. I sorted the mail to Johnny Hammond's "Los Conquistadores Chocolates" while also wondering if Harrison would approve of the playlist. I put the bills in my satchel with the charities Granny liked to donate to. Those would get checks in her name even as I stacked the discards and placed them in the recycling. I caught myself having trouble remembering who exactly it was who had so much trouble letting go of the past. I found empty boxes stacked in a broken down and flattened condition in storage by the book case. I didn't remember putting them there, but judging by the prints and lack of ability to seal, I guessed them to be left over from months of Costco trips I had blocked out after a carton of menthols and some the most expensive Turning Leaf the big box store could offer in a four pack.

I found the packing tape in the drawer in the kitchen mid-way through Oby Onyioha's "Enjoy Your Life" and taped the boxes into weight-bearing shape. I grabbed the repetitious pack rat items and placed them in boxes by category. Soap and shampoo went into the detergent box, hand towels into the wheat box, table lamps and night lights went into the beer boxes and Dolette McDonald went into "Xtra Special." Once I had every box filled, I brought them one by one to the curb in front of the house, hoping a sign wasn't required to describe the charitable donations. On my way back in I caught the tail end of Tamiko Jones with "Can't Live Without Your Love." I did the next record manually due to my smile at the sweat housecleaning can bring. Unlimited Touch, *Searching To Find The One.* Then I began vacuuming. It was getting late and the neighbors would complain if they weren't already making noise themselves. None of us really did quiet at night too well.

Dusting needed something spacer. I compensated by letting go of manual. Foreal People *Love Begins With You.* That left the sun porch to consider. The dead plants I tossed, which struck me as sad for a real reason. Dried dead plants that had been sucked of life by the sun, not unlike some people in my family. Lotti G *What It Worth.* I opened the windows and let the air circulating work on my mood. I dumped both cat boxes in the green compost can and washed the both of them out with the short expanse of hose in the back yard. After drying both cat boxes with a cleaning rag, I refilled them with new litter and vacuumed the floor of the sun porch. As I turned off the machine and wrapped up the cord, I took inventory with my eyes to see what might be left. Mystik Merlin *Mr. Magician*. The garbage cans were boring because I can see in the dark now and there was clearly nothing to be afraid of in the gloom of the back yard that needed a haircut. If I thought I was that dude and started my lawnmower at the later part of eleven o'clock, despite the firecrackers and gunshots, I would be deemed the tweaker. Better I talk to reborn Egyptian deities in my head, right?

The walk back into the house was equally boring if not more so because I was running out of things to clean and keep the peace. The Joubert Singers *Stand On The Word*. The refrigerator was a whole other issue. Shelves had to be soaked. The water and bucket took an easy refill of really hot water, but scrubbing the interior was the hard part. Janice McClain *Giving My Love*. The metal shelves needed to be scrubbed in addition to the scrubbing. Either that or I was being impatient. I put them aside on a new dish towel to dry. Then the large plastic drawers needed a scrubbing. Steven Abdul Kahn *Gotta Have Your Loving*. Bopping my head, moving my arms in sync to where the drums provoke the bass. The plastic drawers got placed on the dish towel shortly after I installed the metal ones. Then the large plastic, I was dancing on my way from the sink counter to the refrigerator. Manhattan Rhythm *Sweet Lady*. The freezer was depressing because the mold from the bottom of the freezer was frozen there. I had been defrosting since I started the refrigerator, having unplugged it when I started. It was loose but if I wanted to get it done I was going to have to tease it.

Into the ice. In between the bonds that hold water molecules together. Heat. Heat. Fire. Nothing. I tried a flathead screwdriver to break the ice, but it chipped it and I worried about punching into the freezer surface. Tee Mac *A Certain Way To Go*. Between what holds the ice together, I wished there was hands pulling it apart. The ice sheet cracked in several places. I spent a while transporting all the pieces into the bucket. Paris *I Choose You*. Scrubbing the freezer reminded me of working in food service and waiting to go home every night. I first learned the joys of one's first job using a punch card time clock. Minimum wage was $4.35 in California then. Gabor Szabo *Keep Smilin'*. I pulled the refrigerator forward by walking it on its corners

383

slowly. I vacuumed and mopped the exposed area of tile, pushed the fridge back into place, fell into a final stare at a house cleaned and realized with one person there it was still a mess. Leon Ware's "Rockin' You Eternally" ended and I found myself staring into space in the living room alone. Finding a seat on my unmade bed, my room seemed too much of a massive project to under take. The beer was half consumed preparing the appropriate metaphor. Half empty or half full. Half occupied, half vacant. One life with explanation and one without. As much as my OCD reveled at the notion of, I questioned the point to where I lived in my head. Then there was the impulse to pack everything and vacate this house. There was no certainty with that. I had yet to see a deed or title for any newly inherited lifestyle where as the power of attorney for Granny and her property stared at me from the desk in my room. Decisions, decisions.

I leaned my head against the headboard, sipping what was left of the bottle in my hands. My eye caught a small shape moving in the corner of my doorway. My sight magnified it after a blink to discover a tiny red spider descending by a strand from the door stand. I couldn't stop watching, hoping it would come my way along the floor when it got to the hardwood. It never did. Its life was quickly ended by the paw of the fluffy male cat that mashed it against the floor.

"Good boy, Stewart," I said in that ridiculous voice I involuntarily use to speak to furry animals. "You caught a spider."

"*I think you have our jobs confused,*" I heard a voice say. It was older and seasoned, somewhere between Harvey Keitel and Willem Dafoe if they had been raised in a rural slum of black Alabama. If Granny had read that she would tell you that Alabama was a rural slum and my statement was redundant. I think that space between Georgia and Florida biased her view of the world; then again I never thought I could live anywhere but San Francisco. I looked around. Empty. Paranoia struck and I felt myself rush outside of the house, hovering hundreds of feet above myself while looking at the top of my head as if I was just a seagull on a wire above a house of glass. Nothing. The city was quiet and no signs of anything. Xochi's soft yellow glowed in the distance but all that told me was she was at her loft. I traveled back down to myself and walked back into the room wondering if I had heard anything at all. Sitting back on my bed, I noticed Stewart was across the room on my dresser. Eye level. We stared at one another until I realized I was still holding the beer. I wondered if I had brought it with me on my astral hot air balloon ride to Windex city. I reached over to the tissue box and pulled out a sheet. I crouched to reach to the floor by the door, wiping the flatten guts and legs of the crawly off of the hard wood floor. *"Yes, you clean up spiders and I keep mice out of the pantry."*

I snapped my head to make eye contact with Stewart at the mention of mice in my head. Granny had owned cats for as long as I had been alive. Some of my earliest memories of caring for pets were being instructed by Granny to clean up the kitchen where her cat at the time had cornered a rodent. After hours of watching the mouse tossed in the air, batted against the wall and futility attempt to flee with the cat's paw on its tail, the cat picked it up in its mouth and sauntered off. Eventually when I came back to the kitchen there were two halves of a eviscerated rodent in key places as separate offerings to each of the cat's pet humans. Granny having seniority was offered the head. It didn't stop at mice. Birds, gophers, rats, crickets and garden snakes were all prepared by the four legged butcher for our viewing. Given all those memories of diced wildlife, I locked eyes with the feline and asked, "Is that you, Stewart?"

"That voice must discontinue if we are to have any serious conversations," I heard again, watching the Birman's lower jaw move. In addition, just under the voice was the faint sound of his throaty gargle I was used to hearing when it was time to change his box or I had been late in feeding him.

"You can speak?" I attempted, removing the baby talk I found myself shifting into when engaging with small furry creatures.

"I speak frequently," the cat replied. *"It's only recently you have had a reply without that condescending dribble."* He licked his paw and pulled it over his fur just above his right eye and combed it back to his ear.

"When did cats begin employing language?"

"We have been using language as long as humans have," said a female voice, raspy and quiet, almost Holly Hunter with a New Jersey accent. *"What you really mean to ask is when did you start comprehending."* Rosie, my fluffier, female Birman with pink tints to her nose and ears walked into the room. She sat by my left foot as she usually does. She stared up at me with her gaze and opened her mouth. *"Apparently only recently."*

"Took him long enough," Stewart replied.

"She said he was slower this time," Rosie shot back.

"*You youngsters are too quick to enable excuses,*" Stewart replied, lying on his belly and yawning.

"Well, she did feed us," Rosie argued.

"Because genius over here forgot to come home for half a month."

"Do you have any idea how volatile things have been for me" I interrupted defensively.

"Tough life, tough life." Stewart rubbed his forepaws against one another. "You hear that? That's the sound of the world's smallest sitar."

"Know much about working a full day do you?" I found myself yelling. "Oh, with the several naps, lack of rent and inability to cook meals . . . ." I stood and paused at the ridiculousness of the prospect of arguing with one's cat. "This is fucking insane." I drained my beer and walked into the kitchen to drop the bottle in the recycling. She waited until I returned to the room.

"Insane until you need another backup body," Stewart answered. Rosie walked past me and climbed up on the bed, using it as a spring board in which to lap on to the dresser. Stewart must have known what she was about because he rose up on his hind legs as Rosie leapt. He wasn't quick enough to do anything effective as Rosie's weight and velocity barreled him over. Two wrestled in a roll for a few moments, making feral sounds with Rose getting the best of him.

"What do you mean, backup body?" I asked sternly.

"We are your family's life insurance providers," Stewart mumbled at me from his position on his back with Rosie's paw pushing his cheek down to the wood of the dresser.

"The triple A of slain attributes," Rosie added still holding her paw on Stewart while slapping him with the pad of her other paw in the space between his left eye and right cheek. "Maybe even the car rental as well"

"So do you two drive as well as well as you speak?" I asked with a wide grin.

Both animals froze to look at me. There was a sarcasm in their gazes I thought only humans could produce with a facial expression. They both froze in mid-scuffle and began moving silently. Rosie sat on her hind legs after backing away from Stewart. Stewart in turn rolled on all fours and sat identical to Rosie. Both animals were tight jawed and staring at me with a dead gaze.

"Can we be serious here?" Stewart asked finally with the indication of annoyance rolling through every last syllable of the sentence.

"He is rather rude, isn't he?" Rosie asked with only a slight head turn toward Stewart to throw her attention on to me.

"Yes," he answered, "very disrespectful. One wonders how he could have developed such a mouth."

I took another kitchen trip and left the next bottle by the counter. My eyes caught the pink vacuum seal pouch of cat treats leaning against where the counter met the wall. It made a crinkle sound when I lifted it from the counter in my hand. I turned in preparation to walk back to the bedroom to conduct a haggle with my feline American roommates when I noticed two sets of eyes watching me intently from the carpet perhaps two feet away. They sat on their hunches, mouths closed, eyes beaming and tails curled on the floor in motion to reveal mischievous thoughts unraveling. I chuckled to myself at the sight of it and the absurdity of feeling outranked by a pair of Birmans. Holding on to the bag of treats, I was reminded how cleverly cats change the dynamic to fool their owners into believing it is them who are in fact the pet.

"Would you two like to play a game?" I asked with a smile.

"Depends," Stewart replied keeping his eye locked to the plastic pouch in my hand.

"What game?" Rosie asked.

"I'm calling it the price is right" I said with a smile.

"How do you play?" Rosie asked.

"I ask a question," I said slowly. "The first one to answer correctly wins a prize."

"What's the prize?" Stewart cut in skeptically. I answered by tossing each cat a treat. "I'm in," Stewart said chewing. I waited until they both had finished to ensure I had their full attention. With a sarcastic smile, I raised a treat to my eye level and held it out.

"Question number one" I started. "For one of these treats, how are you insurance for Attributes?"

"We keep you from making very bad fashion decisions," Stewart fired off.

"That's not true!" Rosie spat at Stewart. "We lend out bodies temporarily when your Carrier is injured critically." Stewart frowned visibly and I tossed the treat to Rosie who caught it with her mouth and broke it with her back teeth.

"Question number," I let out with a smile enjoying the clarity competition produced, "what if you are not in the area? Say miles away?"

"The nearest cat will do," Stewart answered loudly, barely allowing me to finish speaking to ensure he talked over Rosie. "If it's the right breed, we will work to get the Attribute to the correct Carrier within our own people." I thought back to my memories of the ritual in Las Vegas, being crushed and the last sights those eyes held being that of a cat. I tossed a treat to Stewart who ate it as fast as it had flown from my hand. I also noted the amount of lost cat posters I saw in cities I had travelled to that I surmised I had once lived in at one point in the timeline.

"Question number three: What is the right breed of cats?"

"In the absence of lions, stick with Siamese," Stewart barked out. I responded with a treat.

"The Aztec uses Jaguars," Rosie added. I tossed her a treat, which Stewart attempted to steal and was rewarded by a slap to his face. *Lions*.

"Question number four," I flew out to keep with the building momentum. "What if there are no felines around?"

"An artifact will do," Stewart replied. "Statues, monuments or even replicas will work."

"Not advised, though," Rosie added.

"Why not?" I asked.

"You can save files to your hard drive but they aren't as mobile. In addition you don't know who or what else is stored there. Better to use a flash drive," Rosie replied.

"And you are the flash drives?"

"In a matter of speaking," she replied. "I couldn't tell you what a hard drive or flash drive is. I'm only using the metaphors your own mind has picked." I nodded and tossed her a treat.

"Next question," I said speeding things up even more. "What does the enemy use?"

"When there was a threat," Rosie said rolling her eyes up to remember, "they relied on canines."

"Filthy creatures," Stewart said disgusted.

"Yet the Concordian attributes haven't had such pressures for nearly forty years," Rosie said solemnly.

"Why not?"

"The Concordians are interested in works and duels, not open warfare. No one has opposed the Partisans for decades?"

"And the Isfet?"

"When they die," Stewart said, "they are gone forever. That is why there are so many."

"Unless they have a Passenger connected to an Attribute," Rosie corrected him.

"Yes," he agreed, "then they exist as long as the Attribute does." I tossed out a bunch of treats to each of them and waited until they had finished scarfing down their portions. Pieces of the game were cementing before and I wrapped my brain how futile this cause could be. Lighting a cigarette helped me to focus a bit more as I watched Stewart and Rosie gobble.

"Final question," I asked with a heavy sense of suspense. "Given what's inside of me and what I can do, why would I need a Carrier at all?"

"For the most part you are invisible in that form," Rosie said. "Only your Passenger reveals your true nature," Rosie spilled out.

"Or the use of your works," Stewart added. "Paradox is one thing but any time you play with reality you put a flare in the sky for all to see, friend or foe alike."

"But not if I'm among the Veil," I argued.

"How much of the Veil have you seen that is free of Isfet?"

"Good point," I replied. "So even minor works in the Sanctuary leave a trace."

"Nothing they could respond to en mass without Paradox," Rosie said, "but who needs to respond directly when they have access to millions of followers?"

"Or the Partisans," Stewart added. Rosie nodded.

I nodded back feeling I had gotten what I needed and emptied the bag of treats on the floor. I walked around the house turning off appliances until only the lamp by my bed side gave any illumination. Finding my coat, I slung it on as Rosie looked up from eating with a look of suspicion. I walked over and scratched her head which she smiled at and followed by nibbling at the treats. Stewart was disinterested in my caress, side stepping and bringing his paw up to brush my hand away as he kept his head low to consume the treats.

CHAPTER TWENTY-TWO

"No hospital can fix that."

-Omid

The air was brisk when I stepped outside to the porch, the sky too dark to decide if the rain clouds were going to open up on me. I made sure to lock one of the door locks and then the security gate. I told myself I would be right back and my gesture was only a measure of paranoia. The garbage cans had been moved to the side as the local urban miners had rifled through the recycling for items. I couldn't complain too far as they had cleaned up after themselves but I did have to align the blue can on the curb again. My OCD was to powerful to fight. All of the charitable discards were removed, nine boxes of hoarder-type shit gone in under two hours; they had even taken the card boxes I used to categorize. Feeling a certain sense of goodwill done combined with fall cleaning, I headed to the car. I chose not to turn on any music in the ride on my way to the store, there was a lot of clarity to silence I was enjoying. Two blocks away from the market across from the banks, my paranoia rose up again telling me to check the rear view mirror. There were numerous cars on Third Street which was no big miracle for the evening. The problem with Third Street was that either side worked like a river with a light rail running down the middle serving as an island. Driving your vehicle down Third became white water rafting in that there were steady currents pushing you forward but one had to paddle to avoid the rapids of people parking their cars in the right lane to hold conversation with the cluster of du-rag clad young people crowding each doorway along the routes. You also had to compensate for a clog in the current when a car stopped in the left lane to hold a full discourse with someone standing on the platform waiting for the train. Often it was someone heading downtown while the car headed south and they never offered a ride the same way they never had a discussion of anything appropriate for public. I was used to the flow, leaving two car lengths in front of my headlights in case a car swerved over as they often did and kept a steady gait on the accelerator in order to leave space for anyone behind me.

Whether conscious of it or not, most of the cars behind me got this concept, appreciating my vehicle as the wagon at the head of the trail finding the path of least resistance down the route. Except for the Benz three cars back. This is not to attack Mercedes drivers; some of my friends fit that description. However, it is important to mention that Mercedes drivers seemed to carry a genetic disposition to not "get it." The red CLK 230 seemed to fit that description as it fought its way back to the left lane every time it moved to the right and found itself stuck behind another car double-parked. Watching its motion in the rear view, I got the sense it was fighting to get closer to me. Quesada was up ahead and I moved to the left lane, one of the few turns I could make in the area. The red CLK 230 shot by when I did and then skidded to a stop two lights down looking to make a hurried u-turn. Windows rolled up and radio silent, I could feel and hear the electronic pulse that can only come from high-energy dance music. I completed the turn, passed the intersection and slowed to make a right into one of the vertically oriented parking spots in front of the liquor store. My hand touched the stick to flicker my turning signals when the first chill came over me. *The strand is disturbed. One slight vibration along any thread and it is felt at the center of the web. The masses of horrific webs and the legs of Propius move in response. It approaches.*

I took my hand away from the signal and whipped the car out of the spot, shifted forward, kept driving and sped the car some. At the stop sign of the next block, I saw the red CLK 230 in my rear view gaining speed. I hit the right and powered down to Williams, making another right on to it. I paused at the red light, unsure if paranoia or a nicotine fit caused so much unrest at watching the light switch. The light turned green with a click loud enough to echo in my ears. I speed through the intersection, crossing Third but slowing on the other side for the approach of a SFPD squad car coming at me from the other direction. I heard the click again and saw the red CLK was trapped at the right light on the other side of Third. Passing the police station, I stuck to the speed limit, checking my mirrors often. I worked my way on to Bayshore and hit the left on to Silver. I told myself it was still paranoid as I slowed in crossing San Bruno to look for parking at my back up store by the Pizza Joint. That calmed my nerves until my eyes caught the CLK in the rear view again, but now it was black instead of red.

I dropped my foot on the gas pedal, powering up Silver Avenue in the hopes of putting some cars between myself and whoever was following. The CLK matched my speed but came to a screech after a few blocks and I hit the stop sign as a white minivan nudged in between us. A man jumped out of the van, banging on the hood of the CLK, obviously protesting having to force his way in when he had the right of way while screaming in Chinese. I watched the window of the CLK roll down half way and saw the muzzle burst shortly after, then the shell pop out and hit the asphalt. Then came the shot that spun away from the car. The CLK pulled around the man and sped in my pursuit, rolling its window back up. I was running stop signs by then, somewhere between not liking bullets and realizing the CLK had no plates. I was glad it was late enough at night that Silver was empty so I myself was not a risk to the neighborhood. At Mission, it got really messy.

I pulled a hard right on to Mission and then hit another right on to Trumbull, going back along the direction I had just come. After three blocks, I hit a left on to Congdon and waited at the light to merge on to east bound on Alemany. This stunt did nothing for my removal of any tail as the CLK crested the hill when the green wave sent me down Alemany. From here I gunned the engine of the Lexus, sliding into the far left lane so I could take the curves tight and fast. At the first light I hit a hard u-turn and sped back up Alemany headed west toward the 280 South entrance. Passing the CLK going the other way, I waved a confidant middle finger at it. The CLK blurred down another block and then pulled the same u-turn, except it drove over the island obviously not caring about the suspension. Perhaps it was adrenaline starting to drip into my blood or the illusion played by streetlights, but the CLK drove over the island like it was a patch of grass, the chassis becoming translucent as it did. I heard the faintness of techno pulsing louder, followed by a muted distant digital gong. I floored the pedal by then terror encouraging me to realize that my pursuers could manipulate works like I could.

Under the freeway and a bunch of hard skidding turns, I blew on to O'Shaunessy, which was a winding uphill my car took gracefully but struggled with a top speed. I was trying to find routes heavy with police and to no avail. I guess that was the nature of SFPD; there when unwanted and absent when needed. The CLK made great pace behind me but I lost them at the Market intersection when I flashed past on to Twin Peaks drive. Another slow climb began as I hit the first slope. The fog was heavy, hiding the city from view and bullying the headlights. It also slowed the car, which was just as well as the gas light came on. I remembered telling myself I would refill it with the next cigarette and never had. I felt the car slowing to a halt and I pulled to the side of the road. Pulling the keys out, I deadened the headlights, locked it up and hit the bushes leading to the slope that rolled to the sheer bluff above the Castro district. Crouching in the grass, I was five feet from a drop of certain death. I saw the head lights come up the hill and span the roadside with unnatural light. Another vehicle had paused near mine.

"He's not in the car," I heard a voice say, throaty and hoarse.

"Spray the area," another voice responded, dull and nasal. "He's in the bushes."

I was scrambling off when I heard the click when the gunfire began. It was muted, like sitting in the bleachers at AT&T ballpark watching the fireworks in the sky. I was not a munitions expert, but I was fairly sure those were the sounds of rounds being coughed through a silencer. It was an easy and very fast act to pedal my body off the cliff face. The air rushed by my ears as I scanned rapidly, finding anywhere in my head that would avoid falling to my death. *Huh.* The bottom of the trench was reaching up to break my body. The sounds of a techno fuckery might kill me first. *Huh!* The rocks looked dark and jagged like a mouth opening to snap closed and crush me. Then I hit.

Lying on my back, I stared at the sign overhead stating: please keep your ticket on your way back to your car. Headlights blinded me directly and I heard a horn before the whine of voices, being surprised that they were crying out loud. I stood up and found myself in the driveway of the Embarcadero center parking lot. There is no subtle way to maneuver from being laid out in the middle of traffic so I took the first doorway I could. It was a stairway leading to the second level of the shopping plaza. There were three floors all together, including an open veranda of white tile and marble clustered with shops, restaurants and theaters. I remembered taking Granny here to see Princess Monoke because she had felt too mature for Disney and enjoyed animation. Sparse groups of two to three people moved through the walkways in Cary Grant slow motion. The music from the fake ice skating rink bled a mockery of winter wonderland into the night, encouraging couples and their children to frequent the area in overcoats more suited for Madison Avenue than Market Street. I steadied my nerves by reaching for my cigarettes, only remembering I was out of them and had lost my light. In addition the screen on my phone was cracked and inoperable. I screamed out an expletive that echoed for a good three seconds after and walked a bit. I found a kid on his break from his pizza slavery shift and bummed a square, remembering the taste of Marlboro Lights to be a smoky gumbo of dirt and wombat asshole. The nicotine content gave me a headache but the exhalations freed my panic.

I was halfway through the cigarette when my eyes caught the sight of a single tiny red spider in between the branches of the bush on ground floor across the street. It stared at me at a distance, tiny plumes of pink smoke shot by miniaturized jets in the joints of its legs tied to every jitter it made in its web. The smoke moved upwards like shards of pink crystal into the sky and out of sight. The carousel music from the ice rink was muted in place of techno. I heard boots on the stairs as I plotted and dropped the Marlboro stick. I don't know what in me started running but I did, just as the shots of automatic gunfire began.

Pieces of stone, dirt and glass exploded around me as I fled. Something hit just above my head, shattering into a powder that spread into my eyes. Half blinded, I scratched at the world in front of me, colliding with a planter or a standing ashtray. I couldn't tell what it was, but it banged my bad leg causing me to stumble and reflexively grunt in pain as my legs started locking up. Limping and unclear what was in front of me, I did my best to keep my momentum forward, using my hands to push me back up when I tripped. The techno had reached an almost ear-bleeding volume to the point where it overpowered the sounds of the gunfire. I made the mistake of looking back to see two men standing on the promenade, viciously unleashing bullets from silenced automatic machine guns. The bullets, most of them missing their targets, hit the scenery and broke it. The others hit the field and did not lodge. They ricocheted off the environment and when they hit the next structure they became Isfet Passengers. Alert and trained, they moved toward their own to build mass and came after me. I turned back to see how much room was left before the second floor ended. Had I been earlier I would have looked for the third gunman in my path. Instead I saw his foot just before it connected with my chin, knocking me high into the air backwards to the third level. I crashed through a glass sculpture and lay unmoving--bleeding, blinded and beaten.

My muscles kept me from realizing the dire consequences of the temporary flight despite the awakening feeling I got from the pain. I had flown through a sculpture and landed with one of its shards puncturing the muscle between my shoulder and elbow. The right leg was weaker than ever and my left hand was broken. As I made slow, delayed movements to test freedom, I realized I had known paralysis before. With my very body working against me to stay in place, the shudders of pain brought me back to the memories I'd worked hard to bury. Yes, these were experienced by me, hidden by me and were being unearthed by me. *The Nest.* I, not unlike my mother and the other members of my family who had resisted the Isfet, had once been cocooned. I had been a victim of noxious psychotropic venom, insipid webbing and suction of life-force through fanged punctures.

I smiled when the three men came in position to view their defenseless mark. The act rolled two of my loose teeth out of my mouth along the mouth full of blood, threatening to choke me if I didn't cough. They each wore all black, faces covered by painters' masks so often adopted by military since they were cheap at any Army Navy supply store. Two of them were the same build: tall and dense, their chests a stretch of steroids and combat-lifting. The third was a bit shorter and lankier but lithe in every mechanical sense. One of the taller ones fanned out to watch the stairs closest to Sacramento Street while the shorter one watched the buildings above us on the Clay Street side. They appeared less concerned with witnesses and more intent upon preventing my assistance, as if I would be so lucky. The third one walked over to stand near my feet, bringing the nozzle of his barrel to line up with my head.

"Cover him," I heard him say, the same voice that had identified me in the bushes. It was older, impatient and pushy with a Maryland accent. Probably career military, a former seal or special-forces.

The gunmen watching the building aimed his gun at me as the center-piece removed his mask. Ice cold blue eyes with an jet black skin tone, peppered with scars most likely from shrapnel, burns and maybe even knives. He stared at my smile and I could tell it bothered him. He smiled back, obviously aware I was bothered with his eye color and complexion, being aware it wasn't contacts. He shifted his eyes around, scanning the area and then walked to inspect the street on either side. When he returned, he slung the weapon over his back in lieu of a serrated hunting knife. He crouched over me, making practicing cuts with his eyes. I noticed the closer he stood, the less he could meet my eyes. Even with the advantage in their court, he smelled of aftershave and stale scotch--fear.

"What are we waiting for?" the gunmen closest to Sacramento Street asked through the muffled cloth of his mask.

"The sentries aren't in place," he replied curt to the inquirer. I took him to mean the Passenger spiders, which were nowhere to be seen. I would be a fool to pretend I didn't know his intent. They meant to create a ritual out of my body, stealing some attribute's hold over San Francisco. "Shoot any cats you see," he added. Then his eyes finally met mine. "I have a message for you."

"Someone doesn't think highly of me?" I said, nearly gargling blood to do so. "I think that got across."

"He wants you to know there will only be one after this."

"Did he add in that I will kill you last when I return," I coughed again.

"Oh, you aren't coming back from this," he replied. There was the sounding of digital gongs that I took to mean the Hollow One disapproved of the works, the gunfire without police response, and the presence of Isfet. If not for works from some unseen source this area of the city should be crawling with police over a cat in a tree and a hundred times so over gunfire.

"That's the signal," the gunmen closest to Sacramento said. The crouched gunmen before me looked to me with a smile.

"He asked me to start with your liver so you would be alive through the rest of it." When he spoke, I didn't see his face but the faceless image of Propius instead, letting me know whom to blame. I nodded the best I could.

"He's going to start with your children. Your son, Curtis--his screams will be breakfast to make sure you never get an independent thought again." It was the last juice I had left, going inside the man's mind and finding his worst fear

which was the source of all that he had going for him--seeing what the price of his loyalty bought and what it did not. If I was my cousin Anpu, that would have been my last words and I would have used my last dying energy to worry my assassin for the last of his days. In the face of my impending death, I was actually secure in the knowledge that I was not my cousin Anpu. I wasn't Set. I wasn't anything like my family, so instead of having my last word, I spent my last energy to keep myself from invading the man's mind.

"The equation has to balance somehow," was all I allowed to leave my mouth. There I let it hang out and prepared to die. Strangely I was curious. I wondered if I would see my parents. Would I pass the filters in place and see through a cat's eyes? Maybe there was nothing for me except quiet and darkness. The assassin nodded at my words, indicating there was a truth in them that exceeded the rules of partisanship. He cut my shirt away from my midsection or what was left of it. He raised the blade over his head, expecting to have to punch through the lower portion of my rib cage. Then it all happened at once. The lead-in was the music, the mind-boggling techno, that went suddenly silent.

"Oh no," yelled the gunman closest to Clay Street.

"What?" said the assassin crouched over me and turned his head to the right. It was a perfect kick, the heel of the boot caught him on the chin, lifting him off the ground and snapping his neck in the process. I looked over to see the gunman who was positioned to watch Clay Street standing over me, bringing his gun to bear on the remaining assassin. He let off a one-arm spray that climbed up the man's left leg, crawled to his crotch, zipped up his front and ended at the forearm. The body flipped over the sundeck and fell top the street below. He brought the muzzle in line with my head and pulled the trigger, not showing any surprise when it clicked multiple times with an empty clip.

"Guess you can't kill me," I whispered, my chest aching with every word.

"Glad you get it now," he said dropping the weapon and removing the mask. There he stood. Soulful and young in the eyes, cheerful mouth and hawk-like nose. He seemed taller now as if he had enjoyed another growth spurt, finally shedding baby fat for an elongated frame. His eyes scanned me with a triumphant hubris before turning to deep concern as he crouched by me and put his hand on my chest.

"Wallace," I choked with surprise before falling into a fit of excruciating coughs.

"I was," he whispered back with concern. I stared back into his eyes, falling into them. There was a private and intimate history inside. A place we seldom spoke aloud. An affiliation of love and friendship that stood tested and succeeded past thousands of years of disappointing heartache. *We were kings once.* Then I knew.

"Heru," I croaked with relief, bringing tears to my eyes in desperate loss of all reason.

"Wal-Heru," he whispered back, wiping my eyes with his fingertips. "Your faithful student. Forever."

"But they killed . . . I thought you left me."

"Never, dear cousin," he said, stroking my forehead. "I cannot die, Sekhem. That is my aspect. Every exodus of the flesh sends me back fiercer than before. I have mastered the lesson you gave me and I thank you for it." There were the distant sounds of music, seemingly launched from the ice rink. Ghostface *Street Bullies*. It rose in volume by an unseen hand. "That is your aspect," Wal-Heru continued, cocking his head to listen. "Our people's second oldest language. The sound of innovation. Do you believe me now?"

"I do," I said, weeping. "I know who we are." I barely lifted my free hand on his and wept for the absence of nodding.

"Then why do you weep, cousin?"

"I am sad. Only at the end did I accept it. In dying, I know that what you told me is true."

"No, cousin," he said with a slow grin. "Your days are not finished. This is the beginning, not the end." The pulsing, rising bass of Ghostface was disrupted by the sounds of sirens headed our way. "On queue, it would seem," Wal-Heru said. "Close your eyes. This will hurt."

I followed instructions, falling into the darkness of my own body. I felt his arms under me and then the lift. The pull up was white-hot iron skewers jammed into every cell of my physical body as he lifted me off the sculpture, leaving a bleeding perforation in my shoulder and my broken leg dangled. My eyes shot open when I screamed, which broke every piece of glass I could see. Wal-Heru cradled me in his arms, walking to the ledge and jumping down to Sacramento Street. He crossed the street and turned the corner on to Front Street, turning again into a dark alley. A black humvee covered with energy drinks and radio station promotional wraps was parked; its engine and lights jumped on as we approached. The door popped open and I felt another set of hands assist me inside. Lying on my back, my vision was blurred by a dark shape passing before it. I felt a warm kiss on my forehead and heard the door close. The hummer pulled forward and made a right. I felt a hand on my forehead.

"Don't worry us like that," I heard Hari-Hari-Khpr say. I struggled to focus my eyes and found his, sitting next to me with a furrowed brow. I smiled and closed my eyes. "How bad?"

"Multiple gun shots, shrapnel and internal bleeding," Wal-Heru replied.

"He could be infected," Hari-Hari-Khpr added.

"No," Wal-Heru countered. "I killed all the Passengers. The rounds in him are mundane."

"We will need to work together," Hari-Hari-Khpr explained. "I can re-move any of the objects in his tissue but you will need to seal the wounds as I go."

"That's too fast," Wal-Heru argued. "His muscles will never let him forget."

"He's bleeding out," Omid yelled from the driver's seat.

"Then the nearest hospital," Wal-Heru shot back.

"No hospitals," I murmured.

"Shhh," Hari-Hari-Khpr said to me with a whisper and continued to stroke my forehead.

"No hospital can fix that," Omid replied. "He will be dead by the first IV."

"Agreed," Hari-Hari-Khpr growled. "Do as I say. We are out of options." I felt his hands move to the shoulder. It got hot, like molten lava in my blood. Liquid metal bubbled to the wound and then shot to his hand like a magnet. I screamed again and then went silent.

"We can end it tonight," Wal-Heru whispered. "Please wake up."

"That may have been too much shock," Hari-Hari-Khpr whispered. "Do not be surprised if he stays in a coma for months."

"Not him, grandfather," Wal-Heru corrected.

CHAPTER TWENTY-TWO

"And why not?"

"Sekhem doesn't quit. You can knock him down."

"But you can't keep him down," I heard myself say. There were the sounds of clapping and exuberance. I let my eyes open to the dawn beginning at Twin Peaks. The sky was a spread of watercolors staying in the blue, grays and peaches. Though the fog swirled around us, keeping a level plane with the parking lot looking out to the city, it was one of those times it hid whether it was dusk or dawn. The tips of the buildings contrasted at the hint of orange on the horizon past Hayward made it clear the day was just beginning.

"Can you sit up?" Hari-Hari-Khpr asked.

"With help," I replied. Wal-Heru and Hari-Hari-Khpr lifted me to place my back against the seat. "Water?" Omid responded by tossing a bottle to Wal-Heru who in turn put it to my lips. "Cigarette." That came as well. I rolled down the window after lighting it, the cold air informing me I was naked. Not just emotionally, but physically and covered with bandages. I did not mind.

"How do you feel?" Omid asked.

"As if a part of me has died," I said, staring at the clouds. "Though I don't mourn its loss."

"This is our time, cousin," Wal-Heru said. "Thousands years of your plan come to fruition tonight."

"Until what," I countered, "we are beaten and forced to run again. I am not waiting twenty more centuries to free my mother."

"No more running," Wal-Heru said, his eyes blazing. "We are at the finish line. The running ends tonight, I assure you." He was animated as was his nature when intent on a goal. "Look at that sun. Even it knows this is our last morning as rogues."

"To what end?" I asked.

"Kemet," Hari-Khpr said.

"Yes," Wal-Heru added. "We are going home."

"You have seen Propius for yourself, youngin'. We are no match," I croaked.

"Strange that you would use 'we' when you believe it is you who is no match. Truthfully, you haven't faced Propius in a group, ever."

"And I have grown tired its victories," I replied, pointing at my bandages with the tip of my cigarette. "I would rather than die than let it win another time."

"I am not the same child you took to Kemet nor are you the same man. We have grandfather as well. Consider, great strategist, can one lose every battle and still win the war?" I turned to Hari-Khpr.

"*I am against it--*" I started.

"It is your plan!" Wal-Heru interrupted.

"Let him finish," Hari-Khpr barked.

"I defer to my elder," I said to Hari-Khpr. "My vote is against but I will follow your command."

"You must stretch your mind past what the parameters tell you are favorable odds," Hari-Khpr said, cupping his hand around the smoke from my cigarette curling his way and forming a screen in the air. "The Isfet abandoned Kemet long ago, leaving Propius as its governance. Though formidable, it has no reinforcements." A bullet point formed in smoke spelling out "lack of supply lines." "From what I was told, you can hold the line with your works. Propius is not prepared for an offensive; he is capable only of defending his position." Surprise became the second bullet point. "We have all we need to take and activate the Throne." Strategic opportunity became the third point. Then it cleared. "If it is up to me, the elder, then I say this: I am as weary of running as you are. Maybe more. It damages the spirit. This war is old, its losses great and its toll threatens to end all that we love. I cannot die in hiding or on my knees fearing a force I was born to thwart. If I am to die, then let me die trying rather than submitting."

"It is decided, then," Wal-Heru said.

"Take the throne to end the war tonight," I said, smoked and stared at the window.

CHAPTER TWENTY-THREE

"It's like adding sugar to apple sauce"

-Wal-Heru

The shower did wonders for the aches. I talked myself through every single step of the bathing, from ordering a part of my body to move to telling the soap not to be too far of a stretch to grab. It was a very slow process. The tank emptied and refilled. I wasn't concerned with the temperature change either time; I just needed the water. Wal-Heru had been heroic about warning me in my dazed state without speaking to me directly. My body, Clay's body, god's body; none wanted to forget the trauma they had been through. I was being shot, cut and kicked all over on mute in finely acute places on my body. Places that did not have scar tissue yesterday. When I was dry and in my underwear, I covered everything below my neck with tiger balm, rubbing it in until my fingertips were sore. Then I dressed using the parameters given; nothing heavier than a thermal shirt, pants with some thickness and work boots. There was lightness to my movements as I went through the element form in my bedroom; I found that I knew all five of them. I was grounded afterwards, not having felt as tied down by the items in my pockets. I didn't bring keys, wallet or phone as instructed, so I felt obligated to answer emails before I departed. My personal emails were empty. I checked the proxy accounts, much of it too numerous to process in the time I had left. As these things have a habit of becoming, one stood out from the rest. It arrived as a folded journal paper that opened up to an empty page. I gave it a coffee bath from the java I had left over from the morning. When I unlocked it, I felt a chill up my neck and knew this one of the two letter senders. It read as a woman's voice, different from the letter I received at school.

You can't trust them. This is our family. It is easiest to create loyalty when you believe you have been left with nothing. Finish this path if you will but consider what you will do when you collide with the truth. You are our king. Do not be deceived, brother. When you serve their ends you will be expendable to all but me.

Your wife,

Auset

A whole new set of numbers to throw into the wonder wheel and spin in front of my face. Pick through some, form a coherent story and find a solution--survival. I couldn't help but notice the timing of such a message, given my commitment level was at its all time highest. In contrast, I had a room full of *my family* who had saved my life waiting for me downstairs while my mind scrambled around the words within letters from an unnamed woman who claimed to be related as well. In fact, it was two voices, each with a distinct voice but only one of which was my wife. Going by my notes to myself, I also had to factor in Neith somewhere. Was she one of the letter writers? Possibly. A name used for Athena? Unlikely. There is no way my heart could belong to energy like that, I decided. The first letter had predicted another woman would stake her claim to me. Two women arguing over him--every man's dream, right? As much as my ego wanted to indulge, I felt a sense of worry. Neither of the voices made a direct reference to one another; they both warned of things to come and they both refrained from firing accusations. Two clear messages: when you are ready I'm all that you got. I understood there was something embedded in order to make me act; it was a trap in one sense, if I wasn't careful. Who the definitive guide was, I couldn't decide.

The most troubling aspect of it all was the claim as to my Attribute. Just as I had come to embrace the voice of Sekhem Ka in my head and renting the life of Clay Durward, I was hit with the notion that this recently letter had implied I was the eldest of the hybrids. My eyes looked past the monitor, out of the office door and into the eyes of the small child walking past the doorway on his way from the bathroom. He bopped his head as he stepped, rocking his head and swinging his arms to some song he had constructed in his head as he washed his hands. He paused when he became aware he was being watched and turned his body to find the eyes on him. Recognizing me, he responded shyly, as if to say that his song was not ready for public consumption and he had not expected an audience.

"They are waiting for you" he whispered, his voice and lisp revealing he was not unfamiliar with the notion of delivering a timetable to me.

"Okay," I said quietly, "tell them I will be down soon." He stared at me for a few moments. I stared back. We were reading each other. Was I so blinded by affection toward young people that I couldn't see the distraction he was meant to be? Was he the balance crammed into a small child's body so compact that the young man's affinity for me blocked the elder's requirement to inform me of the poison I was letting grow in my psyche? We both pondered what to say to one another and thought better of speaking at all. I gave a strained and tired smile. I could feel it tighten my face and motioned my chin to the stairs. Desta smiled back, dropping his chin at the demand as his shy response to any warmth I sent him. His legs began to move and he padded out of my view along the carpet.

I was left staring at the screen, rereading the email. I clicked the reply button and considered every line I had read carefully. Spend too much time on it and I would give in to the doubt the sender was espousing. Spend too little time and I would hand over a bit of information to a faction I did not fully understand. A reply was required none the less and lack of an answer felt like yesterday--like running. I breathed out, closing my eyes and letting go. The typing began, the words forming themselves through the fingers with minimal guidance.

"It began with the word. Spoken and thus heard. Any message of value should be delivered in the same manner. It is clear you know how to locate me." In review, I found that I was proud of myself. I did not have names or faces to my hidden messengers. I could read a person or the appearance of a person in direct contact. The cold format of type front on digital pages gave me nothing. I was tempted to follow the email back through the servers but thought twice about putting myself inside a machine. In stalemate, I clicked Send and logged off.

I didn't speak when I came downstairs. I used my eyes and hands to greet my relatives as well as the three teenagers with them. Apparently they had been summoned to retrieve my car as I slept all day and recovered. I greeted Cornelius, Nigel and Candace with silent pounds and following hugs. The plan was to leave them with Desta. It was the only option I had for a babysitter with security functions in the absence of Xochi, who had taken a trip to Southern California. I didn't ask much; I knew it was a bit of a homecoming. After our stint in the Nest, I wouldn't blame her. I expected contact from her when she got the lay of the land. Her presence was for this activity was preferred but not required. Fully aware of my promise to keep her aware of all activities I conducted within the Sanctuary, I almost knew she wouldn't approve of our mission within her bounds. I had rehearsed the semantics several times and it came down to one truth: there is a biological family and a logical family in life. Biological is linked by shared ancestry and a household. Logical family is the people who stay consistently in your corner but won't cosign your bullshit. Xochi was certainly logical family. In a biological sense, I knew better than to think that one human being was complex enough to be that genetically different from its ancestors; we were all descended from one small core of ancestors, so Xochi fit the bill again. She was from Tenochtitlan. I was from Kemet. This was about Kemet. Kemet had brought the Isfet. I would end the Isfet and Kemet would take care of its own.

Omid had exchanged the hummer for a Suburban, a nice vacation in Napa with the family-type car. I sat in the front seat, playing with the window switch every fifteen minutes or so. It was a simple but unsatisfying game. I rolled down the window, lit a cigarette, took three drags within a space of two minutes in between, decided I hated the taste, tossed the cigarette out the window to upset Gavin Newsom, rolled the window up and repeated. Hari-Khpr sat behind me, smiling the entire trip. His eyes had lost their sadness, though they moved slower now when he shifted them. His head was turned with his nose toward the open window, chin tilted with the wind blowing into his nostrils. Registering every sight and refusing to ignore, those ancient lights in his eyes shifted from the roadside to my own in the rear view.

"Just checking on you," I sent him, still not convinced speaking was a necessity.

"Enjoying the moment," he sent back with a wide smile. There so much of a young man in the theatre in his grin that I felt the skin around my eyes flex when I smiled back. *"Memorizing the smells in the air . . . pulling apart the blossoms from the apples . . . the grapes . . . the ocean."*

"You can find such details?" I asked through a send. All I saw was the special International Orange of the bridge leaving the north of the San Francisco peninsula around us.

"Before I got sick? No. I took so much for granted. As much as I love cornbread, I couldn't remember the smells of my mother's cooking. Then something put stains on my memory. My freedom went with it. All the rose bushes at the Shores can't replace the ability to walk outside and sniff any flower available. Freedom becomes like a rose. Even tarnished and stained you have to stop and get a whiff or you will lose that smell."

I sniffed the air, closing my eyes and sitting back in my seat. The movement rippled from my legs sending ghost spasms up my body. I smelled the wind first. It was warmer than San Francisco already. The Bay was nowhere improved, catching me with its oil and fish gut aftertaste. Then I caught the trees and then the grass. Then a rose bush somewhere. One could almost put their hands around each scent and follow it to its source.

"I had forgotten," I sent back, opening my eyes, nodding my head. "Thank you." Khpr leaned forward, patted my shoulder, rubbed my head and leaned back. I smiled.

"I feel I should be thanking you. This was a good thing you did. This hasn't happened before."

"Ah, so you are in on it, too."

"Not telling you what you instructed me to not speak about?" He reached forward and put his palm on my chest over my solar plexus. *"Yes, there is something you are trying not to repeat but keep your head in the game regardless. This conspiracy you are implying gave me my mind back. Why would I turn around and hurt you for it?"* I patted his hand and he leaned back into his seat nodding slowly. My eyes left the mirror so I could return to my stupid game with the window and cigarettes.

The road to Stinson was winding and sheer at times. Omid took it at a speedy clip but expertly. Heru watched the road but his palm was aimed at Omid who was able to keep over sixty miles per hour on every curve whenever we were alone on a stretch of road. I didn't worry once, though I still held my fear of heights. I told myself Proxies or not, if this car flips off the road into that ocean, I am peacing out with a wisp faster than a motherfucker. I hate the distance to the water. I am not a little boy anymore. I can't find my father, which means I get to choose which way to die I hate the most, not you. Heights sucked. I studied the beach from afar when we drove across the bridge. We needed a location outside of the Sanctuary but relatively free of Isfet. I selected the beach due to its proximity to Muir woods. By hiding under the nose, we would be that much harder to spit at. I watched the water on the waves as we approached. It was the height of winter and the onset of evening, so the park was legally closed. We stopped the car well before the gate in a turnout under the deep shade of some healthy trees. From there we hiked a quarter of a mile in a single file. Heru led, striking his arms in the air stridently, his aural canal plugged by the unmistakable white ear buds leading to some gadget in the back pocket of his jeans. His sweatshirt seemed like a flag of black cotton draped around his body. His hood was pulled overhead so far that it covered his forehead.

I wondered where his head was at. The cycles made sense but the recovery did not. I wasn't sure Heru had ever adjusted to his father's absence. Ausar spoke through him, not to him. His mother had been a very integral part of his early life and I had been there but I was more of an older sibling than a father figure. Wally on the other hand knew his father but the man had been a complicated role model. I wondered how Wal-Heru reconciled those extremes. I always worried that he hid his grief in his sense of justice, replacing loss for vengeance. He was born ready to take his uncle's head before he could breast feed; his small arms practiced sword strokes from his swaddling cloth, even though his eyes had not opened. He was born impatient too--sharp as hell. He tempered that with being ultra-respectful and taking deep reflection in our lessons together in the cave near the water. However, he always tried to skip steps. I learned with time he simply couldn't help it. It was his nature: if I gave him step number one, his aspect required him to jump to step seven without the ability to back track. Maybe he could treat maturity the same way.

It was that spirit that forced me to submit to his will and return to Kemet to make war against Set--a war with terrible losses that lasted longer than it should, forming two kingdoms in the process. Even after unification under my father's mediation abilities, Heru stayed itching for another go at Set. In many ways, the Isfet invasion was the best thing possible for Heru. I felt he was never content with a reality where he was not after Set's head. Then if he killed Set, he would be miserable as well. The invasion guaranteed he would stay at odds with Set. *For the first periods of the conflict, we tried it Heru's way.* Yes, we did. We set up new kingdoms, raised armies and assaulted Kemet. We met Set where ever we could. Sometimes we won, often we lost. We were never able to build enough momentum to finish it. Then we tried it Sekhem's way, running and establishing ourselves elsewhere, searching for battles where we controlled the parameters and took the least losses. It would seem that strategy had found its end as well. This walk through the grasses and ground cover the sand dunes was the walk of a new way. It was a compromise: a merger of our aspects that attempted to find synergy between mentor and student.

Still. Still I worried. I had witnessed little or no interaction between Wal-Heru and Desta. They occupied the living room like two guests at a dinner party waiting for an introduction. It was not possible they were unaware of each other's true mind. I wondered if the expectation was too stiff, shoving such profound primordial energy into bodies that had not known the full breadth of the human experience. Was it lack of experience that polarized the both of them or some waiting period I was not privy to? Wal-Heru turned his head to the left and, noticing I was watching him, removed the left ear bud and reached into his pocket presumably to turn off his music.

"Lines ripple across your forehead," he said. "Having second thoughts?"

"Not a one," I replied in a whisper. "I am learning your new form."

"Your thoughts go to Horace Marshall."

"Your father was a tangle of complexities. I am still sorting them all out. This transition from him to you is even more tangled."

"Was he a good man?" Wal-Heru asked rhetorically. "By definitions of saints and mystics, no, he was not. Was he an evil man? Those same experts would also say no. Compare him to Hitler or Stalin? Ramses even."

"What a coward he was. Why bring him up?"

"You are biased. He cut off your feet at the ankles."

"I am still limping centuries later." He chuckled.

"Horace was not an evil man given those examples. His path at its inception had a noble cause but he got sidetracked. Isn't that the way our enemy's world leans man's heart?"

"True."

"It was Horace's time to for redemption. He did not run from it. He ran towards it."

"So you believe his murder wiped the slate clean?"

"No, but when he abandoned violence it defended his life better. It may have been in his best interests, but transcending inflicting injury did not compound his heart's weight. His sacrifice is noted."

"So we all deserve redemption?"

"All who seek it with commitment and integrity."

"Even our enemy, the Isfet? How about your uncle?"

"Set seeks redemption? Really? That's a new one."

"Can we assume they do not?"

"There is no accident to these Carriers my Attribute comes back in. For a true rebirth, my aspect can't occur in the in the already enlightened. It's like the dudes who come by the Boys and Girls Club. They tell the kids in homework club to study hard. Those kids are already doing they homework. They already studying--they ain't playing ball outside or in the studio. Dude should be on the block hollerin' that, not a roomful of kids getting grades." Now I was chuckling. "It's like adding sugar to apple sauce; the flavor was already sweet." He put his arm around my shoulder, a gesture reserved for those he held dear. "But to turn thief to generosity or a pimp to equality, that is a rebirth right? Rii? Do you remember our days in Harlem?" The images flashed by in quick succession, ending with my dead body in Vegas and Heru bleeding in a ballroom in Harlem the same day. "I sense your sarcasm, cousin. You will tell me that those days ended with four gun shots for every name change."

"More like seven shots for each. You know me well."

"I will ask you how many millions reconsidered their role in the world and what they could do to better others for every time we fell."

Lists of names, faces and dates flashed before my eyes. Some of them I had been, sharing their thoughts as I rented their bodies toward a common goal agreed upon in the beginning of the lease terms. Some had been Heru's occupancy from birth. They were clear that their path through life would be difficult and explicitly leadership-based. All had died violently, some publicly while others in the privacy of a town square. Others had been friends, true confidants and allies who carried the way, knowing success might be marginal at best and the personal cost exorbitant. Redemption was more than the pages describing a life-changing event captured on Wikipedia for a book report and open for interpretation. It was a culmination of thought processes occurring in the minds of the mortals touched by the influence of Attributes. It was an evolving discussion shaped by current context and compared through historical precedents.

One link was not more important than any other in the chain because without the connection it all bordered on obsolescence. These individual movements were irrelevant unless there was a spine in which to align the body of work. Take it as it comes. All works have an underlying progression in the same vein as the chords one pulls from all the background music on a walk to the neighborhood corner market. Heru and I had not invested in infrastructure; we had invested in the people, in the country. It was a beginning to come together in my head. History was the wall and great people were our graffiti.

The grass gave way to the sheer pygmy sand cliffs down to the sea shore. First Wal-Heru, then Hari-Khpr lowered himself to Wal-Heru's hands and I was last. Omid left us at the bluff, tossing the messenger bag he was carrying down to Wal-Heru. He saluted and turned on heel when the bag was caught, walking out of sight back to the vehicle. By the time my eyes had turned back to Wal-Heru, he was finished opening the messenger bag and dumping its contents on the sand. He pulled a roll of black duct tape from the pile on the sand, starting the strip and then pulled what appeared to several leather belts from the pile. Hari-Khpr raised his arms directly over his head like a small child having a shirt removed by a parent and Wal-Heru buckled several belts from his shoulders to his sides forming an x on his chest. The belts were then wrapped by the tape, covering Hari-Khpr's entire torso in it. Wal-Heru then pulled several gadgets from the pile consisting of a digital clock radio, a hair dryer, an old sim chip based cell phone and a bedside lamp. He placed the items back into the messenger bag and placed the strap on Hari-Khpr's shoulder letting the saddle hanging below waist.

Next he turned and covered this distance between us too fast for the normal eye. His hands came up with the fingers pressed uniform and straightened by a flat palm, each of his blade-like hands sliding my arms upward, then outwards until they straightened as well as turned my body into a cross. He pushed a twenty-five pound circular black metal weight on my chest and taped it to me making my abdomen look like the largest floppy disk ever. Heru gave no explanation when he pushed my shoulders and spun me on my toes I faced opposite as I had been. The same weight and amount of tape was applied to my back. When finished he pulled my hood over my head and safety-pinned a towel to hang from around the back of my shoulders.

"Now set me up," he said, standing back with his arms upraised with a proud smile. Hari-Khpr held the first weight to Wal-Heru's chest and I began wrapping in tape.

"We look like shopping carts," I mumbled. Wal-Heru snorted a laugh out.

"You have a great sense of humor about this," Hari-Khpr he replied to me. "We'll need that." I finished taping and attached his towel. The last things left were two cleavers in the sand that Wal-Heru was picking up by the time I finished the roll of tape. Unfortunately we left the cardboard mold and the i-whatever in the sand. Then he looked to Hari-Khpr who was watching the horizon. "How are we on time?" he asked the elder.

"Considering how fast things move there," Hari-Khpr answered, "we have just under two hours for a window."

"Well, then," Wal-Heru said, turning his bright eyes to me. "We'll need a way home, Mr. Door."

"You want me to draw a door to Kemet?" I asked.

"Yes," he replied, "put us exactly the same location as where we came in from the jail." I nodded and closed my eyes. *Huh.* I remembered the patch of sand we fell on to. I remembered rushing to break away in the hills above Moreland. *The door opens in Kemet first; it scales back to the hillside in San Bruno and it connects to the beach we stand on. The frames placed before us, the forever-blue I have come to know--that is the color between permutations contrasted by the black fill to remind me that we are leaving the Pacific Ocean. It is beach to beach now.*

"I will go first to scout," I hear Wal-Heru say, which opens my eyes. He is one step from the door when I find him with my sight and gone before I can speak.

"Be my guest," I say with obvious hesitation, causing Hari-Khpr to laugh, which makes me want to laugh.

"All clear," Wal-Heru announces a second later, his voice carrying crystal clear through the door. Hari-Khpr walked through next and I followed, stepping on to the beach by the Nile. There was far less vegetation growing now and the water had become darker; the water line was down quite a bit.

The land was sick. Behind me, the door was shooting its forever-blue beam back up into the night sky and back to Stinson.

"Close it," Hari-Khpr said to me.

"What about our exit?" I shot back.

"That door won't lead us out," he replied. "Save your energy." Wal-Heru stood with his back to us, watching the darkness due to the moon and stars hidden by clouds. Time had stopped. No, time didn't exist here in Kemet. Time was for Egypt. We were in a place of ideas, not materials. *Be here now.* The door closed and I felt as one. "When you are ready, grandfather," Wal-Heru said with tenacious urgency.

"Yes, yes, yes, of course," Hari-Khpr replied and walked forward. As he did the garments on him began to glow. Each section of his body glowed with its own color like flashlight under a thin sheet. *The buckle's silver, the leather's brown, the tape's black.* It all began to liquefy, staying just above his skin and spreading. The liquid formed a gel- like substance on his bare skin which took on a translucent quality. When he reached out to Wal-Heru, he was no longer the Harrison I recognized. His sketchers were replaced by dark leather sandals; slacks had given away to a shendyt of aquatic green, his chest covered by a breast plate of hardened forest green leather. Swirling about him on a continuous corkscrew spiral were the rings on planets, all composed of tiny pieces of metal, glass, clay and plastic in liquid form of varying degrees of temperatures. Hari-Khpr reached his glowing hand out. His arm was covered by a rippling clear gel blob and touched Wal-Heru on the shoulder. The area began to liquefy, creating a blob that covered Wal-Heru's whole body. Hari-Khpr turned and headed my direction, stopping less than a foot in front of me. "Do you have your pen?" he asked.

I looked down and grabbed it from my left pants pocket, where I clipped it against the seam to keep it from falling when I walked. I handed the Pilot to Hari-Khpr and in doing so viewed Wal-Heru. His black high tops were gone in lieu of black boots that came just below his ankles. The boots were Chinese in design. He also wore a shenty, though covered by a black war skirt of hard leather that matched the black iron breastplate across his chest. His hood was gone for the long aqua-blue cape he wore to match his father's skin. On his head, he wore the crown of the upper kingdom over the hood. In each of his hands were giant cleavers, two-handed butcherknife-like swords that I knew him to be more than comfortable handling. That was all I could take in before a liquid blob blocked my vision. When it pulled away, I could already see the changes taking place. I wore an identical set of armor as Heru, though my breastplate was etched with a woman between giant wing--son of Ma'at. My cape was a pastel lavender to signify my mother's house, the priesthood. Hari-Khpr stood before me still, holding a giant blade in its scabbard out to me. Taking it from him, I attached its belt at my waist and drew the blade a few inches to see the familiar cross etchings of Chinese and Mdw Ntr.

"You used raw materials to create armaments for us," I said, puzzled as I let the sword fall back into its scabbard. "How did you create the blade?"

"As far as the armor and garments, yes. All of our possessions fell into their particles and built what we needed," Khpr said with a smile, "As for the sword you brought here, you two are linked. Using tools is your aspect."

"A tool of war . . . "

"Have you not heard the tongue is a sword? It can cut the enemy."

"Or cut you."

"A reflection of your heart. Then the tool is always available"

"And if the heart changes?"

"Then the blade does as well." I looked to Wal-Heru who was scanning the gloom of the night.

"Trouble?" I asked.

"Not yet."

"What then?"

"I had always envisioned music when this day came. It's a shame I can't play mp3's here," Wal-Heru said.

"You're not worried about giving us away?" I asked.

"No, cousin," he chided me. "Propius is stranded here. It cannot leave here and it cannot call for help. Kemet is forgotten. That is our mutual prison, Propius included. Surprise does nothing for us."

"Well, then," I said with a smile and let my eyes relax. He was startled when the lion roared just under the sound of the snippet of speech by an Ethiopian emperor. Then there was the call in the night from Capleton, delayed through an echous harmony. After a few pulses of the bass, the bass line kicked in on the one with the drums. Wal-Heru nodded his head on beat, smiling exceptionally wide while he moved his hands in front of him. When his whole body found the rhythm, his hands pulled the clouds away as if wiping a counter while I thought of my father in order to bring out the moon's light more intensely to light things around us. Damien Marley *It Was Written.*

"He's got his father's fire," Hari-Khpr said, delighted at the sound of the music. "Excellent choice. He might be the only one who conveys his father's compassion and sarcasm."

"His brother did the production, so maybe more than one can do it?" Wal-Heru replied.

"Then again, looking for a sequel to a great artist like Bob Marley is blasphemy in some circles."

"Can nature blaspheme?" I responded. Hari-Khpr looked around, nodding his head, visibly disturbed at the vague presence of ruins and webs.

"We certainly can, apparently," he said aiming his eyes at the Veil tower in the distance.

"How were we to know," I tried in an attempt to comfort him.

"You knew," Wal-Heru said looking into me. "So did your father. Publicly he supported Ausar, but privately he told us you had him convinced."

"Me convince Djeuti? Not possible."

"He thought your objections were sound," Hari-Khpr said.

"Then why did you two build it?" I asked Khpr.

"I wanted to see if it could work," Khpr said, ashamed. "I also agreed with Ausar. As for Djeuti, you will have to ask him why." He placed his hand on the middle of my opposing arm, which I had learned was his way of telling me to keep moving. I thought about asking if he should be waving his hands in front of my face, telling me that these were not the droids I was looking for before I told him to move along. Instead, I wet my finger tips and rubbed his knees as a gesture to demonstrate how ashy they were. He frowned at me and Wal-Heru laughed hard.

Then we walked quietly for a time. My companions had seen fit to leave me my cigarettes which I smoked back to back the whole trip using my hands to light them. My thoughts must have been on repeat because the music played on loop until we arrived at the road. It was a crossroads, in fact, linking four distinct avenues at the axis. Along the causeway we walked were soldiers, wearing Heru's coat of arms in formation along either side of the road. They were a smattering of men and women, mostly older, spears and bows, a few chariots drawn by horses, but no sign of an infantry. They all resembled the people we had met my last trip to Kemet, smooth ebon skin with bright hopeful eyes. I noted one figure at the end of the train, standing in the center of the road. Though in salute, his wide nervous smile at our approach was unmistakable. Wal-Heru hastened his pace, walking directly to what appeared to be the army's commander. He wasn't that much older than Wallace, showing signs of being just a few years under twenty-one. There was also a familiarity to him beyond the physical traits of his people; then again, they all looked like friends I could not name.

"My prince," the boy said, bowing low and returning to upright. "We have carried out your orders and were successful."

"Excellent. Any causalities?" Wal-Heru asked.

"More than three-quarters of our total forces. Our infantry is gone," the boy replied.

"Dead or captured?" Wal-Heru asked.

"Dead mostly," the boy replied, his eyes catching mine. "General, it is an honor to finally meet you," he stammered at me.

"I haven't held that title in quite some time," I corrected him, looking to Wal-Heru with skepticism before looking back to the boy, "Clay will do just fine." He appeared confused and looked to Wal-Heru for clarification.

"Clay is one of my cousin's aspects," Heru said, almost covering for me as if I was lying.

"I am indebted to you, sir," the boy said. "My grandmother always spoke of your bravery and kindness to our family."

"Grandmother?" I asked, curious.

"Yes," the boy added, "you exchanged places with her so she might live."

"What is your name, son?" Hari-Khpr inquired.

"Dejene, son of Adanech, who was daughter of Sessen, who was daughter of Wagaye. I am chief of the tribe of Heru."

"Two generations" I said, turning to Hari-Khpr.

"As I mentioned," he reminded me, "things move much faster here."

"We thank you for your courage," Wal-Heru said to Dejene. "Move your troops to outside of the city and await the signal." Dejene saluted and walked to the front of the line. One call and his formation were marching south. They aimed toward the source of the Nile and our ancestral temple. In front of us lay the matted mess of web strewn above our building we knew as the first Nest. Signs of the fire that had been here once were sparse. New webs had been woven with signs of skeletons hanging from cocoons to warn off any considered insurrection.

"Population control," Hari-Khpr said, catching my stare at the skeletons. "They demand one woman sacrificed to them every one of the years here. Without the women--"

"It keeps the childbirth rate down," I interrupted, "which keeps the population from exceeding the resources."

"Terrorize the girls and send them home," Wal-Heru added. "It keeps the warriors demoralized."

"Slavery," I said. "We invented slavery with our absence." My grandfather and cousin nodded their heads; you could smell the shame among us. "The plan again?" I asked to make sure my exuberant prince stuck to the script.

"Wait for the first waves to enter," Wal-Heru said, bored. "Gather them around us."

"Why?"

"Propius is dangerous enough alone, but he will have legions of Recluse nearby serving as infantry and bodyguards. We have to remove their ability to prevent us from engaging Propius directly."

"Then?"

"Divide and conquer. Grandfather and I limit the Recluse while you take him on directly."

"Good."

I was down to my last two cigarettes when we stepped into the same plaza facing the mouth of the Nest. I pulled out a cigarette and lit it, taking a very long drag and exhaling a large cloud that hung by my head. When my lungs were empty, the cloud formed into an arrow, the kind you see drawn on the floors of parking lots to direct traffic. It oriented itself to face the tunnel into the Nest and then flew into the dark passage way. I cleared my throat like I was bringing the classroom to attention, took a few more drags and then tossed the cigarette into the mouth of the tunnel. Wal-Heru took note, gave me a cocky grin and guided the cigarette along, using works to ignite the mouth of the tunnel. He stepped forward, just a bit ahead of me on my right and moved into his stance, with one blade level with his forehead and the other level with his waist. Hari-Khpr's spiral narrowed its diameter but grew in height, spinning faster and looking like a drill. I drew my own sword again and held it above my head. I shifted into a stance, keeping my left hand forward with two fingers extended into a sword hand for the trick. Hari-Khpr then moved to place his back against my own and began mumbling. I felt the sword become lighter in my hand, my muscles able to lift more, my reflexes sped up and my focus enlarged. I knew it was a result of what Hari-Khpr was doing to all three of us.

"I am bringing the Ntr incense and netjeri," I called out. "I expel the foul smell from their mouth. Therefore I come in order to expel the evil in my children's hearts. With this I remove the Isfet which clings to you. With this I bring you Ma'at. I present justice to you." I knew the charm by heart as I had learned it from my parents to guide our human wards through the afterlife. I knew it was a honor to the Nun and an insult to the spiders. However, I couldn't stop the provocation there; it wasn't in my nature. "Announcing the king of the black land and the king of the red land," I bellowed out, "lord of the day, Heru, son of Auset, lord of Kemet."

Pink smoke erupted from the tunnel and the sounds of wet coconuts hitting one another faded away the sounds of reggae. Millions of eyes made themselves known, crawling from the tunnel. They came from all directions this time: before us, above us, and behind us as the Isfet appeared. It was Phantoms and Daddy Long Legs first. The Passengers made the mistake of thinking we did not see them positioning afterward. Then came the lines of Recluse and behind them the abominable image of the giant tarantula that wasn't so grim anymore with its faceless rider.

"*Was our last encounter not enough, Neteru?*" Propius boomed out, without a mouth, "*or are you offering me your Prince's life for your own?*"

"No," I said, the sound echoing and killing the sound of the wet coconuts. In its place, as Damien Marley faded out the drums of Wu Tang's Heaterz faded in. "We have come for yours." Wal-Heru was a blur when he moved, chopping, weaving and slicing. He ripped through hundreds in one stroke, the blow pulling an arc of reddish-yellow fire through their ranks before stepping backward. I brought the orb up around us a free dome of solid unbreakable glass projected from my heart. Wal-Heru dodged the sweep of one of the Daddy Long Legs' blades at his ankles by performing a one-handed cartwheel on the head of his right blade. The act brought his cape up in a long ribbon that burst with flame like a theater curtain of fire signaling the end of the show. He then moved in circles from the interior of my orb outward, slashing wide slices that cut some Isfet and set others on fire.

The Long Legs were attempting to create a perimeter, though frozen by something Hari-Khpr was doing; thousands of them were held in place by planetoid ring spirals around their body in lieu of the large one that had previously been around him. Passengers flew though the air, bouncing off my orb like rain drops on steel garbage can lids. Wal-Heru kept pace with the music, his blades following the strings that introduced the speed-up sample of Gladys Knight saying *when you*; upcut, upcut, big swipe, down cut, hold position and step forward low in the stance. He was marvelous at targeting the Isfet that Hari-Khpr kept frozen at the rim of where the orb touched the surface of the sand under our boots. I shifted my focus to the places the pressure built, sometimes holding three places plus the entire orb until Wal-Heru could step there to clear away the pressure.

When I shifted to behind me, I knew not to take my eyes off the vanguard front. As flanks of Passengers assailed the upper part of the dome I'd put up, Phantoms assailed the upper part of the dome, blinking out of sight and blinking on to the surface of the orb. Where there was space between Long Legs on the ground, the Phantoms blinked out and blinked in against the dome like a battering ram. Wal-Heru responded by moving in long arcs, running along the front holding one blade out past the dome like he was turning the cog of an enormous mill wheel: clockwise from eleven to three, then zagged back from thee to twelve counter clockwise and then zip past back clockwise doing a full three hundred sixty degrees. The Recluse began to temper their attacks as their companions' bodies stacked on the outskirts of my orb.

In the periphery near where the eye turns when it's time to get creative, I spied Propius on the move. His giant shape cast an indelible shadow as it moved from the tunnel's opening to the silk wall and then began an ascent. I didn't let my eye leave the execrable steed or its faceless rider.

"Grandpa," I growled, expecting an action rather than a response.

"Not yet," he said, annoyed as if I was asking him to stop working on his model trains and take me to a movie.

"Above," I spat back at him, finding myself sweating and sore while standing in place. I could feel he was watching Propius as well as I was. The front lines of Isfet that were still undispatched by Wal-Heru came unfrozen and stepped backwards, retreating from the orb. They surged, gained numbers from the rear, and then swarmed in with frenzied blows that chained attacks against the base of the orb. Wal-Heru became slightly less deadly as they were able to coordinate parries and dodges with the blades on their joints. The Recluse enjoyed the gaps and added pressure, using their double arms to add four blows for each swing that were synchronized in places all around the orb. Propius was above us doing some foul works that spilled out in a green gas-like shape that grandfather was able to neutralize. *No. Absorb. Absorb.* I didn't dwell on how it came to me for too long, for fear of losing focus on the mounting attacks to the orb. Hari-Khpr put out works that met the works that Propius sent; though grandfather's sought neither to dominant nor recede. *Both.* This dissipated whatever Propius kept sending down at us.

Long Legs began to scale the orb, getting as high as three tall as they clamored on siege engines of their own dead and locked on Phantoms. In places where there were a bridge of three of more Isfet, the Recluse climbed on and formed an upper ring so they could drill in their attacks. The pressure on the orb was mounting, Wal-Heru not quick enough with the body count to keep the attacks from banging against my mind. My muscles were sore and sweat was dripping in my eyes. I found myself kneeling to keep my focus, the moonlight disappearing as the last of my orb was covered by scurrying eight-legged beasts.

"Ready," Khpr shouted, his voice trembling as his body shook in place by holding off Propius' works. Wal-Heru halted his slicing stepping back and swung his blades together as one, crying out as he did as if lifting the last bookshelf up a flight of stairs during a move. The force pulled a swirl of flame in the air around him much like a child blowing bubbles with a baton hoop dipped in soapy water. The flame shot out in a wide beam when Wal-Heru stepped and sliced, blasting through the bodies in its way through to the web and making contact with the canister of temple oil that had been left by Dejene's men during their distraction of an assault. Wal-Heru struck downward with the blades, thrusting the head of both cleavers into the sand, causing a shockwave that ripped outward, pushing a few Isfet off the orb but more effectively colliding with the wave's intended targets. The rest of the ceramic canisters that been hidden in the web by Dejene's men shattered in the wake of the wave, their contents suspended in spinning orbs full of explosive force by something Wal-Khpr was doing. The igniter orb, the one Wal-Heru had touched with his flaming stroke, touched the nearest suspended oil orb and burst into a miniature fireball. I felt Hari-Khpr switch off from negating Propius and I attempted to adjust, putting the last of my unoccupied mind into blocking whatever the draining works the Isfet commander was throwing down at us. This freed Hari-Khpr to duplicate the fiery orbs to fill up the space between the web and the dome my orb had transfixed. With a clap, Hari-Khpr brought his hands together and released the flaming spheres, filling the night with hundreds of synchronized explosions.

I felt Hari-Khpr shift back to negating Propius. I changed my works to adjust for the incoming wave of flame, though I wasn't nearly fast enough. Hari-Khpr knew it; I wasn't going to close the gap in time and he shifted his intention to me. Then the explosion came forth in a hot wave of white light.

CHAPTER TWENTY-FOUR

"Whether for their mutual improvement or self destruction, humans work well as a group. That is their unique sustainable competitive advantage."

-Sekhem Ka

When I opened my eyes to the sight of a burning Phantom carcass inches from my face, it caused me to scan the battlefield. I was on my side laid out on the ground. I wanted to jump up away from being so close to one of those things, but the pain in my body kept it slow. Take it slow. John Legend. The night was a different complexion all together in light of so much carnage. The web canopy was all but gone except for the last burning pieces holding on to buildings. As far as the eye could see were dead Isfet. In the absence of bodies were their ashes. I oriented myself, noting the tunnel that was once existed was gone and revealed a circular door to a building. The doorway was behind me and I faced the way we had come from the road. There was a group of Isfet rallying where the road met the entrance to the building site. Turning on my heels, I saw Wal-Heru. He swung that giant cleaver in his right arm, though his left arm looked bloody and limp against his left side. His breastplate was gone with his legs and arms looking burnt, his cloak all but cinders. In his wake was Propius on his mount with another section of troops, attempting to surround Wal-Heru. Between both sections of Isfet, their total troop mass was down to less than a quarter of their original size. Hari-Khpr was nowhere to be seen. Isfet had lost three-quarters but we had lost a third. A personal third.

Dizzy and unsure of my footing, I made my way to Wal-Heru, cutting my way to standing at his back. My blade was quite heavy in my grip but I managed to replace the orb. I put my attention at Wal-Heru's rear and waited as the rallied second wave prepared to rush at us. Wal-Heru was much slower in his killing, his face contorting in pain with every stroke. I was not a full bill of health myself; my skin was burned in several places, first degree on my legs and third degree burns on my hands. The breastplate on my chest was hot to the touch and dented in places, making it very hard to move without burning myself. There was dry blood on my face above my lips, the cause of which became apparent when the Isfet began their second assault. The blows against the orb moved like arms on a Tyco drums in temples of my skull, causing blood to trickle from my nostrils and ears.

The Isfet no longer had the numbers to scale the orb, but they triggered their blows in sequence nonetheless. Wal-Heru was back to his circular strokes, although with one arm. Each arachnid took ten times as long to fell. In addition, Propius was at the vanguard, using both its steed's fangs as well as its swords to damage the orb and slow Wal-Heru.

"Children?" I heard a lucid and worried voice call out. My eyes searched for the source, spotting a lonely figure on the road where the charge of the rallied Isfet had begun. Hari-Khpr crawled on all fours toward us, his gorgeous old man silver afro burnt from his head. He was nearly naked except for what was left of his djenty, scrambling with his hands in front of him on the sand. The blood on his face along with the scrap of cloth tired around his face indicated his eyes were damaged to the point of blindness. "Heru...Sekhem? Boys? Are you near?"

"*Rear!*" Propius yelled out, "*take their elder!*" He threw his gauntleted hand forward, aiming a sword at Hari-Khpr's defenseless crawl. The rallied charge that had just started assailing the orb from Wal-Heru's rear broke off, taking a section of troops as well to aim at Hari-Khpr. As they charged back along the field, they formed into ranks, sending half of Propius' force at grandfather.

"Heru!" I screamed, my voice panicked and my throat drier than the sand I stood on. The boy could not be reached. He fought for his life, zoned out against the possibility his family still lived. He was locked into the belief it was up to him alone or that he dare not stop his fight. Every step and swing he took spoke to that. I attempted to run to Hari-Khpr's defense, but found the burns too painful, falling to one knee again, using my sword to catch me from falling flat. With such speed as the Isfet employed, I would never intercept them in time. I tried throwing my orb over him, but it fizzled like an old television every time I took it off of me and attempted to send it elsewhere. There were just moments left between the Isfet horde and Hari-Khpr. I screamed in frustration.

Standing over Harrison in Merritt Shores, his diagrams laid out before us. "Find you competitive advantage," he says to me.

"I'm not sure what that is," I reply. He shrugs and goes back to drafting at his desk. I walk from his room and make the turn into Granny's. It's blood test time. A couple of them because the nurse has several vials ready. Granny is awake and vocal, fighting every step she can. They have assembled orderlies who are preparing the restraining straps to hold her in place. I feel a shadow on my left, turn my head and see The Stranger. His hat is over his chest and he carries a bouquet of dead flowers.

"The best is what you gave," it says, not making eye contact. "Who could ask for more?" Granny becomes focused and catches his words as she fights off orderlies.

"You a quitter?" she asks me, her eyes fiery dots locked on to me.

"Not for you," I say, feeling the tears catch in my throat as I speak.

"How much more can you do?" the Stranger says moving past the nurse next to Granny's right and my left side. He attempts to stroke her head, earning a punch near his ribs. He is able to step out range of at the last moment.

"If you quittin'," Granny says disgusted, with spit foaming at the corners of her mouth, "let me know so I can first." She pushes all of the attendants away and finds her hands on the IVs in her arm.

"He has quit," a new voice chimes in. He stands opposite the Stranger, with a hand over Granny's, preventing her tube removal. Slightly shorter than me, wiry build, broader at the shoulders and better dressed. I stare into his face and recognize a man I know from photos only; vague memories my mind unlock when the numbness of alcohol outweighs the pain of recall. "He has quit doing things his way," Clay's father says.

"What more can he possibly do?" the Stranger says to me.

"What is the unique sustainable quality of the human?" Clay's father asks me, completely ignoring the Stranger, assured he would get my attention. The Stranger falls silent, narrowing his eyes. "He can't answer me, Clay," Mr. Durward says to me. "He can't answer because he is not a human. He does not live with them; he enslaves them. What could he possibly know?"

"To observe, learn and respect," I find myself replying.

"And if pursued with an open heart?" Roland Durward presses me.

"To love. To accept and see in the mind's eye without limitations." He smiles at me and puts out his hand. I take it and he draws me close, so I am at Granny's bedside with him. She holds my other hand.

"What is there to love about us, baby?" Granny asks guiding me in. I start to answer, but my father cuts me off.

"Don't think, Clay," he whispers. "Just be, then answer." Thousands of years and hundreds of empires. From the first hunters to the ones who learned to plant crops. Whether turning the first wind mill or opening day at the Louvre. Shapes come into play. Dynasties rise and fall. Chicken soup kills sickness and penicillin the bugs in the blood. Symbols on scrolls and type fonts of the Macintosh. Charting the stars in Mali and signing the Declaration of Independence. The journey across the Himalayas to discover Cathay was only Nepal and the first boot on the surface of the moon. Walls so high that Mongolian ponies mean nothing and openheart surgery rediscovered. Time is subservient to all of humanity's faculties except for one undeniable truth.

"No species on planet Earth can cooperate in groups better than the human," I say. "Whether for their mutual improvement or self-destruction, humans work well as a group. That is their unique sustainable competitive advantage."

"And the line in between?" my father asks.

"Innovation," I answered, "using time, space and the material works to come anew." He smiles and wraps his arms around me. I embrace back and hiccup out a hard sob before crying into his chest.

"I love you, Clay," he whispers, "don't forget."

"I can't," I say through the tears. He squeezes me hard and falls into me. I see myself kneeling on my sword and panting on the battle field. Time is frozen around us. Behind me the Isfet and Khpr do not move, nor Heru and Propius in front. I walk to my knelt self, who looks up when I stand over him. I step behind him and kneel, our essence becoming one. The orb is up afterward. To innovate is to absorb. The orb hardens, taking a brownish tint the color of watery coffee. I see the earth spinning in space, rounded and molded by its magnetic poles as it negotiates the gravity of a sun with eight other heavenly bodies. The magnets in the heels of my feet charge as I rise to stand up, the force meeting when I drop my weight and spiraling up to my legs into my waist. It climbs up my spine, ignoring each chakra along the way and surges to the magnets in my palms. I am moving now, feeling the element forms that the Monk gave me to work on and master. As I shift weight, the orb rolls and I roll back, then uproot. The orb rolls forward, a giant marble of coppery glass speeding down the stone and sand battlefield with me at its center. The orb builds in momentum, pulling up stone, sand, grass, dirt, clay and pebble with it like an earthen snowball. It smashes body upon body of Isfet under its weight, flattening their exoskeletons and drawing in their very life-force into the orb. This in turn feeds the orb's momentum. The absorbed energy speeds the construct. As the edge of the orb threatened to crush Hari-Khpr, I made the section of it closest to him porous, using where he passed through the barrier to scoop him up on to my left shoulder. I continued to roll, Khpr over my back, crushing the last of the Isfet before reversing course back the way I came.

Excellent timing. Heru was being beat backward towards us, using his blade to parry and block, every once in a while able to cut. I saw his left upper thigh had been blackened by two punctures, Propius' ghastly steed scoring with its fangs. The venom weakened him and his legs looked unsure as he continued to block from every angle. I sped the orb's momentum stopping just before reaching Heru's back and dissolving the orb. I let Khpr slump to the sand and ripped up stone. I waded in ahead of Heru, my blade dancing like a pulse on an EKG machine in my left hand while using my right hand to shove Heru backwards. He stumbled over Hari-Khpr, which had been my intention, forcing him to catch his balance and then understand. Forming a perimeter around grandfather, Heru kept his defense tight and his strokes accurate.

The Long Legs surged against me first. I switched the blade to my right hand and threw up the orb. Again the creatures attempted to scale the construct upon Propius' command, his steed needing no helping in climbing the orb to my twelve o'clock. *To innovate is to absorb.* I swung my blade into a guard and found my posture. *The globe swirled before me again. The magnetic poles sending out waves that attracted and repelled the ore buried deep within its crust. The same metal cooled as ice melted upon mountains, cooling liquids into deep and precious deposits.* I swung my blade in my hands, forming a fan like motion before me. Three feet in diameter circles opened up all over the surface of the orb, resembling a giant kitchen drain. Each circle held a cross hatch of sharpened metal that began to spin and pull; inward. The Passengers were first to go. The aerial ones and those that were not in flight were too small to fight the intake, vacuumed in and chipped like mango in a food processor. The Phantoms were next finding out that their surprise teleportation only put them in the path of the intake and not away from it. The Recluse were smart enough to flee but in doing so blocked the potential exit of the Long Legs who were pulled in next. They jerked as they were grinded to a spray of arachnid blood and exoskeleton confetti which pulled the vital energy from their bodies and fed back into the orb. The Long Legs who had attempted to scale were trapped by their legs being vacuumed in from all eight directions. Propius' mount had lost half of all eight legs before the faceless villain leapt back ards, landing in a crouch with his swords drawn as his steed was chewed into oblivion.

"*Take the wounded,*" Propius screeched, pointing with its sword toward Wal-Heru who was struggling to stand over Hari-Khpr though his area was all but bereft of Isfet due to the orb. "*He is weak. My venom has him.*"

The Recluse broke from their commander's retinue, falling behind him and forming up. Then using buildings and arches, they climbed up and around avoiding the orb in a chase for Wal-Heru. I dropped the orb and brought my blade up, stepping to rotate on Propius.

"It will be over soon," I said with a smile. "Your aspect shall be no more."

"*Arrogant Neteru,*" Propius rang out from his face with no mouth that I knew to be sneering. "*You are no match for my violence works.*" Then he ran forward and swung so that his arms became a blur of cuts. I stepped, parried, blocked, blocked, parried, bought space, stepped over and held guard. This last stroke was a thrust, coming high from three o'clock at a downward pierce aimed for the soft spot in my armor under my right shoulder. I watched the blade enter my vision and ensured Propius had committed. Less than a second. Less than a moment, I spoke to myself. *The spinning orb in space with its two magnetic poles, covered by three-fourths water. The power to soften beaches or drill under a tree's roots. It climbs mountains or finds the earth's core. Formless and seldom contained; water itself was the container. It purifies and drills.*

The orb shot out with an aqua-tinged light. It was smaller now, maybe six feet in diameter but solid with warm water and me at its center in posture. Propius' arm was stuck, unable to move in the element, engulfed up to his shoulder and its sword short of its mark.

"I don't have to match you," I whispered where its ear should be, and then switched elements. *The explosion Hari-Khpr has catalyzed had gone into my very being, connecting me to the spark in the water that had brought the Nun which began Khpr and Ra--Ra who had given birth to my mother and why I was here. The explosion had brought me to the very underpinning of nature itself. Though more than twenty centuries, it was not that long ago I had traveled to the mountain in the Middle above Indus Kush in search of troops to assault Kemet. The Monk, our guide among the land, displayed life as he knew it on the back of a turtle's shell. Five elements connected his world, the fourth of which lived at the Earth's core and in the Sun above.*

The orb detonated outward with a red hunger, flames licking its outmost surface. The initial blast blew Propius through the air, leaving its left leg burning on the sand where the epicenter of the explosion had been. Propius spun through the air and landed on its one leg shaking. It screamed in enraged madness. "That is pain," I said, my voice warping from the orb's heat. "Know it. It is a part of human form you have never experienced. I came to teach you. The lesson is not difficult; pain is your nature." I considered how many thousands of generations of young women had been offered to Propius's torture as some false promise of protection from his violent ways. Thugs and charlatans. The Isfet, the harbingers of pain, had no tolerance for it themselves, I found.

"*I can hear your thoughts, son of Ma'at,*" Propius challenged. "*My Passenger in your neck betrays you.*" His voice still shook but the confidence was unmistakable. I saw pink smoke forming on the cauterized stump of his left leg, moving like the forming of a tiny web. Each crosspoint fizzled with translucent drops, which formed new cells. "*One tissue cell for every life of your people. Use that sight of yours and see,*" Propius taunted, putting sharp inflection on the word 'sight.' "*By the time you're done counting, my entire army will be reborn with this form even stronger than before.*" He sent forward a work at me, the same kind that Khpr had wrestled with before--some type of drain. It came blooming sickly green, a flower with teeth, the edges the color of Heru's cloak but the interior that resembled an infected chartreuse.

I put the orb up, attention up front contrasting with the feeling of rollback in my legs. I was imitating what I sensed Khpr had been doing. The orb caught Propius' intention to dampen my vital organs, almost the opposite of healing me with Kwk works that Wal-Heru had performed on me the night before. My orb met his works and spun it from its mass into a stretched cord around the orb. It was not able to penetrate, but I could not disperse it either. The stump on Propius had slowly begun to regenerate, bubbles of hot liquid popping off like grease from frying fish. In the absence of the steam, his leg was on the march to return. *Water feeds trees.* It took less time to connect the meaning now. I knew wood--strong in how it defies height but flexible from its roots. Keeping the orb rolling on the anti-Kwk maneuver, I dropped my intention on the apex of the dome, turning it into a ring spinning the green thread from Propius onto a spool. Magnets at the feet, waist, hands, between the eyes. *Under.*

Propius prepared for me to sink under the earth to burst up at him. Instead I left the spool twisting and rose up in a simulacra double, leaping from my crouch into the air as my other matching component stayed in posture, rolling the enemy's energy on the spool. One was on the ground and one leapt through the air in mid-flight at Propius. The aerial self waited until his knee was just below the enemy's neck before he swung his blade down. It would have been a body slice, cleaving Propius in a diagonal but the Isfet was able to bring his parry to bear at the last moment, thus dropping the works he was sending at my sentinel standing a few feet behind. That same stationary self felt his works plummet and leapt. Instead of the previous arc, it snapped to its double, forming one like the launch of a paper clip from a rubber band. The move solidified me, doubles in one. I diverted his parry into a quick slice down as it felt the orb draw tight around my whole body like a jumpsuit. The right arm of Propius was lopped off and fell to the ground, causing its owner to let out another curdling scream and fall, unable to execute the physics necessary to stand upright.

"*Curse this form,*" Propius raged, frustrated and unable to regain its footing. "*Weak, pitiful, fragile humans and their Neteru wet nurses.*" Taunts were all it had. I watched carefully as the left leg had reached a knee's length of regrowth. I folded my blade under my right arm.

"*This is why you chose our form, yes? Our bodies, so you can complain when your day comes?*" I kicked him off the ground on my last words as he tried the new leg and failed. He flew against the wall above the opening to the Veil building and bounced off, falling splayed on its steps. I stalked over, hearing his voice out loud and in my head.

"You can have it; you can have it, son of Ma'at," he groaned, *"I will travel your lands no farther."* I started to speak but he kept going. "I am content to know I will be a part of you forever." He laughed as he pushed himself up slowly on the steps, picking up a sword from a half-chewed Recluse in his left arm.

"You are the first, but I assure you, you will not be the last, Propius. If I can beat you here, imagine what I have in store for your species." I shared the shape of things to come for the first time willingly. Through our link in my neck, I compared losses over time with interest. How many of my family and my people had suffered and what was it worth with the delay of justice? How much should the Isfet really be expected to pay? The indignation of a people once conquered, but never subjugated. The vision to search down every possible origin of the Isfet, find the one that was their true source and send every one of them back. As Propius screamed in terror, it was a chorus of a devastated child and a hateful old man.

"Spare me this body, son of Ma'at, merciful of the Neteru," Propius cried out, backing away from me, his sword game looking phony.

"No, I don't think I will," I said, swinging my blade and lopping off his head. *"You will stay, but not with me forever."* His head hit the ground, causing his legs to fall with pink smoke spraying out of his neck. His body became limp and shrunk--a balloon being released to spill out noxious air. The shrinking paused once it reached the size of a brick. In his body's place was a glyph, deep red lines with black fill. I bent over to pull it closer to my eyes, a spark licking up my arm when my fingers made contact. Back to blackness.

There were wind chimes in my head. I considered opening my eyes. They had a warmth and a comfort to them, so I decided not to open my eyes. A lazy dream state--sleeping in on Saturday. I waited there in the dark for a voice that never came. It was then I determined that the chimes were external rather than inside. I was surprised by the light when the first eyelid cracked. It was bright with a warming that led to heat. The second eye caught the sun--it was pulling over horizon. Dawn. I brought my arm up to shield my eyes and found that my head was lying on soft material. A pillow had been placed under my skull, my back lying along a cot. I smelled cooking meat and detected smoke somewhere to my right. It hurt to crane my neck, but I pulled it off. It appeared I was still in courtyard before the Veil building lying on a cot under a lean-to of canvas. The courtyard had become campsite of roughly a hundred people, most of them men in armor, setting up tents and ushering in cars drawn by horses or oxen. In addition, I saw a few war chariots circling on the outskirts down the road by the entrance to the plaza. Scanning the faces, I thought I recognized them as Dejene's troops, though it seemed some had brought their women and children. The sounds of little people laughing gave me the courage to try to stand. First I was able to sit up, and waited a time for my head to stop swimming. Getting off my back made me realize how much my back hurt, especially my shoulders. Once I felt I was stable and had balance, I tried standing on my legs.

It was not successful, but it did earn a familiar face. As I fell back on my ass, I turned to the left and caught the gaze of a young man sitting in a lean-to on a cot. He grabbed a walking stick when my legs went out as well as a water skin and hobbled my direction. As he approached, I could see he bandages on his leg, arms and his back. It was then I realized I was lying without my armor, most of my body covered in bandages. The boy hobbled closer until I realized it was only his body that was a boy here.

"Cousin," he said--the first time I had ever heard him exhausted, "let me help you." He was in pain when he hurried, but he swallowed it, urgent to put a hand out to me.

"You look in no better shape yourself," I said in a whisper, finding that moving my lips at all hurt. Heru stood over me and then lowered himself to the ground at my side, leaning against my cot. He uncorked the water skin and tilted my head back, pouring into my mouth. I took a long series of gulps and then lifted my eyebrows slowly, indicating I wanted to know what he was looking for.

"Grandfather was not certain you would awaken. He wanted me to prepare for the worst, which I did but I had trouble with it. He thought it best that you moved as little as possible. I just thought it wouldn't be fair if you didn't awaken. I'm glad to see you." I blinked to say I understood. "It's not a lot, but I learned to do your music," he said, unsure of himself, more

Wallace than Heru. I heard the distant animals sounds they put into nature shows and Star Trek episodes to make you believe it's another planet instead of a Paramount lot. Then the flute, rolling into a drum set that brought up images of Paul Simon's 50 Ways To Leave Your Lover. Pianos and Nas's voice explaining how we were not alone. I looked to Heru and blinked my eyes as I nodded my approval.

It was a good long while before we spoke again. We sat, just hearing the music and staring off into the plaza at the people. We eventually moved again, Wal-Heru knowing when I was ready for another drink. A meal was brought to us and Heru fed me, followed by his own meal. I guessed it was noon when two of Dejene's men helped me up so I could lean on them and get some time standing. Heru worked his palms over his legs, drawing out venom to his palm and letting it drop to the sand. I took the time to just practice being upright and trying my legs. When I felt like walking, Heru had healed his leg enough to support me but his left arm was still in a sling. Although he did not have enough juice after repairing Khpr's arm, he was still in far better shape than I was. Khpr got the best deal, rightfully so as he was our elder. I guessed he would require less energy than Heru healing himself because Khpr's aspect was to magnify things, which would require less of Heru. His smile was contagious when I finally made it over to where he stood, giving me a long, silent hug before kissing the tops of my feet and then the dirt they stood on.

"The land," he whispered so impassioned that he almost wept, a man possessed to dig his fingers into the ground and expose the dark rich soil under the sand.

"The land," I agreed as loud as I could manage and caught a fit of coughs.

"You probably still need this," he said, rising and pulling a single cigarette from his satchel. He lit it with his hands and lifted it to my mouth. I took a drag, feeling the headrush that led into normalization. The Passenger in my neck rumbled and silenced, allowing me space to recharge for the moment. "I have more of the stuff you are used to, but for now this will do the trick."

"This seems stronger than what I smoke," I whispered.

"It is stronger," Heru said.

"How would you know," Khpr asked.

"You put in the stuff we picked and kept the paper?" Heru returned with his own question.

"Yes," Khpr said.

"Well, if it's from here, it's stronger. Sekhem is the one who figured out tobacco nullified the passengers. I was just the one who realized smoking it rather than eating it was a safer alternative."

"No," I whispered, "I did. You figured out the pipe."

"Same difference."

"How is your energy, grandson?" Khpr asked me, concerned.

"Slow, but I can play with a few things," I replied, surprised that water, food and a smoke made it easier for me to speak.

"I require a door."

"Sure. Where to?"

"Every safe each of your aspects has set up."

"Excuse me?"

"I require the glyphs you've collected and hidden."

"I can grab those for . . ."

"No, you cannot," Khpr said with seriousness. "Your last attempt nearly split you."

"Any idea why?"

"No," he said at Heru, meeting his eyes and then dropping them. *Do not be deceived, brother,* I heard the letter voice say. I studied Heru and pursed my lips.

"We don't know enough yet," Heru said, catching my expression. "You want answers we do not have at this time. You didn't leave instructions for that one." I nodded and decided to drop it, feeling a pit growing in my stomach despite just eating. I opened several doors, each to the interior of a safe, each in different locales of the world, each owned by a different me. Khpr collected them and handed each glyph to Heru who placed each in a wooden box on in cart draw by a horse. In total there were seventeen, fourteen like the kind Athena gave me and three similar to the kind I had seen Propius turn into-- the same kind I had seen fought over at the Grand Concord, the same kind Athena attempted pass through and found we had bugged her. Heru lifted the box off the back of the cart and motioned with his head toward the Veil building at the center of the site. Poking into the sky, it was a combination of mercurial blue and tapioca swirl. I saw its conical and antenna-like structure driving down into a square building with a wide circular opening that had once connected to an Isfet tunnel. It was the Veil. We walked, Heru leading with the box, I leaned on his shoulder and Khpr lifted me under my left arm pit to the extent he could. We went slowly up the circular disc-shaped steps and I was reminded of where I had felled Propius's head. Up the steps we were followed by troops with spears who aligned at the entrance, protecting our backs. Once I had walked down these stairs, I thought of the person I sought to hear me speak the most--my father.

Our throne. Our meeting hall. Our street corner. Our barbershop. Our cipher. Our back set of the jeep. Let's go. Up the stairs and through the long hallway that led to where the Narmer had met for generations and beyond into its enormous round chamber with rising pews from the ground so the center was never mistaken above the voice of its audience. There in the center of the room stood the Auset. The throne of Kemet that unified two kingdoms and more. It unified where we had come from to where we had yet to go. From among the children in the south of black gold, he walked up bring with him his wife who was the only guaranteed proof of his connection to the kings of Ta-Seti and therefore his commitment to the land. The commitment to the people and therefore the way. The throne was named after her wife, knowing we could always return to the source when either our way was lost or our work accomplished. Made of stone, clay, alloys, crystals and stored gases, the throne stood in dutiful observance of whoever sat on it. The ruler of the throne had charge of the day here in the afterlife and in the world before.

Behind the throne, perhaps ten feet from the wall, were a set of what appeared to be consoles. In the floor space the wall and the consoles were two rectangular panels of stone. The left was surrounded by recessed crystal and the right appeared sealed closed. There was one rectangular indent on the left and one on the right. The left rectangular panels contained cuts within it each showing a series of symbols like Excel sheets. Heru stopped at the throne, indicating I should wait there and lean on the object's head rest for support. It seemed like a fair request, so I obliged. Khpr made his way to the consoles, blowing on his fingertips as he reviewed it. Heru set the box down by the left panel and began matching shapes to glyphs. Every time he found a pair, he placed a glyph on its matching symbol and its top began to fill out a shape. Eventually all fourteen pieces were placed and a man's calcified but mummified form lay in the left panel. Green light spilled from between the cracks in the pieces of the body, sealing it together so it looked like a stone replica and retracting into the floor as the right panel opened. When the right panel locked into place, the left had sealed closed. Heru made his way over to me and stood on the other side of the throne. I realized he had left me on the throne's right and placed himself on the left.

"It's ready," Khpr said, staring at the console and moving his palms over it.

"One last door, cousin," Heru said.

"Desta?"

"Yes."

"This better not hurt hi--"

"You are weary," Heru said loudly, cutting me off. "But do not let that be an excuse to doubt my character." I nodded and opened a door to my living room. The clock on the microwave showed we had been away perhaps a total of three hours. That was the same amount of time as the drive to the beach's length. He was already watching for me when I found him, sitting on the edge of the couch to himself, as the rest of the room was clueless. He lowered his body off of the couch and walked directly to me where I was crouched, hopping in my arms and walking with me back through the Huh door. I placed him on the throne, the bottoms of his feet barely touched the edge. He straightened his back against the seat while sliding his butt until he was comfortable and then patted my hand.

"We'll be okay," his little voice rasped and lisped at me. I took my hands off him to stand back. Khpr moved his hand and a ringing began in my ears. We all seemed to notice it except Desta. A circular door in the roof of the chamber opened to allow a shape to descend. Conical and nipple-like, it contrasted against rows of feathers on either side going upwards to a golden disc at its top. The atef crown descended, suspended by a ring of mercury blue energy that stopped its route just above Desta's head. He reached up and placed the crown on his head.

The ringing disappeared, followed by a loud click and then a hum that began to rise. The panel on the left made sounds from its closed doors and then the room lost all its light. An aqua-blue glow came from its center in the place of the throne given off by a man standing facing us, green in complexion, small in stature and familiar in expression.

"Father," I heard Heru ask. The man nodded and smiled. Heru reached over to embrace the man and was pulled close. We watched the two hug for a long time silently as they held each other. Heru had never met his father. Ausar had been conspired against and murdered before Heru was born. Here and only in the Veil could Heru embrace his father without having to be his voice in the world of the living. The Veil had been built for this purpose, to have Ausar walk among us again. Finally they separated and his son was first of us to speak.

"What is your bidding?" Heru asked.

"Provide for our people," Ausar replied.

"We have lost our foundation glyphs," Khpr replied. "Can you rebuild?"

"How much fuel do we have left?" Ausar asked. Khpr waved his hand over the console and studied the lights.

"Nothing is stored and their outer casings have been stripped. They have collected nothing all this time," Khpr replied, disappointed. I caught his glance. "The pyramids," he explained. "They were supposed to be a power plant as well as a battery."

"Keep hope," Ausar said. "I can charge the first foundation glyphs based on your aspects."

"We will not have Djeuti for the languages," Khpr replied.

"We have his son," Ausar said, smiling at me. Somewhere in there was Desta and somewhere was the man who had visited my house. They both gave me a look of utmost faith. "The rest is up to our people."

"Amen," Hari-Khpr replied with a bow. Heru followed suit, but I did not bow. Ausar walked to the console, stepping past to the right panel which had fully opened, showing a black and red grid. Wal-Heru placed three glyphs in the panel and looked to Ausar moved him out of the way with his gaze. He beckoned me over, taking my hand and holding it over one of the glyphs. I could feel him reaching into all of the principles, each category of work at once, and reaching into me. Then it went into the glyph and I heard him whisper, "Know the bush at the edge of the Nile. Its dry leaves give us parchment and its berries ink for our thoughts. Know then the foundation of language." The glyph glowed in deep red and cast the image of the glyph on the ceiling itself before locking in place turning mercurial blue as the light died down. He let go of my hand and I stepped away. He beckoned Heru over and held his hand over the glyph depicting a hunt. "Know the mine and the working of soft metals," he continued, "that so your mind knows the tools of the hunt." The glyph glowed deep red as well, sealed to the panel and turned forever blue. Last was Khpr who came over and held his hand over the last glyph. Ausar did not need to touch him to perform the works. They both spoke together. "Know the clay of the river," they said together, "to know the creation of containers and buildings." The glyph depicting the working of clay glowed red and went to blue like the rest. Then by himself he spoke the last works. "Know beasts of endurance and friend unto their gifts." A glyph appeared, filling the last piece in that section of panel, displaying an oxen in red light, then a horse and then turning to blue when it sealed like the rest. I noticed slabs of stone opening in the walls above the consoles, revealing depressed and smoothed clear crystal. The crystal sheets turned black and then lit up with stars until the focus fell on one shaped and zoomed in--the Earth. There were screens all over the chamber staring at multiple views of the world. Standing erect again, Ausar turned his attention to a glyph in the box Wal-Heru had not placed.

"What's that one?" I asked, pointing to at the glyph Heru had left in the box.

"I was going to ask the same thing," Ausar said nodding and looking to his son. "That language is not Mdw Nfr."

"Nor Mdw Ntr," Khpr added.

"It's Isfet," I answered before Heru could speak. "The closest it can be translated would be Latin: 'Appropriatio.' "

"To take for one's own uses," Khpr mumbled under his breath, shaking his head. Then I studied it again and saw the characters in my mind, remembering their match to the glyph that had fallen when I killed Propius's body.

"Is that what I think it is?" I asked Khpr who kept shaking his head, drawing the same conclusion.

"Yes," he answered, visibly disturbed. "You told us we weren't going to like it and I don't."

"What is it, nephew?" Ausar asked. I grabbed Ausar's arm and limped him over to the box, pointing at the glyph while looking into his eyes and his past, my vision looking through him into thousands of years of errors.

"Through me and this monster in my neck," I said to him, "the Isfet invented racism. They use that to steal ideas from cultures and use them to tear people one from another. They use it to divide and create the conflict they feed upon. Propius plugged that idea into the Veil and built exactly what you thought you could stop."

"And you just killed racism," Heru said, picking up the glyph and walking over to the panel.

"Just what the fuck do you think you're doing?" I barked and limped after him. "What is this, Heru? This isn't the end, is it? This fucking machine can't send them back, can it?" I was yelling now. "It's not going to get this out my neck, is it? How about freedom for the rest of the family? Or bring us back together? Bring my mother or find my father? Is it, Heru?"

"Not today," Heru whispered not meeting my eyes. "No, it won't."

"You mean to steal from them? The fucking Isfet?"

"You can't steal what was never yours," Heru yelled back.

"Is that what this is?" I screamed. "All a play to get the very thing that started this mess working again? A machine? Another fucking machine so you can hack into the Veil? So you can be Prince again? Rule a forgotten time? You lied to me, cousin," I said, livid.

"I did no such thing. I . . . "

"Then why the charade of telling me what I want to hear to get me do what you want?"

"Your instructions," Ausar said, quietly breaking the ping pong of shouts and outrage. "We are all following your instructions. Some of them cross over and some do not. We turned on the throne because you wrote it down." Heru turned and placed his hand on my shoulder.

"And you were correct, cousin. It worked just as you said," Heru said with shaky smile, wary of my temper.

"To what end?" I rasped out.

"We shall write our name back into history," he whispered. "Look at it, cousin. This throne of stone, of clay, of metal, of crystal, glass, gases and the power of the sun. It offers us a say for once. We have a say: we write our own destinies in this stone."

"No, cousin," I said walking away toward the exit. "If it is we who write such destinies then throne is not made of what you say."

"What then?" Ausar called after me.

"It is made of paper. It is a paper throne," I whispered and walked back outside.

CHAPTER TWENTY-FIVE

"A classic is a book that doesn't have to be written again."
-W.E.B DuBois

Her pager rings again. It has gone off for the third time in four minutes. Half asleep she is avoiding opening her eyes to admit it's time to check in. Having just fed, the male beside her in bed breathes shallow having been ravaged by her will. She brushes the one bang of hair that always wants to choke her right eye away from her skull and reaches over to pick up the pager. She avoids phones until absolutely necessary; years of being on call have taken her ability to be objective about it at all anymore. *This is all for nothing. He is gone.* She shakes her head as she frowns. *If I exit.* Her hand finds the pager and brings it to her eye level as she lifts her face from the pillow. The numbers refers to a pay phone in a city but the code refers to the street in the neighborhood. She closes her eyes and regrets in the darkness.

Outside it's hurricane season again and the island is catching its wake up. Rain hits the window hard and dissuades anyone from leaving the house. She still went out, danced up a storm, kept the room warm, saw one of her loyalists, felt an urge, and decided to indulge. She has come to accept storms as part of her business. It's her streetlight in the corner of the window that shines in when her mind is trying to sleep. She taps her fingers against the shoulder of her Saturday entertainment, rousing him immediately with the force.

"Time to head home," she says as his eyes open. He was disoriented and sleepy if drugged. His skin smelled of alcohol but he had burned most of it out of the system.

"Thought I was staying over," he replied with a one-eyed half smile, trying to play into her detached sense of flirting.

"You thought wrong," she says, pulling the sheets away and sitting herself up. She catches her own eyes in the mirror, teal orbs of centuries of beauty and pain. He looks over at her in the dark, nods to confirm his disappointment and rises. She feels nothing as he dresses reluctantly and heads toward the door. She stares at the flashes of mock lightning outside the balcony and waits for the click of the striker against the lock. *Alone*. It starts by stretching: loosening every muscle in her body and straddling the bed forces her to view the tattoo on her ankle. A Chinese character on one ankle and a Japanese character on the other, both sad reminders of where the trail ended. Next the shower, where she finds her composure. Somehow it is not crying if hot water is constantly blasting into your face. It's necessary for her to remind herself of why this always feels hard.

Out of the shower, she pulls the white terry cloth bathrobe around her body in a fresh hug of comfort. It smells like fabric softener and reminds her of simple things she does to play nice human. Laundry. She can do some folding but hates ironing. Sitting on the bed, she pulls open the bedside drawer for some items. Staring back at her is the glass block encapsulating a tattered piece of paper. Papyrus. She reminds herself looking at its frayed and burnt edges. Across its face are symbols, random text to the ignorant eye and a math equation of necessity to her. It starts with a scepter over a three-sided box with no lid, then the small heart, the water over the loaf, the bow and the quiver. If a museum curator saw this, they might foam at the chance to possess a cartouche from the first dynasty, valuing it at over ten million dollars. She had that in her checking account alone and the item was priceless to her. The same curator or linguist might read it as: Ka heart determinative Nth immortal determinative or "the heart of Sekhem Ka hunts for immortality." This translation would forget that text requires context, avoids tense and allows possessive nouns for speech. Instead, the message was quite clear to her: "Sekhem Ka the immortal's heart is the she hunter Neith the immortal." She wasn't an expert or anything, she was just there when it was written--for her. Her eyes massage the parchment to remind her of the purpose of this service before taking the memory and hiding it deep inside her mind. The pager chimes again.

"All right already," she groans out loud in a high-pitched drawl combining the accents of the cities that have made her. Her hands find the pieces of the inactive phone, which is followed by inserting the sim card which allows for complete anonymity. The phone assembled, she watches it come to life after holding the power button. Her brain holds a map of the city and a number to every pay phone there as she dials and hits send.

"Donde vas?" the thick Puerto Rican accent on the end queries, the sound of other dispatchers in the background.

"The Desert," she replies, annoyed and bored. There is the sound of the phone placed on a table. A few minutes later, it is picked up.

"Penny," the deep, cold and whispery voice states from the corners of its mouth, "How are you my love?" She wants to scream at him, but the words are only meant to upset her. This is his jab at her, the constant reminder of his cooperation. He knows she hates being called Penny, but he insists as a form of proving his affection.

"I am well," she burns back into him. Her words are acidic, meant to salve his ego just enough until when she can drive a blade through the window into his heart. While she hid her utter hatred from him behind her own guilt, she could easily fool him with the notion of a rejected hurt. "How are you?"

"We draw closer, as it should be," the voice returns. There is a long pause. "I am requesting you come back to California." Great, she thought, back to Cali--another reminder of what she could never accomplish. As a whole she enjoyed the state with its beaches, sun, open mountain ranges, allure of the great skiing she would never try and memories from college years. Secretly, she could smell something in the wind that never led her to what she really hunted. A return would open a wound she preferred to leave closed. *Such thoughts are dangerous this close to him.* She cleared her head and prepared her voice.

"A trail?" she asks, emotionless and inquisitive.

"A possible," the voice responds. "The free zone is shielding it from my sight."

"I don't know San Francisco," she answers. She really didn't. "Pull from what we have in Los Angeles."

"I've already sent the hound ahead," the voice replies, "but I need this one to go before me, alive."

"Him, then?" she asks, sending that she wasn't happy about working with the hound.

"Yes."

"I'll send him back with your puppy."

"No, Penepole" he says, using her preferred name. She waits through a very long pause "This one must follow you of his own choice." A siren's call. Breaking hearts was the least of her desires and far from how she would like to see her time used. She had never had to lead a mark across country before.

"I see," she says. "I thought that was no longer necessary." There came a long chuckle, condescending and terrible. "So your word holds nothing now?"

"*My word shall remain true to my family,*" the voice challenges, "Have you forgotten why we are all here?" *Liberation.*

"No," Penepole replied in her I-guess-so tone, "I'll make arrangements and leave tonight."

"Excellent. I will abide."

"Thank you," she says and hangs up. She breaks the phone into its pieces, places it back in the drawer and pushes it closed. Her hatred consumes her, turning her skin hot to the touch. Ripping off the bathrobe, she walks naked to the balcony door and slides it open to have her chest greeted by the cold drops. Standing on the balcony, she brings her hands to her temples, massing the pulsing madness growing in her aching head. *Who the fuck did he think he was?* Frustrated and lost, she succumbed to the pain letting out a scream. *Where are you! I am so tired . . . .*

"*Yes, you are,*" the Silhouette says from the canopy of a tree hundreds of yards away from Penepole's balcony. The Silhouette chuckles to itself, knowing she cannot hear him even if it wanted her to. It reaches within the recesses of its shadowy physique and produces a small cylinder. A few words and a flicker of light is all that is needed to ignite the cylinder. The Silhouette leans back against the tree in which it is sitting and smokes. As if enjoying some inside joke, the Silhouette laughs again and says, "*you are tired.*"

The End

Among the Veils

Book I of *The Paper Thrones* Series

MEET THE AUTHOR

Bret Alexander Sweet was born in San Francisco, California. He is the son of prominent Bay Area civil rights attorney and social entrepreneur, Clifford Charles Sweet.

Bret combined his passion for music and entrepreneurship at a young age by earning an internship at PolyGram Group Distribution's San Francisco office in the summer of 1995. Three months later he was an artist development rep focusing on the company's urban division associated with Island Def Jam artists. He left PolyGram shortly after the merger to focus more on his college career at San Francisco State University and open his own label, House Kemetic Suns.

In 2002, Bret began teaching entrepreneurship to youth and young adults from under-developed communities. In 2008, Bret began certifying new cohorts of future NFTE instructors as a NFTE (National Foundation for the Teaching of Entrepreneurship) CETI (Certified Entrepreneurship Teacher Instructor). Bret graduated from the University of San Francisco in May 2009 with his Master's of Business Administration with a dual emphasis in Marketing and Entrepreneurship.

Currently, he teaches entrepreneurship at Cogswell Polytechnical College, the first professor of Entrepreneurship at the school. Bret certifies NFTE teachers, writes for publication and is an outspoken advocate for Alzheimer's research toward a cure.

From the Author: Thank you for joining us on this journey. Find us and stay engaged in coming explorations of the realm of Paperthrones at: www.paperthrones.com

You can also follow us on:
Facebook at Among the Veils
twitter, tumblr, and instagram (@ThePaperThrones, @AmongTheVeils)